MITCH'S MOUNTAIN

MITCH'S MOUNTAIN

KEN GALLENDER

Copyright 2015 by Ken Gallender
www.jerniganswar.com

Special thanks goes to Betty Dunaway Gallender whose devotion and collaboration help make this and subsequent books possible.

Special mention goes to Marie Downs whose help and direction made this book possible.

ISBN: 1514792648
ISBN: 9781514792643
eBook ISBN:
Library of Congress Control Number: 2015912314
CreateSpace Independent Publishing Platform
North Charleston, South Carolina

BIOGRAPHY

KEN GALLENDER HAS always been able to spin a yarn. As all good Southerners do, Ken likes to "visit" with people putting them at ease with his warm personality and subtle wit. Ken lives in Gulfport, MS, with his wife, Betty, a dog, a grand dog and two grand cats. Being an avid outdoorsman, he has spent countless days walking turn rows, hunting and fishing on his Grandfather's farm in the Louisiana Delta. His great love for family and country has guided his entire life. Ken's motto has always been "Family Comes First, Take Care of Family." His greatest fear is having his country descend into chaos at the hands of witless voters and corrupt politicians willing to take advantage of them.

1

TONY SAT AT his desk facing the computer screen and logged in his time for the hours he had worked the day before. While he was typing in his password and ID, his phone buzzed. A message from his hunting buddy simply read: "Made it to camp; chasing out the mice." Tony texted back: "Great, got my gear, will leave straight from work." The little cubicle was cramped, but it served its purpose. The cubicles allowed forty or so people to conduct the business of the company in a small efficient area. He had two desk drawers that could be accessed if he rolled his chair out of the cubicle, but first he had to make sure that no one was coming down the walkway. A reminder popped up on his screen reminding him that he had a meeting in the conference room coming up in thirty minutes. He pulled up his company e-mail and downloaded memos for the day. He also checked the news of the day on several websites. He left his desk long enough to fill his coffee cup and returned with fifteen minutes to spare for the meeting. Most of the people who worked in this office lived in the New Orleans metropolitan area. A couple dozen of them commuted from neighboring cities and suburbs. Along with Tony, a small handful stayed during the week and went home on the weekend.

His office was located in one small corner of a five story building that was full of similar offices and larger ones for the management team and owners. In all, the building housed about five hundred employees. Like everyone else in the office, Tony hated his job, but in these times, any job was a good job. So like hundreds of others in the building, Tony kept his head down and tried to do the best job he could.

The meeting kicked off on time. The conference room was centrally located, and it seated twelve people around a large rectangular table. The table looked expensive, but in reality it was heavy particle board with a laminate covering that gave the appearance of expensive cherry wood. The chairs were faux leather and added to the fake opulent illusion. A computer projector dominated the center of the table, and a conference telephone sat next to it.

The speaker was a typical bureaucrat from a State agency, whose life mostly consisted of making procedures more complicated. The process was quite simple: drag out the project and burn more government money by creating spreadsheets. In order for the manager to create his spreadsheets, he required that everyone present at the meeting prepare and create supporting spreadsheets. The project would soon grind to a halt whereupon consultants would be employed to straighten out the mess. Sometimes, they would hire a consulting firm to come in to analyze everything, and make recommendations. The government bureaucrats would take it all into consideration and make decisions that didn't have anything to do with the recommendations. All in all, it was very efficient methods of burning government money and for making small people feel big. However none of it really didn't matter because the money was created out of thin air and was all part of an endless process.

Everyone had just brought their attention to the graph projected on the screen when the lights went out along with the projector and the telephone. A loud boom from an electrical transformer shook the building.

The boss said, "Great; it looks as if the transformer has blown; we may get the day off. Let's try to conference in by speaker on my cell phone." He fiddled with his phone. "That's strange; my phone is dead."

"Can't get a signal?" Tony looked down at his phone and it too was dead.

"No, it's dead as a door knob."

Everyone in the room pulled out their phones and found them completely dead. One of the guys dropped his phone. The battery was overloading, and the phone was smoking before it sparked and died. One of the inspectors removed his hearing aids and started checking the batteries.

"That's strange; the batteries seldom go out at the same time."

None of the emergency lights had come on either. At that moment Tony realized that an EMP (electromagnetic pulse) event had taken place. Tony started to mention to the group that he thought that an EMP had hit, but decided against the idea. He figured that everyone would think he was a nut. He went back to his office and tried to fire up his laptop; just as he feared, it was dead, and so was the portable radio that he carried in his computer bag.

After several hours, people started giving up on the lights coming back on. Tony sat at his desk as people gathered their belongings and headed to the parking lot to leave. They were all surprised to find that most of their cars wouldn't crank. One guy had a very old Mustang that he had been restoring. It cranked. He drove out of the parking lot and disappeared around the corner. Tony watched from the window and waited as people returned to the building at a loss for what to do.

He walked into the lounge, commandeered an un-opened five gallon bottle of water for the water cooler, carried it to his desk and hid it out of sight underneath. He then went out to his truck and unlocked it using the key. The FOB didn't work, nor did anyone else's work. He tried to crank his pickup, but it wouldn't start. He hung around as people carpooled with the two or three cars that would crank, and eventually most everyone who couldn't catch a ride started walking home in orderly fashion. One older woman had a slight limp as she made her way down the road.

Tony had his backpack and hunting gear, including: a rifle, shotgun and pistol, stowed in the back seat of the truck. This weekend was opening weekend of deer season. His plans had been to leave for the deer woods after work. He took out a pocket pistol he kept in his glove box and put it in his pants back pocket. He carried the pack into his office and then retrieved his shooting bag which contained his rifle, shotgun and big pistol. He also brought in his boots, coat and hat. He closed the door to his office wing and by the light from the window cleared his desk so that he could inventory the contents of his pack. He laid it all out so he could sort through it. He had five changes of under clothes, long underwear, three boxes of trail bars with twelve bars each, and sunglasses. Tony thought *I was worried I was carrying too much gear, now I wonder if I have enough.*

After going through an extensive pile of equipment and clothes, he set aside four 20 round boxes of .308 ammo, four loaded 10 round magazines for his rifle, two loaded 13 round magazines for his 9mm Browning pistol and a large hunting knife in a scabbard. He made one last trip out to his truck and brought back his tool box. He knew it would be just a matter of time before all hell would break loose in the city. From his tool box, he had enough tools to overhaul a bus; he would have to figure out a way he could carry a fifty pound tool box. He stripped off his office clothes and put on his jeans, canvas shirt, boot socks and boots. He put on a heavy leather belt and strapped on his knife and Browning high power 9mm pistol.

Tony was still a few years shy of fifty. His wife had left him several years earlier, and his kids were grown and lived away. His daughter lived in the New York City area, and his son was working in the North Dakota oil fields. His ex-wife was living in a retirement community in Florida with her soul mate and more than half of his life's savings. He pretty much stayed to himself, lived in an old motor home during the week and went back to his home on weekends. He kept the home because it was paid for, and he planned to retire there one day.

He took a heavy wrecking tool from his tool box and went to the snack vending machine. Late in the afternoon, the only other person left in the building was a single lady, about ten years younger than he was, named Cheryl Jacobson, who commuted to her home about twenty miles away each day. Like everyone else, her car and cell phone wouldn't work. Tony didn't know much more about her other than that. He had found her attractive and would occasionally join her for lunch in the break room. He never let the relationship progress to the point of discussing personal matters. He thought it best to just mind his own business and leave well enough alone. Normally, he would have just nodded and went about his business.

She looked distressed so, to break the ice, he asked her, "Are you hungry?"

"I'm starved."

He told her, "Grab an empty box from the copy room and clean out the fridges of anything that has not been opened. If you look on my desk, there is a flashlight that should work. If it doesn't, there is a lighter and a candle lantern. I'm going to empty out this snack machine." With that, he burst out the glass with his heavy wrecking tool and proceeded to fill up an empty copy paper box.

"Aren't you afraid you'll get fired for vandalizing the machines and wearing a gun?"

"It's a chance I'll take. If we don't act fast, we are going to get stuck here with no food, and we will fall victim to the mobs. The pumps aren't working, and the city is already starting to fill with water. Unless they can get the backup pumps cranked, this city will be underwater in no time. We are going to have to get out of the city tonight, and there may not be any food wherever we go."

"I don't know if I want to leave; I think I am going to wait until the lights come back on."

"Suit yourself, but I am almost positive the lights will not be coming back on any time soon and maybe not in our lifetimes."

She looked at him as if he was crazy. He took the next thirty minutes explaining what an EMP was and what the ramifications were. The conclusion was very simple. If virtually every integrated circuit in the US and Canada were blown, the supply chain that keeps everyone fed is dead. People in hospitals, airplanes and nursing homes were already dead or dying. Most of the rest of society would soon follow.

She stood befuddled for a long thirty seconds, chunked her phone in the garbage and headed to the copy room. After cleaning out the fridges and the vending machine, they carried everything back to his office and proceeded to eat the yogurt and other items that would spoil. Tony took out his rifle suspended it on his shoulder and watched while she unlocked her car and retrieved her gym clothes and tennis shoes.

"Before I pack my gear, I want to go through the building and try to locate a coat and cap that will fit you and anything else that is useable. You can come with me, or I will get you outfitted as best I can. Do you have a gun?"

She stared at him. "I am scared of guns."

He reached into his back pocket and pulled out his Ruger LCP .380. He unloaded it and handed it to her. Motioning to the water cooler, he said, "It's unloaded. I only have seven bullets for it so I am going to let you practice dry firing it. Just bring it up to eye level and keep that little bump on the end between your eye and the cooler. Pull the trigger slowly and notice that it tries to move to the right when you squeeze. If you are using your left hand, you would tend to pull it to the left. Concentrate on keeping it straight as you pull the trigger."

She took aim and pulled the trigger. The gun snapped, and she smiled. "That was one dead water cooler if you ask me." She dry fired it a dozen or so times before Tony reloaded it and told her to keep it in her pocket where she could get her hands on it.

"There is no safety or hammer to cock; the only thing you have to worry about is the trigger. It will shoot seven times. If you have to shoot someone, it is a good idea to keep shooting until they are down or running the other way. Do not threaten anyone with the gun. If you pull it out, start shooting."

They searched the building floor by floor where they found items left at fellow employees' desks. They were able to outfit her with a down vest, leather jacket, Saints ball cap, and gloves. They located a butcher knife in the kitchen and made a scabbard from a computer bag and some staples from the copy and binding room. He gave her the leather dress belt from his pants. He shortened it and punched some holes with his knife and a screwdriver from his tool box. They found a couple of two wheel dollies in maintenance, several computer bags and one large briefcase that could hold the equivalent of four laptops.

"Cheryl, I need to know before I start packing what your plans are."

"What are your plans? I live about twenty miles from here; I can't possibly get back to my house any time soon. I live only one block from a pumping station."

"I plan on walking about five miles down this road to the marina near the Lakefront Airport and then find an old boat. If I can't find a boat that I can crank, I will spend the night on an empty one and try to make it to my old motor home in the morning. It has an old diesel engine and almost no integrated circuits on it. It will probably crank, and I may be able to drive it out of the city. The problems we will be facing are roads blocked by disabled vehicles. I have no idea how far I can get."

"Do you mind if I come with you, Tony?"

"I don't mind at all. Two of us will have a better chance of survival than going it alone. One of us can stand guard at all times."

He methodically repacked his back pack leaving out the dead GPS, and his hunters orange vest. On the last trip to his truck, he retrieved a half a dozen bungee cords he used to stow tools and gear. Using the bungee cords, he strapped the five gallon jug of water, lying on its side, to one of the two wheel dollies. On top of this, he put his pack and strapped it to the dolly as well. He rolled up and tied his oil cloth coat and sleeping bag to the top. The wrecking tool was secured on one side of the dolly with paracord and a machete on the other. The three boxes of trail bars were secured in his pack. He loaded the large briefcase on the other dolly, and he filled it with the rest of the food and snacks from the vending machine.

After one last trip through the building, he found several stadium blankets in the office of one the owners. He also discovered an expensive putter in a golf bag and an aluminum baseball bat in another office. He figured they would make great fighting clubs if they ran out of ammo. He filled the other computer bags with toilet paper, napkins, wooden pencils, paper clips and various sizes of binder clips. He gathered up unopened bags of coffee, filters, creamer and sugar from the break room. In addition, he found left over candles from an office birthday party. He mounted the tool box on the second dolly with the briefcase and computer bags on top. He knew he could discard it if it became too cumbersome to pull. He wanted to keep as many tools as possible in the event he needed to work on an engine or if he needed to dismantle or construct something.

"Cheryl, pull this behind you and tell me if it weighs too much. It probably weights fifty pounds."

She grabbed it and pulled it around the room. "This isn't too heavy; I don't think I'll have any trouble."

"We'll eat off your dolly first. That will lighten the load as we go. I don't want to abandon any of the food. I want you to put what you need out of your purse in one of the bags--that will be your new purse and will save some weight."

They put the butcher knife on her belt and made sure she could get to the pistol. She placed it in her vest pocket. She rolled up the jacket and secured it to the dolly. The preparations to leave were coming together.

2

MITCH CRAWLED OUT from under the old Jeep after running a new ground wire to the frame. He set the battery from his new pickup into the battery box and strapped it down with a black bungee cord. He hooked up the red battery terminal wire and then hooked up the black ground terminal. The oil dipstick showed the proper amount of oil even though it obviously needed changing. He climbed into the driver's seat and bumped the transmission into neutral. He turned the key and was relieved when the 1970 six cylinder engine turned over. He pulled out the choke knob, and the engine burst into life. After goosing the throttle a few times, he was able to push the choke knob back in, and the engine idled smoothly. The exhaust stank as the old fuel from the tank was consumed.

It was a cold, windy day, and the weather was getting nasty. Tonight would be a great night to build a fire in the fireplace and enjoy a shot of whiskey or two. His dad had a big fireplace in the house for cold nights such as this on the bayou. Living on the water always seemed to feel hotter or colder depending on the time of year.

When the lights went out, Mitch was listening to his radio while he inventoried his father's workshop. He was cleaning up the shop, yard and house in anticipation of the upcoming estate sale. His father had died six weeks earlier; his mother six months before that. Mitch was thirty-five years old, and his parents were both eighty when they died. His mother called him "their little surprise" because he came along after they had given up hope of having a child of their own.

He didn't have any brothers or sisters so this chore was an emotional roller coaster. He was an electrician by trade and traveled from job to job working for several large construction companies. When they needed an electrician, they would call him because he would drop and go wherever they needed him. That lifestyle was not conducive to having much of a love life. He made good money, but it involved periods of intense work for months at a time and periods of time off with nothing to do but wait for the next project. When he wasn't working, he lived on an old boat down at Grand Isle, LA. He had managed to care for his parents until they died. His time between projects worked out so that he was home when his parents needed him the most.

The home, located near Slidell, LA, on a bayou off the Pearl River, was the house he grew up in. It was on a raised foundation about twelve feet off the ground with parking underneath. His dad's shop was out back, and it was designed to float. There were two large telephone poles on either end of the shop that went through the deck on each end and through the roof overhead, so that when flood waters came, the shop simply rode the poles up and back down when the water receded.

Both his parents were born during the great depression, and as a result, they were very conservative and fearful of losing everything. His dad had every nail, screw and nut that had ever passed through his hands. They were all neatly stored in jars and bins on the wall behind his workbench. He had storage cabinets all around the shop. His power tools were on one side and his sports and camping equipment on the other.

Mitch opened the gun safe and pulled out his dad's old M-14. It was a rifle like the one his Grandfather had carried during the Korean War. His dad had accumulated at least a hundred 20 round magazines for it and had no less than five thousand rounds of ammo. He used the rifle for hunting, as well as for target shooting. It was equipped with a 4 power scope sitting on a see through mount so one could also see and use the iron sights. Mitch's hunting gear was also stored in the shop because every hunting trip started with his dad here at home. His personal hunting rifle was a Ruger bolt action with a telescopic sight in .308 caliber. The M-14 carried more fire-power so that is what he would choose to carry. His dad's fishing boat sat suspended in the boat lift out in the boat house.

For as long Mitch could remember, he and his dad traveled to their deer camp up in Mississippi to hunt. His dad bought an old farm in Franklin County, near Meadville, MS, back in the 70's. It was about as remote a property as was available and was surrounded by national forest lands. The property was comprised of about three hundred acres and had a small stream running across one corner. The old house was built back in the 1880's from old growth cypress. The interior was lined with heart pine and still had the old fire-places that ran through the center of the roof. It was two fireplaces in one: one was in the kitchen and the other in the living room. The two fireplaces shared a common flue. Wood heaters sat in the three upstairs bedrooms. The large bedroom downstairs had a fireplace on its outside wall. His mother insisted that they be modernized, so each of them had stainless steel flues installed, and the hearths were reworked twenty years earlier. They would still be safe working fireplaces for another hundred years. Sometime in the early 1900's a large wood stove was added in the kitchen, and it sat to one side with the flue plugged into the side of the chimney about halfway to the ceiling. A water heating reservoir on it kept water hot when it was needed. Although the house had a hot water heater, they frequently used it for old times' sake. The fireplace in the kitchen still had the racks and Dutch ovens that were used a century earlier. His dad fre-quently cooked a pot of baked beans, chili or stew in a Dutch oven over the coals in the kitchen hearth. The food was especially enjoy-able on cold winter nights during hunting season. The wonderful memories of their hunting and fishing trips flooded back.

After his parents retired, they spent more time at the farm, as they called it, than they did at home. For health reasons they kept their home in Slidell for its proximity to their doctors, hospitals and Mitch's elderly aunts and uncles. Everyone was gone now, leaving only Mitch in the area. His cousins were scattered across the country and were much older than Mitch, so he was pretty much alone at this point. He didn't have a girlfriend or ex-wives and very little baggage. His only obligation was a big old blue leopard Catahoula Cur named Bacon. Bacon had one white eye that locals referred to as a glass eye. Bacon was about three years old; Mitch had had him since he was about six weeks old. One of his friends had brought Bacon home to surprise his wife and kids. His wife pitched a fit and insisted that he get rid of the dog. Mitch agreed to take care of Bacon until his friend could find him a home. So three short years later, Bacon was still around which suited both him and Mitch just fine.

Several hours had passed since the lights went out. The old diesel generator cranked fine, and he ran it long enough to warm it up in case he needed it to keep the freezer and refrigerator cold. He turned it off to save fuel, and if needed, he would tap into his mother's box of hurricane candles. The home had a water well with a pump that ran off the generator. The TV and radios were fried, so there was absolutely no word on when the lights would be coming back on. This power outage was different; the question in his mind was *why did all the new electronics die?* All the old stuff was still working fine. A gut feeling told him to load up the old rifle and his dad's old Colt 1911 pistol. He had a nagging feeling about what happened after Katrina, so he put the pistol on his belt and leaned the rifle against the fender of the Jeep. He muttered *are you becoming a nutcase now that you are an orphan?*

He looked across the lawn to see Mamie and Hannah McGregor walking across with a paper sack that was no doubt full of something tasty. They would stop by every so often to drop off cookies or cake. Mamie was concerned that Mitch needed some extra attention since the loss of his parents. He looked forward to the visit, because her daughter Hannah would usually be with her. Hannah had recently moved home after losing her job in Jacksonville. She was twenty-eight, single and didn't have a boyfriend or children. Mitch found her attractive, but with his parent's illness and work, it was only with a passing thought that he considered the possibilities.

Mamie called out, "I cooked banana nut bread before the power went off, and I made an extra loaf just for you."

"Ms. Mamie, I am going to have to go on a diet if you don't stop trying to fatten me up."

Hannah grinned. "Sorry, but you have to eat it, or we'll get our feelings hurt."

Mitch blushed. "How are you guys making it with the lights out?"

Hannah looked at her mother. "She's got plenty of candles, and dad has a new generator. It won't crank. We are going to leave the refrigerator and freezer closed so we won't lose the cold."

Mitch pointed at the old diesel generator sitting on the deck of the shop. "Dad's old diesel generator runs fine; if the lights don't come on, I'll make room in my fridge and freezer. What won't fit; we can put in Bacon. We won't get any complaints out of him."

Bacon wagged his tail at the mention of his name. He was a steady visitor over at the McGregor's, and they were always good for a handout. Mitch watched as Mamie and Hannah walked back across the lawn. Hannah's snug fitting jeans made it difficult to look away.

"If you need to use the restroom, shower or the washer and dryer; let me know, I'll fire up the generator."

"Thanks," they yelled as they disappeared around a hedge of azaleas. A brisk wind blew across the yard bringing with it a wave of leaves from the oak trees along the road.

A storm was brewing; tonight would be cold and lonely. He carried up several loads of firewood and soon had a fire going in the big fireplace. He walked out on the deck that surrounded the house and looked down the bayou. The wind kicked up little waves on the water, and leaves blown from trees were floating on the surface. Like little sail boats some would scoot across the black water.

The weather was unsettled, and so was the feeling in the pit of his stomach. Something wasn't right. He couldn't put his finger on it, but he had learned years ago that his gut feeling was never wrong. Something was going to happen; he just didn't know what.

Bacon stood beside him and then bounded down the stairs to conduct his dog business. Mitch knew that he would bark when he was ready to come in. He went inside and dug out a can of ravioli from his mom's hurricane pantry and heated it on the gas stove. He poured himself a bourbon and coke and sat by the fire with his pistol nearby. Bacon barked at the door so he let him in and sat out his dog food. Mitch went back to his chair, nibbled on a slice of the nut bread and gazed into the flames and embers. In the light created by the fire, he could see his parent's wedding portrait and a picture of the three of them taken when he was in the first grade. He was mesmerized by the flames as the wind and storm raged outside. What tomorrow would bring he did not know.

3

SINCE THE SUN was disappearing on the far side of the great lake, the evening shadows were long. The moon was already showing overhead. A wind was blowing off the big lake and made it feel colder than it was. Tony hoped that the cool weather would keep some of the local population bottled up. Walking to the marina would take them four or five hours. He wanted to walk under the cover of darkness so as not to draw the attention of the local gangs who would be using this as an opportunity to loot. The odds were that they would be trying to get to the malls, drug stores, sporting goods stores and jewelry stores. The dollies made travel fairly easy. If they had to abandon the dollies, they would have to discard about seventy-five percent of their gear. He stopped one last time at his truck, took out his hunting jacket and loaded the cartridge loops in the pockets with 20 rounds of the .308 rifle ammo. He already had two loaded 10 round mags in the pockets plus one in the rifle. He also put the two loaded 9mm magazines for his Browning pistol in the inner vest pockets. He put the oil skin cap on and pulled out a baklava from one of the pockets so Cheryl could cover her ears. He checked the Trijicon orange dot scope to verify that it was shining bright. He took a small pair of binoculars out of a coat pocket and put them around his neck. The Trijicon scope had no magnification; it had only the orange dot that appeared as a hologram projected on a target. Where he hunted, they only shot big bucks or doe's; he didn't need a telescopic sight.

Cheryl couldn't help but ask, "Why do you have all this gear?"

Tony shook his head and laughed. "Tomorrow is, or was, opening day of deer season; I was on my way to the deer camp. My plans were to leave today after work. I want you to carry this rifle hung on your dolly. I'll pack my 12 gauge pump shotgun."

The final item he picked up was a 25 round bandoleer of buckshot and slugs. He slung this over his head and put on his coat to cover it. His Remington 870 twelve gauge was a slug gun with an eighteen inch barrel with a magazine extension. It already had six buckshot in the magazine.

"We better keep moving. If someone approaches us, let me do the talking; don't tell them we are heading to the marina. As far as they are concerned, we are just heading home on foot. I am sure there will be people thinking about the marina, especially after the city starts to flood. The advantage we have is we are pretty close. I just hope all the people in New Orleans East don't head this way right away."

They quietly walked along Lakeshore Drive. He kept his shotgun dangling behind him under his coat, and his pistol in its holster on his belt was out of sight as well. The wind was cold, and they could taste the salt spray as the wind whipped the waves into the sea wall. They saw only one guy on a bicycle who was wearing his riding outfit. Evidently he was out on his nightly exercise ride oblivious to the disaster that was unfolding. The rider was a classic example of someone with a normalcy bias. Some people have no way of conceiving that a catastrophe could occur around them or even recognize it as such until they were adversely affected by it.

When they got to the first bridge, they looked across the city; it was dark except for a few large fires. Several sets of headlights were slowly making their way across the high rise. When they left the parkway, they started running into people trying to walk home.

One lady asked, "Where are you going? It looks like you are going a long way."

"We live in Mississippi, and are trying to get back."

She invited, "You can stay with me until they get the lights back on."

Tony didn't have the heart to tell her that he didn't think they would be coming back on. "Thanks for the offer; but we love to camp so this will give us an opportunity to vacation at the same time."

They didn't get in a hurry but continued down the boulevard and veered toward the airport. Everyone else turned south and was walking toward the neighborhoods. People were moving in both directions. As they headed down the road, he noticed that several men separated from the crowd and followed in their direction.

While moving his 12 gauge pump into position, he whispered to Cheryl. "We have some company following. I want you to take out your pistol and hold it by your side out of sight then move around behind me so that my body and our gear is between you and them. If I start shooting, get down behind me and behind my dolly."

They stopped as if to take a break and allowed the men to catch up. As they approached, Tony noticed one of them pulling out a pistol. He racked the slide on the 12 gauge loading a round of buckshot into the chamber. As the distinct sound echoed from the shotgun, the pistol quickly disappeared, and the trio turned and ran back in the direction they had come. One of the men was wearing a long sleeve white tee shirt that almost shown like a light under the full moon. The white shirt bobbed up and down as the man ran. Tony turned around to make sure Cheryl was okay.

"Would you have shot them?"

"I was within a hair of pulling the trigger; they have no idea how close I was to hosing them down with buckshot."

She smiled. "Did you see those bastards run?"

Lowering the shotgun, Tony answered, "Do you remember what happened here after Katrina? Civilization broke down and that was with help on the way. If what I believe has taken place, there will be no help coming now or ever. Do you understand?"

She looked up at him. "I don't want to believe that it is over; I keeping hoping that the lights will come back on."

Gunfire could be heard from several different directions.

Tony cautioned, "Listen."

Looking back at her, he stated, "I don't expect you to agree with or like what I have to do, but I have no desire to die in this city. At any time you like, I will outfit you as well as possible and let you go on your way."

"I want to stay with you."

"I want you to stay with me also." She hugged his neck, and they continued into the night.

The marina sat on the east side of the Lakefront Airport. A few people were milling around, and they could see some men trying to get an old seaplane cranked. Tony thought about trying to help them but decided that his initial plan to find a boat was the prudent thing to do. He had spent a couple of lunch breaks here near the marina and remembered a motor sailor, named *Lucille,* which was docked on the west side. Luckily, the bright moonlight made walking easy. He took the bolt cutters off his dolly and quickly cut through the chain link fence. He could see several boats lit up and could hear generators running. Some of the boats were old and had pre electronic engines and generators. None of the modern electronics on the boats would be working, and most items with integrated circuits that were connected to the grid wouldn't have survived the pulse. He came up to the boat named *Lucille* and knocked on it with the golf club. A red, FOR SALE sign was taped to the windshield. No sound came from the boat. If the owner was not on board, chances were that they would not get here any time soon. He noticed a lock and hasp on the door, and taking his bolt cutters, he cut the lock on the cockpit door. Just as he hoped, he found that it had an old diesel engine. The boat was probably fifty years old, but it appeared well maintained. It looked to be about thirty-five feet long and had been a grand boat back in the day. Although it had seen better days, he couldn't find any rot. Someone had evidently taken good care of it over the years. He fired up the generator and found that most of the analog gauges were working fine. The radio, GPS and radar were fried. The diesel tanks read full, as well as the water tanks. It had a toilet, shower and bunks. Clean linens were in the cupboards. They stowed their gear and were looking things over when a knock came on the hull.

Tony walked out and met an old codger who asked, "You plan on stealing this boat?"

Tony looked him square in the eye and lied. "Not if I can buy it instead; I saw the sign, and the door was open."

"I must have forgotten to lock it. This boat belonged to Sam Jones. He died several months ago, and his widow wants to sell it. She absolutely hates it and is practically giving it away. She didn't like Sam spending time over here taking care of it. He planned on taking it around the world, but he had a stroke and died out in Houston at his home."

Without missing a beat Tony asked, "How much is she asking for it?"

"She wants $30,000."

"Do you think she will take $20,000 cash for it?"

"She won't take a penny less than $25,000. She just wants to get rid of it."

"Does it include any of the gear and supplies on board?"

"Everything here stays with the boat."

"Will she take a check, and can you get me a bill of sale?"

"I am the yacht broker. Yes, she will take a check, but you won't get a bill of sale until the check clears."

Tony reached into his pocket and pulled out his money clip which had several folded up checks next to the credit cards and cash. He reached out his hand. "Deal, my name is Tony Jackson."

"I'm Jake Finley."

Tony filled out the check and gave it to the old man. "I need a signed sales agreement, and I will take possession tonight." He let the old man copy down his name and mailing address off his now useless driver's license.

After taking the check and hand writing a sales agreement, the old man casually mentioned, "You do realize that writing a bad check is serious business here in Louisiana; they will lock you up in a heartbeat."

"Yes sir, I do. If the lights come on and if you like, we can run down to the bank for cash in the morning."

"Alright, that's a plan. I live on that blue sailboat on the next pier."

"It's a pleasure doing business with you. Where is Mrs. Jones located?"

"She is still in Houston and won't be coming back. I'll deposit the check tomorrow unless you want to wait until the bank opens back up and get me a certified check."

"I'm in no hurry to get a bill of sale unless you are. When's the rent due on the slip?"

Jake turned to go. "The rent's due in two weeks. You'll have to go to the marina office and sign a lease if you want to stay. Widow Jones was paying month to month since it was for sale. I've got supper in the oven; give me a shout if you have any questions about the boat. The keys to everything and the manuals are in the cabinet over the helm in the salon. You can also operate the boat from the helm overhead. I sure hope the lights come back on soon; I hate burning up precious diesel as expensive as it has gotten. If you can't figure things out, I'll be around tomorrow."

Tony waved him goodnight and returned to the salon.

Cheryl hadn't said a word until Jake left. She turned to Tony. "What just happened?"

"I just bought a boat."

"You said that the electricity wasn't coming back on. How's he going to cash the check?"

"He's not. In the event he is able to, there is, or was, $30,000 in the bank, so the check's good. Our only other option was to shoot him or try to convince him that the lights aren't coming back on. As it sits, we have a roof over our heads, and a means of escaping the city. The temperature is dropping, and the wind is howling. I think our best bet is to kill the generator, turn off the lights and stand guard as best we can until morning. In the morning we can see what we are doing, and I can move the boat out into the lake where we will be safer. With a little luck, we should be able to follow the shipping channel out into the Gulf. We'll look around in the morning and see if we can use anything else lying around."

She looked at him and shook her head. "I've worked with you for two years, had lunch with you in the break room, sat in meetings with you and waved to you in the parking lot. It never occurred to me that you were anything other than a quiet loner. You never missed a day, and all the managers spoke highly of you. No one knew much about you. Who would have thought I was working with a survivalist."

"You might not believe this, but I have never thought about shooting anyone or swindling anyone out of a boat before in my life. Believe me when I tell you; I'm winging it. This is completely out of character for me, but under the circumstances I have to do what I have to do."

They put fresh sheets, pillow cases and blankets on the beds. The water tanks appeared to have two hundred gallons of fresh water, and the four 150 gallon diesel tanks were full. The two thirty pound propane tanks, that were also full, fueled the salon heater, water heater, stove and oven. With a little luck, Tony hoped to locate a few more propane tanks around the marina in the morning.

The temperature dropped into the mid forty's which was very cold this time of year in New Orleans. The wind was blowing about thirty miles an hour off the water which made it feel as if it were in the teens. A slow drizzle started making the night miserable. The boat had battery lights from a bank of batteries located in a ventilated compartment next to the generator. He lit the salon heater and the water heater.

"Cheryl, I can't sleep; why don't you grab a shower and take the big queen bed in the front salon and try to get some rest. My adrenaline is still pumping from the all the excitement."

"I don't know if I can sleep, but I can use a shower."

"Go easy on the water. I think I saw a reverse osmosis filter that will turn sea water into potable water, but I am not certain. Just wet down; turn off the water, soap down and then turn it back on just long enough to rinse. It's called a navy shower; I'll shower after you finish."

Sometime after midnight, fatigue took over, and they slept. Cheryl slept in the queen bed, and Tony was on the couch with his pistol in his hand. Their luck held out. The stormy weather got worse as the cold wind and rain continued unabated. What was good for them was bad for the city; the canals overflowed as the pumps sat silent. Once again people retreated to the safety of their roofs, and many died from exposure during the blackness of the night.

The next morning they rose early and spent several hours prepping the boat and stocking up on what they could scrounge around the dock. They cleaned out another snack machine at the marina's coin laundry and found some food in several of the nearby boats. They also found Cheryl some more clothes, soap, linens and toiletries. His nature was not to loot and steal, but at this point, he and Cheryl had to survive. They could not let the masses win. The weather was breaking, but whitecaps were still on the lake. Jake Finley stopped by and sold Tony two more thirty pound bottles of propane.

"We're taking the boat out on the lake; we'll be back later. I want to see how she handles in rough water."

Jake showed him how to use the water filter and how to pump out the holding tank. He showed him how to take up the anchor and explained setting the sails.

Tony told him, "I just want to run on the diesel in this weather. I am going to wait until better weather before I try to sail her." He then looked at Jake. "I hope you realize that the city is filling up with water after last night's storm. You will probably be overrun before the day is out with desperate people. You might want to think about taking your boat out in the lake until you know the lights are back on."

"I thought about that. Is that check you wrote me any good?"

"The check is good, and if the lights come back on I'll be back. Make sure you have a gun, or you'll get boarded. I don't have to tell you that we are in a city with one of the highest murder rates in the world, and a disaster is unfolding."

Jake held out his hand. "Good luck, and thanks for the advice."

The boat had a ten foot dingy on top with a davit to launch it. The dingy had an old six horse mercury outboard with two six gallon cans of mixed gas stowed inside. The main engine was a six cylinder Perkins diesel engine that appeared to be about seventy-five horse power. It fired right up, and according to the manuals on board, its alternator would charge the batteries and power everything, but the AC. A person didn't need to run the generator unless he was anchored and needed to top off the batteries or run the AC. The fridge ran off propane, 110 volt AC or 12 volt DC; it had not been powered up when the EMP hit, so it survived. Anytime they were underway the engine powered it too. It had a solar panel on top, but the controller was fried. If they used it, they would have to be careful not to overcharge the batteries.

They idled out of the slip and turned toward open water. Although the old boat had a fairly shallow draft, Tony stuck to the channel markers and ran dead slow. He put on his hunting coat and sunglasses and steered from the helm above the salon. The sun was breaking out from behind the storm front, and there was a stiff wind. The shallow lake was very choppy, but the wide hull helped even out the waves. A large Bimini top covered the entire upper helm. The mast stood directly in front of it. He kept his rifle within reach and wore his pistol. Once they were well out in the channel and several hundred yards away, he looked back through his binoculars and saw that Jake had followed his advice. His old blue sail boat was leaving the dock, and several other boats were following. Evidently, Jake had told his friends about the danger. Tony could also see groups of people walking down the road in the direction of the marina. Occasional gunfire could be heard between the gusts of wind. Several shots splashed the water around the boat as he slowly progressed out into the lake. Fortunately, none of them struck home. He ran the boat just over a fast idle because he wanted to make the fuel last, and he wanted to learn how the boat handled. He understood the basics of sailing since he had sailed with some friends when he was in college. His friend owned a Hoby Cat. The principles were the same on it as they would be in this boat; only this boat would handle differently and would be much more stable due to its increased size and weight.

One of the boats, behind Jake, turned and ran aground near the seawall apparently a bullet had found its mark. At one time Tony would have turned around and tried to help, but these were not normal times, and they would probably never be normal again. A new normal was being established, and along with it new codes of conduct and behavior. Sure there were good people, but no one would ever be given the benefit of the doubt again, especially in the big cities. Cheryl joined him at the helm as the boat slowly chugged its way out into the lake. The only navigational instruments that worked were the compasses at each helm location. He anchored several miles offshore. He could make out the causeway to his west, and he could see the shoreline in the distance to the south. He waited until Jake caught up with him. The old man pulled along the starboard side and tied off to his boat. The other boats kept their distance and headed for the North Shore. Dock bumpers were still hanging off the side of both their boats.

Jake called out, "I owe you my life. You were sure right about what was about to happen."

Cheryl nodded in agreement. "I would probably be dead or worse if I hadn't listened to him."

Tony replied, "I just considered the ramifications of what was happening. I thought about what had taken place in the city after Katrina, and I realized that in the right circumstances the city could become 'Hell on Earth' again. We need to get out of the lake as soon as we can and into the Gulf. Already, people are heading across the twin span, the interstate highway bridge that crosses a corner of the lake. If we hurry, we may get under the bridges before the masses of the population start crossing and trying to stop us."

"Come on," Jake said, "let's go." He set his sails and started tacking off in the direction of the bridge.

Tony told Cheryl, "I don't want to attempt setting sail canvas until we are out in the Gulf. I think we need to stay under power until we are past the bridges and are safe in open water."

"I'm with you; tell me what I can do."

"I want you to keep your eyes peeled for any boats approaching us. We can't assume someone is friendly just because they are in a boat. They may want a boat they can live on. We are going to stay on *Lucille* as long as it is safe to do so. The fuel isn't going to last forever, but we can anchor somewhere safe and hide."

"I figure we have about two weeks' worth of food. What do we do then?"

"To start, we need to limit our daily intake. You don't have much padding, and I've got about thirty pounds of fat on me. We start with you eating about fifteen hundred calories a day and with me eating no more than fifteen hundred. You won't lose any weight, but I will. We can stretch our food supply out to about a month. Every extra pound I am carrying is good for three thousand calories. That gives me an advantage over you. So unless we catch some fish or find some more food, we will have to stretch what we have."

They watched as Jake's boat slowly outdistanced them. Tony maintained the boat at what he estimated to be five or six knots. The fuel gauges still showed full; the diesel engine was very frugal. After several hours, they approached the twin spans. He found some channel markers and steered toward the highest span that was high enough for the sailboats to go under. His mast was much shorter than the one on Jake's boat. Jake had dropped his sails and was motoring under the bridge. The Hwy 11 Bridge was already open. He hoped that the bridges were open on the other side of the Hwy 90 Bridge as well. If Jake could make it under, so could he. Jake's boat slipped under without hitting, so Tony proceeded. Some people were already walking across the bridge. Tony had no way of knowing if they were leaving or returning to the city. He reassured himself with his hand on his pistol as he passed under the bridge. The people on top only watched as *Lucille* slipped under and continued on its way. They followed the channel on around and under the tall bridge. When they got to the Hwy 90 Bridge, it was also open. It was soon apparent why all the bridges were open. The Hwy 51 Bridge stayed open most of the time because of construction on the bridge and roadway. The bridges over Hwy 90 and the next bridge were open because a tow boat with barges was navigating the waterway when the lights went out; the tow boat and barges lay against the bridge where the tide had deposited them. Fortunately, the bridges were open and not blocked. A couple of fishermen in ancient crab and shrimp boats were busy loading up and were getting ready to head into the Gulf and into South Louisiana to escape the exodus of starving people who would be coming.

Once out in the Gulf, Jake motored up to them. "I can't believe we lucked out and got past those bridges. I was afraid we were stuck in the lake, and this is the only way out. We at least have a chance to hide. I am going to my son's camp down at Grand Isle where I can fish, and where we have a few supplies. Where are you folks heading?"

"I am not sure. The first thing we have to do is find more food and supplies. Can you spare a couple of hours and show me some of the ropes on sailing my boat? It has been about twenty-five years since I sailed on my friend's Hoby Cat."

"That's the least I can do. Let's get out of sight of land before we start. Tie about forty feet of line from your bow to my stern, and I will set sail and tow you out. That way you will save fuel." It didn't take long before they were well away from shore and prying eyes. Jake anchored and boarded Tony's boat. Over the next two hours, he showed them how to deploy and set the sails. He also showed them the sea anchor and when to use it. They bid Jake farewell and watched him wave as he headed off into the distance. That would be the last time they ever saw Jake Finley. That night they stayed anchored with the lights out. The night was cold on the open water, but they were warm in their beds.

4

THE STORM RAGED all night, and Mitch woke to a windy and clearing day. The cold air blasted him when he opened the door so he grabbed his jacket and stuck the .45 behind his belt. The wooden steps creaked as he gingerly went down with Bacon leading the way. The old diesel generator fired right up and ran like a champ. It was attached to a five hundred gallon, gravity fed fuel tank that sat in a stand about eight feet off the ground. His folks installed propane gas when they built the house back in the 70's. It was hooked to a thousand gallon tank in the yard that had eight hundred gallons of propane in it. His dad wanted to set up some solar panels, but they never got around to buying and installing them. He had enough propane to heat the house, run the stove and feed the water heater for several years. Sitting in the utility room, was a Servel gas refrigerator that had never been turned on. He would use it if the lights didn't come back on soon. There were several wall mounted propane lamps that he could use if it became necessary. He trotted up the stairs to the deck. The brisk cold wind encouraged him to hurry his step. He raided his mom's hurricane pantry and cooked some biscuits made from one of the many boxes of Bisquick she had stored away in vacuum sealed containers. A can of canned ham was soon sliced and fried in a skillet, and a spoon full of honey topped off each biscuit. That he had food, fuel and supplies was no accident. His mom was a "Prepper." He thought she was foolish, but she had been one her entire life. Having been born in the great depression, she lived in fear of going hungry and doing without. He figured it was a harmless pass time, but after Katrina they were back home in just a couple of days with lights and running water. He was now tapping into the supplies she had put back for this emergency. In fact, the farm was a product of her prepping. When he was younger, he took for granted that she would spend a lot of time, energy and money preparing for bad times. She would tell people in a minute that she was not afraid of the apocalypse because she was ready for it. Growing up with parents who had a farm and hunting camp was great. He enjoyed getting to hunt, fish, camp and shoot. It was a wonderful life for a boy. After riding out the night, he changed his mind about selling the house and would instead make this his home and use his boat down at Grand Isle as his fish camp. He could see his mother and dad smiling at his decision; after all this was the only home he had ever known. The only other place that he felt at home was at the farm in the old farmhouse.

He ran the generator for about six hours to make sure the fridge and freezer were kept cold. He was surprised that the lights were still out. He thought *maybe all the wind last night had knocked down some power lines prolonging the outage.* While sipping on a cup of coffee, he remembered that his dad had an old short wave radio that he had bought at a garage sale about thirty years ago. It was stored in the hurricane pantry with all the emergency supplies. He found it sitting on the top shelf in the back of the room; there were batteries in a Rubber Maid bin along with flashlights and spare bulbs. His parents must have set up nights worrying about what to stick in this room. He managed to tune in some HAM radio operators who were describing what was taking place.

One operator reported, "The lights are out all over the country; the only radios operating are the old units and some EMP protected military equipment."

Another operator chimed in. "Did anyone pick up anything from overseas last night?"

He was answered by the first operator. "The only other broadcast I picked up sounded like Chinese, but I am not sure."

Mitch slowly turned the dial through the entire radio spectrum. He would pick up a signal from time to time, but nothing he could understand. He tried on short wave, weather, police scanner, AM, FM and all the TV frequencies, but found nothing. At this point, he became concerned. He flipped off the generator to conserve fuel. Until he got a handle on what was happening, he would conserve the diesel and use it only to power the water pump when he was bathing, washing clothes and dishes. As a precaution, he inventoried the contents of the freezer to determine what he could cook, can, dehydrate or eat right away. He lit the Servel refrigerator and transferred the contents of the electric fridge over to it. His dad told him that the Servel would probably run for several years on a full tank of propane. This situation looked as if it was going to be serious.

Taking stock of his gasoline, he found that he was coming up short. His dad had about fifty gallons of stabilized gas in five gallon jerry cans. Another thirty gallons were in the boat and about twenty more in his truck. He had already sold his dad's old truck and his mother's old Lincoln after they died. So all he had was his new Ford truck and the old Jeep. He also had an old Kubota tractor and a riding lawn mower. The Kubota had a diesel engine that cranked up just fine. He was getting ready to air up the tires and give the old Jeep a test run when he heard gunshots coming from the direction of the McGregor place. Instinctively, he picked up the M-14. At that moment Hannah came bounding over the fence that separated the two properties. Two men were chasing her, but they were slowed by the fence. He could see that one of them had a shotgun in his hand.

With a look of terror on her face, she screamed. "They shot Mama and Daddy." Mitch tightened his grip on the rifle.

5

THE NEXT MORNING Tony and Cheryl went through *Lucille* from one end to the other looking into every compartment and corner. They found two cases of MRE's (meals ready to eat) in a compartment beneath the couch. The MRE's expanded their food supply by almost two weeks. They now had almost six weeks of food. In a locker above the couch they found 5 fifths of George Dickle bourbon, and 2 fifths of Grey Goose vodka. In the bathroom vanity, they found more toiletries and first aid supplies, including a dozen or so boxes of feminine products. Cheryl quickly confiscated them and tucked them away in the front berth. They found books, charts and even a sextant with a manual. Tony hoped he could figure out how to use it. Lockers on the deck held fishing equipment and cast nets. Even though much of the equipment was well used, everything was still serviceable. Stowed in the engine compartment, were a full tool box and extra oil, oil filters and fuel filters for the engine. *Lucille* also had kerosene lamps mounted to the wall in several key locations. In one of the lockers they found 5 one gallon jugs of lamp oil. Considering how they had started out the day before, they were living well.

They could only imagine the carnage that was starting to unfold back in the city. The largest portion of the people would be sitting around waiting for rescue that would probably never come. More would be cleaning out the stores, while others were trying to escape the city. A significant number of people would be preying on the survivors.

Looking at the charts of the Gulf, Tony was relieved to see they had been updated since Katrina. Katrina had created and destroyed islands as the wind and current changed the geography of the Gulf. A satellite photograph in one of the charts helped him orient the islands to the region. Tony estimated that in less than two months, everyone on land would consume all the readily available food and start starving to death. If they could hold out that long before going back to shore, a significant part of the danger would be over.

Tony asked Cheryl, "Do you have any family back in the city?"

"I have some distant cousins; my sister and her family live in Atlanta. They aren't much better off than everyone else in Atlanta. My parents were killed in a car accident when I was just out of college. I was married for a short while about twelve years ago, but that fell apart pretty quickly. I don't have any children yet, and my clock is ticking."

Tony laughed and told her about his family. He added, "I have no way of getting to my children. I know they are resourceful because we spent a lot of time camping, shooting and boating when they were young. I made sure they had rifles, shotguns and pistols. My son is single, and my daughter has been married a couple of years. I don't know if they will try to come home or not, probably not. They would have to walk for months unless they could get to a river with a canoe or boat and float down the Mississippi river. If we can get to my home up the river in Mississippi, I have a few supplies on hand, and the population isn't nearly as dense. You have to realize that the populations of New Orleans, Baton Rouge, Jackson and Memphis will be spreading out across Mississippi looking for food. It won't be pretty. My brother has a family; they live in Tennessee near Nashville. He is a big "prepper;" he's been ready. What little preparations I have is because of his insistence. I have been preoccupied getting my financial house in order after my ex-wife and her soul mate tried to clean me out."

Cheryl smiled. "Your wife had a soul mate, too. My ex-husband left me for his soul mate. I think she is a stripper now, and I heard that he's a bartender somewhere."

They split an MRE and mixed up the fruit punch powder mix. They bumped their cups together, and Cheryl toasted, "To soul mates everywhere."

After eating, they pulled up the anchor and set the sails. Tony cranked the generator to top off the batteries. He figured an hour every other day would be enough to recharge them. Once they found a safe harbor, he would try to charge them directly off the solar panel. An old pre integrated circuit voltmeter showed that their output was twelve volts. He figured he could hook it up for about an hour each day to juice the batteries to capacity.

They ran out past the Chandelier Islands and anchored on the downwind side of an island that had pine trees growing on it. He anchored far enough out that he would not be blown aground in the event the wind switched direction. At this moment the wind was coming out of the southwest, so he was anchored on the northeast side of the island. Tony climbed up into the upper helm and peered through his binoculars. There was no sign of anyone anywhere. There were no tracks that he could see in the sand beach on the island, so he went into the lockers and broke out a couple of fishing rods. He managed to throw the cast net which came back full of croakers, each of them were about four inches long. He put a couple dozen of them in a large ice chest full of water; he released the rest. Using a popping cork, he threaded a croaker on the hook and cast it out perpendicular to the shore. He had only popped it a couple of times before a five pound speckled trout snagged it. Five trout and thirty minutes later, he was filleting them on top of the ice chest. The remaining croakers were thrown back into the Gulf to resume their croaker business. They fried the trout and washed it down with a cocktail made from vodka and another MRE pouch of fruit punch.

They stayed anchored for the next three days. The weather held out and the fishing was good. They saw some sail boats off in the distance, but none of them slowed or gave any indication that they were seen. A large container ship drifted by on the third day. It appeared to be one of the banana boats from the port at Gulfport. Tony pulled out his binoculars from his hunting pack and watched it as it floated past. There was no sign of life on it. Two of the life boat racks were empty; he had no way of knowing if they had been deployed. He couldn't help but wonder what sort of supplies were on board that they could use. There was no ladder hanging down, and he didn't have one on board *Lucille,* so the thought of boarding the container ship was an exercise in fantasy.

He called down below to Cheryl. "We're pulling up anchor; I want to follow that ship and see if there is a ladder on the other side. I bet it's loaded with things we can use."

"How are we going to get on it? It must be twenty feet up to the rails."

"That's what we are going to look for; if the Jacobs ladder is extended, we can climb aboard."

The diesel engine in *Lucille* cranked right up, and they rapidly caught up with the runaway. The Jacobs ladder on the other side of the boat was extended to the water line. The crew had evidently abandoned the vessel while they were close to land. The dock fenders were still deployed on the sail boat so they eased up to the side of the ship and shut off the engine. Tony tied off to the ladder, and the two boats drifted along together.

He climbed the ladder wearing his pistol, and told Cheryl, "If you hear shooting, I want you to cast off, crank the engine and take it out several hundred yards until you see me wave. If I don't come back, you are to take the boat to safety. Remember, going north will take you to land."

"Ok, but be careful. I can't do this by myself."

Tony climbed the ladder and went aboard. There was no sign of life on the boat. He found the bridge and the captain's log. As he suspected, the crew had put ashore in the life boats while they could safely do so.

Tony ran back and waved to Cheryl, "It has been abandoned; you stay with the boat, and I'll send stuff down by rope."

As he expected, all the electrical systems were dead. He ran to the crew's quarters and found clean linens in a locker. He loaded up the pillow cases with all the food left in the galley. If anything was edible, it went in the pillow cases. He found five, 5 gallon jugs of peanut oil and lots of rice, noodles, onions, potatoes, can goods and all the staples that a galley feeding a dozen or so men would have. His proudest acquisition was an extremely well equipped first aid kit. It even had sutures, surgical instruments, antibiotics and mild narcotics. After six hours of hard work, he had picked the ship clean. He found twenty, 5 gallon cans of oil for the banana boat's engine. He emptied these and filled them with diesel from the fuel tanks. Tony also found many other items: rope, soap, toilet paper, paper towels, plates, silverware, pots, pans, cups, saucers, kitchen supplies, flare gun with flares, eight bottles of tequila, a bag of oranges, bag of limes, boxes of salt, pepper, spices and a short wave radio that still worked. The radio, stored in a metal locker, had been shielded from the EMP pulse. The last bundle was a sheet tied up to contain the extra clean clothes he found, as well as any personal items he thought they could use or trade. He had so much gear that they might have to discard a lot of it because the sail boat would simply not have enough room. Out of one of the remaining life boats, he found a survival kit that had a good knife with a scabbard for Cheryl. There were no guns or ammo on board. On the last trip, he brought down a case of bananas from one of the containers.

"I feel like Santa has just come," Cheryl squealed as she went through and sorted the supplies.

"Our life expectancy has just increased from weeks to months." Tony peeled a banana from the box. "We had better enjoy these, as they will probably be the last fresh bananas we will ever see."

Grabbing one herself, Cheryl decided to educate Tony. "We can dry these in the sun and enjoy them for months. Get back up there and get us several more cases."

So after offloading several more cases of bananas, they shoved off from the runaway banana boat and motored back to the shelter of the island. For three days, they sorted through and stowed all the food and gear. They tied down a sheet and covered it with thousands of slices of bananas. These slowly dried in the sun. Fortunately, the days were fair and warm, and in no time, the banana chips were dry and sacked up in spare pillow cases. They did the same thing with the sacks of onions and potatoes. In the coming weeks, they would concentrate on eating the things that would spoil first.

"We are going to be sick of eating eggs; we have twenty four, 18 count cartons to eat."

"I hope we can think of more ways to eat them than fried, scrambled or boiled," Tony mused.

The short wave radio would occasionally pick up a transmission. The word was the same from around the country. The lights simply went out. Some protected military machinery was still working, but there was very little the military could do. Some people speculated that a solar event had happened, and others had heard that a nuclear exchange among the super powers had occurred, but whatever the reason, their world was now plunged into the medieval ages, and widespread starvation and killing was transpiring. Guns still functioned, and men had reverted to their primal roots. Tony just wished he were better armed. If they were confronted, he would be out of ammo quickly.

Although the deck was cold, the sunset was beautiful so they sat bundled up in folding chairs. As they watched the sun set, Cheryl reached over and slipped her hand into Tony's.

He turned and looked in her eyes. "I am not worried any more. In fact I am happy; just think no more spreadsheets ever again!" They both laughed, and then they kissed.

6

M ITCH PULLED BACK the bolt on the M-14 and released it. The bolt slammed forward loading a .308 hunting round from the magazine into the chamber. He took two steps aside so he could aim around Hannah and found in his scope the one with the shotgun. When the man's torso filled the field of view in the scope, Mitch squeezed the trigger. Nothing happened. He had forgotten to flip off the safety. He quickly flipped his trigger finger forward and disengaged the safety. Instantly regaining the target, he squeezed off a round. The big rifle barked, and the action cycled flawlessly. The bolt extractor grabbed the spent brass casing and threw it from the ejection port on its journey rearward. When it reached its stop, the strong spring slammed it forward and it picked up a fresh cartridge from the magazine. All this occurred in the time it took Mitch to get back on target. His first target collapsed in his tracks. This time he peered under the scope and used the iron sights; he squeezed the trigger again. The second one dropped like a sack of rocks, and the great rifle cycled out another empty hull and picked up a fresh round. A pistol he hadn't seen went flying from the hands of the second man as he went down. Hannah collapsed about twenty feet away. Mitch ran over and checked her. She was only in shock from what had happened, and she was hyperventilating.

Mitch told her, "Hold your breath." He gently placed his hand over her mouth and asked, "Are there any more?"

She could only shake her head "yes" and point.

"How many?"

She held up three fingers. He walked around behind her, scooped her up with his right arm and pulled her to her feet. He half dragged her up the stairs into the house and pulled out a revolver that was kept in a fake book on the bookshelf. His father was proud of having found a way to hide a weapon within reach.

"If someone tries to come in after I leave, just point it at their belly and pull the trigger. Keep pulling it until they are down. I'll be back."

He called the obviously agitated Bacon in to be with Hannah. If someone broke in, Bacon would tend to business. He put the .45 on his belt and proceeded at a dead run down the stairs and around the side of the house. By running behind the bushes, he tried to keep out of sight of the McGregor house as long as possible. He kept glancing around as he ran towards their house. He mentally kicked himself *crap, I'm wearing a light blue shirt and white tennis shoes; damn it to hell; I've got to start to start thinking better.*

When he reached the edge of the yard, he held back hidden between the azalea bushes. His heart was beating ninety to nothing as he peered through the scope. He couldn't see any movement or anyone through the windows. He reasoned that they had to have heard his rifle's report. The house was also on a raised foundation, and the McGregor's cars were parked underneath. He carefully looked under and in the cars and saw no movement. He was looking at the home from the right rear corner. At that moment, three men made a run for it. They ran down the front stairs and out the front driveway. He got off eight more rounds and knocked one of them down. He ran under the house and popped off ten more at the retreating men. He could see one man dangling an arm that obviously had been hit by a 150 grain .308 bullet. He raised the gun again, but the trigger was dead. He had run out of bullets. Once again, he mentally kicked himself *damn it again. With all the magazines and ammo, why the hell didn't you pick up more?* He leaned the rifle against the front steps and drew the .45. Chambering a round, he ran over to obviously dead man on the ground. A round had struck him in the back of his head; there wasn't much left to identify. Mitch reached down and snagged his pistol. It was a Smith and Wesson .38 revolver, but it only had one unfired round in it. He ran after the two running men. He quickly ran up on the wounded man, who had bled out. He didn't have a gun. The gun was probably with the one who got away. There was no sign of the other man; he was probably still running. Mitch double timed it back to the McGregor's and bounded up the stairs. The front door was still standing open. Jack McGregor, Hannah's dad, lay in the hall with a hole in his chest. Mamie had a bullet hole over her ear and one in her back. He could do nothing for them. He pulled a table cloth off the dining room table and covered Mamie, and he used a sheet from the hall closet to cover Jack. Now, he had the grim task of telling Hannah.

He ran back down the front steps, bounded across the yard and up his stairs. He yelled out, "Hannah, it's Mitch; don't shoot."

She looked up with tears streaking her face. "Are they? Are they?"

Mitch held her. "There was nothing I could do for your folks; I got two more of the killers, but one got away."

"Do you think the police can find him?"

Mitch looked her in the eye. "The police aren't coming; we're on our own."

She slowly sat down at his table. "What are you trying to say?"

Mitch explained to her what he had heard on the radio, "The lights are not coming back on. We are on our own. I am going to kick on the generator; I want you to get cleaned up and collect yourself. We've got to take care of your parents and get your things moved over here."

He showed her the guest bathroom and pointed to the door. "I want you to keep that pistol I gave you within arm's reach at all times and keep that door locked at all times, do you understand?" She nodded, and he continued, "I'm going back to your house to take care of your parents. I'll come get you when I'm ready." She could only nod.

He left the heavy M-14 in the house and went down to the gun safe and retrieved a Remington pump twelve gauge. He removed the long barrel and replaced it with a short 18 inch barrel that he had picked up at a gun show. While the barrel was off, he removed the plug and reassembled the gun. He then thumbed in four rounds of buckshot. He shucked the pump to put one in the barrel and thumbed another into the magazine. This shotgun had a strap so he could sling it on his back. It was the one he used for turkey hunting. He had a leather bandoleer with thirty- five more rounds of buckshot that he slung over his shoulder. The M-14 was one of the finest battle rifles ever made, but the shotgun would allow him to engage targets within fifty or sixty yards without having to aim dead on. With the twelve gauge he would probably have killed or wounded the one that got away. Two more seven round mags for the .45 went in his back pocket. He gathered up the dead man's Winchester twelve gauge and the Taurus .22 lying in the yard. He took a piece of rope and tied it around each of their necks, and using the tractor, he dragged all of them across the yard and down the road to a vacant lot where he left them out of sight. They didn't have anything of value to salvage.

Mitch then ran back to the house and told Hannah, "Stay put with Bacon and that pistol. I am going to make a run up the road to see what I can see."

Crying, she said, "Please hurry back."

He aired up the tires on the Jeep and cranked it. With the shotgun on the passenger seat, he ran towards town. Just as he feared, he ran into throngs of people just walking along with what they could carry. When a group started running in his direction, he quickly spun the Jeep around in the road and raced back in the direction from which he had come. He had not made it ten miles from his house before the enormity of their situation settled onto his shoulders. He pondered *we're in trouble, and it is only going to get worse.*

Mitch returned to the house which, fortunately, was not on a main road. It was located on a rather remote and secluded road.

After checking to make sure Hannah was still okay, he went back to the grim task of burying the McGregors. As gently as possible, he pulled the couple out of the house and down to the back yard where they had a small meditation garden next to the bayou. It was a quiet, beautiful place. He wrapped them in the sheet and tablecloth, leaving only their faces exposed. They looked peaceful. He cleaned up the blood in the house and burned the paper towels and newspaper that he had used in an old barrel out back. Now, he had to go back to get Hannah and a shovel.

When he returned, Hannah was sitting at the kitchen table. She was slightly composed, but her look of despair was heartbreaking.

"I have everything cleaned up; we've got to lay your parents to rest. I have them in their little meditation garden. We can't get them to a funeral home, and we have no way of calling the police or an ambulance. Do you think that would be a good place to put their graves?"

She sobbed. "I can't believe this is happening. Are you sure there is no one we can call?"

"As best as I can determine all modern electronics have been fried; there is nothing we can do. I can wrap them in plastic so we can recover and move them later if the lights come back on."

They walked hand in hand down to the garden. Hannah dropped to her knees sobbed and gently stroked her mother's hair. Mitch had placed a Band-Aid over the bullet hole near her ear.

"Is this a good place for their graves?" Hannah just nodded.

He led her back to her house and told her, "I want you to gather your things while I prepare the graves; I'll come get you when I'm ready."

Over the next three hours, Mitch excavated two graves. The ground was soft, and he quickly cut through the surface roots. He wore the .45 and had the pump shotgun within reach. When he finished, he went to his dad's shop and retrieved a large roll of plastic sheeting. He lined the graves and gently lowered the McGregors into them. He created a cocoon for each of them, and then he was ready to get Hannah.

Together they recited the 23rd Psalms:

"*The* LORD *is my shepherd; I shall not want. He maketh me to lie down in green pastures: he leadeth me beside the still waters. He restoreth my soul: he leadeth me in the paths of righteousness for his name's sake. Yea, though I walk through the valley of the shadow of death, I will fear no evil: for thou art with me; thy rod and thy staff they comfort me. Thou preparest a table before me in the presence of mine enemies: thou anointest my head with oil; my cup runneth over. Surely goodness and mercy shall follow me all the days of my life: and I will dwell in the house of the* LORD *forever.*"

Mitch closed the graves while Hannah, sobbing quietly, sat on the garden bench. Bacon sat soundlessly with his head resting in her lap. Just as Mitch was finishing, Bacon raised his head and a low growl rumbled in his chest and the hair on his neck rose as he looked down the road. Several men were heading in their direction. Mitch mentally prepared himself to light them up. He slipped the bandoleer over his head and thought *I won't run out of ammo this time!*

7

TONY WOKE AND, for a moment, didn't realize where he was. Realization soon returned when he felt Cheryl's naked leg slide across his body, and her warm moist lips on his ear and neck. He turned toward her and eagerly sought her mouth with his as their bodies met once again. He never thought that he would experience physical pleasure such as this again.

They didn't leave the warm covers until mid-morning. He lit the cabin heater and the hot water heater. While she showered, he cooked some eggs and canned ham. A pan of biscuits made from biscuit mix, found on the banana boat, was in the oven. She came out of the shower with a towel around her head and wearing one of his tee shirts. The tee shirt was just long enough to cover her buttocks, but not long enough to quell his desire.

"Grab a shower while I eat. You can have desert in a little while." Tony grabbed a biscuit and headed into the shower. When he finished, he found that the heater was off, the cabin was cooling and she was back under the covers. She tossed him the tee shirt, and he had his desert.

All was quiet that day. Tony could not remember a more enjoyable day in his life. Late that afternoon, they noticed that storm clouds were brewing to the west. A stiff wind from the southwest had blown *Lucille* around so that the tail of the boat was pointing away from the island. The waves were beginning to kick up, so he cranked the engine, took up the anchor and moved *Lucille* a little farther out. He didn't want her to hit ground when the waves bottomed out. He was on the north side of the island. He estimated the wind to be around fifty miles per hour. The waves were kicking up about ten feet tall, and being aboard *Lucille* was miserable. They had to tie everything down and take down the Bimini top. Thank goodness, the anchor held. Lightening lit up the boat and the island. Each time the lightning struck, they could see the island and trees. That was the only way they knew that Lucille was not being swept away. The intense storms lasted all night. The next morning the storms let up. The wind had switched back to coming from the north so they cranked the engine and took the boat around to the south side of the island. Several large containers from a ship were resting on the beach. They scrambled ashore and found that they were full of bananas. The banana boat had evidently sunk in the storm, and the containers had broken free and floated.

Cheryl asked Tony, "What would have happened if those containers had hit us last night?"

Tony just shook his head. "The honeymoon would have ended a little sooner than I anticipated."

She laughed. "What do you think we should do?"

He began studying the charts. "We need to see if we can locate a safe anchorage or a bay that we can get *Lucille* into. We need protection; I don't want to take a chance on stranding her out here. We have the dingy for an emergency and to run back and forth to shore, but I don't want to be out in open sea in a ten foot boat with an old six horse motor. We can last out here for several months so long as everything works, and we keep supplementing the food with fish. It is going to take a couple of months for the hordes of people to starve to death and kill each other off."

"I wonder what is happening to everyone we know? Aren't you worried about your children?"

"Yes, I am, but there's nothing I can do, short of trying to reach them. I might be able to get to my daughter by sailing up there, but there are tens of millions of big city people going berserk about now. It will be like a zombie movie up there. I just hope she and her husband have enough food and ammo. I sent pistols, rifles, a shotgun and a supply of ammo to them last year. I know they had a thirty day supply of dehydrated food in case of emergency. My brother sent everyone in the family five gallon buckets of the stuff for Christmas last year. Mine is sitting out in my shop under a bench. My son is in North Dakota, and he has all of his hunting and fishing gear with him. He has an old motor home like mine. Being in a low population area, he will have a leg up. He is in more danger from the cold and snow than the population. Food will also be a major issue for him. He is very resourceful and a very good shot, so I am not as concerned about his safety. He is also into canoeing and camping. If he can get his canoe into the Missouri River, he can make it back in a few weeks."

That evening they broke out the short wave radio to see what they could hear. After dialing through the frequencies several times, they picked up some HAM radio operators talking. Everything was just as they feared; the lights were out all over the country. There was speculation that a major solar event had taken place. The government had declared martial law, but there was little they could do. Although much of the government equipment was EMP protected, they could only do so much when everyone everywhere was starving. Entire cities of people were fanning out across the country in search of food. Every store was emptied in a matter of hours. Virtually everything with an integrated circuit was dead. Reports that some of the military units had gone renegade were being circulated. In most areas the local authorities were confiscating food and weapons for redistribution primarily to themselves and their families. Troops were going AWOL in droves to try and reach their families. The HAM operators were conjecturing that those that survived would soon be living a medieval lifestyle. In a matter of time, equipment would fail, and neither replacement parts nor gas for generators would be found.

Tony looked at Cheryl. "It looks as though my fears are coming true. What can we do, and where can we go? The EMP failure happened a few days ago, and we have months of food if we are careful. If my kids make it back to my house up in Franklin County, they may have a chance to survive. It's located in the country with thousands of acres of woods, rivers, ponds and creeks surrounding it. We will not be any help to them if we go racing back, get caught up in the chaos and get ourselves killed. I am not anxious to start killing people either."

"What about your ex-wife? Will she be trying to get back there?"

"I don't think I have to worry too much about her trying to walk back. I inherited part of the property from my parents; it was my father's home place where he grew up. I bought out all my cousins after I had to sell off everything from the divorce. She took her half and left with her soul mate. I understand that he helped her invest it in condos down in south Florida. She'll never figure out how to get back. Her soul mate will be busy looking for hair gel and cologne. They'll know the time though because she bought him a Rolex as a wedding gift. Rolex watches don't run on batteries because they have a mechanical movement. If we get back to the farm, I think we can survive. It even has the old water well with a bucket. The house has a fireplace and a wood cook stove, as well as a barn and two old diesel tractors. I have been going home every weekend and working on it so I could retire there one day."

Cheryl hugged his neck. "I'm sure it's wonderful. I can't wait to see it. How about we mix a cocktail and relax? There's nothing we can do tonight."

They blew out the lamp and climbed up on deck. The sky was alive with stars as far as the eye could see. The moon was low in the sky and reflected off the water. A fish jumped somewhere off the bow. There were no blinking lights in the sky from aircraft. A small star slowly crossed almost directly overhead. It was a satellite still locked in its orbit; it would continue its silent orbit for possibly thousands of years before it would succumb to gravity and be drawn into the atmosphere to burn up. On shore, some people were huddling in the darkness, some were around fires and others ran in fear. The food was rapidly disappearing, and mankind would be reverting to their primal roots. If it weren't for the cloud of worrying about his children, Tony would have been content. He never realized how much he hated his job and life until he was unshackled from it.

8

BACON TROTTED OUT in the yard with his tail high and his ears up. He barked a deep series of barks that let the men know that he meant business. Mitch commanded, "Get back here."

Bacon trotted back and stopped, keeping himself between the men and Mitch. Mitch had the shotgun cradled in his arm so that the men would have no doubt about his intentions. They stopped in their tracks as soon as they saw him.

One of the men called out, "I'm Deputy Jones with the sheriff's department; I'm going to have to ask you to relinquish your weapon. We are gathering weapons and food. We will be redistributing the food from the convention center."

Mitch remembered what the government did after Katrina and wasn't about to relinquish anything. He told Hannah, "This could get ugly; I'm not going to relinquish my weapon. We have no way of knowing if they are on official business or personal business."

Without taking his eyes off the men he yelled back, "We aren't relinquishing anything. This is the last house on this road; you need to turn around now and slowly make your way back the way you came. We don't need assistance, and we will not be seeking any."

Deputy Jones stammered, "Are you threatening an officer?"

"No, I am not threatening anyone. I am exercising my constitutional rights as a citizen of the United States of America. You cannot simply walk up here and take away my firearms and food, so unless you want to shoot it out with a man who has the drop on you with a twelve gauge shotgun, I suggest you go back the way you came."

He raised the shotgun to his shoulder and clicked off the safety. The men, obviously taken aback started backing away. They were not in uniform, but they were carrying rifles and pistols.

"Hannah, start running to my house and get behind the shop. I'll be right behind you. As soon as they think they are out of shotgun range, they are going to start shooting."

Hannah broke and ran. Three heartbeats later, Mitch and Bacon followed. When he reached the shop, he put down the shotgun and bandoleer and grabbed the M-14 and a pouch holding six 20 round magazines.

He quickly acquired the men in the scope and watched. As he anticipated, they moved apart and turned with their rifles. They were about a hundred and fifty yards away, past the McGregor place, and down the road. Mitch ran under his house and aimed across the hood of his dead truck. The engine block would give him some degree of cover should they choose to start shooting. A muddy hole in the gravel road was full of water from the recent storms. It was directly in front of and between them. He placed a round into the puddle. Water and mud showered over them.

He yelled, "The next one hits meat; the choice is yours." They glanced at each other, turned and retreated the way they came.

Hannah came up beside him. "What do we do now?"

"We head to the farm; we won't last a week here. Do you know how to shoot?"

"Yes, Dad bought me a .22 rifle when I was twelve so I could go hunting with him. He bought me a .22 pistol when I moved to Jacksonville."

Mitch went back into the shop and dug out four large duffel bags and two Alice backpacks that he and his dad used to pack when they were heading to the farm. He handed Hannah two of the bags.

"I will stand guard while you pack up your things. We are going to have to take the Jeep and the four wheeler trailer and head to the farm. If those guys were law enforcement, they will come back with help. Even if they weren't, others just like them will be coming."

"What should I pack?"

Mitch looked at her and explained. "You won't need any dress clothes; we are going to be on the run and possibly on foot. I want you to pack your heaviest duty clothes, toiletries, tennis shoes, boots, etc. Everything needs to fit in these two bags. In the pack, I want you to put in two changes of clothes including underwear, socks and a pair of shoes. This pack is what you will grab along with your rifle if we have to abandon the Jeep and go on foot. I want you to include a towel, wash cloth, toothpaste, tooth brush, medicine, toilet paper, matches, etc. Load it up with everything you can think of. We'll also add food, water filter and canteen when we get back to the house. I want you wearing jeans, tennis shoes that are broke in, a light jacket and a heavy coat. You'll need something for your head and ears. My mother had some gloves that should fit you."

She sobbed and hugged his neck. "How do you know all this?"

"It's easy. My parents were survivalists; lunatics you might say. They believed in being prepared for anything."

While he stood guard, she gathered her things. Bacon was outside; he would bark if anyone approached.

"What about all our stuff? We have pictures and things that have been in our family for generations."

"We can make room for a few photos. Put some of them in a big envelope; I'll do the same. We are going to have to abandon almost everything or die here fighting. There are a couple of million starving people heading out of the city in every direction. We have only had a taste of what we can expect. Get your rifle and pistol."

As she packed her belongings, Mitch reminded her to pack all her feminine products as it would be unlikely they would find any on the way.

She looked at Mitch and began to cry. "I have to pack the sum total of my life into two duffel bags and a backpack. I can't believe what is happening.

"We'll come back if we can, but until then we are going to have to stay alive."

They went into her father's den and opened the gun safe; inside were her .22 rifle and pistol. The pistol was an older H&R that held nine rounds and had a break open top and what looked like a nine inch barrel. The rifle was a Ruger bolt action .22 with 4X scope. A ten round rotary magazine was in the gun, and ten more rounds were in a drawer in the cabinet. There was also a five hundred round brick of plain .22 long rifle ammo. The rife had a sling, and the pistol had a holster that would fit on a belt. Her father also had a Winchester 94 lever action 30-30 with a Bushnell scope and an old Belgium Browning A5 twelve gauge. He only had forty rounds of 30-30 ammo and a box of squirrel shot for the shotgun. They also took out all the jewelry stored in the safe, as well as ten silver dollars that her dad had saved over the years. The .38 S&W pistol that her dad kept by his bed was gone.

As they were leaving, Mitch said, "We'll leave the house open; there is no need in locking it up. People will just kick the door down to get in. Since we are taking all of the valuables and the safe is bolted to the floor, I'll leave it open too. If we get back, it will probably still be here."

They went back to Mitch's house and built a fire in the fireplace. They left Bacon in the yard. He had a barrel under the house that he normally slept in. His barking would alert them to any activity. Mitch closed the hurricane shutters on the house and pulled all the blinds and drapes. They lit some candles and raided the hurricane pantry. Tonight biscuits, beef stew and brownies were on the menu. To take her mind off the events of the day, Mitch insisted that she prepare supper while he filled his two bags with his belongings and made a list of everything he wanted to take to the farm. Everything would have to fit on the four wheeler trailer. That night he insisted that Hannah take a couple of Benadryl so that she would sleep. He didn't expect trouble tonight, but tomorrow was a different story. He put her in the guest room, and he dozed in his chair by the fire. Tomorrow they would have to pack up the Jeep and trailer. He loaded up the magazines for her rifle and filled her pistol. He found an old wide leather belt that once belonged to his father and punched some more holes in it so Hannah would have a pistol belt. Fatigue soon took its toll; he blew out the candle, and he slept sitting in his chair with the twelve gauge within reach.

The next morning there was a cold wind blowing off the Gulf; Mitch thought *this will dissuade people from doing any unnecessary walking.* The temperature felt as if it were in the twenties. Breakfast consisted of pancakes made from the biscuit mix, fried canned ham and hot coco made from powdered milk. Hannah looked a little better considering what she had gone through.

"I am going to hook the trailer to the Jeep so we can start getting it loaded. It's going to take some time."

She reached over and touched his hand. "I am as ready as I'll ever be."

He showed her the belt with the new holes. She put it on, and they adjusted her pistol holster to fit. Her rifle already had a sling. He gave her a box of .22 bullets and had her dump them loose in her pockets. She had a large canvas purse that she could position across her shoulder where he put ten spare magazines for the rifle.

"Try not to lose the magazines if you are shooting and changing them. I don't expect we'll be finding any more."

He took the rifle and sighted down the bayou at a stump sitting in the water. The stump was about fifty yards away. He squeezed the trigger, and a piece of the stump burst loose and fell in the water. The little rifle was hitting dead on. He was confident that the rifle was safe and accurate. He removed the bullet in the chamber placing it and a replacement for the one he shot in the magazine and returned it to the gun.

"If you have to use the gun, just cycle the bolt to load it. I am keeping my shotgun and my .45 pistol fully loaded, so please be careful if you move or hold them." Hannah nodded in approval.

Mitch went down the stairs cranked the Jeep and backed it into the shop. He changed the oil and the filters. His dad had everything needed to fully service the Jeep including the hoses and belts. Mitch changed these also. He then pulled over to the four wheeler trailer. The trailer was fourteen feet long with a wooden bottom and two foot high sides. It was designed to carry two four wheelers or the small Kubota tractor. The four wheelers were already at the farm as deer season was right around the corner. The old Jeep hadn't been used very much in the past few years. His Dad had bought it back in the early 70's before sportsmen started buying ATVs. Mitch liked to ride around with the top off in the summer time. His dad let him use it while he was in high school and college. A metal top was stored in the top of the shop, so with Hannah's help, he got it down, and they set it on top of the jeep. After securely bolting it to the jeep body, he went back in and retrieved the rack that mounted on top. He aired up the two spare tires, threw them on top and secured them with bungee cords. He wrapped a twenty foot chain with hooks around the front bumper and mounted a large jack to its mount on the side. Another mount on the rear spare tire held two cans of gas. He stuck a shovel in another bracket installed on the driver's side. He mounted the battery and battery box from his dad's boat to the fender well of the Jeep. He ran the winch power line and a switch directly to the battery. He then ran a power line and switch from the main battery over to the new battery so it could be charged while the Jeep was running. He checked the wiring on the Warn winch, flipped it to free spool and pulled out all one hundred and fifty feet of wire cable. While Hannah held down the retrieve button, he re-spooled the cable as neatly as possible to make sure it was working properly in case they needed it. He took out the back seat of the Jeep and set in a large black plastic toolbox. In it he placed various tools and equipment, as well as the extra guns and ammo. On top of the box he put all the food he could squeeze in. Once this space was full, he secured all of the items to the floor with straps. Packing took them all day and into the night to finally get the Jeep, trailer, duffel bags and backpacks full. Bacon would have to ride on the toolbox between the backpacks. There was a tractor with diesel fuel up at the farm, but in a pinch the Jeep would also serve as a tractor. They also managed to pack all the food in large plastic barrels with screw on lids. They had at least a year's supply of food if they could keep it, and there was at least that much more waiting at the farm. He spread a large canvas tarp over the trailer and secured it with bungee cords.

A terrible thought crossed his mind as he was mentally going over everything in his mind. He looked at Hannah and asked, "Are you okay with leaving and going with me? It didn't occur to me that you wouldn't want to go."

"I'm not staying here with everything that's happened, and besides I've been waiting for you to ask me out for the past couple of months. I assume you feel the same way, or you wouldn't be looking out for me. I know Mama and Daddy kept hinting that you were available."

Mitch grinned. "Shouldn't we kiss or something to make it official?"

She smiled and gave him a big kiss on the jaw. They made one last run through both houses. They were satisfied that they had everything they couldn't live without. The last thing they loaded was Bacon. As they were leaving, rain started to fall, and before long the weather became stormy. The temperature was about forty-five degrees, and the wind was blowing about thirty miles an hour. This miserable weather was perfect for their escape.

The Jeep had automatic locking hubs so putting it in four wheel drive was simple. The Jeep wound up to speed slowly since it was pulling a heavy load. About a mile down the road, Mitch turned off on what was little more than a trail. He bumped the Jeep into four wheel drive high range as they splashed through the light mud and water. The trail led down to a one lane gravel road that ran alongside a pipeline for about three miles. This route would keep them off the main road where he had encountered the throngs of people earlier. He knew this road from having worked on a pumping station electrical system a couple of years earlier. This road led them to a quiet country road that threaded north more or less parallel to the river. During periods of high rains, this road would flood so there were few homes or people here. There were only hunting and fishing camps, and these were few and far between. The windshield wiper blades thumped away. Mitch and Hannah didn't speak as they drove into the night. They had almost two hundred miles to go. The Jeep's heater worked fine and stayed ahead of all the air leaks around the window and door frames.

The farther they traveled from New Orleans the safer they would be. Soon they would be farther than most of the throngs of people could have walked by now. The fact that many people would not realize what was taking place would work in their favor. Most people were still waiting for the lights to come back on. Very few would have short wave radios; fewer still would have HAM radios with which to communicate.

The past few days were just a blur as they ran for their lives into the night. The storm continued unabated. The headlights of the Jeep punched through the darkness, and as they anticipated, they saw no one. After stopping once to study the Atlas and to top off the fuel a couple of times, they made it to the gravel road leading to the farm. They traveled this road for several miles before turning down yet another road that led to an old lane that headed to the farm. This lane went through several miles of national forest lands. Other than stopping to move some fallen limbs, the trip went smoothly. Daylight was pushing through the forest as they approached a small spring that formally ran through a culvert that was now washed out. The rain had swollen the stream, but it was not so deep that they couldn't cross. The rain was letting up; it was down to just a drizzle. He put the Jeep into low range four wheel drive.

Hannah gripped his arm. "What if we get stuck? Aren't you afraid we'll get stuck?"

"That's what the winch is for. We should be able to make it just fine so long as we don't stop; just hang on."

The Jeep ran into the little stream, and steam billowed out from under it as the water hit the exhaust pipe.

"We're on fire!" she cried.

"No, it's just steam coming off the hot exhaust pipe; don't be alarmed. Hold your nose because the mud and water will stink."

The Jeep stalled a moment as the wheels searched for traction. The bottom of the stream was clay with a lot of gravel; so as soon as the wheels cut through the sand on top, they bit, and the Jeep started moving again and made the crossing. It only stalled once more when the back of the trailer caught on the bank as its wheels dropped into the stream. Suddenly, the bank gave way allowing the trailer to drop into the creek. After a bounce they continued up the lane and out of the creek bottom. A quarter mile further down the lane, they came to a large metal gate at the boundary of the farm. Mitch turned the key in the old lock and it sprung open as it had a thousand times before. He had not been back to the farm since his Dad died. After locking the gate behind them, they drove up to the old farm house on the hill.

It looked lonely up on the hill, but it beckoned to Mitch as he remembered all the years of playing here with his parents and friends. A deep sadness rolled over him. The last time he was here was at his dad's funeral. A couple of weeks before that he brought his dad up for one last visit. He recalled the trip and recalled his dad struggling to climb the old steps. They drove around the old farm in the truck instead of walking or on the ATV's. They had cooked a good pot of chili in the fireplace and enjoyed sitting around the fire talking about old times and old hunts. The weekend had been a wonderful one; his dad had a stroke and died two weeks later.

The farm had a backup propane generator that was fed by a thousand gallon propane tank. The tank, having been topped off during the summer, was full, and the generator could be cranked from the house with remote control switches. There was also a water well with a pitcher pump located in the kitchen. A tank on a raised platform sat next to the old two story barn up on the hill. Gutters on the barn roof fed into the tank so that it usually remained full to the brim. This provided pressurized water for the toilets, showers and sinks. A gas water heater could be lit if needed. The house was fitted with gas lamps throughout, as well as electric lights from the generator. They also had a gas refrigerator that could be fired up as needed. A huge water cistern sat next to the house and was fed from the water tank overflow. It had a hand pitcher pump on top of the old cypress wood cap. The leathers had been replaced recently so it could be used to water animals or flowers. In times past, the cistern pump would fill a horse water trough.

What Mitch considered the house's greatest asset was not what was in it but what was under it. The house sat on a hill, and beneath it was a huge basement. He and his dad had created a hidden staircase when he was a small boy. They had turned the old stairwell leading to the basement into a closet. All one had to do was flip a hidden lever, and the entire closet would pivot aside revealing the staircase into the basement. Down there were shelves stocked with a lifetime of supplies, food and equipment. It was also a place to retreat in the event of bad weather, and it had an escape tunnel out the back. There was even a large bed and a bunk. A person could retreat and live there with no one, living above, the wiser. If they could manage to stay alive for a few months, they would probably make it for the long haul. Mitch thought *maybe my crazy old folks weren't crazy after all.*

9

M ITCH WOKE, STRETCHED and sat up in the old brass bed. The bed and most of the furniture had been in the home since its earliest days. Although the mattresses in all the beds had been replaced in recent years, the old iron and brass beds were still sitting where they had been placed generations ago. The goose down comforter felt good. The house would be cold until the wood stove in the kitchen was lit and warmed up. The upstairs bedrooms had wood heaters that could be fired if necessary. He could hear Hannah's feet hit the floor, and he looked forward to hearing her come down the stairs. He was wearing his insulated long underwear. He climbed from under the covers and shivered as he rose. He padded over to the chair in the corner where he had his clothes laid out. In the background he heard Bacon's claws hit the floor as he trotted down the stairs ahead of Hannah. He had taken to sleeping in Hannah's room since she had a wood heater that kept the room warm all night. Mitch opened the bedroom door in time to see Hannah step from the bottom step straight into his arms. She gave him a big good morning kiss and a hug.

"How about some breakfast, big guy?"

"That would be great." He couldn't help but blush.

They had made it okay for several days. No one found them due to their remote location. The first visitor they had was a small black and white tom cat kitten. There was no telling how far he had travelled or where he was from. He was half starved, and other than Bacon treeing him on the porch, his arrival was good timing. They needed a cat; the old house had a good crop of mice that had moved in for the winter. They had trapped four or five, but late in the evening, they could still hear some running in the attic and walls. After a couple of days, Bacon became convinced that having a cat was acceptable. They named him Rover after a goofy cat Mitch had had as a child.

The first week was peaceful. Mitch felled several water oaks that he cut, split and stacked for several months' worth of stove and fire wood. The next week was spent hunting and walking the old fence lines. The ones that needed repairing would be put back in order. All they needed now was some livestock. Wild hogs were on the farm so pork would not be a problem. There would be plenty of deer until starving people thinned the herds. The old farm house seemed to come alive as the young couple's love grew, and they turned the old homestead into a home.

The old farm was the homestead of Dugan and Kathleen Kelly, a couple of settlers to the county back in the 1800's before the civil war. The couple started with little more than the land they stood on. They built the old house with lumber sawed from trees that were felled on their land. The bricks for the chimney came from clay dug out of the banks of the nearby Homochitto River. Dugan Kelly traveled to America while in his early 20's from Scotland. His bride Kathleen, who was Irish, was migrating to America to meet her family who was living and working in New Orleans. They met on a ship from Europe. *Marie* was a huge three mast schooner that was sailing for New Orleans where it would drop off its cargo and pick up cotton to carry back to the mills in England. It was returning from its latest voyage when a hurricane drove it aground off the coast of Mississippi. The surf broke up the vessel and landed the passengers in the Mississippi sound. During the catastrophe Dugan came to rescue the owner of the vessel, Zachariah Cameron, who was a wealthy merchant and landowner in Natchez, MS. Zachariah had been hopelessly trapped under some rigging. Everyone else had abandoned the ship and left him to die. Dugan dove into the water, swam back to the stricken vessel, cut him free and swam with him to the small landing boat. Dugan had no idea whom he rescued; he had only seen the man from time to time aboard ship.

With Cameron and Kathleen on board, he rowed the boat toward shore. The storm surge carried them almost a mile inland. They tended to Cameron's injuries before the three of them walked north to find help. Zachariah was so thankful that he repaid Dugan with the deed to the three hundred acres of land in what was then considered a wilderness. He outfitted him with a mule, a cow with a calf and enough tools and equipment from his warehouse for them to homestead. Zachariah introduced them to Father Christopher Chevalier, the Parish priest, who performed a lovely wedding where they consumed a lot of wine before the young couple set out for Franklin County, MS.

Cameron threw in a wagon as a wedding present and sent the couple on their way with a map and the deed to the three hundred acres. Zachariah Cameron also owned several thousand acres of virgin forest surrounding the farm, so Dugan had a job supplying him with timber from the land. Dugan and his sons spent their lives farming cotton, raising cattle, cutting timber and making lumber for Cameron to sell. Dugan turned out to be the best investment that Cameron had ever made. The friendship endured and resulted in the marriage of one of Dugan's sons and one of Zachariah's granddaughters.

So as it was, Dugan and Kathleen traveled down the same trace that Mitch and Hannah traveled to get to the farm. Here the Kellies had hacked a living from the land, raised their children, lived, died and passed on their life's work. So here, in this hidden farm in the middle of nowhere, generations of Americans were spawned. The Kellies were scattered all over America and the world. From this union, descendants of the Kellies fought the Nazi's in Europe, the Japanese on Guadalcanal, and the communist Chinese in Korea. Three more were priests and one a professor of English. Generations later, the Kelly's great, great granddaughter had sold the farm to Mitch's parents. Dugan and Kathleen lay buried in a small graveyard down the hill behind the farmhouse along with their children and a handful of their grandchildren. Mitch's parents were also resting there as would Mitch one day. The love and reverence for the old place was now entrusted in the hands of Mitch and Hannah. They had no idea what had been started here nor about the future.

With an arm load of wood, Mitch stood in the yard and looked at the old home. The smoke from the old fireplace rose into the sky. He had never felt more connected to the old farmhouse and his parents than he did at this moment. He loved the old house back in Slidell on the Pearl River, but there was something about this place that felt magical. He took the brick steps to the porch, walked up to the kitchen door, opened the old rusty screen door and the wooden door behind it. Hannah was standing behind the old sink with the hand pump. A pan of hot biscuits was sitting on the shelf next to the wood stove. He dropped the wood into the wood box and sat down to a breakfast of hot biscuits, bacon and scrambled powdered eggs. Afterwards Hannah came around and sat in his lap. She looked into his eyes. What came next, he couldn't explain. He was lost in her dark brown eyes. His situation became hopeless; he scooped her up in his arms and gently carried her to the bedroom.

10

THE NEXT MORNING Cheryl and Tony were awaken by the sound of something hitting the hull. Tony had his head buried in the pillow when he heard the cabin door open.

The next thing he heard was "Don't move a muscle people."

Cheryl gasped as they turned to see source of the voice. Tony tightened his grip on the pistol that was under his pillow. He knew what he would have to do. He just hoped that he could keep from panicking and blowing his plan. He turned in the bed and looked into the eyes of a grinning fool. The idiot was a tall man with about a two week beard. His unwashed body filled the room with its pungent aroma. His semi toothless grin told of a life of neglect and probably meth addiction.

Tony kept his hand holding the Ruger .380 under the covers and positioned himself into a firing position; he placed his other hand across Cheryl's body and said, "Don't move."

He felt her body stiffen as he returned his gaze to the intruder who was holding a revolver and was waving it around while barking orders. Tony wasn't listening to the orders but was watching the weapon as it bounced around while the man was babbling. On the third swing of his arm, his pistol aim left Cheryl, passed to Tony and then slightly away. The instant that its aim left him, Tony pulled the trigger on the pistol. In rapid succession he kept pulling the trigger. The rounds passed through the quilt and into the torso of the man who had the opportunity to pull the trigger on his gun twice. The intruder's first bullet passed harmlessly through the wall of the cabin and on into the vastness of the Gulf of Mexico. The second bullet passed through Tony's shoulder narrowly missing a major artery but clipping his clavicle. He recovered enough to see the man crumple in place. Tony's seven bullets had found their mark. He knew he had been hit, but he shrugged off his first impulse to cradle his wound. He got to the door and grabbed his shotgun that was leaning against it. Tony stepped over the dying man kicked the pistol out of the man's reach and then clubbed him in the head with the butt of the shotgun stilling him forever. Tony's left arm was weak so he put down the shotgun in favor of his 9mm pistol. He heard an outboard crank as he made it to the door leading to the rear deck. A man in a sixteen foot skiff was running parallel to the shore and was hightailing it away from *Lucille*. The skiff evidently had an old engine built before there was an integrated circuit installed in outboards. Tony leveled the pistol on the escaping man. He was almost through the thirteen round magazine when the engine went dead. The man leaped from the boat and swam to shore. Tony waited until he stood up in the shallows to run ashore. He fired off his last four rounds emptying the pistol. Before Tony could turn to retrieve his other magazines the man stumbled, slowed, stumbled again and stopped. Staggering, he turned toward *Lucille* while attempting to raise his pistol. Instead of firing, he fell flat on his face and rolled down into the water.

Cheryl came out with his rifle.

Tony said, "Thanks," and handed her his pistol.

He cycled the action of the rifle and sighted over the rail of the boat. He put a .308 hunting round into the torso of the fallen man. The man's body bounced when the bullet struck; the threat was silenced.

"Check my shoulder and see how bad I'm bleeding. I want to retrieve his guns, ammo and boat. If possible, just tape me up; my arm is weak, but it hasn't starting hurting really bad as of yet."

Cheryl pressed a clean washcloth on the wound and using some duct tape secured it to his shoulder. "They're both dead. Why don't we just leave it?"

"I just expended a third of our ammo. What if this happens again? We have to scrounge whatever we can whenever we can."

When he tried to stand, she said, "You're staying put. I can launch the dingy. The bad guys are dead. You can stand guard with the rifle." When he tried to protest, she gave him a stern look, "I don't want to hear it; I'm in no mood. There's a dead man in my bedroom, and my future husband has been shot. You're going to listen just once, okay!"

He couldn't argue, so he simply directed and helped her launch the dingy from its davit. The little Mercury outboard motor started on the second pull. She was back in a few minutes pulling the sixteen foot skiff. The pirate had a Glock 9mm with four full magazines and a Beretta .380 with fourteen rounds of ammo in it. Their boat held some canned beans, sausage, ten pounds of rice, a twenty-five pound bag of pinto beans, ten pounds of sugar, two boxes of crackers, a box of 380 ammo less the fourteen rounds in the man's pistol, a case of twelve fifths of unopened Smirnoff vodka, and five, 5 gallon cans of gas, and oil for the engine. The boat did not have any holes below the water line but the engine had taken a round through the block—it was toast; however, it could be a source of parts should they luck up on an old Johnson or Evinrude outboard. They retrieved the dingy and secured the boat to the rear of *Lucille*. The dead man in the bedroom had a Smith and Wesson .357 magnum with a six inch barrel. It was loaded with .38 full metal jacket bullets. There were four unfired ones left in the gun. There was a quick loader with six .38 caliber bullets in his pocket. Other than a wad of hundred dollar bills and a wallet, there was nothing else in his pockets. They dragged him from the cabin and unceremoniously dumped him over the side. The tidal current carried him out to sea, and he disappeared from view. The other body was consumed by the tide and was soon following its companion by drifting away in the current. Their bodies would join countless others claimed by the seas.

Tony looked at Cheryl. "You do realize that this could have just as easily gone the other way. That could be us floating off into the sunset."

She gazed back and ran her hand through his hair. "No, you would probably be the one floating off, unless of course they were gay guys. If they were gay guys, then I would be the one floating off. Thanks for saving me again." She gave him a kiss and said, "Now let's get you patched up."

Using the first aid kit from the banana boat, Cheryl dressed his wound. The kit from the banana boat was an advanced set similar to what would be in the hands of a combat medic. The .38 bullet had passed almost cleanly through. It had taken a small plug out of his clavicle, and when she irrigated the wound, some bone fragments rinsed out. She liberally applied antibiotic cream and elected not to suture it closed. A gauze bandage covered the entry and exit holes and was secured with medical adhesive tape. She fashioned a sling from a beach towel and fixed him bourbon on the rocks.

"This is going to get sore, real sore; I want you to sit on that couch with a gun within reach while I change the sheets and mop up."

Tony started to object, but she handed him his pistol, a fresh loaded magazine and the drink. "Stay put. Drink your bourbon and load your gun."

"Yes um," was all he could say.

Just as she said; the pain steadily grew until he could count his heart beats from the throbbing in his shoulder. She had the boat and bed cleaned up in no time. She washed out the bloody sheets in the sink and soon had them hanging up to dry. They spent the rest of the day sitting around standing guard. The events of the day made relaxing impossible.

Their worry was that the men had others with them, possibly even camping on shore. They pulled up the anchor, cranked the engine and motored away from the island. They had the pirate boat with them, and since the water was cold, anyone swimming from the island would be unlikely. Once they were anchored, they could still see the island in the distance. They glassed it using Tony's binoculars; there was no sign of anyone. There was no smoke from fires that they could see. When the sun went down, they didn't see any light from either a fire or flashlight. The night was bitter cold with a strong wind from the north. The only way they could be safer was as if it were raining.

Tony took some aspirin from the medical kit and mixed another strong drink using a bottle of the pirate's vodka. They locked the cabin door and positioned pistols and weapons within quick and easy reach.

Tony advised Cheryl, "Any time one of us is outside this cabin, we have to be wearing or holding a weapon. Inside we are only an arm's reach away from a weapon."

"I'm not going out without one. I seemed to have lost my fear of handling a weapon; in fact, I hungered for one when that bastard woke us up," Cheryl chimed.

Tony reloaded his pocket .380 from the box of ammo scrounged from the pirates. It saved them once; it may do so again. Cheryl gave him some anti-histamine and put him to bed. He was soon asleep. She walked out onto the fantail of the boat holding the small .380. All was silent this evening. Only the gently lapping of the waves against the hull could be heard. Clouds were blowing across the sky and were illuminated by the bright moonlight. Cheryl was having difficulty comprehending what had taken place. She turned on the shortwave radio and ran through the dial until she picked up a HAM radio from somewhere in the Idaho mountains. A man was talking to someone on an island in the Bahamas. She listened as they described the unfolding disaster from each of their locations. The man in Idaho was fairing reasonably well. He was located on a ranch bordering the mountains. He was at least a week's walk from any town, and it was unlikely anyone would head in his direction. The man in the Bahamas did not reveal which island he was on as he didn't want anyone trying to find him. He had a fresh water cistern and access to plenty of seafood as he had good fishing and nets at his disposal. He stayed hidden during the day and was running his nets at night. He had a twelve gauge shotgun that he had kept illegally. He had to use it to shoot the police who showed up to steal his food. Now, he had their guns and the food they had already stolen from other islanders.

Cheryl thought *it's funny how the local authorities seem to go bad as soon as a disaster strikes.* She walked back into the cabin, locked the door, and slipped under the covers. She didn't know what tomorrow would bring, only that it would come, and they would face it together.

About a hundred miles south and seventy-five miles east of where they were anchored, a cruise ship drifted along with the current and wind. The passengers had consumed all the food and most of the water. The ship was dark so they just sat around on the decks wrapped in blankets. All the toilets were topped off with sewage, and human excrement was flowing in the halls and down into the bowels of the ship. The pumps weren't working; as a result, the great vessel was slowly sinking. Unbeknownst to the passengers was the fact that the ship was floating directly toward an offshore oil platform. The engineers and crew of the drilling and production platform had managed to stabilize it by releasing the massive anchors. The GPS stabilization thrusters were dead. A couple of the old, hands on engineers used torches to cut the anchor chains free. Even with the platform temporarily safe, they were just one storm away from total disaster. Underneath their feet were ten deep sea oil wells. If the blowout preventers gave way, an environmental catastrophe of biblical proportions would occur. In fact, the massive production and drill pipes were helping anchor the platform. The men on the platform had about an hour's notice that the cruise ship was bearing down on them. One of the lookouts spotted the great ship in the twilight. The men only had time to evacuate to life vessels that were not powered, because the engines in the other boats would not crank. They all watched helplessly as the current and wind carried them away. They quickly lost sight of the platform and the cruise ship as they drifted into the night. The next thing they heard was the echo of steel hitting steel.

11

CARL BENSON SAT at the table in the corner of the bar room. The double doors were closed to keep out the cold. An old diesel tractor was set up on the side of the building with a welding machine generator running off the power take off. The compressors on the beer coolers and refrigerators hummed in the background. A light was hanging over the former poker table. Carl had been a small time gambler, bookie and owner of the Blue Flamingo pool hall and bar. It officially became a bar after the EMP. He had always sold alcohol under the counter to his customers and got away with it by paying off the local police. There was no such thing as a dry county now that the lights were out. He made small loans, pawned items and had a crew of thugs he called collection agents working for him. When the lights went out, he didn't panic like everyone else. He knew there was profit to be made in the chaos and was in the perfect position to make it. He had weapons, plenty of alcohol, a large pantry and a crew of thugs willing to follow his orders. The local police disbanded, almost right away, and went home to save their families. Carl had several girlfriends who lived upstairs and weren't going anywhere. His thugs had some girlfriends and managed to find a few more once the girls realized there was food and electricity at the bar and in the houses around it.

Unlike most people, Carl did a lot of reading and research. He recognized the EMP event for what it was. Carl and his thugs had managed to steal a sizeable stock of food and spent a good part of the last three weeks robbing the locals and people walking through. While they had honed their skills of robbing and killing, they had had only two casualties.

Carl gathered his three lieutenants. "How are we coming with cleaning out the town?"

A big, potbellied, redneck by the name of Tub Johnson was the first to speak. "Boss we have about got the town picked clean. We have rounded up and stored in the hangers down at the air strip every engine that will crank. We have every scrap of food stacked and stored in the warehouse behind the bar. We have an electrician and the HVAC man rigging up a working walk-in freezer and cold storage. We have Sam, the butcher from down at the grocery, lined up to slaughter and butcher any livestock we can gather up."

"That's great Tub. What did y'all do with the mayor and the sheriff?"

Tub grinned. "The sheriff didn't make it; Pete shot him the first chance he got. He never got over the sheriff busting up his meth lab. We dropped the mayor off in the Homochitto River with his wife. The last we saw of him, he was paddling downstream in an old aluminum boat. I don't think he's coming back."

Carl laughed at the thought of the old pompous Mayor disappearing down the river. "What about Doc Brown; did you get him set up? We got to have someone to patch us up and doctor on us."

"We have him set up down the street in a house near the old hospital. The electrician is running lines now, and we found a plumber to hook up some running water. Doc isn't happy; we had to slap him around a little to convince him to stay."

Carl grinned. "I want you to start working on the surrounding country. I am sure there are plenty of farms we can clean out. Be careful; all those folks will be armed to the teeth. Okay guys; empty your pockets in the barrels: jewelry to the left, gold in the middle, silver to the right. If you aren't sure, put in the fourth barrel in the back. I'll sort through it later. I better not get wind of anyone holding out. Your women look like gypsies as it is. I want it all put in the barrels. The time will come when we will need it to trade for stuff we don't have."

Hazel came in about that time. Hazel rode an ancient Harley and had half a dozen lesbian bikers who followed her. There wasn't a tougher bunch of women in the state, or men for that matter. Without saying a word the girls unloaded their pockets in the barrels.

Carl asked, "You gals hungry?"

Hazel grinned. "You betcha, Daddy."

Carl nodded at Spike. "Go wake up the cook and get him busy."

Silently, Spike Hobbil went into the kitchen, roused the cook and had him busy cooking.

Spike was an interesting character. He was a quiet operator. He did some work for Carl, but it was common knowledge that he was there because it was profitable for both Carl and him. He had two girlfriends who were twins and extremely loyal to him. They stayed in a large house down the highway. Spike had developed a reputation of being a lady's man prior to the blackout. He was Carl's best collector. Each time Carl made a significant loan or covered a large bet, Spike would be called in to explain the collection process. Very few of Carl's customers failed to pay back their loans once he turned them over to Spike. The few who didn't pay Carl back left the county for good. Spike was paid ten percent of what he collected, and Carl didn't ask questions. Spike had the services of the other two enforcers if he needed muscle, but that wasn't necessary.

Carl nodded at Hazel. "I want you girls to make a run around the county and make note of which houses are occupied and which ones are vacant. We've 'bout got the town cleaned out, so we need to clean up the county next. I want you to stop killing everyone and cleaning them out. I just want you to get their extra stuff; we are going to be tax collectors. Until now we've been slaughtering the sheep. I think we can start shearing them now; don't leave them on starvation. I want to be able to show up and get their extra produce and animals ever so often. In turn, we won't kill them or burn them out. Let them know that we are serious and let them know we can provide them some security."

Unknown to his crew, Carl was beginning to think of himself as a king and in many ways he was. He had tax collectors, and he had the power of life and death over them. With only a word he could dispose of anyone. The only thing he needed to do was expand his sphere of influence. He would soon have complete control of this county, and the surrounding counties would be next.

After eating a hearty lunch, Carl looked across the room at Hazel, Tub, Pete, and Spike. "Guys, we are taking this to the next level. So long as the lights stay out we're in control. Once we lock down this county, we'll move into the counties that surround us. Each of you will be granted your own county; you will be barons in charge of your own county estates. I will be King, King Carl the First. I know you are thinking that this is nonsense, but how do you think the original Kings of England came to power? Do you believe it was from divine providence or was it from seizing power? I got news for you; God wasn't involved. It was from power. So the choice is yours. We have this county; the state is next and the Southeast after that. Are you in or out? Now is the time to lead, not just hang out."

In unison they gave him thumbs up. Carl's three girlfriends surrounded him and they all toasted with a round of cold beer. Carl sat back down at his former poker table and kicked back a cold beer. Michelle, his first girlfriend, brought out a hand full of the stolen jewelry from the fourth barrel. Carl pulled out his jewelers loop and started separating the good jewelry from the costume. Michelle looked down at her swollen belly and smiled. She was carrying the next heir to the kingdom.

12

MITCH PULLED HANNAH close; he couldn't be happier at this point in time. He was at the old farm, and he had enough food and supplies to live comfortably for the next two or three years. He had the most beautiful girlfriend he could possibly imagine, and she was lying beside him naked and bedded. Hannah snuggled up and kissed his earlobe. He melted on cue and realized that he was ruined for life.

He started to get up when she said, "You aren't going anywhere handsome."

All Mitch could do was grin and submit. They left the bed mid afternoon. Mitch couldn't remember a better day in his life. The rest of the day was spent sitting around the fireplace in the living room.

That evening as they sat next to the fire, Mitch said, "We can live comfortably here for a long time, perhaps forever, but we can't get complacent. Before long someone will hear us shooting or cutting firewood. The smell of our wood smoke will carry for miles. I want to establish another bug out location. We need to keep our packs ready to go at all times. We are already in the habit of carrying weapons twenty four hours a day."

Hannah was sitting with her pistol strapped to her waist and Mitch was wearing his .45 in a shoulder holster. Bacon and Rover were each lying next to the fire.

"Do you have any place in mind?"

"As a matter of fact I do, there is an old brick kiln a couple of miles from here, near the Homochitto River. Dad told me that the bricks in this chimney and the bricks used in the foundation and walks around here were made in the old kiln. I haven't been there in a long time because it can only be reached on foot or on a four wheeler. At one time there was an old logging road, but it has long since grown up. We'd have trouble even getting the Jeep through there now."

"Can we build a shelter there?"

"We may not have to build anything. There was an old log structure built from cypress logs taken from old growth cypress trees that grew in the swamps nearby. I hunted around it for twenty years and took shelter in it during a storm seven or eight years ago. The old shake shingle roof only had a couple of leaks. It has a dirt floor, but a layer of pine straw could make it habitable very quickly."

"When can we go see it?"

"Tomorrow, we'll leave with our packs and guns and carry a load of supplies back there. We'll go on foot so as not to create a trail."

The next morning they were up with the dawn and soon had a couple of rucksacks loaded on a game carrier. Mitch took the M-14 and he let Hannah carry her .22 rifle and pistol. If they ran across any small game, they could use her rifle. Anything big would fall to the old battle rifle. Bacon led the way and poked his nose into every hollow and thicket. He jumped deer several times, but Mitch resisted the urge to make a kill as they made their way to the kiln. Two miles wasn't very far, but because of the terrain and the need to take detours, the trip took them several hours. They stopped at the top of a ridge overlooking the bottom where the old dwelling sat. This was national forest land, but Mitch knew that under the present circumstances it belonged to no one. They sat for a few minutes and peered down through the hollow. The old shake covered roof was green from the covering of moss that had been on it for a century. A plum thicket surrounded it; the old brick kiln was not obvious at first. A century of leaves had buried and hidden it.

They made their way down to the old log structure and kiln. The kiln could hold several thousand bricks for firing. The gaping hole was spooky, and they didn't know what lay within. Hannah shined a flashlight through the hole. The flashlight illuminated a low roof and a floor covered with leaves and debris. The kiln would be a great place to bury provisions for later use. The old log structure was not large, only a fifteen by twenty foot room. It was built as a shelter to work from. A ceramic nipple in the wall indicated that a wood heater had at one time been sitting in the building. It was probably a shelter for the men who were logging and shipping timber back in the late 1800's. An old cross cut saw was hanging on some spikes in the wall; its handles had long since rotted away. The remains of an old wooden table sat on the floor. The kerosene lamp that once sat on it lay in the debris and leaves on the floor.

When they finished, they had two months of food and supplies hidden in the old kiln. They raked leaves and debris inside to hide any evidence of their work. Taking care not to leave a trail, they left the kiln and climbed back up the ridge the way they had come. The game carrier held their two packs and the empty rucksacks they had used to ferry their emergency supplies. From a point down the ridge, they could see a green field off to the west. A farm house in the distance had a column of smoke climbing from its chimney; someone else was alive and surviving.

"Tomorrow, I'll give them a visit. Maybe they'll have something to trade. I want to get back and make sure we haven't had company. When we get back, Bacon and I will go in first. You'll stay hidden up on the mountain until I give you the all clear."

"What mountain? I haven't seen a mountain around here."

"My mom called the big ridge behind the house, Mitch's Mountain. When I was little, I thought it was a mountain and would climb it every time we came up here. We'll be approaching the house from the east and take a trail up the mountain. You can see the back of the house from there. I'll go down, make a quick run through the house and if everything is okay, I'll wave to you, and you can come down. If not, you will stay there with your rifle where it's safe and play it by ear. If I'm dead, you can sneak in through the tunnel and hide in the basement after dark, or you can go back to the kiln and camp out until you can figure something out."

They took a trail up and onto the mountain. They stopped when they reached a point where they could see the back of the house. "We'll sit up here a while and watch the house to make sure there is no one around."

Their caution paid off. They spied Tub Johnson walking down the back steps munching on one of Hannah's biscuits. Behind Tub, a man stepped out that Mitch didn't recognize. He knew Tub from the truck stop back in town. Tub owned the lunch counter and had some slot machines hid in the back. He was one of the people who knew about the farm, because he sold and delivered the old diesel tractor to Mitch's dad many years ago.

Mitch told Hannah, "I want you to stay up here with your rifle. My dad told me not to trust Tub Johnson. I don't know what my dad knew about him, but my dad was a great judge of character. Stay up here hidden with your rifle loaded, and I want you to watch everything through the scope."

Mitch walked down the trail toward the house. When he was within earshot, he pulled back the charging handle on the M-14 and released it. The spring pulled the bolt closed and in the process loaded a .308 hunting round with a 150 grain soft nosed bullet. The sound of the rifle bolt slamming shut brought both Tub and the man behind him to a stop.

While aiming through the scope, Mitch called out, "Tub, what the hell are you doing in my house?"

"Who are you? What do you mean this is your house? This entire county belongs to Carl Benson now; the only people who can stay here have to pay rent. Me and Luke are here to collect, and we'll be by every month. We'll start with what's in your kitchen and that Jeep of yours; you won't be needing it anymore. In return we'll provide you protection if you need it. All you have to do is get word to us in town, and we'll come running."

"You mean to tell me all my worries are over? You guys are now the law and my landlords? I guess this is my lucky day."

Tub grinned. "I'm glad you see it our way."

"Tub, I remember you from the truck stop. My dad bought that old diesel tractor from you; I am now claiming all the land from the river to the highways east, west and north of here. If I catch you or any of your people here again, I'll kill you. The next time I see you or Carl on this land, you're dead."

About that time, Hannah's rifle cut loose, and a man Mitch had not seen hit the ground. The man had fallen from a bedroom window upstairs. His shotgun lay beneath his body. Tub turned to run, and almost without thinking, Mitch pulled the trigger, and in quick succession five .308 hunting rounds hit Tub and the man with him. Other than a few involuntary twitches from the dying men, the encounter was quickly over. Bacon who had been sitting with Hannah came at a run and stopped next to Mitch. Mitch's heart was pounding as he considered what to do next.

"Hannah, are you ok?"

"I'm fine, baby."

Mitch called back. "Stay put; until Bacon and I check out the house."

Pulling out his pistol, he stepped around the dead men and went into the back door. Bacon led the way. They didn't find anything but a ransacked house.

He called to Hannah. "Come on down; the house is clear." Hannah soon joined him, and together they hugged.

"Hannah, I want you to clean up the house while I haul off the garbage."

Hannah looked at the one she shot. "You know it was easier than I imagined. After what happened to Mama and Daddy, I don't have a single regret."

"I know. It's never a good feeling, but we are just going to have to do what we have to do. We have no other choice--be victims or die."

Mitch walked to the barn. His rifle was loaded with a fresh magazine and suspended on his back. He swung open the two double doors and climbed into the seat of the old diesel tractor. It cranked right up as there were no electronics on this old beast to be damaged. He grabbed a length of rope, drove around the yard, through the gate and backed it up to the dead men. After unloading their pockets, he took the clothes, belts and shoes that weren't soaked in blood. None of them would fit him, but he could use them for trade or the material for mending. He tied the three of them together at their wrists and tied them to the implement bar on the back of the tractor. Then he pulled them down the road. The lock on his gate had been cut.

Just across the creek sat their old Ford truck. To his great delight, he found that their truck was full of stuff they had been stealing from other farms around the county. There were three large dog crates that contained twelve hens and three roosters. A little female Australian Sheppard puppy was in a box on the back seat. Mitch named her Pinky and knew that she would be a great addition to the family. There were also canned goods, tools, and more ammo and weapons.

He got back on the tractor and proceeded to drag the bodies almost out to the highway. He turned up a forestry side road and stopped where he could turn around. Here would be a good place to dump the dead. This location would be his bone yard; he hoped this would be the end of the killing. In his heart he feared it was only the beginning. He drove back to the farm and parked the tractor in the barn. He crossed the creek and drove the Ford truck across and parked it next to the Jeep under a shed roof off the far side of the barn. He put the chickens in the old chicken house and put out a bucket of water. They would soon be roosting, and once he fed them, they would stick around.

He called out. "Hannah, come see." When she came to the door, he held up Pinky. "Look, a new baby."

Tears welled up in her eyes as she grabbed the little puppy and snuggled her to her neck. He hauled in all the food and stored it in the basement. Everything else was stowed away in its proper place.

After supper they sat by the fire pondering the day. "They are clearly not operating alone. Tub was just a thug; he was working for Carl Benson who is just another low life taking advantage of terrified people. I'm proud of the way you took care of the one aiming at me."

"I just thought about what happened to Mom and Dad. I won't hesitate to shoot from now on."

The bad guys' rifles were leaning in the corner, and their pistols were laid out on the mantle. They now had two Bushmaster AR-15's with twelve full thirty round, magpul magazines and two thousand rounds of ammo. Each of the AR-15's was outfitted with suppressors and Eotech red dot sights. Tub and Bob had left their rifles leaning on the porch rail while they were eating Hannah's biscuits. The dead guy had a Remington 870-12 gauge and a bandoleer of buckshot and a pocket Ruger LCR in .38. They also each had a pocket of loose silver and gold jewelry. If things got worse, Mitch and Hannah would move into the basement to sleep. In the meantime, they would make sure the downstairs windows were shuttered, and the doors barred at night. In time, life would return to some sort of normalcy.

13

THE CRUISE SHIP and oil platform crunched and ground together and rapidly turned themselves into one huge jumble of iron, oil, bodies and death. The friction ignited the natural gas which in turn ignited the thick oil. Almost immediately, the entire Gulf was lit from the conflagration created by the two vessels and the untold billions of cubic feet of natural gas and millions of gallons of crude being released into the water and atmosphere. A huge fireball erupted as the natural gas and crude oil exploded into an inferno that rivaled a volcano in its ferocity. Both vessels were ablaze. Passengers were forced to jump into the cold waters of the Gulf; none of the life boats had been deployed. The cruise ship succeeded in ripping up the production strings as well as dislodging several of the blowout preventers. In the span of about twelve hours, the platform and the cruise ship were settled in a heap on the floor of the Gulf. The huge ship was almost a thousand feet long and was no less than ten stories tall. Almost as much oil as the US normally used in a day was now bubbling to the surface every twelve hours. The torrent of hydrocarbons would continue unabated until the bowels of the earth were empty or the geological structures miles beneath the earth collapsed sealing them forever. The natural gas was still burning at the surface. Most of the oil just billowed out into an ever increasing oil slick that just got larger and thicker. The ecosystem of the Gulf of Mexico would be permanently altered until the noxious oil stopped. For the bacteria in the Gulf to consume the millions of gallons of crude oil would take decades.

Cheryl was the first to wake to the smell of oil in the boat. She punched Tony to wake him. "Do we have a fuel leak? I smell something."

Tony rolled around until he could get into a position that allowed him to get up with his wounded shoulder. "I don't think there's a leak on board."

He painfully rolled out of bed, went on deck and became alarmed when he realized that he was looking at an oil slick that spanned to the horizon. He had been shot seven days ago. He was doing better, but he was still in no shape to do much more than lie around. He couldn't believe what he was seeing. Several bodies in life jackets were floating within sight of the boat. He grabbed his binoculars, went up to the upper helm and looked around. He didn't see anyone alive, and as far as his eyes could see, all he observed was debris and oil.

He called Cheryl. "We've got to get out of here; this is only going to get worse. We can try to run through it going south, or we can head up the Mississippi River."

Cheryl had made it up the ladder. "How do we know it's not coming from the Mississippi River?"

"We don't, but my bet is that it is from an off shore platform; especially since we've seen people in life vests. Let's get dressed and prepare to shove off. I'll get out the charts and try to figure out which direction we can go."

The charts were clear; however, the difficult part would be figuring out the landmarks. GPS and Lowrance were worthless now. Tony and Cheryl would have to depend on the landmarks and current to find their way. The oil would only make the puzzle harder to solve. He turned off the water filter because he didn't want to contaminate it with the oil.

They hastily dressed and prepared *Lucille* to sail. Tony cranked the engine and took the slack up on the anchor line. Cheryl cranked the winch and retrieved the anchor. *Lucille* pushed her way through the oily sheen. After they got around to the opposite side of the island, the going was easier. On the other side of the island, the wind had piled up the oil into a thick carpet that turned the surf into a brown, churning, pudding of oil, sand and foam; here they were in a thick sheen instead of a thick carpet of oil.

"We are going to have to set sail; we can't waste fuel. We are going to need every drop to motor up the river. This is a large boat, and it will take a lot of fuel to get us all the way up the river to where the Homochitto River empties into the Mississippi."

Cheryl headed for the front sail. "I'll be the muscle; just tell me what to do."

"Ok, muscles, take the cover off the sail on the spar."

She looked puzzled. "Are you sure this is called a spar?"

"I'm not sure what it's called. I'm new at this; we'll call it a spar for now until we find out what the hell it is. Anyway, once you get the cover off and stowed, I need you to flip the lever on that winch, insert one of the handles and crank it to pull the sail up the mast."

Remembering Jake's instructions and with Cheryl's help, Tony had the boat moving away from the island. *Lucille* leaned slightly as the wind filled the sail and pushed her through the water. Locating the mouth of the river would be difficult. They kept the coast in sight and plowed through the oil and noxious fumes. Everywhere oil covered birds were floundering in the water. Thousands of dead fish were floating on the water's surface. A huge sea turtle poked his head up through the oil for a breath and quickly submerged to get away from the oil and fumes. By late afternoon, the slick started to thin out which indicated that they were nearing the mouth of the Mississippi. The fresh water stream was pushing the slick away from shore where it would soon be nothing more than an iridescent sheen on the water reflecting the late afternoon sun shining across it.

While still in the Gulf, they set anchor. They were free from the worst of the oil. A strong wind from the north, along with the freshwater from the river, was keeping the spill away. That night they made their plans. Cheryl pulled out a notebook and pencil and made a quick inventory of their supplies. "Do you think we can get to your home out in the country?"

"If we can get that skiff up the Homochitto River, it will take us to within a couple of miles of my house. The problem we're going to face is if that little six horse mercury outboard can't push the skiff up the river. If it can't, we'll be pulling and pushing the boats. The Homochitto River is really shallow, and we will have to get out and push it through a lot of places. Even then, we might not be able to move it. The dingy would probably make it okay, but it won't hold many supplies. So we would have to make a lot of trips to get our stuff to the house, and I don't know who or what we'll face."

Cheryl reached over and ran her hand through his hair. "I guess we'll just do what it takes. How long will it take us to motor up to the mouth of the Homochitto?"

"I'm not certain, but I would say a week. For one thing, I am not sure we can find the Mississippi River. Once we find it; it'll still take a couple of day's travel north of the bridge at St. Francisville. The other problem is the hole in my shoulder. I don't know if it will be healed enough to push a twenty two foot aluminum skiff upstream in a shallow river."

"What if we find a place to park *Lucille* and just hang out for a month or so? There's bound to be somewhere we can tie up out of the way."

Tony thought for a minute and consulted the maps. He found a lake off a channel in the river below New Orleans. Tony looked up while holding his finger on the map.

"As I see it, that's our only choice. Let's anchor here for the night, and tomorrow morning we'll try to head up the river. All we have to do is go against the current, stay in the clear water and it will lead us to the mouth of the river. Since we are within sight of land, we can't show any light at night so we need to cover the windows and the door glass. We'll take turns sleeping. We can't take a chance on getting boarded again, and our odds of getting boarded just went up a lot."

"Ok, baby, sounds like a plan; what is plan B if we can't find or get up the river?"

"Plan B is we sail flat out for the Caribbean. We'll go straight south until we hit land and then track east and southeast until we are well away from the oil. I just hope the current sweeping through the Gulf isn't flowing faster than we can sail. You sleep first; I'll be up on the helm where I can see."

She gave him a hug and a kiss and helped him get his coat on. He was wearing his pistol and took his pump shotgun; he could shoot from the waist with it if the need arose. He climbed up to the upper helm and unfolded one of the deck chairs. From there he could see in every direction. The sun was a deep red and looked ten times its normal size. It was shining from under waves of clouds as it set in the west.

In the grand scheme of the universe this was nothing. The earth would continue spinning on its axis on its journey around the sun. In a million years, the earth would still be circling the sun, and life on earth would probably still continue in one form or another. Man will have come and could be gone, but everything that is taking place at this time will amount to nothing. No one would remember anything that was happening here today. The oil flowing from the earth would be long gone having been consumed by the environment. The molecules of their bodies as well as that of the boat and their equipment would still exist; they would just be changed and altered and scattered all over the earth and possibly the universe. Just as the elements of their bodies were created in the super nova of the ancient universe, these same atoms would be dispersed once again. The water they drank, and the water they were floating in was the same water that once flowed through the veins of dinosaurs. Theoretically, every breath he took contained air molecules from Caesar's last breath. But for now, all that mattered was what happens to him and Cheryl. Death was inevitable. Just as surely as he had had to take his first breath, he would one day have to take his last. His goal was to stretch those two events as far apart as possible. He knew that in the coming weeks, months and years he would be tested and retested. For a few weeks his shoulder wouldn't allow him to do much more than poke around.

When Cheryl touched him, he jumped; he hadn't realized that he had fallen asleep. He looked out across the water. The bright moonlight lit the water in every direction. At that moment, he saw the brief flair of a cigarette as its owner drew a puff.

He squeezed her hand and whispered, "Don't make a sound we have company." She tensed and eased down into the chair next to him.

"Where?" She whispered.

"On the bank," he answered as he stood and carefully surveyed the water in every direction.

The bright moonlight made it impossible for anyone to sneak up on them. Unfortunately, that same moonlight also made them visible from the shore. They sat concentrating their eyes on the spot where the cigarette would flare from time to time. Before long, a fire was lit on the shore. The group of people around it were either unconcerned that they would be seen, or they hadn't spotted *Lucille*. Tony couldn't see a boat, but he could tell that the men were packing rifles. He decided their best option was putting distance between themselves and the men. The anchor would have to be winched in, and it would make some noise. The wind was blowing from the north, so all they had to do was pull up the anchor and let the wind push them out of range of the rifles on shore. The winch had a ratchet mechanism; therefore, when they started cranking, there would be no turning back.

He told Cheryl, "I want you to start cranking. Just go one click at a time and pause between the clicks. I'll be aiming with my rifle across the rail. If they hear us and start shooting, I want you to crank as hard and fast as you can. I'll open up on them. With a little luck, they won't hear, and we'll get away clean."

When Cheryl started to turn the crank, the first click echoed across the water.

14

CARL WAS SITTING in his customary spot at his table in the corner. Pete, Spike and Hazel came in and sat across from him.

Pete said, "No sign of Tub, boss. He and his guys have dropped off the face of the earth."

Carl raised his head and ran both hands back through his hair. He pounded the table with his fist. "Have you checked with his women? He wouldn't leave them behind."

"They are all upset. He and his boys have been missing for three days now; none of Tub's women or their women have seen hide nor hair of 'em."

"Did they say where they were going?"

Hazel said, "We saw them cross the river heading east; they were in the old Ford 4x4 pickup. Luke and Sam were with him."

Carl shook his head. "Well, we know that whatever happened to them took place on the other side of the river. I bet they got themselves shot. Tub isn't the sharpest pencil in the box, but he was smarter than those idiots with him. Each one of you guys has three or four men or women that you can rely on. I want you to find someone to replace Tub and his boys. I want you to recruit someone in Amite, Adams, Lincoln and Pike counties. We've got to start expanding our operation; I want you to look for some small time operators. If they don't want to play, you know what to do."

Spike who was usually quiet spoke up. "What if we find some big time operators?"

"If you can't recruit them, find out how many men they got and let me know what we are up against. Now would be the time to take them out; they won't be getting any weaker than they are right now."

Spike already had a good idea what the competition looked like, because he had connections one hundred and fifty miles in every direction. He also knew that Carl Benson was likely to be getting in over his head. A lot of country people were armed to the teeth, and most of them could and would shoot. Spike knew the road that Tub and his boys were working when they disappeared. He made a mental note to avoid that area. He would let the other boys take on the rough characters. He wasn't afraid of a fight; it just had to be on his terms.

Carl told them, "I want you guys to get started tomorrow. I want another twenty guys working here. I know y'all have a bunch of friends and relatives that you've been looking out for, and we're going to put them to work. I expect the men to fight if we need them. They will get paid in food and protection. We're going to set up a trading post; we won't be accepting money unless it's gold or silver. We'll take anything of value. If someone tries to go in competition with us, it'll be their ass."

Spike had six brothers-in-law that he could put to work. Every one of them owed him money, and they and their families were eating only because they were brothers to Spike's women. Spike went back to his house and called them over to lay out the game plan. When they arrived, he called them all into his den and pulled a bottle of bourbon out of his desk. He retrieved some shot glasses from his bar and poured a round.

He looked at them and made a toast, "Here's to a prosperous future." They bumped their glasses and Spike motioned for them to follow, "Follow me out to my warehouse."

Spike led all of them across the back yard and through a gate located in a ten foot tall chain link fence that was topped with three stands of barbed wire. He had a mini storage complex and had rented the units for many years. When he was collecting for Carl, one of his ladies managed it. There was also a storage yard with RV's, boats and trucks. The back dozen or so storage units were the ones used just for his private possessions.

Spike had been accumulating things for years. He had at least eight large safes bolted to the slabs that were full of gold and silver coins, jewelry and other items of value. The stacks of hundred dollar bills in them would make good toilet tissue. In the middle unit, he kept his armory. Spike was in the first and last desert war and was involved in what could be best described as special operations. He mustered out as a Sergeant and went back into Iraq working for a private contractor. As a private contractor, he accumulated many assets. In fact he shipped back five shipping containers of what many people would consider contraband. The five containers were still sitting on the back of his lot and were full of ordinance. From time to time, he would carry a truck load of ammo to the gun shows when he needed some cash for a project or holidays. Keeping up two girlfriends was not inexpensive. Even though they were identical twins, they were always jealous of one another to some extent. He learned some time ago that their jealousy could be both good and bad.

He raised the door on the middle unit. No one, not even his women, had ever been in these. The wall was lined with new Colt M-16 shorties. There were boxes of Beretta 9mm pistols--all new. Another rack had Remington 870-12 gauge shotguns with extended magazines and short barrels. All the military weapons were in vacuum sealed packages and were in pristine condition. Underneath the gun racks were some large airtight steel cases, all painted olive drab. He threw these up on a table in the middle of the room. Inside were shoulder holsters, rifle slings, and Trijicon military weapon sights. His brothers-in-law were speechless. They figured he had had a checkered past, but they had no idea the real nature of the man to which they were beholden.

"Boys, each one of you get a rifle, a shotgun, a pistol, a Trijicon rifle sight, a holster and slings."

He pointed to his youngest brother-in-law and tossed him a key ring. "Mike, you, Greg and Lucas go out to the container on the far right and haul in four cans of 5.56 and two cans of 9mm. Look in the middle container and look for some unopened cases of 5.56 and 9mm magazines. Also, bring in a couple of those sealed cases of 12 gauge buckshot."

Pointing to another case under the shotgun rack, he nodded to Bob. "Grab that case with the yellow numbering and one next to it and get out eight of those Kbar knives and eight of the leather shotgun shell bandoleers."

Before the afternoon was out, each man had sighted in a Colt M-4 and had acquired two pouches with six, thirty round magazines loaded in addition to the one in their rifle. They were wearing matching pistols in shoulder holsters that also held two magazines in addition to the one in the pistol. The shotguns already had slings and would be used as their daily carry. The rifles were for any offensive action they would take.

He pointed to Mike. "I want you to pull out an extra rifle, shotgun and one of all the gear just like we have."

"What for? We're all equipped."

"If we don't take Carl Benson an outfit, he will think we are holding out on him. Do I have to tell any of you that no one is to know about what you have just seen? I'm going to tell Carl that I got these off a National Guardsman that I ran across over in Lincoln County. If you catch any of his men nosing around the warehouse, let me know. Kill them if you see that they have broken in. Our lives won't be worth a plugged nickel if they find out what I've got. I haven't even told your sisters what I have."

Mike asked, "How on earth did you get your hands on this stuff?"

"Let's just say it was a bonus for a job well done. No one on earth knows what's here but us. I was in charge of shipping one hundred fifty containers of ordinance to friendly forces in Northern Iraq. Five of them were accidentally shipped here in error. Do I have to tell any of you what will happen to you if word gets out I have this equipment?" They all nodded "no."

"Another thing, no more drinking. If we do any drinking, it will be here in my game room. No drinking down at Carl's. The first time I even think you are drinking down there your tail will be mine. If we're going to be alive this time next year, we've got to be on top of our game. Carl is just a redneck thug; Pete and Hazel are no better. Not even your wives and girlfriends are to know about what we have here. They might slip and tell some of their friends. If you love your families and want them to survive, we have to keep our secret."

Lucas spoke up. "What do you want us to do?"

"You do what I tell you, exactly what I tell you. Is there anyone here who doesn't think I will pop a cap on you if I hear that you're talking?" They all listened in silence; they knew that he would do exactly what he said he would do.

Continuing, Spike said, "I am going to put two of you down there with Carl. Do what he says and report to me every day what is going on. So long as it's to our advantage, we are Carl's men. He'll try to work us against each other; that's his way. Just keep me posted on what's going on. The rest of you are with me. We are going to figure out who is left alive around the county. We'll be trading, not robbing and killing. Bad guys will be coming through now that it has settled in that modern life is not coming back. Tomorrow, I will take Carl his new rifle; you guys put the Trijicon and sling on it and get it sighted in. I'm going to hang out with the girls and relax."

15

AFTER A PEACEFUL night Mitch and Hannah woke and started the day. Mitch made a run out to check on the chickens. Bacon wasn't too sure about the new puppy that was insistent on attacking his tail. She treed the poor cat every time he showed himself. The cat was well out of Pinky's range so long as he stayed on the porch rails. Mitch spread some corn, that was originally intended for the deer feeders, around the chicken pen, and the chickens quickly ate it. He would feed them in the coop for the next two evenings, and they would be forever imprinted that the coop was home. Today, he was carrying one of the AR-15 shorties that he had taken from the dead men. He also wore his .45 1911 pistol in a holster and a vest with six additional magazines for the rifle and two for the pistol. A large hunting knife rounded out his gear.

He called in to Hannah. "Lock the door; I'm heading up on the mountain to see what I can see of the farm down the river. There was smoke coming from the chimney yesterday, so I want to check on it."

Hannah poked her head out of the door. "Don't be long; I'll have breakfast ready in half an hour."

'I won't be that long."

The hike up the trail didn't take but a few minutes. From the high point of the ridge, he could see up the river valley and the chimney top of the neighbor's house in the distance. As expected, he could see a faint trail of smoke coming from the chimney. Off to his right, he could see the smoke gently rising from the chimney in his own house. Bacon came trotting by. He was patrolling the area looking for a deer trail or a careless squirrel. The cold fall air fogged from Mitch's breath. Everything indicated that this year's winter would be cold. Turning back, he followed the ridge where it ran behind the house and down to the small graveyard. His dad's grave was still fresh; the grass had not grown to cover the grave before the cold weather started. He paused a moment in reflection before heading down the trail back to the house. He thought about the house down the river valley; he knew the owner of the house from all the years of staying at the farm. That farm belonged to Tony Jackson and had been in the Jackson family as long as he could remember. He hoped that Tony had survived to make it to his farm. He would try to make a run over there after breakfast. After the run in with Tub and his boys, Mitch did not want to leave Hannah alone at his house. After breakfast, they shared the chore of washing the dishes, and then they geared up.

Mitch looked at Hannah. "We are going to upgrade your fire-power; I am going to outfit you with the extra AR-15. It doesn't have much recoil, but it has a lot more knockdown power and a much greater range."

"You're going to have to teach me how to shoot it. What about my pistol?"

"I don't have a pistol that is small enough for your hands. I've got a couple of big revolvers. I think the .22 pistol you have now would be better. You've shot it and are more comfortable using it. I think it's more important to hit what you're shooting at. Bad guys with holes in them are less likely to continue their offensive. It's hard to concentrate on attacking if you're busy trying to stop blood from coming out of your body."

"Great, I want you to teach me how to shoot all the weapons we've got."

"I think that's a good idea; we'll start with your new rifle. We also need to see if we can locate or trade for one or two more so we can have replacement parts. We'll need extra parts if one of our guns breaks."

They spent a couple of hours making sure the rifles were sighted in, and they learned how to break them down for cleaning. If he ever made it to town, he would try to find a manual that detailed the complete breakdown and cleaning of the rifles. The Jeep cranked immediately. Bacon hopped in the back; he knew the drill. This wasn't his first Jeep ride. Hannah set Pinky over in the back. They headed through the open gate and across the creek; the Jeep really had to dig in to scramble up the far bank to get out of the stream. One of the next projects would be to build a bridge or replace the washed out culvert.

They ran down the trace and then exited on to the highway. Mitch pointed to the bone yard trail as they passed by it.

"I dragged the bodies down that road and left them at the dead end turn around. That will be the place we drag any future bad guys."

"I hope there won't be any more."

"I'm afraid that they are only the first of many. If we can survive the next few months, we'll make it for the long haul."

The trip down to the turn off that led to the Jackson homestead only took about five minutes. The Jackson farm was down near the end of a long gravel road. When they got to the driveway, they turned and went up to the house. An Australian shepherd ran out from under the garage door; behind her bounded three fuzzy puppies about the size of Pinky. Tony Jackson's son Larry walked out on the porch. He instantly recognized Mitch and the Jeep. Mitch and Hannah stepped out of the Jeep. Bacon hopped down and Pinky quickly joined her litter mates.

Larry grinned and pointed at Pinky. "I see you met Tub and his boys. How much did he steal from you?"

"He was all set to clean us out until Hannah dropped the one that was getting ready to shoot me. Tub and his other friend didn't make it. Their tax collecting days are behind them, so it looks like I owe you for a puppy."

"You don't owe me a thing. I owe you for capping those bastards; I would have if they hadn't had the drop on me."

"Your father was at the graveside service at my Dad's burial. He said you were in North Dakota; I'm surprised to see you."

"The oil rig I work on is undergoing an overhaul; so rather than lie around for a month or so, I decided to surprise my Dad and show up at the deer camp. I found the Aussie and her puppies on the highway on the way home. My truck is dead; I don't know why it won't crank, so I've just been hanging out here at the house. The phones are dead; my only other choice was to take a four wheeler or tractor to the truck stop in town where I could call a wrecker. I figured Dad would show up in a day or two. I wouldn't have expected the days to turn into weeks. I've just been hunting out here around the farm waiting for him to come or for the lights to come back on."

"Larry, I've got some bad news for you. The lights aren't coming back on."

"What do you mean? I know we had some bad weather, but they'll get the lines fixed sooner or later."

"Larry, the lights won't be coming back on in our lifetime; everything with an integrated circuit is fried. That's why I'm in this forty-five year old Jeep, and not in my new truck. This Jeep doesn't have anything electronic on it. I heard on Dad's old short wave that an electromagnetic pulse event has taken place. Life as we've known it is over, probably forever."

Larry just shook his head. "That's why my cell phone, truck and Dad's weather radio are dead. That was why Tub was confident when he told me they would be coming by every month to collect my taxes."

"Tub wasn't acting alone; Carl Benson is the ring leader."

"Who is Carl Benson?"

"Carl owns the Blue Flamingo back in town. I'm sure he has some more thugs working for him."

"Crap, that's all we need! That means that Dad may be stuck in New Orleans; but if anyone can get out, he can. He was always pretty resourceful. He and my uncle were always buying stuff just in case. My crazy Mama will still be in Florida with that whoremonger she ran off with. They are probably already dead. I don't expect to ever see her again. Maybe, dad will show up in a week or two; it'll take him that long to get here on foot. There's nothing I can do, but wait. I'm worried about my sister; she's in the closest thing to 'Hell on Earth.' The high population in the New York area will be in worse shape than New Orleans. The cold weather and starvation will wipe most of them out quickly." Mitch nodded in agreement.

Hannah called Pinky who came running with all her litter mates. Bacon had hopped back in the Jeep to avoid the onslaught from all the puppies. Larry motioned for them to come in the house. When they entered the living room, a low fire was burning in the fireplace, and the room was warm. The house was smaller than Mitch's farmhouse and was built in the 1920's. Like Mitch's house, it had a working wood cook stove, but unlike Mitch's it had seldom been used since the 1950's.

Mitch suggested. "You might want to drop a couple of trees across the road near the highway. Is there anyone else living down this road?"

"No, this is the only house anyone lives in. There are a couple of old abandoned farm houses on down the road. I guess I'll go look in them to see if there is anything I can use."

Hannah asked, "Do you think we'll be seeing other people? Other than Tub, we haven't seen anyone at all."

Mitch spoke up, "The only reason we haven't seen anybody is because we got out early and are very remote. We only saw Tub because he knew about our houses. Folks from Natchez, McComb and Brookhaven will be arriving at any time. I'm afraid hoards from the big cities will be showing up on foot during the next few weeks. We've had to kill seven men so far, and this catastrophe is just starting to unfold."

Larry looked at the floor. "Starving people will be going berserk, and we will have to contend with all the crooks like Tub and his boys. What can we do?"

"You're going to have to stay hid and fight. Many more people will be descending on us. We can expect people hunting deer and game to stumble upon us at any time. Don't let them know what you have; you are going to be at a disadvantage living here by yourself. What else did Tub steal from you? We may have it at the farm."

"I lost some can goods, a few boxes of shotgun shells and the puppy. One of them wanted to take the puppy to his girlfriend."

"Run by the farm when you get a chance and get your food and shells. I'll have them boxed up ready for when you come by. If I were you, I would cut through the woods; we need to block these roads to discourage people walking down them. Use that old logging road that runs along the river. It curves up to the back of the farm. If you get out, look for some livestock. We are going to need some cows and horses. Come get me, and I'll help you round them up. I've got a running truck and tractor if we need to pull a stock trailer. I'm glad you made it, and if you need somewhere to take shelter, you know where the farm is."

Larry nodded. "Thanks. Y'all can come take refuge here as well if you need to."

Hannah gathered up Pinky. "You can have everything back, but Pinky; it's finders keepers with her."

Larry watched as they joined Bacon in the Jeep. As they drove back Hannah commented, "We're lucky we found somebody who's not trying to kill us."

"I've known the Jacksons my entire life; they are good people. Don't let on to anyone, including the Jacksons, about our basement. It is our family secret. Not even my friends who came to the farm with me as a child knew about it. It is the one place we are safe to hide. We can camp out there even if the house is occupied by an enemy."

The ride back was calm. They didn't see anyone. When they arrived home, everything was as they had left it. Mitch dropped

Hannah off, took the Jeep around back and parked it. He grabbed a chain saw and hopped on one of the four wheelers. He ran up the road and dropped a huge pine tree so that it fell across the road. The fallen tree was in a section where he could drive up through the woods and back around should he need to take a vehicle out to the road. To a casual observer, it looked as if the tree had been knocked down by a storm. The sun was getting low, and the day was getting colder. Tonight would probably be the season's first frost. He got back to the farm house, ran around back and put the four wheeler and chainsaw away. Using a funnel setting in the top of the fuel can, he poured the gas from the chain saw into the can to store it. He then cranked the saw and revved the engine until all the fuel in the carburetor was consumed. That was the only way to make sure the fuel wouldn't go bad until he needed it again. The sun was not quite down so he lightly fed the chickens in their coop and closed the doors. He went all around the hen house to make sure there were no holes that a fox, coon or possum could get through. To his knowledge, this was the only flock of chickens. If something happened to these, they may never have eggs again. He knew that fresh eggs and live chickens would be as good as gold one day.

When he got back to the house, Hannah had a fire going in the cook stove. The kitchen was good and warm. Bacon, Pinky and Rover, the tom cat were all stretched out by the stove. Pinky and the cat had called a truce. Bacon sat with his tail lightly wagging and tried to be invisible because he didn't want to get put out in the cold weather. Mitch dropped the bars behind the large wooden doors and closed the heavy wooden shutters on the downstairs windows. He didn't want any surprise visitors in the middle of the night.

16

T HE SECOND CLICK from the winch echoed across the water. One click after another rang out as the anchor line was cranked around the spool. Tony kept his eyes peeled and rested the rifle on the top rail of the boat. The people were still milling around the fire. After a few minutes, they stopped walking around and starting facing the boat.

He called to Cheryl, "Our secret is out! Wind it up fast."

She quickly wound it up, and the wind started moving the boat. Other than watching from the shore, the people did nothing provocative. Tony let the wind push them out until the bonfire on the beach disappeared from view. Only then did he drop the anchor. They were still not out of danger. There was always the possibility that the people on shore would put in a boat and look for them. Tony spent the rest of the evening alert for danger and waiting for the dawn when the danger of pirates would increase. As he paced the deck, he looked to the southeast where he could see a dull glow on the horizon. The burning oil and gas lit the distant sky. The wind switched back from the south, and with it came the stench of the oil and a haze created by the smoke. They had to get away from the air and water pollution, so he made the decision that today they would take on the Mississippi River.

Dawn came, and they pulled up the anchor, cranked the engine and continued along the coast. A tug with a string of barges came into view. It was not under power and was being carried along in the current. This was one of many out of control vessels being carried to the

Gulf of Mexico by the river. Most of them would become stranded or sunk by collisions with sandbars, bridges and other vessels. Tony turned the boat in behind the tug and headed upstream. After a couple of hours, he was in a recognizable portion of the river. He could see the river banks on both sides. At this point, the river was immense with the banks almost two miles apart. They kept *Lucille* running dead slow and were careful to avoid debris in the water. Huge trees, being carried downstream, were a testimony of storms from somewhere upstream. If they were going to anchor, they had to do so out of the main channel which was filled with debris, trees and vessels. Any of those items coming down the river could destroy or capsize their boat. *Lucille* was large and fully capable of cruising on the river, but nothing could take on what the Mississippi River was carrying in its current.

They located a canal off the channel of the river that appeared to run through a cypress swamp. It was evidently a short cut that was created by oil companies to reach remote wells. The current was calm in the canal so they proceeded at a dead slow pace for an hour until they were well out of the river. They passed a few abandoned camps and found several families living on shrimp boats who had taken refuge back in the swamp. All of them were armed and defensive.

Tony called out, "Ahoy, we're not looking for trouble; just shelter."

A man with a strong Cajun accent answered from the first boat. He had a twelve gauge shotgun cradled in his arms, "We don't want no trouble either. The oil in the Gulf just chased us up here. We were taking shelter in the Gulf until the oil overtook us."

"How many families do y'all have here?"

"There are three families here; we made our living in the Gulf until all this started. The only things we can get to work are the old diesel engines; nothing electronic works."

"That's because an electromagnetic pulse has taken out everything with an integrated circuit. The lights aren't coming back on;

once you are out of diesel, you will be stranded where you sit. I don't want to disturb or bother you folks. What will I find if I continue down this canal?"

"You won't be bothering us. We are trying to figure out what to do and where to go. If you keep going up this canal, it will take you back into some bayou country where there are camps and more canals that head off into the Gulf and marsh. This is going to be the most remote section; that's why we are here."

"I just need some time for me to heal. We were attacked a week or so ago, and I took a bullet through the shoulder. I've just got to heal a little before we head up river."

"The only way anyone is going to get here is by boat. There is nothing but miles and miles of swamp in every direction. Unless someone has a running boat engine, they aren't going to make it very far in the river. I am Herb Herbert, and my two brothers and their families are on the other two boats."

"Glad to meet you. I'm Tony Jackson, and this is Cheryl. What do y'all have to trade?"

"We've got plenty of shrimp and trout. We're trying to eat them up; we've been keeping the ice machines running with the generator."

Tony grinned. "I'll trade you a sack of banana chips for a sack of big shrimp."

Herb called over his shoulder. "Scoop up ten pounds of d'em big shrimp; I've got us some bananas coming."

They made the exchange. Tony cranked the boat and idled a hundred yards further down the bayou where he tied off to some old piling next to the north side. They boiled up the shrimp and used salt and crab boil from the kitchen to season them. Tony flicked the switch on the refrigerator to the gas setting and listened for the puff of the gas coming on. An audible pop echoed from behind the unit, and a little glow could be seen through a sight tube. The gas burner in the fridge was working. For now they would have the refrigerator so long as the gas held out. He hoped the propane gas would last until they could evacuate to the farm. That night they stayed in the warm cabin. They weren't worried about the shrimpers up the bayou. If they were up to no good, they had had plenty of opportunity to attack them during the transfer of the shrimp and banana chips. There was always the fear of attack; they knew that one of the few places of refuge from the starving hordes was the bayou country. The only advantage was the fact that they were only approachable by water.

That evening the weather once again turned stormy. They hunkered down in the cozy cabin and turned on the short wave radio. As before, there were few stations to listen to. They occasionally picked up broadcast from HAM operators who had dug out obsolete equipment they had not discarded. Most old radio guys never throw away the old equipment; it winds up in a barn or attic just in case they need to resurrect it for some unforeseen event. The news was only getting worse. The cold winter and the lack of electricity were wiping out the populations of the big cities in the North. This was of grave concern to Tony because his daughter was living there.

The only light in the room came from the dial of the radio. Cheryl could see the look on Tony's face in the dim light and knew that he was worried. "Is there anything that we can do to help or get to her?"

"No, even if we tried to sail up there. I wouldn't have any way of finding her. I tried to instill some self-reliance in her. I just hope she has more common sense in her from me than her idiot mother."

"What about her husband?"

"She married someone from up there; that means she probably has to take care of him. Few of those big city guys will know anything about living off the land nor do they have any mechanical skills. I met him at the wedding. I think he had big city living mastered. I don't believe he would last a minute outside that environment."

Cheryl grinned. "I bet he is a lot like that guy from New York City we had working in IT. He didn't believe in self-defense; he said that was what the police were for."

Tony shook his head. "I bet he is having second thoughts about all of that now, if he is even still alive."

"Probably not, he would have been bewildered by the bad guys until it was too late. He would also be one of the first ones demanding that other people need to feed and protect him."

"We have to stick to our plans to get back to the farm with as much of our supplies as we can. Without communication, we can't do anything but hope she can make her way home."

"Do you think she will try and reach her mother in Florida?"

"I hope not. My son Larry said she wasn't very fond of her new step-father. She spotted him fooling around with one of the neighborhood women behind her mother's back. When she told her mother, she didn't believe her, and they all had a big blow up over it. She flew back to New York. All of that happened about a month ago, so she will probably not be heading in that direction."

Their attention was captured by someone speaking on the radio with news from Atlanta. The city was in a dire condition; grocery stores had been picked clean as well as all the food warehouses. What people had on hand was all they would have unless they started taking it from others. The speaker estimated there would be a lot of dead people in the next thirty days from starvation alone.

Tony looked away from the radio. "In the morning we need to tell the Herberts what we know. There will also be people in small boats trying to escape the cities, and this area is the only one in the region where they can seek refuge. I think we need to head north on the river right away. The sooner we can get to the farm the better. We can pull the big skiff with the dingy up the Homochitto."

They went to bed with the troubling news weighing heavily on their minds. They were awaken by gun fire erupting from where the Herbert's boats were tied up. Tony reached for his shotgun.

17

SPIKE RODE DOWN to the Blue Flamingo in his old Ford Bronco. He parked it just outside the door next to the Harleys that belonged to Hazel and her gang. He had Carl's weapons in a duffel bag. Although it was early, Hazel and the girls were already drinking and shooting pool. Carl came down the stairs from his apartment above. His oily hair was slicked back and culminated in a short ponytail. "Spike what brings you out so early?"

"Got a package for you; I ran across something you'll like."

Spike sat the duffel on the table and unzipped it. He pulled out the fully automatic M-4 and passed it to Carl as he pulled out the Beretta pistol, shotgun, Kbar and accessories.

Carl put the M-4 to his shoulder and adjusted the stock length. "Where did you get this gear?"

"I ran across a former National Guard supply sergeant. I bought out his stock; there was enough for me and my guys with an extra set for you."

"Spike have you been holding out on me? What did you trade him?"

Spike's just looked at Carl. "Carl, we've always done business, and it has always been profitable for both of us. Do you really want go there?"

Carl nodded towards Hazel. "Spike, I can't treat you any different than I treat Hazel and the other guys."

Spike recognized what Carl was doing. He was playing Hazel and him against one another. "Carl, I don't care how you treat Hazel and the other guys. I will work with you so long as it is beneficial to us both. I don't ask you about your business, and you better not ask me how I conduct mine. So, do you want the gift or not?"

The Beretta in Spike's hand was loaded, and Carl's answer would decide if he would use it or hand it over.

Carl laughed. "Just kidding, Spike. Thanks for thinking of me."

Hazel who hadn't said a word starting laughing and made her pool shot with a crack of the cue ball against the eight ball.

Spike grinned back although he knew that the day would come when he would have to use force. "The guns are loaded; there are extra loaded magazines in the bag. I'll send a couple of my guys over later this morning; go easy on them their first day." Carl called to the cook back in the kitchen. "Rustle us up some breakfast. Spike, are you hungry?"

"I've already eaten; I'm going to do little exploring today."

Spike hopped in his Bronco and headed back to his compound. When he arrived, he again gathered his men in the den. His girlfriends had prepared breakfast of biscuits, bacon and coffee for the meeting. All the men, including Spike, were wearing their shoulder holsters and Beretta pistols. Spike explained to them what had taken place down at the Blue Flamingo and illustrated Carl's methods of intimidating people and playing them off one another.

"I am warning you again. Do not reveal to Carl what we've got here. If he finds out, he won't hesitate to kill you, me and your sisters to get it. I told him that I bought our gear off of a National Guard supply sergeant. I didn't tell him who or where; he is going to ask you. Everyone knows I went on a trip last Thursday to Pike County. The story is real simple; all you know is that I showed up with it all last Thursday when I got back. That's all you know; any questions?"

Josh spoke up. "How long are we going to be working for Carl?"

Spike grinned. "Men like Carl have a tendency to die young. I think you all know me well enough to know that I don't play mind games or attempt to manipulate people. As long as what we do keeps us alive and fed, we'll do it within reason. I'm not going to rob or murder anyone unless they just plain need killing. I don't expect you to do it either."

Mike asked, "If Carl orders us to kill someone, what do we do?"

"You'll just have to play it by ear. If you have to kill Carl, Hazel or Pete, I will understand. At this point we are going to do what it takes to keep them from killing us. If he doesn't believe we're on his side, he'll come after us. So we will eat his food, guard his chickens and cover our rears. Does everyone understand? If any of you tell him about our provisions, he will be glad to get the information, and he will also know that you can't be trusted. He won't hesitate to pop a cap on you. He thinks he is establishing a kingdom here in the middle of nowhere. Maybe he is, but I doubt it. Mike and Greg take your shotguns and a bandolier of buckshot and hang out at the Blue Flamingo."

He turned to Bob. "I want you to hang out here and guard the house and storage yard. The rest of us are going to round up some big campers and motor homes; we're moving them to the back of the lot and set them up for your families. I believe it's going to get bad; everyone is on foot right now. This little community is off the beaten path, but it won't be for long."

Spike reached in his pocket and tossed Lucas a set of keys. "Go get my old Ford diesel wrecker; it should crank right up. We can use it to drag up some motor homes that we can't crank. Josh, will that old Dodge truck of yours crank?"

Josh turned. "Sure. I'm glad I didn't get rid of it."

"Good; go get it. It has a hitch on it that we can use to pull trailers with."

They spent the rest of the day looking for and gathering up campers. They took an old working generator so they could see which of the campers had working refrigerators, air conditioners and water heaters. By the end of the day, they had found a dozen RV's that had everything working. The next job was to get them cleaned up and outfitted with food and good mattresses. They spent two more days getting water, sewage and electrical lines run. The natural gas lines in town were still under pressure because they were all being fed by natural gas wells throughout the region. So long as the gas wells produced and the lines didn't break, they would have gas to cook and run generators. A large, forty-kw natural gas power plant hummed between the house and the campground.

The next order of business was to drag up abandoned cars to block the driveways so that anyone trying to drive in would have to weave in and out around them. The cars would prevent anyone from being able to quickly approach the compound unless they were in a tank. The blockade would give the men on guard time to react.

Since Spike rotated his guys working down at the Flamingo, none of them had to spend too much time under Carl's influence. Up until now, they hadn't had to kill anyone, and Carl was content to take what Hazel, Pete and their crews were hauling in.

Hazel and her girls came riding into the camp just as they finished working on some of the defenses. The girls dropped the kick stands; the big bikes leaned as they climbed off. They walked over to Spike. "Looks like you boys have got yourselves a fort put together over here?"

"Yep, there will be throngs of people showing up here anytime now. What we have seen so far has been a trickle. Do you girls have a place in mind if it starts getting bad?"

"We've been helping Carl fortify the Flamingo; we've been hauling in concrete blocks and bricks around the place."

"That sounds like a good idea. What brings you around?"

"I've found out what happened to Tub and his boys. We were making a run out Hwy 98 and saw a bunch of buzzards circling just off the highway. We found what was left of them off one of those US Forestry roads. I recognized Tub from that big gold tooth he had."

Spike grinned. "Let's see it." He knew Hazel would not have left it to disappear.

She dug down in her pocket and came out with it. "It has to be worth something as big as it is. They were picked clean; whoever killed them took everything they had including most of their clothes. I checked down the road, but it was impassable from downed timber. I think someone may be camping down that road, or there could be a house back in there someplace."

"Hazel, I'd be careful if I were you. If they could take out Tub and his men like that, they might not be someone you want to mess with. I bet there are easier pickings elsewhere if you know what I mean."

Hazel nodded. "I think you're right. Carl isn't going to be happy; he'll probably send some of us back there to look around."

"Tell him that a couple of my boys and I will check it out. That'll get you off the hook. If you tell him about the tooth, you are going to lose it. Tell him you recognized the body as Tub's because of that missing pinky finger on his left hand. Everybody knows he lost it by getting it cut off with a chainsaw last year. That way you can keep the tooth as a souvenir. How far out is it?"

Hazel grinned. Her two gold teeth shone in the morning light. Her intense blue eyes were framed by the black doo rag that covered her shaved head. The silver spike earring accented the brow rings that looked at first glance like mosquitoes resting on her eyebrows. The leather gloves she wore had the fingers exposed, and the nails were short and painted black. Hazel was not the sort of girl one could bring home to meet Mama. She pointed to the road on a map that she had pulled out of one of the saddlebags on her bike.

Spike nodded. "I'll head over there in a couple of days and check it out."

"Those bodies stink like hell; you don't want to get too close."

Spike gave her a wink and watched as Hazel and her gang hopped back on their bikes. Soon the familiar lope of the Harley engines filled the air. They left in a cloud of dust and roar of exhaust.

Spike's brother-in-law Mike spoke up. "Why do you suppose she came by here to see us?"

"Oh, I imagine they are a little curious about what we're doing, and finding Tub and his boys have made them a little nervous. She doesn't trust Carl any more than we do."

"How did you know she had Tub's tooth in her pocket?"

"I've got a good handle on the people around me and what they are capable of doing. I just know Hazel and her type; there's very little they won't stoop to. I know they will be heading back down that road to see if there's a house back there or if someone is camping. They figure there may be a haul to be made, and in her mind they aren't going to let me beat them too it. I assure you; they don't bring everything in and give it to Carl."

"Do you think we need to try and find that road and check it out?"

"We have to finish things here first. It might not be good for someone to go busting in there. Hazel may wind up biting off more than she can chew."

18

MITCH WOKE EARLY. The room was cold, and his breath fogged as he slipped out from under cover. He took the poker and raked the ashes off the coals beneath. A rush of sparks raced up the chimney as oxygen reached the newly exposed embers. He tossed several sticks of wood on the coals, and smoke started pouring off, before the wood erupted into flames. Mitch walked to the thick wooden shutters that had a small diamond shaped hole in the center. The diamond shape was formed when the two halves of the shutters met in the middle. He looked out and made sure there was nothing moving and that no one was on the porch. He pulled the shutters open and let the fall sun light come streaming through.

Hannah stirred at the creak from the old hinges. "Good morning, baby. What are we going to do today?"

"I'm going to set up an early warning system. I'm tired of trying to sleep with one eye open all the time. My dad showed me how to rig a simple trip wire alarm using some fishing line and some party poppers. The party popper has a string that attaches to a tiny friction activated explosive charge. If we take out the confetti and replace it with black powder, it will pop real loud, alert us and scare the daylights out of whomever or whatever is sneaking up on us."

He went to the kitchen door and let Bacon and Pinky out. If anyone was lurking about, Bacon would quickly have them cornered. All was serene at the farm. After a good country breakfast, they sat up an assembly line on a long table in the basement and started making up the black powder filled poppers. The final step in the process was dipping them in paraffin wax to make them water tight. With some fencing staples, fishing line and some nails, he created simple triggers to set off the poppers once they were tripped. The rest of the day was spent deploying the poppers on all the roads, lanes and trails leading to the farm house. They were just finishing with the last one up on Mitch's Mountain when they heard one of them go off in the distance. Although it was several miles down the road, the topography of the ridges funneled the sound down to the farm. As usual, they were armed for battle. He and Hannah made a quick run back to the house where they locked in the dogs.

Hannah picked up a can of brown shoe polish and grabbed Mitch by the sleeve. "Let's tone down these shiny faces and hands before we head out."

Mitch grinned. "That's not a bad idea; let's put on some camouflaged coveralls as well." Shortly, they were geared up and ready to go.

Mitch's Mountain was a large ridge that ran down behind the house and flattened out before getting to the old cemetery. Just past the cemetery it fell off again and eventually played out at the little creek that ran across the road coming into the farm. On the opposite bank another great ridge ran down and ended in the creek as well. Sometime in the distant past someone had cut one of the large cypress trees that grew along the creek, and when it fell, its trunk spanned the creek. Using limbs from the great tree, someone had attached a rough handrail. The axe hewn notches still held the limbs in place. It was a crude, but very effective, footbridge crossing the creek.

This ridge was every bit as large as Mitch's Mountain and ran more or less parallel to the road coming to the farm. This area of the forest had a huge number of the Old Plantation Pines. Many were planted back in the 1930's and had never been harvested. Their canopies touched high above and shaded out most of the underbrush. The pine straw was deep and cushioned every step. Here in the low light, ferns and wild azalea grew. Magnolia trees were interspersed among the giant pine trees. Occasionally, one would find a tree known as a Giant Leaf Magnolia. The open woodland was not a good place to be, because there was very little cover unless one was hiding behind one of the giant trees. The advantage the woods gave Mitch and Hannah was speed and silence. They probably wouldn't run into anyone here because the land on all sides was surrounded by cut over timber. The cut over timber had once been like this section but had been harvested about five years earlier. It was now so thick with briars and small trees that no one could walk through it. It would make a great place to hide, but one would have to be on his or her hands and knees to crawl into it. Even then the going would be next to impossible. It was, however, a wonderful habitat for deer and game.

They reached an area where the ridge meandered close to the road. At this point they could look over the cutover section and look down upon the road. In the distance a person could see the old Hwy 98 that went over to the little town of Bude, MS. From here one could also see the big pine tree that Mitch had cut to block the road. Behind the tree, a small group of people had set up camp using the tree to shield themselves from the road. They counted four men, three women and several children. The adults were arguing, and one of the men was pointing down the road and giving a gesture that appeared to be a resounding "no." They were gesturing in the direction of the first popper booby trap that one of them had obviously triggered.

An old yellow school bus came into view heading down the highway; Mitch could see people in the bus, but couldn't see how many. Shots rang out from a gunman that he hadn't seen. The bus careened off the road and disappeared down the embankment on the other side of the road. All the men took off toward the road and crossed down the road bank where the bus was wrecked. Mitch and Hannah looked at each other as gunfire erupted from across the highway. The men were hauling up gear and supplies from the attacked bus. A small child could be heard crying at the top its lungs. A shot rang out, and the ensuing silence was deafening. Hannah was raising her gun to fire, but Mitch stopped her, put his finger to his lips, and told her to be quiet.

Hannah whispered. "What are we going to do?"

"To start, we aren't going to alert them to our presence. We can hit them from up here, but we have to careful. I don't want to hit the children, and I don't want them shooting back. They might get lucky and hit us."

Mitch reached into his pack and pulled out the suppressor for his rifle and screwed it on in place of the flash hider. As he attached the suppressor and watched, the child killer crossed the highway and started down the gravel road towards the camp. Both he and Hannah's rifles were equipped with Eotec red dot scopes. He raised his rifle, put the red dot on the child killer's chest and squeezed the trigger. The rifle bounced, and the man collapsed as the 55 grain bullet turned his heart to jelly. The rest of the people scattered. They couldn't know from which direction the shot came, so Mitch waited. After about thirty minutes, they started yelling back and forth to one another. The women and children quickly gathered their things and started for the highway. The men followed suit. The trailing man turned and shook his fist in the air; Mitch dropped him with a shot through his head. Another man started shooting wild; Mitch silenced him as well. The others started running and didn't look back. Mitch put in a fresh magazine and looked at Hannah who was shaking.

"I wish they were all dead; I hate them."

"We'll leave the bodies where they lay. We have more of our popper bombs between there and the house. Maybe those bodies will act as an early warning to anyone wanting to come looking our way."

"Mitch, when's it going to end?"

"It won't end for a long time; I'm afraid there is no shortage of bad guys."

They didn't speak much on the way home. People from the cities were starting to reach the country. Since this was one of the most remote places in the South, only the smart and tough would have survived to have made it this far. When they were back at the house, they made sure that it was secure. They closed the shutters and barred the doors. Hannah wouldn't put her rifle down, but instead wore it hung on her back.

Mitch pointed to her gun. "You plan on sleeping with that thing?"

"I'm scared Mitch. I was hoping we would be safe here."

"We are safer here than anywhere I can imagine. We'd have to be out West in the mountains and out of walking range of the cities to be more secure. Short of that, we are as safe and secure as we're going to get. We are at the end of the road, and we have an early warning system that works. We have dogs, and we are armed to the teeth. If we come under attack, we can escape through the basement and attack them from the rear."

Hannah hugged his neck. "We've got to make sure that we aren't caught off guard."

The next morning, Spike Hobbil walked out on his back deck and looked across the back of his storage yard at the collection of RV's that were housing his extended family. A heavy frost covered the grass and the tops of the porch rails. Steam blew from his breath and drifted off the top of his cup of coffee. The drone of the generator was the only thing disturbing the quiet morning. Today would be a good day to check out the road where Tub and boys met their demise. He wanted to beat Carl or Hazel and her girls to the punch. He loaded up his old Bronco with his rifle, and he was wearing his pistol. His brothers-in-law were up and stirring so he gave them their orders.

Spike pointed to Greg. "You're with me; bring your rifle. We're going scouting." He walked to the back door where Lisa handed him a sack of sausage biscuits to carry with him. She also handed him a thermos of hot coffee; she and her sister Lacy could always read his mind. They said he was the only person other than their mother who could tell them apart.

He fired up the old Bronco, headed out and crossed the Homochitto River on Hwy 98. He passed the lake and turned onto the road marked on his map. He came upon a school bus that was wrecked on the left side of the road.

He stopped on the road above the bus and told Greg, "Keep your eyes open while I check it out."

He walked down to the wrecked bus and found the dead family. A small girl about four years old had been shot between her eyes. A cold chill ran up his spine. The bus contained a lot of things they could use. He wouldn't leave it for someone else to scavenge. He climbed back up the road bank, hopped back in the Bronco and turned down the side road. Three dead men lay in the road; Spike and Greg stopped and gathered the weapons and ammo off of the dead bodies.

Spike commented, "Whoever killed these men were not robbing them; it was more likely they were executed. These men were hit by small diameter bullets. Those people in the bus were killed by the deer rifles carried by these guys."

Greg looked apprehensive. "Are we in danger of getting shot?"

Spike grinned. "I wouldn't be surprised if we are being watched at this moment. Keep your rifle slung on your back; don't appear to be at the ready."

"Are we going to investigate further?"

"Sure, but I want these folks on my side; I don't want to have to wonder about who or what they are. I'm going to take a walk. Take the Bronco back home and get a truck and trailer and a couple of the guys to help; I want you to load up the rest of the supplies in the bus and get them stowed back at the house. When you get back, hide the Bronco here in the woods and hide the key inside the trailer hitch tube."

Spike watched as Greg disappeared down the highway. He crossed the fallen tree and headed down the road. He munched on one of the sausage biscuits as he walked. About a mile and a half down the road, he came to a thin piece of monofilament line. He only spotted it because a leaf that had fallen from a pecan tree was hanging on it. He followed the line over and realized that he was looking at an early warning system. He didn't disturb it, but he removed the pecan leaf hanging on the line. He continued down the road and spotted three more poppers. He followed the road until it came to a small lane leading up through the woods. The lane had been well traveled over the years. The trees completely covered it from above. When he reached the creek, he saw where the road crossed and spied the washed out culvert lying twisted downstream. Farther down, he could see the footbridge across the stream. He strolled down to the foot bridge and crossed over. He walked back to the lane and up to the metal gate. It was also booby trapped with a warning popper, so he climbed over the fence to the side. Once he cleared the fence, Spike walked up the lane and reached the yard of a farmhouse. A small column of smoke drifted from the big chimney in the center of the roof. He was standing and wondering whether it would be safe to just knock on the door, when the decision was made for him.

Bacon came bounding across the yard barking. A moment later he heard the distinct shucking sound of a twelve gauge pump shotgun. He gently squatted, laid his rife on the ground and slowly removed his pistol from his shoulder holster and laid it next the rifle.

Mitch called out. "Move away from the guns and put your hands on top of your head."

Spike said, "I don't want any trouble; I just wanted to see who was staying up here."

Mitch came out from behind a huge pecan tree growing near the house. "Who are you, and what do you want?"

"Some men we know were found dead up near the highway; I just wanted to see who was back here."

Mitch studied him. "It seems to me that the dead bodies would be a good reason not to come here."

Spike nodded in agreement. "Under the circumstances, I would say you are absolutely right, but there are some people I know who will come here in force once they realize you are back here. I'm sure Tub and his boys deserved what they got; they were working for Carl Benson."

"Are you working with Carl Benson?"

"Let's just say, I have a truce with him. Right now he needs me more than I need him. As you know, we are starting to see people from the cities showing up. Carl and his men have killed, robbed and run off most of the people in town and have been robbing and killing people here in the county. I bet Tub was out collecting taxes when you had to kill him."

Mitch noticed that Bacon had quit barking and was instead just lying in the grass unconcerned.

Mitch motioned for Spike to put his hands down. "Bacon is a pretty good at judging people. Leave your guns where they are lying and come have a seat on the porch." Hannah appeared from behind a tree off to the left of Spike.

"My name is Mitch Henderson, and this is my girlfriend Hannah; she'll be my wife if we find a preacher."

"I'm Spike Hobbil. I live near Meadville with my family and extended family. You've managed to get the attention of Carl Benson, and that's going to be a problem."

"I'm not afraid of Carl Benson. Why is he interested in us out here in the middle of nowhere?"

"He's not after you so much as what you represent. You've got resources that he doesn't control, and you have single handedly taken out three of his best men."

Hannah spoke up. "They were stupid and tried to kill Mitch; we didn't have a choice."

Spike grinned. "I have no doubt they needed killing. Carl Benson thinks he is starting a kingdom here in Mississippi. He has gathered up a group of about twenty men and women who are nothing more than a bunch of killers. He's trying to establish similar groups in the surrounding counties, and they intend on collecting taxes in the form of food and equipment. Another problem you are going to have is the city people heading this way. The food is exhausted in the cities, and people will have to leave there to keep from getting killed and to keep from starving."

Mitch nodded in agreement. "I figure there will be people trying to live off the land. They will be seeking refuge in the Homochitto Forest and will be camping around Okhissa Lake and the one at Clear Springs. What about the people living in Meadville and Bude?"

"Carl's men have either killed or run most of them out. Carl's men haven't ventured too far out in the county for fear of being shot by the locals. The problem is most of the people who live out don't have huge gardens or animals either. Those that do are targets for those who don't."

Hannah spoke up. "Where does that leave us?"

Spike shook his head. "I don't know; you are going to be a target not only from Carl but also from anyone who happens to stumble upon you. You have what everyone is looking for--a working farm."

Mitch agreed. "Where does that leave us with you?"

"At this point, I will want to trade with you and maybe think of this place as somewhere to retreat. I am well supplied and secure where I am, but all that can change in an instant. All the food that Carl and his men have accumulated isn't going to last forever; I fully expect there to be groups traveling the countryside attacking and stealing what they can find. I'm going to tell Carl that you guys are on starvation and are looking for a handout, and that you have no idea what happened to Tub and his boys. You need to keep alert; trouble is coming."

"Thanks, how do I find you if I need you?"

"We're located at the mini storage out on the highway past Meadville. I live behind it. Be careful if you come visiting; it's well guarded."

Mitch pointed west. "There is another farm a couple of miles downriver. Larry Jackson lives there and is expecting his father to come walking in at any time. I'll give him a heads up."

Mitch stepped into the kitchen brought out a map of the county and showed it to Spike. "Here is a map of the county. Here are the boundaries of this farm. He pointed out the highways in three directions and the Homochitto River. These are the boundaries I am establishing as belonging to this farm. I don't need that much land, but I want a tremendous buffer around this farm. No one will be allowed to stay unless we invite them."

Spike nodded. "I agree, and I will respect the boundaries. I'll tell my men."

"The Jackson farm lies to the west across this road."

Spike shook Mitch's hand. "Understood, I'll try to get word to you if I hear trouble is headed your way. If you need to abandon the farm, bring what food you can carry and head to my place. Good luck, folks."

With that, Spike headed out, picked up his weapons and retraced his steps to the highway. The bus was gone, and in its place were four graves. The dead men still lay in the gravel road where he found them earlier. His Bronco was hidden where he expected. It cranked, and he wheeled back out on the highway being careful not to back over the dead men. The mud grip tires whined as he headed back. He hoped that Carl would buy his story.

19

MAKING SURE THAT there was no light, Tony opened the door and with his twelve gauge shotgun at the ready, stepped out on the rear deck. Gun fire was erupting from the shrimp boats. A loud boom from Hebert's shotgun was followed by a loud splash. A spotlight popped on from a boat and a stream of machine gun bullets with tracers lit up the night. Tony almost didn't see the man in black coming over *Lucille's* fantail. He jerked the shotgun around and hit the man with a full blast of buckshot in the chest. The blast of lead propelled him backwards and back into the boat in which he was riding. Tony emptied the shotgun into the boat and its occupants.

He yelled back into the cabin to Cheryl, "Get below the water line and keep your pistol handy."

"What are you going to do?"

"I'm going to help the Heberts fight."

He strapped on his Browning pistol, knife, coat and rifle. The coat pockets held his spare magazines and ammo. He immediately sighted across the water; the orange holographic dot from his weapons sight completely covered the spot light that was sweeping the Hebert's boat. He squeezed the trigger and the rifle bounced. The light went out in an instant. The kick from the shotgun and now the rifle had set his wounded shoulder on fire, but it wasn't slowing him up; the adrenalin from the gun battle was doing its job.

He scrambled over the fantail and into the boat with the slain attackers. The weather was still bad, and the rain was soaking him.

His waterproof coat shed the water, but his bare head and pants were soaked. One of the attackers had a small flashlight that was still burning. Not wanting to attract extra attention, he used it to quickly look around the boat before switching it off. The boat had an aluminum hull; his shotgun blast had been absorbed by the men and the floor deck of the boat. It had a modern inboard jet drive and was obviously a military or government vessel. There were no obvious leaks from the gunfire, but it would be daylight before he would know for sure. The boat's motor must have been EMP protected or repaired. The men all carried Colt M-4 carbines with the Trijicon battle scopes. They were all wearing Beretta 9mm pistols, the standard issue for the US military. He left the four bodies in the bottom of the boat, took one of the paddles and started heading for the Herbert's boats. The machine gun had quieted, but there was still gun fire from the boats. He resisted the urge to pick up the rifles in the boat. He felt that fighting with the weapons he knew was better than using ones with which he was unfamiliar. Lightening streaked across the sky and lit up the boats and the black water of the canal. In the brief intense flash of lightening, Tony saw bodies floating in the water. Another large aluminum boat was tied up to the rear of the nearest shrimp boat. It was larger and had a machine gun, on a mount, in the middle, in front of the center console. As his boat drifted towards the larger one, a flashlight came on illuminating two men setting another can of ammo on the machine gun. In one smooth motion, Tony raised the rifle and pulled the trigger the instant the orange dot crossed the torsos. The two men went down, and the flashlight disappeared behind the gunnels. He cycled the action, and he fully expected to come under fire, but none came. He could still hear gunfire from inside the three shrimp boats. The current carried him up to the larger boat. He looked over into the big boat where the flashlight was still shining, and in the reflected light he saw what the hunting round had accomplished. The round had passed through the torso of the first man, through the machine gun mount and finally through the chest of the second man. Both men had collapsed in the bottom of the boat. He thought about climbing into the shrimp boat, but in the darkness there was no way to know friend from foe, and he did not know the layout of the boats. The gun fire had ceased, and an engine cranked up in the bowels of the shrimp boat. Lights came on in the shrimp boat as the generator energized the circuit and lit the area. Herb Herbert appeared over the back of the boat and aimed his shotgun at Tony.

"Hold up Herbert; it's me, Tony."

"Sorry Tony, I thought some more of those bastards were still out here. I see you took care of them already. They killed one of my brothers, his wife and one of my nephews. He got off a shot before they got him. His shot warned us, and we were able to start fighting before they were all on board our boats. It's a good thing we always keep someone on guard; otherwise, we'd all be dead."

"It's a good thing you started shooting; I was able to stop these just as they were boarding my boat. From the looks of their boats and equipment they appear to be government men. I can use this boat and some of this gear to get up the river to my farm. Do you need any help tending to your family?"

"I'll call if we need you; go back to your boat and stay alert. This might not be all of them. We're going to kill the lights as soon as we get everything back in order."

Tony cranked the jet boat, powered back over to *Lucille* and called to Cheryl, "It's okay. I'm back; the battle is over for now."

Cheryl came barreling out. "What happened?"

He clicked on the flashlight and pointed to the dead bodies in the boat.

Her hand came up to her throat and neck. "My God, who are these men?"

"Looks like they are some of our government people gone rogue. This is Katrina on steroids all over again. I am going to start handing you guns and gear; this boat will allow us to take all our gear up the

Homochitto River all the way to my farm. It has a jet drive that will run in shallow water; this is our ticket home."

"Why is this boat engine running? I thought all modern engines are toast?"

"I think all the electronics are on the motor down in the engine compartment. This boat is all metal including the hatches. By being in the water and surrounded by metal on all sides, the boat acted like a Faraday cage and protected it. I am just thankful that we've ended up with it."

He took his time and unloaded the Colt M-4 rifles and pistols before handing them up to Cheryl. He took all the usable gear off the men and out of the boat. He even removed their belts and clothes. He rinsed these out in the canal, wrung them out and spread them out to dry. He passed the bodies over the side. He then cranked the generator, powered up the deck wash hose, rinsed away all the blood from the craft and cleaned himself up. The water was bitter cold, but he was still running on an adrenaline high. He finally came in and warmed up with a shower and hot cocoa from an MRE. He finished his tasks by cleaning and oiling the rifles, pistols and knives. He could go through the balance of their gear once the sun came up.

They turned off the generator and sat on the couch. The twelve gauge shotgun was cleaned, reloaded and within arm's reach. In the darkness they held one another and waited for the dawn. Sometime in the night, they dozed and eventually retired to the bed. The next morning they woke to a sunny day.

Cheryl looked at Tony, "Happy Thanksgiving, handsome."

"I've lost track of time; it's a shame we don't have a feast planned and a house full of people."

"Don't worry. Thanksgiving next year will be at the farm, and hopefully it will be a lot quieter than this one."

Tony groaned as he rolled out of bed. His left shoulder was in agony after all the night's activity. He took some aspirin and some of the pain killer from the banana boat's first aid kit. After another hot shower, he was moving again, so he finished going through their newly acquired tactical gear. He now had twenty-eight, 30 round, pmag magazines to go with the four Colt rifles. There were also twelve magazines for the four Beretta pistols. Each of the government men had had large knives in polymer scabbards, a tactical vest and assorted gear. Two of the vests were too shot up to use, but the others were fine. He adjusted them to fit him and Cheryl. They moved the extra gas from the skiff and their dinghy over to the new boat.

This new boat was large enough to hold all their food and gear when they made it to the Homochitto River. It was twenty four feet long, eight feet wide and had virtually no draft, and it had the capability to run the river all the way up to the farm. The boat had a small leak from a buckshot hole at the water line that caused the bilge pump to kick on from time to time. After the bilge pump finished pumping out the water, it raised the hull so that the hole was right at the water line again. He took a hammer from his tool box and beat the metal on the outside of the hull back into shape. He found a piece of dry driftwood up on the bank and whittled it into a plug that he could drive into the hole. It quickly swelled from the water and stopped the leak. He whittled off most of the excess; the repair, although crude, would hold until they got back to the farm.

They solemnly watched as the Herberts transferred the bodies of their family to the large government boat. Tony and Cheryl paddled down in the skiff that they were preparing to abandon.

Herb Hebert looked down from the large captured boat, "We're taking them over to the bank and will bury them there; thanks again for helping us last night, after the burial I'll come over for a visit."

"I'll stay on guard with my rifle until you finish."

Herb choked up and could only nod his head in agreement. Tony and Cheryl didn't really know the Heberts, but they were sad just the same. They both knew that they had had a very close call. From *Lucille's* deck, Tony could see up and down the canal in both directions. With his .308 deer rifle leaning on a rail within reach, he maintained his vigilance.

The Heberts moved the dead up the canal bank to graves that the men had prepared. A woman could be heard wailing and sobbing. The sound made the hair on the back of Tony's neck stand on end. The Hebert family returned to the boat and attended to getting the mess cleaned up. Bodies of the dead government men were stripped of gear and clothes and dumped into the canal. The lifeless bodies slowly floated towards the river where they would wind up in the Gulf of Mexico. The sun was burning away the light mist that was hovering just above the water. Herb Hebert climbed into their small boat and paddled over to *Lucille*. Tony caught the rope and held it as Herb climbed over the side.

Cheryl poked her head out of the door. "Could you use some coffee? I'll put on a pot if you like."

Herb nodded. "That would be great! We ran out of coffee last week; I didn't expect to taste it again anytime soon."

Tony pointed to the government boat. "I think we lucked out. That boat should be able to carry us all the way to our farm in Mississippi. I'm going to tow it with this boat all the way to and as far up as I can travel in the Homochitto River. I should be able to get to within a half a mile of my farm."

"We don't know what we are going to do," Herb said. "I'm thinking that we can put all our fuel and gear on one of the boats and head for South America. I think we can get to Belize where we went on vacation one time. If we head out now, we can go around the oil on the west side of the Gulf and head into the current off the coast of Mexico until we get clear of it. We will burn a lot of fuel, but with one boat and all the fuel from the other boats, we should easily make it. If we can keep from getting attacked by pirates, we should be fine."

Tony pointed to the machine gun on the other boat. "You should be able to stop anyone thinking about attacking you with that machine gun."

"Don't worry, we are going to spend the next few days fortifying my boat and stocking it. We want to load you up with all the shrimp you want. They'll just go bad when we turn off the generators, and we'll have to dump them."

"All we have room for is another sack of them we can cook today. We are stocked up on food and gear now." Tony pointed to the skiff he had taken from the men who tried to rob them. "I am going to abandon that skiff if you want it; between that jet boat and the dinghy we are set."

"Thanks. We may take you up on it."

Herb shook their hands and climbed back into his boat. He called over his shoulder. "Thanks for the coffee. I'll send one of my boys over with a sack of shrimp later."

Cheryl hugged Tony's neck. "What's next?"

"We eat some shrimp, finish going over that new boat and get ready to head up the river. I think we'll sit tight here and plan on leaving in the morning."

20

SPIKE RETURNED TO his storage yard and found his men working on the bus. Before long they had cleaned it out, stored the contents away, hosed out the blood and serviced the engine.

"Good job, guys. See if you can find some dark paint and get that school bus yellow covered up. We might need to hide in that thing one day. I walked down that road, and all I found was an old farm house." He pulled a map out of the glove box, gathered them around and showed them the boundary of Mitch's farm. "Stay out of the area within these highways and the river. The people there can and will kill you. Don't say a word to Carl about this. As far as he knows, there is only a starving couple and an abandoned farmhouse. We may have to partner up with these folks to survive. I'm heading down to the Flamingo; I'll be back later."

His guys waved him off. He wheeled out of the drive and ran down the road to the old bar. When he arrived, he saw, parked out front, Hazel's old Harley along with bikes that belonged to a couple of her girls. His two brothers-in-law, Josh and Bob, were sitting off to one side guarding the front door.

He shook his finger at them. "Don't sit out here in the open standing guard. Get back in one of these empty building where you can see out of a window. You are sitting ducks out here in plain sight!"

Bob pointed with his thumb at the front door of the Flamingo. "Carl wants us out here where we can be seen."

Spike shook his head. "He is using you as an early warning system. If someone starts shooting at you, he will hear it and go hide; I'll deal with Carl."

He pulled open the front door and walked in. As usual Hazel was at the pool table, and Carl was behind the bar popping the top off a bottle of beer.

Spike motioned to Hazel. "I found where they left Tub and his boys. I also found the bodies of three men out in the road just down from them. It looks as if they were the ones who may have killed them. I walked down the road, and all I found was an old farm house with a starving couple who were looking for food. I don't know who killed the men I found dead. By the way, I just told Bob and Josh to get out of sight when they are guarding the front door. If you don't want surprises, I would lock the door and answer when somebody knocks. I don't want my boys getting shot for no reason."

Carl grinned. "Anything you say. Why are you getting so testy lately?"

"I've seen a lot more killing and action than you guys have. You want the element of surprise; if we had used your tactics in Iraq, we wouldn't have lasted a week."

"Spike, this ain't Iraq."

"Carl, this is going to be worse than Iraq. Over there all we had to worry about were some idiotic religious fanatics; over here we are going to have starving people. Nobody is going to have to trick them to come looking and fighting for food. You managed to murder and scare a bunch of people here in town into running. I imagine some of them will be coming back, but you will also have millions of people walking out of all the major cities. They are going to be heading out here with the mistaken idea that they can live off the land. What do you think is going to happen when they run out of deer and squirrels?"

"That's what I have all you guys for. As long as we can gather food from all the people out in the county, we will be fine. We can tend to the masses when they start arriving."

Carl's collector Pete came busting through the door. "Carl, we ran into some trouble. I lost one of my men. The people started shooting the instant we pulled up; they didn't even wait to see what we wanted."

Carl walked out from behind the bar. "Did you kill 'em? What did you get from them?"

"Kill them? We barely escaped with our lives!"

Carl was red in the face. "You get back there and wipe them out; you hear me."

Pete gave him an incredulous look. "Those guys obviously had military backgrounds. They had us in a cross fire. Bullets were flying everywhere; look at my shirt and hat." He pulled off his hat and ran a dirty finger through the hole in the brim.

Carl looked over at Spike. "Take some of your guys with them and go tend to this."

Spike headed for the door. "Follow me, Pete."

Pete followed him out the door. "I'm not going back there."

Spike simply said, "Be quiet; follow me." He motioned to Bob and Josh and pointed at the Bronco. "Get in boys; Pete, as soon as you get your man buried meet me at my place."

"We already had the funeral. He fell out of the truck after he got hit in the head, and we left him in the road."

Spike just shook his head and headed to his Bronco.

Josh spoke up, "Ain't we working for Carl today?"

"No, he thinks we are going to fight those men that shot up Pete and his boys."

"Aren't we going to go kill them?"

"No, boys, I have no intention of risking our lives. The fight will be coming to us real soon, but it will be on our terms."

"What about Pete?"

"Pete's no fool. He's a coward and a murderer, and his men are just like him. Hazel and her girls are in the same boat."

Bob grinned. "When I think of Hazel and her gals, the word girl just doesn't spring to mind." They all grinned and laughed.

Pete came pulling up in the yard behind Spike. He climbed out of his truck; it was missing a windshield and had numerous bullet holes in the cab. Blood was on the seat where his man had been sitting when he was hit.

Pete walked up rubbing his chin. "I was thinking; maybe your guys can hit them first, and we'll back you up."

Spike gave him a stern look. "First off, quit thinking; all that will do is get you killed."

"Carl told us to go kill them."

"Where did you run into them?"

"They were out on the four lane between here and Natchez."

"How many of them were there?"

"We thought there was only three or four because they were the only ones we saw at the truck we came up on. The ones we didn't see were off to the side on a forestry road. A half dozen more were in another truck. I think there was another van full behind them. Lester started out the door with his pistol, and before we could spit, he was dead, and they were lighting us up. Melvin and Robert got off a few shots, but I got the hell out of Dodge."

Spike could only shake his head. "You idiots, from the looks of your truck, I don't see how you weren't all killed. Why would you come barreling up on a group of men without first observing them from a distance? Also, why would you come out with guns? Hell, I'd probably have shot you myself. Have you looked at yourselves lately? When was the last time you shaved or had a haircut? You look like a bunch of redneck heathens. Take a shower every now and then."

Spike walked around shaking his head while looking at Pete's truck. "Were there any women or kids that you could see?"

"No, just men wearing camo."

"Were they in uniform? What kind of truck were they in?"

"I don't know; it looked like a new Ford truck."

"Pete, you and your guys go home. Tell Lester's people that he's dead and not to collect his body until we're sure the road is clear.

For God's sake, get cleaned up! I know you have power and water; my boys and I will check on the bad guys. Tell me exactly where you ran into those men."

"They were stopped in the road over there by the fire tower out on the highway towards Natchez. What do you want us to tell Carl?"

"Nothing, y'all take the day off. I'll update Carl once I know something."

Spike watched as Pete and his crew of thugs headed out of the driveway. His thoughts were not about Carl or even Pete but the arrival of the military and why they were at the fire tower.

He told Bob and Josh, "Gather the guys; we have to talk."

Without a word they nodded and headed in different directions to find the other men. Spike went into his den and opened his closet door. He pulled out a medium sized backpack and carried it over to a large table that sat against one wall. He cleared the table and dumped the contents of the bag out. The huge old Victorian mansion echoed with the sounds of men coming in. Spike loved to hear the sound of creaking and popping wood as it received the weight of the walking men.

He opened the door leading into the foyer and called to his girls. "I want you to hear what I've got to say; come on in here."

Spike's den was formally the library in the old house. The home was built by the owner of a lumber company back in the 1890's. No expense had been spared in its construction, or its size. The fireplaces were designed to burn fire wood, and the house still had wood heaters. The kitchen had a wood stove with another one just outside on a large, now screened, porch.

When he had all of his crew gathered around, he pointed to the pack on the table. "I'm afraid it's going to get very exciting around here quickly. Bob, Josh and I are going to make a run over to the fire tower out towards Natchez; if I see what I think I am going to see, we can expect trouble. I believe we have military heading in. This can be good, or it can be bad. If they are good guys it may be good; if it is as I suspect, it's going to be very bad."

He pointed to the table and the backpack and all its contents. "In the shipping container on the far left out back, are hundreds of packs in various sizes. I have enough gear to outfit two hundred and fifty men. That's the reason all you got hunting and camping gear every year at Christmas instead of soap on a rope and useless stuff. In the second container you will find field kits that will contain things like mess kits, towels, soap etc. Over in unit twenty-seven of my mini warehouse you will find dehydrated food and cases of MRE's. I bought these to sell on the internet before the lights went out."

Pointing back to his backpack and contents he continued, "This is what is known as a bug out bag. When we were in Iraq, we kept one of these ready to go. All you have to do is grab a rifle, ammo pouch, tactical vest, camel back, bug out bag and run. Each bag contains enough food and supplies to keep a man alive for one week."

His girlfriend Lacy held up her finger. "What do you want us to do?"

"I want each of you to put together a bug out bag like the one I have. You will find everything you need in the storage units. For the kids, I want you to use their backpack book bags. I want you to be able to grab and go at a moment's notice. Hopefully, we can drive, but if we have to we can go on foot. You ladies need to remember your toiletries. Don't waste space for makeup or hair curlers; it will be better to carry dehydrated food if you are going to be on foot. In three hours, I want everyone outfitted and ready to roll in an emergency."

Lisa asked, "We want to be armed as well; can we get guns?"

"Great idea; Mike and Greg, you are veterans; dig out rifles and pistols for your sisters, wives and girlfriends. I want you to teach them gun safety and how to shoot. If you look around in the unit where I dug out your knives, you will find suppressors for the rifles. Outfit all the rifles with suppressors and remember don't let on what we're doing if any of Carl's people decide to show up."

Spike opened up a desk drawer and pulled out a suppressor for his rifle. He took out his knife and used the blade to break loose the flash hider on the end of his rifle barrel. He replaced it with the suppressor.

"This will not make this rifle silent, but it will make it silent enough that you won't need hearing protection; we're burning daylight, get started."

He reloaded the contents of his bug out bag and grabbed his ammo pouch. He replaced his shoulder holster with a tactical vest and dropped his pistol in the vest holster and magazines in the pouches attached.

He called out to Josh and Bob. "When you get your bags and vest loaded, get back here with your rifles and gear; we've going for a ride to see what's going on." They both gave him the thumbs up from across the yard.

Within the hour, they were heading down the highway in the direction of the fire tower road. The lug grip tires on the old Ford Bronco sang as the aggressive lug pattern of the tires bit the pavement. He backed off the throttle as they approached the crest of the hill and wheeled into a side road that meandered around through the national forest on the south side of the Homochitto River. The road zigzagged through the hills and hollows of the old forest. They had to stop twice and cut through locks on government gates, but they eventually made it to a road that led back toward the fire tower. If Spike's instincts were correct, the men for which they were looking would be using the fire tower as a platform to observe the surrounding countryside. They drove for what he estimated to be half the distance to the tower. The forest road down which they traveled went through thick timber, and at no time could they be spotted from the tower. This road was previously used by forest rangers to access the deep recesses of the forest and was used as a logging road at one time. He backed the Bronco into a branch trail to hide it from view, reached into his bag and retrieved a camo makeup kit.

"Boys, knock the shine off those cheeks and noses. We're going to see what's going on. Screw the suppressor on your rifles."

After applying the makeup and attaching limbs and leaves to their vest and hats, they started out down the road. All three of them had received tactical training in the army. They spread out about a hundred yards apart and adopted a leap frog pattern as they made their way toward the tower. Soon they were in sight of it. Its steel legs could be seen through the forest where it perched at the top of the ridge they were climbing. They left the road and crawled into a grove of wax myrtles and watched. Just as Spike suspected, there was activity at the tower. Men wearing camouflage uniforms and packing AK-47 rifles were milling about. Spike motioned for his men to stay put and cover him. Slowly he crawled through the underbrush until he was within earshot of the men. Two of them came walking up to the steps where they greeted two others who were standing guard at the bottom. Spike listened. *Russian! They were speaking Russian!* The implications hit him like a ton of bricks. *Was this EMP event a prelude to invasion and were these the first scouting parties?* He thought about killing the four men he could see, but he didn't know how many more were within hearing. He slowly crawled back to where Josh and Bob were hidden in the thicket.

"We may have a big problem; those guys are Russians."

Josh cocked his head towards the tower. "Russians; what in the hell are Russians doing here?"

Spike looked back and forth between the two of them. "I think we now know why the lights went out."

Bob made a motion with his rifle barrel. "What are they doing in Franklin County of all places?"

"They must be conducting recon and using the tower as an observation platform and possibly as a radio tower. We know there are four on the ground and one or more in the tower. Let's head back to the Bronco and get back out to the highway. We need to know how many we can see from over there; I don't want to start a gun battle not knowing how many we are up against. I imagine they are setting up recon locations near or on all major highways in the country. The tower gives them a commanding view of the whole area."

They took extra care and caution returning to the Bronco. Presently, they were back on the highway and driving toward the tower. At this point, they were below the crest of the hill and out of sight of it. They pulled over onto the side and proceeded up the hill on foot. Once near the crest, they moved into the tree line and wormed their way to a point where they could see west down the highway. The fire tower was on top of the largest ridge near the highway. The road leading up to it had two vehicles at the entrance, and a third was parked on a crossover in the middle of the four lane highway. All three vehicles were late model Ford trucks. Lester's body was nowhere to be seen. Another Ford truck came down the highway pulling a trailer with barrels in the back; it stopped, and the men started pumping fuel into all the vehicles.

Josh asked, "How is it possible that they can get those new Ford trucks to run?"

Bob, who was a mechanic before the EMP, answered. "They probably brought spare computers. It would have been simple enough to buy up a bunch of them and protect them until they were needed."

Spike agreed. "That would explain all the Fords. They wouldn't have to ship in a bunch of trucks for an invasion, just the electronics. New Ford truck dealerships are everywhere; they could take their time shipping in their military vehicles. All they really need to do is send in teams to observe and report while we starve to death and murder each other. It looks as if we have at least four out here on the highway, four around the tower and one or more up on the tower."

Josh looked concerned. "Are we going to try and kill them now?"

Spike grinned. "We can probably kill the ones we can see, but we need to get the rest of our guys and attack from the woods and from here at the same time. We aren't starting anything unless we can get them all. They probably have radios that work. Besides, your sisters would never let me hear the end of it if I let any of you get hurt."

Bob shook his head. "We dang sure don't want to get you in the dog house!"

From down the highway an old Bluebird Wanderlodge motor home came into view with a Jeep Wrangler in tow behind it. When it reached the peak of the hill, it stopped dead in the road. The

Russians scrambled. Some soldiers, that Spike hadn't seen, moved from the woods on either side of the road and assumed positions where their sniper rifles could cover the bus.

Spike whispered. "Spread out. I count eight; if they start shooting, we are going to take them down. Josh take the three on the right; Bob the three on the left. I'll take the two in the middle and follow up on any that don't go down. Once they're all down, stay put and focus all your fire on the fire tower. They'll have a sniper or two up there. I'm not going to let them murder any more Americans. Empty two full magazines on semi auto fire into the fire tower house. We'll then fall back into the woods and get back to the Bronco." They spread out about a hundred yards apart and waited; suddenly gunfire erupted.

After shooting the Russians in the road and emptying their rifle's magazines into the fire tower house on top of the platform, Spike and his men retreated into the forest until they were well hidden from any snipers who were still in the tower and from the two guards who would have been standing out of sight at the base of the tower.

Spike praised. "Good shooting, guys. Everyone that we can see has multiple holes in them, and the tower house has been riddled. Now we have a choice-- we can go in and try to finish the job or retreat to the Bronco and get ready for a retaliatory strike."

Bob looked puzzled. "Retaliatory strike? What are you talking about?"

"They are obviously an advance military unit. They will have reported our attack, and we can expect them to send for help. This is the same thing we were doing in Iraq. When our guys encountered resistance they called in the big guns. So we can spend a couple of more hours here and try to wrap this up or we can head back and start evacuating our families into the forest. Bad guys are on the way."

Josh pointed to the Bluebird Bus on the hill. "What about those folks?"

Spike pointed out. "If they are hurt they may start shooting at us, I know the Russians got off half a dozen or so shots before we started shooting."

Suddenly, Bob pointed to the steps on the tower. A Russian was running and half falling as he propelled himself down the steps. All three of them fired in his direction, but he was below the tree line before they could hit him.

"Let's grab the two nearest trucks and head back home. Those Russians will be heading into the forest in the opposite direction. I'll cover you guys from here. As soon as you get moving, swing by here and pick me up and drop me off at my Bronco." With military precision, Josh and Bob broke over the hill, ran to the nearest trucks and were back at Spike's position in less than two minutes. Spike jumped into the truck Josh was driving and hopped in the Bronco when they arrived at it.

"Guys, go back home and get everyone packing; I'm heading up to that bus, and I hope that I don't get shot."

Bob shouted back. "If you get killed, what do we do?"

"Take your family out to the most remote farms or roads in the county and hide with as much food and supplies as you can manage. Fill that school bus with everything you can put in."

"What about Carl?"

"If he shows up, kill him and whoever is with him. If I don't get killed checking on the bus, I'll go see Carl before I come home."

Spike waved them off and cranked the Bronco. Its tires dug in, and he sped down the highway and over the crest behind which they had been hidden. The fire tower was off to his left as he passed the lifeless bodies of the dead Russians. He crested the ridge and saw the bus sitting on the ridge.

He ran up beside it and hollered out, "Don't shoot, I'm American."

There was no answer. He glanced up and saw a small child looking down from a large side window. He ran around to the front and realized that the front window had been shot out. A man and women were dead in the front seats. He opened the side door and found a young girl lying dead in the aisle between the couches. The small boy standing in the seat was crying and scared.

Spike touched him. "Stay here. I'll be right back, son."

He quickly went through the rest of the bus to make sure no one else was inside. The little boy looked to be about four year old. His face was smeared with the blood of his sister, and his tears had cut little lines down his face.

He hopped down and tried to shake his sister. "Sissy wake up; Sissy wake up."

Spike looked around and found the boy's coat and shoes. He told the little boy, "You've got to come with me; we can't stay here."

Two big tears ran down his cheek, and all the boy could say was, "Mama and Sissy won't wake up."

Spike went into the bath and retrieved a wet cloth and towel. He squatted down and held the little boy close. "Your Mama wants you to come with me, son. I'm Spike. What's your name?"

The little boy said, "Roger Randal."

"I'm going to clean your face, and then we're going to get your things packed up."

Spike quickly located a small backpack and stuffed it full of the boy's clothes and what he assumed was his toiletries from the bathroom. Soon, he had the child buckled into the front seat of the Bronco, and they were barreling back to town. The little boy was silent; the shock of the attack had him traumatized. Spike didn't stop at Carl's, but continued straight to his home where he wheeled around back. Little Roger sat in the seat quaking with fear.

"Roger, we are home. I'm going to take you to meet two very nice young ladies who will take good care of you."

"What about my Mama?"

"Roger, was that your Mama, Daddy and big sister with you in the bus?"

The little fellow nodded "yes."

"Roger, they are all dead and have gone to live in heaven."

Roger looked up. "Have they gone to live in heaven with Grandma and Grandpa?"

"Yes, son, that's where they are."

"Why didn't they take me with them?"

For the first time in his memory, tears burst from Spike's eyes. "I don't know; all I know is that they wanted you to stay with me. I'm going to take you inside. I've got two young ladies who will want to meet you."

Spike unbuckled him and carried him up the stairs to the back door and into his den.

He called to Lisa and Lacy. "Girls, I need you to come meet someone."

Lacy and Lisa came walking in, and Spike looked at them. From his bloodshot eyes, they knew that he had been upset.

"Girls, I want you to meet Roger Randal. His parents and sister have gone to heaven to live with his Grandma and Grandpa. His parents want him to stay with us."

"Roger, this is Lisa and Lacy. They will get you squared away."

Lisa squatted next to him and gave him a big hug, while Lacy accompanied Spike back to the Bronco. When Spike told her what happened, tears streamed down her cheeks as she took the boy's backpack.

Spike said, "I guess we have a family now. Have you got everything packed up and ready to go?"

"Yes, how much time do you think we have?"

"Not much. One or two attack helicopters can pretty much level this town; I don't want to be here when they show up. We may have more time, but I doubt it. We're not far from the Natchez airport. They will be using every airport that can support heavy jets as the invasion progresses."

"What about Carl?"

"I'm going to explain to Carl how the cow eats the cabbage first thing tomorrow."

21

THE MOON WAS bright and streaming though the diamond shaped lookout hole on Mitch's shuttered window. He was awaken by a deep growl coming from Bacon. He placed his hands on his muzzle to quiet him. He scooped up Pinky and handed her to Hannah.

"Keep her quiet, we've got company. Get your gun."

"I already have it."

He looked around in the twilight and saw that she was clutching her rifle, and her eyes were wide open with fear.

The afternoon before, when he had walked up on the mountain, Mitch had heard the crackle of rifles off in the distance. The rifle fire had come from across the river in the direction of the fire tower. From his vantage point, he could see the top of the tower where it protruded through the canopy of the pine forest.

He knew trouble had once again come to the farm. A shadow crossed across the diamond shaped beam of moonlight, and it was followed by three more. A board on the floor of the porch cracked and popped under the weight of footsteps. He tightened his grip on Bacon's muzzle. Resisting the urge to open up with his rifle, he waited.

He slipped his feet into his boots and whispered to Hannah, "Quietly grab your gear; we're heading to the basement."

The hinge to the basement door made a faint creak when they pushed it open. The sound of the locking mechanism gave them a sense of relief as they descended the stairs to safety.

Hannah touched Mitch's arm. "What do we do now?"

"We are going to finish quietly getting dressed, and then we are heading out the back door. You hang on to Bacon and Pinky, and don't let them bark while I dress and gear up. Then I'll hold them while you dress. After we dress, we're heading out the tunnel and up on the mountain. I'll circle back to where I can see what's going on once you're safe. If they are smart, they won't try and break in because they don't want to get shot. My bet is that they will sneak around, hide, wait until morning and try to pick us off. That was the reason they were tiptoeing around the porch; they were trying to determine if anyone was home."

Without a word, they completed their task and headed to the tunnel entrance. The tunnel ran about a hundred and fifty feet and was made of sections of sixty-inch concrete culverts. The opening was revealed only by pulling aside a set of shelves. The tunnel was slanted downward toward the creek and came out in a cane thicket that completely hid it from view. The cypress hatch was barred from the inside and could be opened from the outside, but only if one knew which board to remove.

They entered the tunnel, pulled the shelving unit closed behind them and headed down the tunnel. It was always damp and cold because it would sometimes leak a bit after heavy rains. The light from the LED cap lights let them navigate the tunnel. They had to walk stooped over to keep from hitting their heads. Spiders and bugs were always living in the damp dark corridor even though they had tried to keep them out. They switched off their lights. Both of them were relieved when the outer hatch swung open, and they stepped into the cold night air. Bacon had made this trip numerous times and was getting ready to head back to the house before Mitch stopped him.

He reached for Hannah, placed his fingers to her lips and whispered, "Don't make a sound. A voice will travel a long way on a still cold night like tonight."

"What do we do now?"

"We're going to take our time and make our way up on the mountain where we can look down on the house. We'll just have to sit tight until the sun comes up in a couple of hours."

"I'm freezing; I don't think we can stand it out here that long."

"I think I can solve that problem. When I was young, my parents let me tent camp up here with my friends. Our old campsite is on the other side of the ridge. My dad found a large chiminea at a garage sale and carried it up to our camp. He didn't want us to burn down the woods by accident. It's in a hollow out of the wind, and no one can see the fire. There're plenty of limbs we can burn."

The small hot fire in the chiminea soon had them thawed out. Squeezing Hannah's hand, Mitch explained to her, "I want you to stay here with the dogs; I am going to slip back over the mountain and get to where I can see the house when the sun comes up. To get out of the wind and cold, they are probably in the barn or the vehicles."

"Please be careful. I can't make it without you."

"Don't worry. I know these woods like the back of my hand. You know how to get back into the basement, and you know the trail back to the old brick kiln where we have our cache. Hang on to Bacon. I don't want him helping. He'll just start barking, raising the devil and alert them to my position. I want you to stay put even if you hear shooting. I'll be back to get you."

He kissed her goodbye and walked away screwing the suppressor on the barrel of his rifle. The leaves crunched under his feet as he climbed back to the top of the mountain. Once he was on the trail that ran the length of the ridge, the going was a bit quieter. Since the pine trees on the ridge were denser, a bed of needles deadened the sound of his footsteps. In the moonlight, he could see the trail created by the four wheeler and occasionally the tractor. The tracks from the wheels had left their impressions from years of use. His quilted, olive drab coveralls kept him warm. The heavy leather belt carried his dad's 1911 .45 pistol and his hunting knife. A pouch with six magazines for his rifle rode across his body from a strap that went over his head and shoulder. Two extra magazines for the pistol rode in his back pocket. He slowed as he neared the point on the ridge where the house became visible. He eased over next to a huge pine sitting at the edge of the trail and waited. The sun was rising so he stayed in the shadow of the great tree. Morning birds were stirring, and a squirrel was barking at something further down the ridge. Someone sneezed up ahead. He slowly crouched down in the bushes near the tree. He gathered up a hand full of dirt, spit on it and created a muddy paste that he applied to his shiny face and the back of his hands all the while keeping his eyes peeled in the direction of the sneeze. The man sneezed again, walked out on to the trail and hit the key on his microphone. Mitch couldn't understand what he was saying because the man was speaking Russian. He was joined by three others who climbed up the mountain from the vicinity of the barn. Their heavy coats were unzipped; they were obviously designed to be worn in a colder climate. All four were carrying AK-47 rifles and ammo packs. They did not have back packs, so they were either not far from their vehicle or were unprepared for being in the field. One of the men had a bandage on his head, and another bandage was around his hand. Mitch recognized a canteen that normally stayed on his four wheeler. He reached down and picked up a pine cone at his feet and tossed it so that it landed in the leaves down the side of the mountain. All four men opened up with their rifles at the sound. The rifles were firing on full auto. Small trees and bushes were falling as the bullets tore through the woods. Mitch opened up from his position and quickly had all four men on the ground. Without leaving his position, he finished them with triple taps to each one making certain the threat was over. He waited for an hour before moving. No sound came from the house, and no movement came from the barn. After a quick look around, he could find no evidence of any other Russians. The roosters were crowing so he opened the hen house and went back to the campsite where he found Hannah waiting.

"What happened? I heard all the shooting; I didn't know what to do."

"Don't worry I got 'em. They killed one of our pine cones though."

"They killed a pine cone?"

"Yep, I chunked a pine cone down the hill beside them. They were so trigger happy they opened up on it. I took the opportunity to take them down."

"We can't keep living like this. I'm afraid all the time."

"I'm fearful it's going to be like this for quite some time. I think I know why the lights went out. The men I killed were Russian soldiers."

"Russian soldiers; what are Russian soldiers doing out here in the middle of nowhere?"

"I heard shooting taking place over in the direction of the fire tower yesterday afternoon. In fact, I heard a lot of shooting. These guys were only carrying rifles and ammo; they didn't have any gear. They must have had to run with just what they were carrying and what they were wearing. They were not equipped to be in the field. Whatever took place over at the fire tower must have sent them running."

When they reached the bodies, Mitch and Hannah hastily gathered the weapons and ammo. Each of the Russians had handheld radios, Vostok watches and personal items. They carried everything into the basement and stowed all of it away for future use. While Hannah cooked breakfast, Mitch cranked up the tractor, took it up the trail to the top of the mountain where he tied the dead Russians to the tow bar and dragged them out to the bone yard. After a hearty country breakfast that included fresh farm eggs, he and Hannah set about cleaning the rifles and inventorying the ammo and magazines.

Hannah remarked, "Who would have thought that in just a couple of short weeks we could kill and dispose of the dead and then eat breakfast without breaking a sweat. There has got to be something bad wrong with us."

"No, I think it is perfectly normal for people to survive. Other than getting ourselves killed or starving to death, we haven't had a choice. I'm not letting it bother me. I don't like killing people. For that matter, I can't say that I like to kill anything. I enjoy hunting deer and game, but we eat what we kill. It's no different than buying a package of hamburger or a box of fried chicken. The only difference is that I paid someone to kill the cow and the chicken."

"What do we do now?"

"We are going to keep on living. We have food, a home, and a farm to work. We can't do anything for a few more months. It will take at least that long for most of the population to finish starving and killing one another. Then the problem will be the Russian army and their immigrants that will be coming. We may even be facing troops from other countries. I'm sure we are being divided up. We don't know what other counties were affected by the EMP. If I were a betting man, I would say that the Russians set off the EMP that knocked out the electricity. I'm certain they aren't here to rescue us. I would think they will start securing every airport that can handle heavy jets so they can move in men and equipment."

"What airports around here can handle heavy jets?"

"In this region, we have Baton Rouge, Jackson, Alexandria and Natchez."

Hannah gave him a puzzled look. "Natchez, I've never heard of any commercial flights servicing Natchez."

"Natchez can handle large jets because it has a very long runway. My dad went to see the first George Bush give a speech at the airport in Natchez when Ronald Regan was running for his second term. Bush arrived in a large airliner. If this is indeed an invasion, they will be securing all the major roads, bridges and airports."

"What are we going to do if this is war?"

"I guess we'll resist; we won't have a choice. I don't think they will hesitate to kill off the few of us who may survive."

"We may be jumping to conclusions. All we know is these four goons were snooping around here and got themselves killed."

Mitch walked over to the kitchen window and looked out across the large pasture that lay beyond the driveway in the front of the house. He could feel the vibrations from the helicopter blades before he saw it suddenly appear above the trees about a half a mile away.

The Russian helicopter pilot keyed his microphone by pressing the button on the center hand control. "*There is no sign of our men yet; they indicated they were at a farm house four kilometers south of the fire tower where they were attacked yesterday. I am looking for it now.*"

The Russian tower commander answered. "*Be careful. The Americans will be armed to the teeth. I didn't believe the stories that every one of them had a gun until I got here. They have them and know how to use them.*"

22

Lucille slowly passed the Herberts' shrimp boats on its way down
the canal. The Heberts were busy transferring items from the two
boats they were abandoning to the one on which they were going to
take refuge. Loaded with gear, the jet drive boat was securely tied to
Lucille's stern and was ready to deploy once they reached the mouth
of the Homochitto River.

Herb Herbert called out, "Good luck, and God speed."

Tony called back, "Thanks for the shrimp and the extra diesel; I
hope to see you again one day."

He and Cheryl waved goodbye as the Herberts' flotilla disappeared behind them. The strong diesel motor in *Lucille* was running at a fast idle as they approached the river. Today was going to
be a good day. The temperature was in the 40's, and a brisk wind
swept across the vast river. *Lucille* dutifully chugged upstream in
the turbid waters; they motored around huge trees and debris that
was coming down stream in the current. They steered as close as
possible to the center of the river as they approached New Orleans.
They observed on the shore an occasional fisherman with lines
in the water. Tony ran the boat from the helm inside the cabin
because the threat of gunfire and attack was foremost on his mind.
Tow boats and barges were grounded on both sides of the river. He
decided to kick the throttle wide open and run the boat at its full
speed. The less time they spent in this section of the river the safer
they would be.

A column of smoke rose in the distance far up the river. As they got closer, they saw that the fire was coming from a ship at the port. Traveling the river at night would be impossible; therefore, their only chance was to make the run in the daylight so they continued heading upstream. Suddenly, when a ship came into view, they realized that a battle was underway. The ship was an American war ship, and it was coming under fire from jet aircraft. Tremendous gunfire was coming from the ship and was directed into the sky at an unseen enemy. An explosion erupted high in the sky above the river; after the bullets exploded the incoming missile, debris rained down. A hatch popped open, and a missile tube fired; the missile popped out of the hatch, and its fuel ignited. The missile took off in a cloud of smoke and raced out of sight on its way to an unseen target. Tony could see gunfire leaving the ship targeting another incoming missile. A second later the ship exploded. The shockwave bounced *Lucille* and cracked several of the windows. Before they could recover, another explosion high in the sky brought a fighter plane crashing down. After the plane hit somewhere in the city, they detected, behind the levee, a huge mushroom cloud of smoke climbing to the sky.

Cheryl clutched his arm. "What do we do?"

"We are going to keep heading north. I have no way of knowing who or why that ship was being attacked. We don't know if those men who attacked us were from that ship. I am sure of one thing; if we head over there, they will find some reason to take our boats, food and guns."

After a couple of hours, they had left the city behind them. They were now passing through industrial areas where refineries and chemical plants lined the river. Several times they spotted helicopters heading toward New Orleans, but they were too far away to tell much about them. While it was still light enough to see and before they reached Baton Rouge, they found a huge debris island on the west side of the river. The debris was comprised of sunken vessels, barges, trees and other items that were deposited by the river. A few brave souls were climbing among the debris and vessels searching for food and anything they could use. After they passed, a group of people took to a small boat and pursued them.

Tony handed Cheryl the wheel. "Keep it in the middle of the river while I start shooting." He opened the cabin door and looked across the stern of the boat and across the captured boat they were towing. He picked up one of the Colt M-4 rifles and fired a warning shot off to the side of the pursuing boat. The men fired back, so he opened up on them and ran a full magazine through the rifle. As he expected, they turned away but continued firing. He slapped another magazine in the gun and continued to engage them as they powered away back down the river. He had no way of knowing if his bullets hit anyone or not; however, the threat had been silenced and that was what counted. He replaced the spent magazine in the rifle and returned to the cabin. Cheryl was shaking as he took over the helm.

"It's over. Calm down and collect yourself. We're okay."

She looked up with tears streaming down her face. "When is this nightmare going to end? Maybe we should have tried to sail through the oil and head south. Are we going to have to fight for our lives every day until we're killed?"

"I am certain we will have more fights before we get to the farm; then we will have to defend the farm. Civilization as we have known it has come to an end. Starvation turns everyone into animals."

"We haven't tried to rob or kill anyone."

"We haven't been faced with starvation yet. We've stolen from vending machines and collected all kinds of stuff that doesn't belong to us. We're riding in a stolen boat. We are surviving only because I didn't wait to see if the lights were going to come back on. I would have looked the fool if the lights came back on thirty minutes after I broke into the snack machine back in the office. I could even be guilty of murder. I don't know if those government men back in the canal had a reason to attack Herbert's boats. I shot first and went with the assumption they were going to kill us. I think I made the right decision, but who the hell really knows?"

"I just pray we can get home."

"We've got to keep trying."

They continued up the river and crossed under the bridge at Baton Rouge before dark. That evening they anchored behind a sandbar island located in an isolated portion of a loop in the river. The banks were wooded, and the loop didn't have any grounded tugs or barges to draw scavengers. The current at this point of the river swept the far bank and deposited sand on the inside of the loop forming the vast sandbar island.

Tony rubbed his sore shoulder after he released the anchor and turned to Cheryl. "We're going to have to sleep in shifts tonight; until we are on the farm, we can't let our guard down for an instant."

She rubbed his neck and gave him a long kiss. "We've got to eat the rest of the boiled shrimp, and I managed to make some banana pudding from the dried bananas and Bisquick."

"Sounds good to me, honey."

They could feel and hear the vibrations from a helicopter in the distance. Tony pulled out a pair of binoculars and brought it into view. The large red star on the tail indicated that it was Russian. He passed the binoculars to Cheryl.

"Russian, look at the red star near the tail. That's an attack helicopter; notice the two canopies in the front. I bet they're the reason the lights went out. Probably an EMP nuclear device was detonated high in the atmosphere somewhere over the middle of the country."

"What can we do if they attack us here on the river?"

"There's nothing we can do, but jump overboard with our life vests on. They can turn this boat into confetti and never get within rifle range. If one of them comes over, all we can do is smile, wave and hope they don't attack. I just hope they think our aluminum boat is a duck hunting boat and not a military craft."

The next morning they continued up the river. They passed a few small boats of people heading down the river. Huge numbers of sea birds, obviously displaced by the oil, were following the river. They met a large house boat containing a retirement age couple, their children and grandchildren. They were heading south down the river. The captain waved them down. Both boats were kept a safe distance apart as neither trusted the other. The old man had a good mane of gray hair and the start of a matching beard.

He called out, "Ahoy, sailboat, please don't shoot."

Tony was running the boat from the upper helm under the Bimini top. He throttled back so that the boats drifted along with one another in the current.

"We won't shoot unless you start. How can I help you folks?"

"We just need some information. How's the river south of here?"

"The river is good until you get near New Orleans. We came under attack at a huge debris field of tugs and barges. Otherwise, it is open to the Gulf. It appears as though the Russians sunk a ship at New Orleans. How far are y'all planning to go?"

"We are heading to the Bahamas. I had a beach house on one of the islands there. With a little luck we can hide there for a while."

Tony shook his head. "You need to know that there has been some sort of blow out of one or more offshore oil wells. The reason we are heading upriver at this time is because we were run out of the Gulf by the oil and fumes. An ecological disaster is underway. You'll need enough fuel to travel south against the Gulf Stream current or go right through the middle of it."

The old man stood dumbfounded for a minute. "I was counting on the clockwise rotation of the Gulf current to carry us near the keys before I had to start burning a lot of fuel."

"If you rely on the current, you will be in oil the entire trip. I'm not sure you could survive breathing the fumes. It's really bad out there. What does it look like up north?"

The old man motioned with his thumb upstream. "We've traveled down the Ohio; we had to go through one set of locks that was pretty tricky. My son-in-law was with the Corp of Engineers and managed to power up the valves and gates from an old emergency generator from years past. The only trouble we had was coming past Memphis. Those people were going crazy; I think the whole city was on fire. The only other problem happened up at Natchez when we had some people try to slip on board while we were anchored just north of the bridge; they weren't successful."

Tony grinned and gave him thumbs up. "We don't plan to go that far; I'm going to take a small river up into the middle of the Homochitto National Forest to my farm. I figure we'll be at the Homochitto River in two days if we don't run into any problems."

They waved. Tony pushed the throttle open and *Lucille* resumed her journey north. Tony really liked *Lucille* and he didn't look forward to abandoning her to the river. Later that morning, he passed under the bridge at St. Francisville. A stream of people was crossing the bridge as they left the Baton Rouge area and headed into South Louisiana. Tony and Cheryl kept their rifles handy, but all they received were hopeless looks. Many of the people appeared hollow eyed and haggard. The struggle to live and starvation were taking their toll on the survivors.

That night found them behind another sandbar that formed an island in the river. This spot on the down current side was located where the water formed an eddy. They tied off to a tree that was mired in the sandbar. There they were protected from the current. No one could approach them from land or in a small boat, so they were safe for the night. Breaking out the fishing tackle and using some shrimp for bait, they caught a half dozen river cat. The eddy provided safe harbor for their boat as well as a quiet spot for schools of catfish.

The weight of the world was resting on Tony's shoulders. He was worried about his children, and he was concerned that he had made the wrong decision to head up the river. The Russians were still flying up and down the river, and their heading back to the Gulf was not an option. They could make it to the farm quicker than they could make it back to the Gulf. Even if they managed to get to the Gulf, there was no guarantee they could survive the oil to make a break for the Caribbean.

Sitting under the Bimini top, Tony listened to the sounds that came from the swirling river current. The moon was a deep red and moved higher in the sky as the night wore on. The deep red, blood moon made the hair on the back of his neck stand on end. He remembered hearing about the blood moons and how they were harbingers of bad times to come. The blood moon set the tone for the night; the only thing that could have been more depressing or foreboding would have been if Dracula were standing next to him.

Tony tried to analyze what had taken place. Here they were sitting in the middle of one of the largest rivers on the Earth. What would have been considered a vacation or adventure two months ago was now a dash for their lives as they ran the gauntlet that was now the Mississippi River. Several times, he thought he could hear jet aircraft, and once he was certain that he could feel and hear a helicopter. All the grounded towboats and barges helped mask them on the river. When they were underway, they would be vulnerable; otherwise, they were just another boat floundering in the river.

He fell asleep in the chair and woke when Cheryl gently touched him and handed him a cup of hot coffee.

"It's morning. I thought you were going to wake me to take over while you got some sleep."

"I fell asleep, and I didn't wake up until you woke me up. I guess we both needed some rest. The blood moon last night haunted me. I'm glad it's morning. You don't see any vampire puncture marks on my neck do you?"

"No, silly, let's get under way, and I'll cook breakfast while we're running."

Shortly, they were back in the current and cruising north up the river. They had both taken to wearing their pistols and knives on their belts. The sight of the Russian helicopters and the thought of the sunken naval vessel weighed profoundly on their minds. They also placed life vests around *Lucille* in case they had to abandon the boat in a hurry. The blood moon weighed heavily on Tony's subconscious as the day wore on. As usual, Cheryl made a great breakfast from their store of provisions. Around mid-morning a helicopter came into view and made a big sweeping circle around their boat. This one was also a Russian ship as the large red star stood out on the side near the tail. It was a general purpose helicopter, not a combat craft. However, it sported what appeared to be machine guns slung under the fuselage. Tony grinned ear to ear as he spoke through his teeth and dropped his gun vest before walking out from under the Bimini top.

"Take off your gun belt and come out of the cabin. Smile and wave; baby, smile and wave."

Cheryl followed suit. The pilot and co-pilot both waved back, and the co-pilot held up a camera. The helicopter turned and resumed its flight north.

"I hope they are just sightseeing; otherwise, one of those attack helicopters will be showing up pretty soon. I figure the only reason they didn't sink us was because they could be trying to locate functioning vessels and engines."

Cheryl sighed. "The sooner we reach the farm the better off we are going to be."

"If they want the vessel intact, they'll keep checking on us a couple of times a day or direct a satellite to monitor our progress. I bet they will simply wait for us at or near the Natchez Bridge. I don't think they will anticipate our heading up the Homochitto River. We'll run aground before we get more than a couple of miles up it."

Cheryl frowned. "I hate to abandon our honeymoon cottage."

"Honeymoon cottage? I don't remember us getting hitched."

"You can remedy that. You're the captain!"

"By God you're right; what I say goes around here."

He grabbed a broom and laid it on the floor. "Hold my hand and jump."

Cheryl gave him a big kiss and laughed. "Nothing like a short, quick ceremony."

As they expected, they were buzzed by the same helicopter on its return trip south along the river. Once again they smiled and waved.

They saw the helicopter two more times before reaching the mouth of the Homochitto. The Homochitto was at least a quarter mile wide where it met the Mississippi. It was late in the afternoon when they made the turn out of the Mississippi and up the waterway that was the Homochitto River. This section of the river was a dredged waterway that gave the river a direct path to the Mississippi and was designed to stop the flooding in the region. This would enable them to get well away from the river and away from heavy current while they made the transition from *Lucille* to the jet boat.

Cheryl looked up the peaceful river with the trees sitting on the banks. Their limbs hung over the water.

"We could stay here for weeks back in these trees and quiet water."

Tony pointed to a log stuck up in one of the trees about ten feet above their heads. "See that piece of driftwood up in that tree?"

Puzzled Cheryl asked, "How did it get up there?"

"That's where the flood waters left it. This river drains a large section of the country around here. It gets that high several times a year, and a good day of rain will put it up there."

Cheryl frowned. "That means the first good rain after we leave *Lucille*; she'll be on her way to the Gulf. Is there someplace close we can anchor her in case we need to find her again?"

"If the river is high enough, we can get her into Old River on the west side of the Mississippi. We can anchor her out in the middle, and she would be safe until we came back or somebody finds her."

"Let's try. I hate the idea of discarding her; she is the only reason we are still alive."

They turned and headed back into the Mississippi and crossed over to the opposite bank where they located the inlet into Old River. They proceeded dead slow until they were well into the old river; they anchored in the middle. The shore was thick with old willows that grew well out into the lake. This big waterway was formed when the river changed its course and left a horseshoe lake in its place. This was at one time a channel of the river. Untold numbers of river boats and sternwheelers had plied these waters in the distant past. Its bottom would be littered with bottles and skeletons of men and animals, but for now it was simply quiet, peaceful back water.

They spent the rest of the afternoon and evening transferring and stowing everything that would fit in the jet boat. The dingy was launched and tied up behind the jet boat where it would serve as a backup in case they lost the jet boat. In the dingy they placed an emergency supply of food, a rifle, pistol and gasoline.

The next morning just as they were getting ready to shove off, a lanky old gentleman in a pirogue came paddling up. In the pirogue were his two dogs-- one was a black lab and another was a Brittany. "Ahoy, *Lucille*, don't shoot."

Tony looked over the back of *Lucille*. "What can I do for you friend?" All the while, his hand was on the butt of his pistol in its holster.

The man said, "I'm Hank Richard from up at Natchez. My friends call me H.R. I escaped with a little food, my dogs and my hunting gear in my old pickup with this pirogue in the back. I've been hiding, fishing and watching the Russian aircraft."

"I know you H.R.; do you remember when you were guiding with your Brittanies and Dove hunting? My son Larry and I were hunting on your dove lease four or five years ago."

"Yes, I remember you. You had the old Browning sweet 16."

"I still have it; or rather it was locked in the gun safe back on my farm when I left a few weeks ago. What's going on up at Natchez?"

"After the welfare crowd went berserk and the city burned down, the Russians moved in at the airport and have been flying in men and equipment. I slipped out and across the river before they closed the bridge. I've managed to stay hidden down here near the water. I don't have a family or children. I noticed that you are cleaning out *Lucille*. I was wondering where you folks are heading in that jet boat?"

"I'm Tony Jackson, and this is my wife Cheryl. We're going up the Homochitto to my farm up in Franklin County. What can I do for you?"

"I can't fight the Russians and the crooks by myself; I'm having trouble keeping watch twenty four hours a day. Can you folks use another gun? I don't figure I'll last much longer out here by myself."

"You're right. It's a miracle we've made it this far. We escaped New Orleans in this boat."

"Why on Earth didn't you just set sail for the tropics and stay out at sea where it's safe?"

"We didn't have a choice. The Gulf is full of oil, and there's been an oil well blowout. A full blown ecological disaster is taking place."

"There goes my plan B."

"What was your plan B?"

"You're not going to like it."

"Why's that?"

"I was going to steal your boat once you guys left."

Cheryl laughed, and H. R. asked, "What's so funny?"

"Oh nothing; we stole it first."

Tony grinned. "We didn't steal it; we bought it. I wrote a check for it."

Tony pointed to the jet boat and the dingy. "How much stuff do you have? We don't have a lot of extra space."

"I didn't get out with much. My big house on Linton Avenue was on fire when I pulled out of the driveway. I watched it and all the others burn from the levee on the Vidalia side of the river. All I have is a duffel bag of clothes, a box of can goods, two dogs, a .308 Winchester rifle, an over and under twelve gauge and my hunting gear; it'll all fit in my boat. I can also drain the gas out of the truck into some paint cans and pull the battery."

"The sooner you can get loaded up the better; we'll pull your pirogue behind the dingy."

At that moment they heard their friend in the helicopter. Right on time it made its lazy circle overhead, and they all exchanged smiles and waves. The copter was evidently ferrying men and supplies north and south along the river. H. R. paddled up to *Lucille* with everything he owned.

"Friends of yours?"

"They've been monitoring us for the past few days. They come by twice a day on their daily north-south run. I'm glad they came by before we make our run up the Homochitto."

"Why do you think they are interested?"

They either need a running engine, or they have their eye on a good sail boat. I figure they were waiting for me to get it up to Natchez where they could take it."

H. R. watched as the helicopter disappeared in the distance. "It's a shame we can't strip out the engine and batteries."

"I figure I would leave it in running condition in case we need to come back any time soon."

Cheryl lamented. "She was only our home for a short while; I'm going to miss her."

After topping the jet boat tanks off by putting the extra fuel from H.R.'s truck into them, they crossed the Mississippi with the dingy and pirogue in tow. The mouth of the Homochitto River was in view.

23

WHEN SPIKE ARRIVED at the Blue Flamingo, he noticed that Pete's truck was parked out front. He pushed open the front door, found Carl behind the bar and Hazel and a couple of her girls eating sandwiches at a table.

Pete called out. "What did you find out; y'all were sure gone a long time."

Carl bellowed. "Did you get 'em?"

"We got most of them, but there are more on the way."

"What do you mean more on the way?"

"Carl, those were Russian troops. They were probably an advance scouting party. I imagine they'll be using the Natchez airport since it can handle heavy jets. I expect they will be taking and holding every airport that can handle the big planes. That way they can control the regions and squash any opposition."

Carl pondered. "I wonder if we can cut a deal with them; there's no sense in us getting killed."

"Carl, are you saying you are willing to throw in with the people who just killed untold millions of Americans by turning off the lights?"

"Why not; I can't bring any of those people back. Spike, I need to know something, are you with me or not? I know you haven't killed or robbed anyone or brought in any loot since all this started. You haven't even asked for food or help of any kind. I think you and your guys are operating on your own."

Spike glanced around the room and saw that there were half a dozen guns pointed in his direction. "Are you planning on killing me, Carl? 'Cause if you are, you need to know that in my left hand I am holding a cocked .38 revolver, and it's pointed at the center of your chest. If you even blink, you're a dead man."

Carl suddenly went pale when he realized that Spike had a hand in his left jacket pocket and what appeared to be the barrel of a pistol pointing at him through the fabric.

"Carl, I want you to ask your friends here to lay down their weapons and turn facing the wall. If anyone does anything else, this trigger will get squeezed, and you will get a bullet in the chest."

Carl said, "Do it."

As they placed their weapons down and turned, Spike pulled out his Beretta pistol and backed towards the door. Carl was visibly shaken and enraged. Spike considered killing him, but he knew that more than one of Carl's men was holding weapons he couldn't see. He went through the door and instantly jumped behind the brick column holding up the roof that was just outside the door. The door to the bar was immediately splintered to bits as the volley of bullets from Carl's gang opened up. Spike counted to five to give them a chance to come to the window and door. He turned and fired seventeen rounds of 9mm full metal jacket ammo back through the door and window before running down the sidewalk and ducking into an abandoned building. He slapped a replacement magazine into the pistol, headed out the back door and around to the back of the bar. The last thing they would expect would be for him to return to fight. Pete and two of his guys came charging out the back door. Six quick shots had them down with the last one lying in the door blocking it open. He emptied his pistol through the door before replacing the magazine once again. Carl opened up with the M-4 Spike had given him; he riddled the back of the bar room wall, but not before Spike ducked back into the vacant building he had just run through. He ran out the front door bowling over Hazel and two of her girls before hopping into the Bronco and gunning it through town. At that moment all hell broke loose as a Russian helicopter gunship opened up on the city block where the Blue Flamingo was located. His Bronco was rocked as the explosive shells from the cannon on the helicopter exploded behind him. Not wanting to lead them to his home and warehouse out on the highway, he turned and drove into the city cemetery where he abandoned the Bronco and hid behind the biggest monument he could find. His Bronco was soon a pile of scrap metal, but none of the ordinance reached him where he hunkered down behind the large monument. Splinters of granite and marble stung his face as the cemetery was raked with fire. They soon gave up and disappeared in the direction of the Natchez airport. He *thought at least they didn't head in the direction of my house and warehouse out east of town.* He scrambled out from behind the shattered monument as Hazel and two of her girls came riding up.

"Hop on, Spike. Looks like you need a lift; don't worry we're on the same side now."

"Thanks, Hazel, are they all dead?"

"The entire block is leveled and on fire. No one could have survived; the Flamingo collapsed and is an inferno."

"Take me home, Hazel. We won't have much time. What about your other girls?"

"They're at my hideout. I took your lead and made sure we had a backup plan."

As Hazel gunned the big bike, Spike had to shout over the wind in his face.

"Hazel, do you need any supplies or weapons?"

"Can you get me some of those rifles and pistols like you gave Carl?"

"Sure, I'll get you all outfitted; we've got a war to fight. I suggest you girls melt into the forest, and don't go up that road where you found Tub. Those folks will be on our side, but I need to warn them about what's happening."

They rolled into the storage yard where the family was busy loading up equipment, food and supplies. Spike asked Hazel, "How many guns do you need?"

Hazel pondered for only a moment. "A dozen rigs will do."

He called out to Bob who came running up. "Bob, do you remember that road where we found the bus?"

Bob, still out of breath from running, nodded "yes."

"Take the campers to the next road past there and take that road toward the river. There is a forestry road about a mile down that road leading off to the right. We can get the campers out of sight from the air on that road, and there's a small stream that runs through there that flows from the Henderson farm. Drive my big diesel motor home around to the front of my house and make sure Lisa and Lacy get it loaded; it's fueled and ready to go. Once we get the families safe, we can sneak back and get more stuff. I'm going to get Hazel some gear."

Spike threw open the doors to his private stash and loaded a dozen large duffel bags with rifles, pistols, ammo and full gear. One of Hazel's girls left and returned with all the girls on their bikes. Each hefted a duffel across their shoulders.

Hazel asked Spike, "Why did you put up with Carl as long as you did?"

"I don't like killing, and I hoped that I could just coexist; I should have shot him when the lights first went out and when he started all the killing and stealing."

"I don't know if it means anything, but me and the girls didn't murder anybody. We robbed a few people of their jewelry and sent them on their way. We only stole food from the abandoned houses and stores."

"Are you sure Carl is dead?"

"I didn't see his body, but I know the building collapsed on top of him, and it was an inferno from the ruptured gas lines."

"We'll know soon enough if he lived through it. He'll be after me for turning on him and after you for not coming back to dig him out. For now, we have to worry about the military that will be coming in to occupy us. Another thing you need to realize, Hazel, is what we are up against. If this is indeed Russian military, they will have sophisticated night vision capability. If you are thinking about sneaking around after dark, they will have the advantage. They'll probably have star vision type scopes and binoculars. They will own the night, so you need to stay holed up at night and venture out in the daylight. You can blind them with strobes or bright lights at night if you need to make an escape. If you hear a helicopter at night, just hunker down out of sight, and keep your fires low and to an absolute minimum."

"How do you know all of this, Spike?"

"I spent a little time in the army and later with an army contractor. We sold and serviced a lot of the equipment; I wish I had managed to steal some of it. I just wound up with stuff I knew I could sell when I got back."

"Thanks Spike. I'll come find you if I need you. We're back off Berrytown Road about five miles from Okhissa Lake on my mother's old farm. We leased it out as a hunting camp for the past twenty years after mother died. It has an old well with a bucket on a rope. We cleaned out the old outhouse, and it works fine. A couple of the girls have set up solar panels so we have lights and running water to the kitchen from rain barrels. You can spot the drive to the house; there's a big cedar tree standing by the road that looks like something you would see in the front yard of a spook house."

"Hazel, try to stay hidden and alive. Don't be a hero. Hit them and fall back to cover. They will have to eventually fort up and only venture out in force. We'll figure out how to attack them and cut their supply line as this invasion progresses. We'll have most of this gear cleaned out in the next two days if they hold off attacking again. I think they are just refueling and will be back right away."

Spike looked across the highway at the abandoned construction company. A large yellow bull dozer sat off to the side with a huge ripper mounted on the back. The ripper was used like a plow to rip open hard ground, asphalt roads and thin concrete slabs. He quickly formulated a plan on how he could cut up the airport runway at Natchez.

The rest of the day and into the evening was spent relocating the families. The campers were pulled back off the road into the surrounding woods and were located near the little stream running behind them down the hill. They would have a potable source of water once they installed a cistern with a filter to feed the campers. This was an area of older growth woods where the canopy was thick from the old pine trees. Across the road was a section of forest that had been clear cut many years ago. This area was mostly hardwood and would supply them with an unlimited supply of firewood and game. The campers were invisible from the air and far enough removed from the main road so as not to attract attention. All they had left to move was the big natural gas generator and the containers packed with food and ordinance. If they could avoid attack and detection for another half a day, their escape would be complete.

24

ITCH WATCHED AS the helicopter made a big lazy circle of the farm. It was looking for the dead Russians. Before he could stop her, Hannah walked out the front door doing her best "Daisy Duke" impersonation.

"Get your rifle, honey; we're fixing to have company."

""Oh crap, baby, what are you doing?"

"I'm getting them on the ground so you can do your thing."

Mitch hastily retrieved his dad's rifle and a pouch containing a dozen or so twenty round magazines loaded with hunting rounds.

He ran out of the back door and yelled to Hannah. "When I start shooting, grab the dogs and head into the basement and down the tunnel."

He was quickly down on his belly and crawled under the azalea bushes that lined the porch on the side of the house. Before long, he was where he could observe the helicopter making its approach. Hannah smiled and waved as the big machine touched down. Mitch put the crosshairs of the scope on the pilot and waited until the side doors sprung open. A machine gun on a mount was swung around to cover the house. Mitch waited until four men had disembarked and were heading in their direction. The big rifle jumped as the first round found the pilot. Without waiting for the result, he sighted on the machine gunner and fired. The gunner fell backwards and then slumped against the harness that held him in position. The four men turned to run back to the helicopter. Another round from Mitch's rifle hit the co-pilot who was trying to get the blades back up to speed. The four men opened up on the house when they realized that the helicopter was going nowhere. Several bullets tore through the bushes above his head. Bits of leaves and limbs rained down upon him. Another shot from Mitch sent one of the men falling hard. The others took off running toward the woods in the direction of the stream. Suddenly, gun fire erupted from the woods, and two of them went down as the third made a vain attempt to get back to the helicopter. Mitch hit him through the torso and knocked him down. Four more shots from the woods silenced the men for good.

Hannah cautiously emerged from the woods with her rifle in hand. "Did we get them?"

Mitch crawled out from under the bushes and met her in the yard. "I ought to kick your butt for pulling a stunt like that."

"Sorry, Baby, it was the only thing I could think of; you and I both know that the next thing was for them to open up on the house with the machine gun or call in more troops."

"You're right. I just don't like using you for bait."

"I don't think they would have landed to come see you in your tight blue jeans."

"I don't know; you might be under estimating me. I need to get the power shut off in that helicopter. It probably has an emergency transponder; I need to either disable it or completely destroy it. If I destroy it, there will be a column of smoke that will be seen for miles."

He quickly located a fuse panel and had all the electrical systems killed. He found a yellow box with a whip antenna attached to the firewall. A small light was flashing; this was disabled by opening it and removing the battery. As a precaution, he unhooked the cables from the batteries that were used to start the engines. The dead men were pulled into the woods with his tractor to get them out of sight; a trip to the bone yard would have to wait. He tied a chain to the helicopter skids which made it possible to pull it into the woods behind the barn with the tractor. Here they covered it as much as possible with tree limbs so that it would not be seen from the air. Hannah brushed out the skids' drag tracks to hide any evidence of the copter.

Mitch was almost overwhelmed by the events of the morning. One moment he wondered if he were justified in attacking and killing the soldiers--what if they were part of a rescue or relief effort. He quickly dispelled that by the fact that they were sneaking around the house rather than just knocking at the door. There was also the fact that they opened fire when he tossed the pinecone down the hill. No, they were up to no good; otherwise, they wouldn't have shown up ready to fight. The other worry he had was if the helicopter's pilots had managed to radio others where they were located and what they found. That question was answered immediately.

Once again they could hear the heavy vibrations from a helicopter's rotor before they saw the attack helicopter appear in the distance. They retreated to the house and watched as the helicopter made broad sweeps of the area. It appeared as though they were searching the entire area looking for the missing helicopter that was now hidden behind his barn. When they were gone, he would add more limbs and boughs to the cover that was now hiding it.

Hannah waved her hand at the pile of Russian military gear that they were accumulating. "We going to be able to corner the market on Vostok watches, AK-47's and accessories. Do you think we can use these walkie talkies?"

"We can probably use the walkie talkies; you just have to realize that the Russians can hear us. So if we use them to communicate, we can't say anything that would give away what we are talking about or what we're doing. It might not be a bad idea to start making some gun and ammo caches around the farm as well. If this keeps up, we may be running and fighting all over these hills and hollows."

"Hon, what do you think of the idea of our setting up some survival shelters scattered out a mile or so in every direction. We wouldn't need anything elaborate, just a shelter out of the wind and rain with basic supplies, rifle and ammo."

"Okay, Hannah, we'll start building one or two a day until we have safe havens all around the farm. We'll take advantage of the cutover timber. There are sections of it in almost every direction. Nothing short of a nuke could get us once we are in there. They would even have trouble using their thermal imaging. They couldn't distinguish us from the deer and wild hogs especially if we were careful with the fires at night." The dead Russians were added to the bone yard, and the first shelter was established in the cutover near the highway.

25

TONY STEERED THE jet boat across the current avoiding the trees and debris being swept towards the Gulf. The boat was a little more than halfway across when they came upon a man, wearing a floatation device, floundering in the water. He was still alive so, Cheryl and H.R. pulled him onboard as Tony held the boat steady in the current; the man was almost dead from being immersed in the cold water. From the American flag on his flight suit, they assumed that he was an American pilot. As they continued across, H.R. stripped him of his wet clothes and wrapped him in a blanket. Once they were well up the Homochitto River, Tony nosed the boat onto a sandbar and built a roaring fire from drift wood. Hot coffee from H.R.'s thermos revived the man.

Tony introduced Cheryl and H.R. and himself before asking the man, "What's your name, and what are you doing in the middle of the river?"

The young man appeared to be in his thirties and looked up with tired eyes.

"I'm Captain Wayne Matthews with the Louisiana Air National Guard. My helicopter was hit as I was trying to make an attack run on the Natchez airport. I lost power while trying to get back across the river this morning; my gunner was killed when we were struck by enemy fire. Thanks for pulling me out; no matter how hard I swam, the current kept pulling me back towards the center of the river. I thought it was over for me."

H.R. spoke up. "We know that Russians are landing. Do you know what has been taking place?"

"As far as I know, several nuclear bombs were set off in the upper atmosphere over North America and a number exploded over Europe; therefore, causing an EMP event. We aren't sure what else has taken place. We assume it was the Russians because their task force is now in the Gulf; we also suspect that the Chinese and North Koreans are involved as well. Before all communication was lost, we heard that there were PLA Chinese troops in California.

Our command and control structure has broken down due to the loss of communication; it is my understanding that many of our satellites were disabled at the same time. The supply chain that brings food and materials to the troops was dependent on the grid and on integrated circuits. We are also facing a number of our units that have gone rogue. The recent purging of our military officer corps has led to the installation of officers who are political socialists. They feel that the communists are our only salvation. Needless to say, they have filled their ranks with officers and men who agree with them."

Tony grimaced. "So what you are telling me is that we can trust no one but ourselves."

"That's exactly what I'm telling you."

Cheryl chimed in. "That's why we have the jet boat. We were attacked by American equipped men one night. Tony got off the first shot or we'd be dead."

H.R. refreshed the coffee cup in the flyer's hand. "What's going on at the Natchez airport?"

"The Russians are securing every airport that can handle heavy transport jets in the region. I was flying out of Bossier; we've knocked out Alexandria, Monroe, Lake Charles and Lafayette airports. They have managed to defend everything else with surface to air rocket batteries. I'm afraid they are going to have to be taken out by ground forces at this point. All they have to do is hold the airports along the Mississippi until they establish a beach head. We don't expect them to start trying to enter the countryside until most of the people have starved to death or killed each other. All the gasoline has dried up, and the people leaving the big cities are doing so on foot. The attack helicopters are shooting up whatever they can find. They are flying in helicopters and troops with those big transport jets."

The flyer pointed at the jet boat. "I'm going to need that boat; I've got to get back to Bossier."

Tony grinned. "We can drop you off on the other side of the river, or you can ride with us up the Homochitto. We can drop you off about thirty miles east of the Natchez airport. You are welcome to the boat when I'm done with it. I'm willing to fight Commies and traitors every day of the week, but I'm going to do it from my farm where I know the country and terrain. I've got children who will be trying to make their way home; they come first. So, what's it going to be?"

The Captain thought a minute. "I think I'll ride with you up the river. Is there any way I can talk you out of a rifle?"

"We'll do better than that. If you'll help us get this stuff to the farm, I'll give you a full combat rig with ammo and this boat or a ride to town if I can get any of my vehicles to crank."

Tony looked over at H.R. "His coveralls are dry. Look in that big duffel and dig out a rifle, vest and seven of those 30 round mags with pouches. Give him a couple of Beretta mags for his pistol; they should all be down in the bottom of the bag."

Shortly, they were cruising up the Homochitto. The shallow draft and jet drive of the boat allowed them to navigate the shallow sections with ease. The only time they met resistance was when they came to a tree that had fallen across the river. They easily jetted across the trunk using the boat's momentum to cross over it, but they had to stop and carry the dingy and pirogue around it. They were at the point on the river that was closest to the farm in a little more than five hours. The sun was getting lower in the sky. Rather than try to reach the farm, they took the time to transfer everything into the woods near the road that ran parallel to the river. They weren't far from the old brick kiln that once had operated near the river. Since the weather looked as though it would hold, they made camp for the evening. As a precaution, they moved the dingy and the pirogue up into the woods and covered the jet boat with limbs to camouflage it from the air. Tony knew from having been raised near the river that it would only stay there until the next flood. Unless they could get it on a trailer or winch it out of the river, it would be lost at the next good rain storm.

They gathered enough pine straw to make adequately comfortable beds for the night. They made a cold camp and waited for dawn. Although they were only about two miles as a crow flies from the farm, in order to get the supplies there, they would need to retrieve his old Farmall tractor and the hay wagon. The trip around by the roads would increase the travel distance to three or four miles. In normal times this would have been an easy trip, but now it could be a gauntlet.

The next morning, they were greeted with a heavy frost. H.R. built a hot fire, and when they warmed up, they got ready to go.

Tony sat down and pulled out a notebook and pencil. "I am going to draw you a map."

He quickly penciled in and labeled the river, major highways, location of the kiln, his farm, and the Henderson farm.

"I'm going down this road about a half a mile where I'm going to cross over to this old brick kiln. There's an old piece of cabin that has been there for as long as anyone around here can remember. I am going to mark the spot where I leave the road with this pine knot." He reached down and picked up a piece of pine that was thick with resin, "You will note on this map that I have a dotted line that leads to my farm. This is an old logging road that I have hunted off of my entire life; it leads up to the back of farm. If I don't come back by dark, it will mean that I didn't make it or ran into trouble. I'll have to bring the tractor and trailer around by the roads." Again he pointed to the route he planned to take.

Cheryl tugged at his sleeve. "Why don't you take H.R. or Captain Matthews with you?"

"Good idea. I might need help cranking the tractor and hooking up the wagon. Captain Matthews, do you feel like a little stroll through the woods?"

"Sure thing, Mr. Tony; you lead the way."

They loaded up with rifles, pistol, water and some snacks left over from the snack machines they had raided back in New Orleans. Cheryl gave Tony a big hug and kiss.

Captain Matthews grinned. "I wish I could get a send off like that."

H.R. grinned. "Come here boy; I'll give you a big kiss."

Everyone laughed as Tony and Matthews headed out. Tony yelled back. "Stay out of sight. What you are guarding is more valuable than gold."

They heard gunfire from the direction of the town, and it was followed by the thumping of helicopter rotors which was soon drowned out by explosions.

Matthews commented, "Sounds like someone is getting pounded by an assault helicopter. Those things have the firepower of a World War II destroyer; they are turning whatever they are shooting at into dirt and gravel."

"I was afraid they would spot the jet boat and attack. They observed us twice a day for several days while we were heading north on the Mississippi."

"They probably were planning on taking and using it once you did the work of getting it close to Natchez."

They reached the point on the road where they were near the old brick kiln and cabin. Tony deposited the pine knot and they pushed their way through the blackberry vines that grew along the edge of the highway right of way. The thick vines were as big around as a man's finger and were lined with thorns that tugged at their clothes. The thorns occasionally found a bare spot of skin on the back of their hands, and one snagged Tony's ear. Once the first vine was stepped on, it mashed its neighbors down so that the next step could reach the next vine and the next. Before long they were through the briars, and other than a bloody ear and scratched hands they were unscathed. Hundreds of little thorns were broken off in the fabric of their clothes much like the stingers of honey bees after an attack. In the spring of the year these vines would be covered with thousands of dark purple blackberries.

Tony pointed out, "For every berry there will be three red bugs, the Yankees call them chiggers. They are delightful creatures that will give you many hours of amusement."

Captain Matthews gave him a puzzled look. "I've never heard of them."

"Where exactly did you say you were from?"

"I was raised in Dallas, and we moved to Shreveport when I was in high school. I've never been much for the outdoors: I was into sports."

Tony looked over at him. "If you're out and about here in the spring, you'll get an introduction to red bugs, ticks, mosquitoes and horse flies. There will also be some copper heads and rattlers thrown in for good measure."

The old logging road was just as he remembered. The old brick kiln and cabin were just ahead; the old road leading through the cutover was thick with sage brush and berry vines. In other areas, it was just a shady lane. A cemetery from before the Civil War lay off to the left where an ancient cedar tree stood at one corner. A dozen or so tall slabs stood over the graves of settlers who were long dead and forgotten. The remains of an old homestead were on the right about a hundred yards farther down the road. All that remained was the foundation rocks on which the old house sat. A cistern sat silent with its old cap made from cypress still sitting on top. What was left of an old pitcher pump lay in the leaves and dirt to one side.

Captain Matthews asked, "Who lived back here?"

"The last name on the grave stones read Calhoun, but none of the Calhoun's living in these parts have any knowledge of those folks.

Those graves date to the early 1800's; the county records don't go back that far. My family has owned my farm since just after the Civil War. This is all forestry land; I guess it's nobody's land at this point. If Mitch Henderson is still alive, we'll be redrawing the property lines back here one day."

"How far are we from your farm?"

"I would say we are about a mile away once we climb this ridge."

As they neared the ridge they heard gunfire in the distance. Tony raced to the top of the ridge to get his bearings. "If I didn't know better, I would say that is coming from my house."

Without saying a word, he broke into a trot with Captain Matthews keeping pace. They stopped about halfway to catch their breath before picking up the pace once again.

Tony stopped and pointed. "This old road opens into a large pasture beside my house. Stay close. We're going to stick to the wood line to the right. One of my kids may have made it back home."

They got to where they could see a couple of men and several women scattered out shooting toward the house. The people were so preoccupied with shooting at the house that they were unaware they were being watched.

A shot rang out from the house. The bullet smacked the tree near the head of one of the men who cussed, "That son of a bitch almost hit me."

He was answered by one of the women. "Keep your head down; he can't stay awake forever. We'll wait him out."

Captain Matthews whispered, "Do you know these people?"

"No, I'm trying to figure out who's in the house. If I knew it was my son or daughter I'd start shooting."

"How are going to find out?"

A twig snapped in the woods behind them; both men dropped and rolled as a shotgun blast tore through the spot where they were standing.

26

W HILE HIS MEN went back to gather their remaining supplies, Spike
climbed in an old Jeep Wrangler that he had owned for years.
Like his old Bronco, this was a pre electronic era vehicle. He went
back to the cemetery and retrieved his rifle, gear and the battery
out of his trashed Bronco. He made a quick run back though town to
see if there was any activity at what remained of the Blue Flamingo.
It was only a pile of burned out rubble that was still smoking, and
the heat could still be felt radiating from its remains. A column of
flame was still jetting from a broken gas pipe down in the rubble.
The gas meter was still intact standing out by what remained of the
cinder block wall of the building. He took a wrench from his tool
box, closed the valve and killed the flame. Not one to waste time
or ponder about what had taken place he climbed into the Jeep and
made a stop to check on Doc at his house down the street. The old
doctor was loading up his belongings in an old station wagon.

He paused long enough to ask Spike. "You gonna make me stick
around?"

"No, Doc, keeping you locked up was not my idea; I see you
found a vehicle from Carl's stash. Be careful where you go, Doc.
The Russians are here, and they are likely to shoot first. Where are
you heading?"

"My family's dead. Hazel has said that I can stay with them, so
that's where I'm heading."

"Doc that should be an interesting bunch to stay with; I bet you will be able to write a book after a couple of months over there."

"I'll give you the first copy."

"Good luck, Doc. I'm sure you'll be seeing me again one day. I just hope I won't be one of your customers."

Spike, heading out to the highway, kept his eyes peeled for danger. When he reached the road that led to Mitch Henderson's farm, he slowed and turned. The buzzards were circling, so he ran down to the bone yard and turned around in disgust. He thought *Mitch has sure been busy.*

He turned around in the road, headed up into the woods and around the tree that lay across the road; he slowed just long enough to lift and go under the trip lines on Mitch's early warning system. He stopped at the stream, crossed the log bridge on foot and climbed over the fence. He paused at the top of the driveway giving Bacon time to bark a warning. He stayed in the open until Mitch came out on the porch.

"What's up Spike? What brings you back so soon?"

"Russians are what is bringing me back. From what I can tell, you have already met a few."

Hannah came out. "We've haven't had a dull minute in the last couple of days."

At that moment, the sound of gunfire came to them from the direction of the Jackson farm.

Mitch reached inside the door and came out with his AR-15 and an ammo pouch. "Hannah, stay here."

"Spike, follow me; we're going up on the mountain where I can see the Jackson's place."

A brisk sprint up the hill brought them to the point where they could see the top of the house in the distance. There was without a doubt a gun battle taking place.

Spike asked, "Can we get there through the woods, or do we need to take the road around?"

"We can drive through here on my four wheeler."

Without a word, they ran back to the house where Hannah waited. "Hannah, it looks like Larry is being attacked. You stay here with the dogs. We are going to take one of the four wheelers through the old logging road to the Jackson's."

She ran out and hugged him. "Please be careful; I can't do this without you."

"I'll be back as soon as I can."

They cranked the nearest four wheeler and climbed aboard. They drove out of the back door of the barn past the helicopter where it was hidden.

Spike asked Mitch, "Is that what I think it is?"

"Yes, we've been awfully busy since I last saw you."

They ran down the ridge and were soon past the point where he killed the Russians. The grass and brush were still crushed and bloody from the fight. Spike felt himself lucky to have not gotten shot that first day he arrived.

"I came to tell you that we have had to leave my place in town. I've relocated my people down the road on the east side of your land. We are backed up to your stream a couple of miles from here until I can find an abandoned property where we can relocate."

"No problem; let me know if I can ever help."

They didn't speak the rest of the trip; they came down off the mountain and onto the old logging road that led to the brick kiln. If they turned left, they would find the kiln; if they turned right, they would go to the Jackson farm. They veered to the right and toward the gunfire that grew louder. When they reached the old cistern where the old farm house once stood, they left the four wheeler and proceeded on foot.

Spike said, "Stay back about a hundred yards until I motion for you to continue; we'll leap frog our way up to the farm. That way we can cover one another as we approach."

When they reached the end of the road, they heard a shotgun blast off to their right. They turned in time to see Captain Matthews and Tony open up on one of Carl Benson's surviving men with their M-4's.

Mitch called to Tony. "Don't shoot; it's Mitch Henderson."

Tony asked, "What are you doing here?"

"We heard the shooting, and I figured Larry needed some help."

Gunfire erupted from the group that had been attacking the house; bullets tore through the woods around them. Everyone dived for cover. A stream of blood poured down Mitch's face from a cut in his scalp caused by a ricochet. After verifying the identity of the dead man, Spike hunkered down behind the largest tree he could find "Those are the remains of Carl Benson's gang. I didn't figure all of them had been killed when the Blue Flamingo was hit."

He called out, "Carl, are you out there?"

Carl called back, "Spike, is that you? We thought you was dead."

"Not yet, but you're fixing to be."

"Oh yeah, come and get me."

Spike looked around at Mitch, Tony and Matthews. "We're going to have to kill them. I should have killed him the last two chances I had. A lot of people would probably still be alive if I had just gone ahead and pulled the trigger on his sorry ass."

Tony called out. "Larry, it's your Dad; don't come out. Are you okay?"

"I'm okay; the house is shot up pretty good."

"Stay with the house."

"Dad, there's several out behind the house as well."

Tony pointed. "I count two men and three women out front. We can assume that the one we killed was with the ones in the back, and they are probably trying to get around behind us right now."

At that moment, they heard Bacon barking from somewhere in the woods behind them. Mitch said, "He must have gotten away from Hannah and followed us. He has them spotted; I hope they don't shoot him."

Shots rang out, and Bacon came running in to Mitch with his tail tucked, but he wasn't hit. Mitch said, "I'm going after those bastards. You guys kill these."

Mitch disappeared into the woods. The shadows were dark in the big woods so he remained hidden to some extent as he slipped from tree to tree. He was still wearing his camo, and his cheeks were now stained dark from the blood he smeared over them. He started to crawl with Bacon bringing up the rear. He had moved less than a hundred yards before he heard two men whispering. He couldn't understand what they were saying, but they were foolishly close together. Bacon started a low growl that Mitch quieted with a quick tap on his muzzle. Ever so quietly, he eased forward until he got a glimpse of them squatting about six feet apart. He waited a few minutes and watched. He wanted to make certain that these were the only two. As he waited in the shadows, he did not feel the fear or apprehension that a deer hunter gets at the first sight of a big buck. This was a feeling of satisfaction one gets when he has cornered a wood rat. He eased the rifle to his shoulder and squeezed the trigger just as the red dot crossed the chest of the closest man and again on the second. Two finishing shots to their heads brought this hunt to a close. Behind him he heard the other guys firing, and then he heard several rifle reports from the house.

Spike called back, "Mitch, need any help?"

"No, I got 'em."

Spike could see one of Carl's men was down. Carl and the other three people broke and ran for their vehicles; they made their escape in an old black Chevy truck. Although they all emptied their guns on the retreating truck, they were unable to stop it.

Tony called to Larry, "They're gone, son."

Larry came out limping with a bloody rag around his leg. "It's a good thing you guys showed up; I was about out of ammo for my deer rifle. I don't know why they attacked me."

Tony reached down and grabbed a hand full of hair on one of the dead man's head and pulled it up so that everyone could see his face. "This is Buster, my ex-wife's new brother-in-law. He knew we had a farm out here and was friends with Carl Benson."

Spike nodded in agreement. "I remember Buster; he spent a couple of years in the pen back in '98 for swindling a widow woman out of her life's savings. I sure wish we had killed Carl. He's probably heading for another farm or back to sift through the rubble at the Blue Flamingo to look for his barrel of gold and silver. He'll round up some more killers. This won't be the last we've seen of him. If any of you ever spot him, the best thing you can do is kill him on the spot."

Tony looked over at Spike. "Spike, if I remember correctly, you worked for Carl."

"I would on occasion help him collect his money from people like old Buster lying over there. It was probably one of the biggest mistakes I ever made."

Tony was still looking at Spike with a skeptical eye. "How do we know we can trust you? It's obvious Carl couldn't."

"You'd be a fool to trust me, or anyone you don't know for that matter."

Mitch could see that the conversation was deteriorating. "Tony, Hannah and I trust him. He warned us to look out for Carl, and he didn't tell Carl about our farm. In fact, he came to warn us about the Russians. Spike and all of his family are camped up on the far side of our place off of Big Pine Road next to my creek where it turns toward the river."

Captain Matthews chimed in. "You guys need to establish some sort of militia with a command structure. Like or not, the war has come to you. If you're going to defend your homes and families from the likes of Carl and the Russians, you have got to stick together. I've got to get in touch with my command at Bossier City or head in that direction tomorrow."

Mitch asked, "I recognize that you are wearing military issue coveralls. What's your rank and duty?"

"I'm a Captain in the Louisiana National Guard and a helicopter pilot."

Spike spoke up. "Mitch may have something you can use."

Mitch grinned. "Tony, send him over to my farm when you finish with him, I've got something that will be right up his alley." He explained to Captain Matthews what was behind the barn.

"How bad is that leg, Larry? Do we need to go get Doc or carry you too see him?"

"No sir, everything still works. I just have two holes in the side of my leg. It's stopped bleeding, and I can put weight on it. I figure I'll be stove up pretty good once I quit moving around."

Tony spoke up. "I've got to go get our equipment, Cheryl and HR. I don't like the idea of leaving them back there all alone."

Mitch replaced the magazine in his rifle with a full one, slung his rifle over his shoulder and headed for the four wheeler. "I think the Captain has a good idea. Can everyone meet at my house tomorrow after lunch? We've got to get some plans in place to fight. This is quickly spiraling out of our control."

Bacon raised his head perked his ears and looked in the direction of Mitch's home. A growl emanated from his throat, and the hair on the back of his neck stood on end; he then bolted into the woods in the direction of the house. A moment later they heard the echo of one of the warning poppers near his farm.

27

HANNAH ROCKED BACK on her knees and wiped her face with a damp face cloth. She hesitated a moment before hitting the flush handle. She got to her feet, walked down the hall to the kitchen and fished around in the drawer where she knew there were some mints. She popped one in her mouth and thought *God I hope this help; this morning sickness really sucks.* She knew that she couldn't wait much longer to give Mitch the good news.

At that moment, she heard the warning poppers down the road go off. She didn't panic until the one at the gate down the hill by the creek went off. She quickly made sure that the windows and doors were shuttered and peered through the diamond shaped hole in the middle. A black four wheel drive Chevy pickup charged up the drive. An arch of mud, gravel and dirt sprayed away from the wheels as the lug grip tires searched for traction. The man blew right through the front gate and stopped at the steps before hopping out with his rifle.

"Open the door or we'll burn you down. I know someone is in there I can see the smoke from your chimney."

Hannah grabbed her rifle, snatched up Pinky who was barking at the front door, and ran towards the cellar door. Carl Benson could hear Hannah running down the wood floor inside the house, so without a hint of remorse, he fired his rifle on full automatic down the wall before returning to his truck for more ammo. He whirled around as he heard a growl and was knocked to the ground.

Mitch and Spike ran the four wheeler flat out and almost wrecked in their rush to get back to the farm. They stopped the four wheeler on the mountain behind the house. Mitch ran down the hill in a murderous rage. He didn't slow down when he rounded the corner of the house and emptied the magazine of the rifle into the three women who were scrambling with their guns to get around the truck. He slapped a fresh mag in, hit the bolt release and was ready for action as he rounded the truck. Bacon had Carl by the throat and down on the ground. He was shaking Carl furiously. Bacon's fangs had penetrated the jugular; the blood was flying everywhere which only fueled his attack and rage. Carl was still gurgling when Bacon released his grip. The last thing Carl Benson ever saw was Bacon standing over him growling.

Mitch called to Hannah. "Open up, Hannah; it's over." The only sound was Pinky scratching at the door and yipping.

Mitch ran down the hill to the tunnel and into the basement. He flipped the latch on the basement door and caught Hannah when she fell into his arms. He could feel that her clothes were sticky with blood. He gently carried her to the basement bed and laid her down. He quickly stripped her shirt away, and his heart sank when he realized there was a bullet hole just above her navel.

Hannah stirred and looked up at Mitch. "I knew you would come back."

"Stay quiet, sweetie; you've been hit."

"I've got to tell you something; I love you more than anything."

"I know, Baby, and I love you too."

"Mitch, be quiet and listen. I'm going to have your baby." She tried to smile as she drifted away.

Mitch held her close and felt her slip away. He started shaking; his only thought was that he had to go with her. His hand settled on his .45 pistol. He pulled it from the holster and cocked it as he lifted it to his head.

Spike caught his hand. "Wait, this ain't over yet. Put that up and get out of my way."

Spike immediately started CPR on Hannah and ordered Mitch, "You've got to go get Doc right now. Take my Jeep and head down Berrytown Road until you see a huge cedar tree that looks like a ghost tree. Doc is down that road at Hazel's house. There is a lesbian biker gang living there. Get Doc and get him back here. If you see Tony or Captain Matthews, send them down."

Mitch opened the front door and met Tony and Matthews running into the yard. He quickly told them what had happened and where he was going.

Tony yelled to Matthews. "Get down there and help Spike. Doc is staying at the house that was our hunting camp. Mitch, I'll drive; you ride shotgun."

Mitch could only nod. With breakneck speed, they raced down the road and over to Hazel's place where they found Hazel and Doc on the front porch.

Mitch screamed, "Don't shoot! Spike sent us for Doc. Doc, we need you badly! My girlfriend has been shot, and they are doing CPR."

Doc grabbed his bag and a large black case, and they were soon racing back to the farm. Hazel and a couple of her girls followed in a Chevy Blazer that she had confiscated from Carl's stash.

When they reached the creek, Tony called back to Doc. "Hang on this is going to be rough."

Hazel had to slow down, but Tony barreled across the creek. Water, mud, sand and gravel cascaded in every direction, but the Jeep never slowed. Doc raced down the steps to the basement with Mitch hot on his heels carrying the large black case.

Spike had stopped the CPR, and Hannah was breathing shallowly. Doc opened the suitcase, quickly hung a saline bottle and had a saline drip started. "I need a blood donor now."

Mitch stripped off his vest and shirt. "Me. Use me. Doc, she told me she was pregnant just before she passed out."

Doc handed him several aspirin. "Ok, kid, chew these up and swallow them we've got to thin your blood. The aspirin will make your platelets scatter so the blood won't coagulate in the tubes. Sit over here next to the bed; this device will let me pull blood from you and transfer it to her. I'm going to take a lot of your blood. If you start feeling faint, say something so one of the guys can keep you from fainting and falling out of the chair."

"Doc, you take every drop of my blood if that is what it takes. You save her at all cost."

"Hang in there; it shouldn't come to that."

In an instant, Doc had the device in Mitch's arm and a stream of blood was coursing through the clear plastic tubing. When it reached the end, he plugged the needle into a port on the side of the saline line. He pinched off the saline and started slowly pushing blood into Hannah. Her lips began to turn pink. Doc smiled when he took her blood pressure.

"Good, we've got her back. I'm going to have to operate to see if I can patch up what's been hurt inside. We're going to have to set up an operating table with a lot of light."

Mitch pointed to a switch on a post. "Spike, flip the bottom switch and then the top one when you hear the engine crank. I have alcohol, hydrogen peroxide and antibiotics on the medicine shelves."

By that time, Hazel had arrived and spoke up. "Y'all might not believe it, but I was an RN before I went Goth. I know what you're thinking, but it's true."

Spike flipped the switch, and they heard a generator come to life out in the barn. The second switch lit the room from a gang of fluorescent lights.

Mitch pointed to the sink, soap and a box of neoprene gloves, "Doc, I don't have anything for anesthesia."

"Son, I have an injectable. If she starts to wake, I can give her enough to kill the pain."

"Don't forget about the baby."

"I won't boy. I'm going to try and save them both."

"Hazel, start another saline on this boy; I want to leave him hooked up in case we need more blood. If she needs more blood after today, we're going to have to do some blood typing, or we'll have trouble with rejection."

They quickly had the table and additional lights set up. Doc's surgical tools were sitting in a cake pan filled with alcohol.

Doc ordered the men. "Help me move her over to the table and hang on to this boy so we can move him over here out of the way. Boy, do you have a cutting torch?"

"Yes, sir, in the barn."

"Someone fetch it; she can use the oxygen."

The oxygen tank was wheeled in, and oxygen started flowing slowly through a small nose piece under Hannah's nose.

After they had her moved to the table, Hazel told the guys, "You guys get upstairs out of the way and send my girls down. They both used to work in the hospital with me."

Tony, Spike and Matthews sent the girls down and went outside to clean up the yard. Bacon had calmed down and allowed them to wash away the blood that coated his neck and chest. When Bacon was cleaned up and Pinky had calmed down, the guys threw the dead bodies in the back of the truck.

Tony said, "Matthews, come with me; we're going to dump these bodies. Then we're going to get my trailer and retrieve Cheryl and HR. This has been one hell of a day."

Spike told them, "If I hear shooting, I'll come running; otherwise, let's meet here in the morning the day after tomorrow. If the girl lives, Mitch won't be in any shape to work or fight because he has lost a lot of blood and may lose some more."

Spike walked into the kitchen and put a large pot of salty water on to boil. He knew from witnessing battle field injuries that the Doc would have to wash out Hannah's body cavity to reduce the chance of infection. He also put some dry cloths and towels into the microwave and cooked them on high to sterilize them.

He found and sterilized a meat injector and a turkey baster; these could be used to suction blood and fluid during the surgery. He carried a bucket and the sterilized utensils and cloths downstairs, "Doc all of this has been sterilized. I'll be down with sterile saline water in just a minute."

"Thanks, Spike, what did you say you did in the war?"

"I did some of everything, Doc. Mostly I kept my head down."

Doc looked over at Mitch. "Do you have a soldering iron anywhere?"

"Yes, there's one on the workbench in the barn."

Doc called up to Spike. "Get out to the barn and look on a workbench for a soldering iron. I'm going to need it wiped down with alcohol and plugged in so I can cauterize the small blood vessels that I can't clamp off."

"On my way, Doc."

Spike ran to the barn, retrieved an extension cord and the soldering iron. After entering the basement, he wiped it down with a rag soaked in bourbon that had been retrieved from a kitchen cabinet. He plugged it in, and handed it to Hazel who was gloved and masked. Spike went upstairs to the kitchen where he filled the sink with water and set the hot pot of water in it to cool. He started a fresh pot of water to boil on the stove and carried the other one down to Hazel.

"Hazel, this has been sterilized and cooled. Check to make sure it is cool enough before you use it."

"Thanks, Spike, we'll call you when we need more."

Spike sat at the kitchen table and mentally kicked himself over and over *if I just had the guts to have shot that goofy ass Carl, none of this would have happened.*

Looking around the kitchen, he found some coffee and figured no one would mind if he put on a big pot. They were going to have a long evening. He hoped that his people were doing okay in his absence. Lisa, Lacy and their brothers weren't stupid and would carry on until he got back. He didn't like to be in charge of the brothers and their families, but it had just worked out that way for some reason.

A couple of hours later, Doc came up from the basement. Spike poured him a cup of coffee. "How's it looking, Doc?"

"She is doing okay. She lost a kidney, and I had to patch some of her intestines. She is young and in good health. If the antibiotics do their work, I think she and the baby will be fine. What are these kids' names? I don't have a clue who these people are."

"His name is Mitch Henderson, and you operated on his girl-friend Hannah."

"I think I remember him. His father is old Curtis Henderson and his mother is Dorothy; they called her Dot. When he was a little fellow, they brought him into my office; he had fallen out of a tree and had broken his arm. It wasn't badly broken, so I just put a cast on, and they took him home. I didn't realize he lived back here. He's lucky to have a place like this."

"I wish I had a farm in the middle of nowhere."

"I'm sure there will be quite a few empty farms before this is over."

"The problem is there are a lot more people like Carl, not to mention the Russians and maybe the Chinese PLA."

Hazel climbed the stairs. "I smelled the coffee. She's starting to wake. I made Mitch get in the bunk bed, and he's out like a light. How much of his blood did you take, Doc?"

"I took too much; he won't be worth killing for a week or so."

Doc disappeared down the stairs as Spike poured coffee in mugs for Hazel and the girls.

28

TONY DROVE AROUND the downed tree in the road and noticed the buzzards circling down the side road before the smell of decay hit them. "Damn that stinks."

He pulled down the road to the bone yard and said to Captain Matthews, "It looks as if Mitch has been one busy man in the past few days."

They dumped Carl's body and those of his women next to the others and headed back out to the highway and around to Tony's house and farm. They pulled into the drive and up to the house. The Aussie and her puppies came out barking. Up until now, the dogs had remained hidden in the old garage.

Larry came out of the house. "What happened at Mitch's place?" Tony and Matthew told him the details.

Larry starred in disbelief. "I wish I had been a better shot. I should have just shot his ass when he pulled up and yelled for me to come out. He threatened to burn me out if I didn't come out. I fired my rifle over his head instead of through it. This is all my fault."

Matthews shook his head. "No, it's that crazy bastard's fault; we can't give anyone the benefit of the doubt again. It's a new world; our paradigm has shifted."

Tony pointed to his equipment trailer by the barn. "Larry, a lot has happened in the past few weeks. I have a new wife. I traveled by sailboat up the Mississippi and then up the Homochitto in a jet boat that I captured from some renegade army guys. Now, we're going to hook up the trailer to this truck, and then we're heading around and retrieve my bride, our gear and H.R."

"H.R.; is he the guy that took us bird hunting a few years back?"

"That's him. We picked him up on the river, and I figure we could use an extra gun hand. We plucked Captain Matthews out of the Mississippi too. His helicopter went down in the river, and we were able to get him out before he froze to death. Have you had any word from your sister or mother?"

"I haven't heard anything; I doubt we'll ever see them again. If it's this bad here, I can't imagine what it would be like in New York or South Florida."

"We're camped just down the road near the old brick kiln next to the river. We'll be back in a couple of hours. Stay locked up until we get back."

"Don't worry, Dad. This leg is starting to get pretty sore; I won't be getting out if I can help it."

Tony and Matthews loaded the dead bodies in the truck attached the equipment trailer to the back of the truck and headed down the highway. Both of them had their weapons at the ready. They stopped when they reached the river road and dumped the dead into the ditch, and then proceeded to where HR and Cheryl were waiting. When they arrived, they found them behind the supplies with their weapons drawn.

Cheryl grinned ear to ear. "We heard shooting in the distance; you had us worried."

Tony gave her a tremendous hug. "We've had a very busy day. My son Larry made it home. Although he is wounded, he will recover. We need to load everything on the trailer and get back to the farm where it's safer. I want to winch the jet boat up out of the river with the winch on the front of this truck. I don't want to abandon it in case we need to use it again one day."

H.R. piped up. "We need to get the gasoline and batteries out of it when we get it out of the river; that will keep someone from trying to launch and use it. They will assume that it won't crank like all the other late model equipment."

They unhooked the trailer and pulled the truck as close to the river bank as possible. They tied on to the tie down hook on the front of the boat and pulled it up out of the river and into the woods. They turned the truck around and tied on with the boat's bow line and dragged it up to the road. From there, they laid down limbs and pine boughs, and using a chain and pulley, they winched it across the asphalt road and up into the woods out of sight. They picked up the limbs and used the boughs to sweep away any evidence that the boat had been dragged across the road. They piled all the limbs and boughs over the boat, so, unless a hunter stumbled up on it, no one would find it. They drained the boat's fuel tanks and topped off the gas tank of the black truck; the rest of the fuel was put in the boat's empty fuel cans. Next, they dumped buckets of river water into the truck bed to wash away the blood before loading the dingy and H.R.'s pirogue. With everyone in the truck, including H.R.'s dogs, they headed back to the Jackson farm. The trip back was uneventful. No one spoke as they passed the dead bodies in the ditch; it hadn't taken long for the buzzards to start investigating.

Cheryl held her hand over her mouth as they passed. "Tell me what happened."

Tony told her blow by blow what had taken place with Captain Matthews filling in some of the details.

Cheryl sighed. "That poor girl; do you think she'll live?"

Captain Matthews spoke up. "I've seen guys live who were in much worse shape under much worse conditions. She is a young healthy woman, and I think Doc got to her in time. Spike performed CPR on her until she came around, started coughing and nodded her head. He listened to her heart and said that it was beating steadily, so we kept her covered until Doc arrived a short time later. Mitch's blood transfusion brought her around."

Cheryl volunteered. "Do you need me to go over and help?"

Tony shook his head. "No, we are meeting over there the day after tomorrow. They have Doc, Hazel, two of Hazel's girls, Mitch and Spike there. We can swing by there tomorrow once we get settled. We need to get Larry's leg cleaned up and bandaged and get some antibiotics in him from our med kit."

Matthews spoke up. "I want to get a look at that helicopter behind the barn. It looks as if it's flyable."

"Okay. Then we will make another run over to Mitch's in the morning."

H.R. hadn't said much on the way back, but as he gently stroked the fir of the big lab sitting between the seats, he said, "Who would have thought that an old fart like me would be getting ready to start fighting a war?"

Tony looked at him through the rear view mirror. "H.R., you should be old enough to have been drafted for Viet Nam."

"I was there for almost nine months. I still wake up at night and think I hear the cans with rocks rattling on our perimeter wires. Those Viet Cong were sneaky little bastards."

Matthews asked, "How many did you kill?"

"I don't have a clue; I know of two for sure. We had a few of them sneak all the way in to where we were sleeping. They slit the throats of three of the guys in my tent, and they would have gotten me, if I hadn't woken up with a full bladder. I beat two of them to death with my trenching tool. I didn't think to just shoot them with the pistol I was wearing; I guess I just went crazy. I know I burnt through thousands of bullets in those M-16's they issued us. On several nights, I just fired at the men and bodies that I could see from the flares. I burnt through three rifles in one night. Those guns would lock up; I'm not sure why. I think the rifles I was shooting just overheated."

Tony could see the emotion in H.R.'s eyes and hear it in his voice as he went on to describe the friends who died and the smell of the dead after a few days in the tropical heat.

"H.R., I think this will be a different kind of war for us. For one thing, we won't have an unlimited supply of men and ammo to back us up. This will be a sniper's war. There aren't enough of us to make frontal attacks, so we will have to fight smart and make their lives a living hell."

H.R. said, "We need to maim them whenever possible. They will have to take care of the wounded. Every one of them that are lying around wounded is a mouth they have to feed; not to mention the medical staff and facilities they will have to have in place to tend to them."

Captain Matthews nodded in agreement. "That's good thinking HR. I can see knee capping them or blowing out a shoulder socket as a good way to side line one of them forever. We won't take prisoners unless we need them to be interrogated. We will simply disable them with extreme prejudice and leave 'em lying. Just make sure they won't be able to return to the field."

The trip back was peaceful; there were no refugees or attacks. The Jackson farm looked and felt differently as they pulled up in the yard; in fact, the whole world was different. The country was at war, and they weren't spectators. Tony remembered watching the news and seeing reports from Viet Nam, Iraq and Afghanistan now it was here at home. He had and would kill people; the only problem he foresaw was figuring out who were the good guys.

They were packed in for the night with Tony and Cheryl taking Tony's old room. Larry was in his normal room and H.R. took the third room. Captain Matthews took the old travel trailer parked in the barn; it was cold, but the bed was warm.

When Larry discovered that the lights weren't coming back on, he hooked up the camper's pressurized water system to the house. That gave the house running water for the toilets, sinks and showers. Once a day he carried water from the old well and filled the water tank on the camper. Using their old tractor, he stole a work trailer from the Forestry Service that had a solar panel and twelve volt batteries that powered a flashing light that said "men at work." The trailer had been inside a metal building, and all the electronics were enclosed in a metal housing, so they were shielded from the EMP. Now the trailer was powering the water pump and lights in the camper.

With the dogs on guard in the yard that night, they were able to get some much needed sleep. The next morning found them up early as there was a lot to be done. Cheryl made an inventory of food and supplies and a list of what they needed to gather. Food was top on the list along with garden seed, needles, fish hooks, etc.

Tony and H.R. made a list of weapons, ammo and gear that men in the field would need to fight and survive. Captain Matthews made some suggestions. Tony and Matthews decided that they would head over to the Henderson farm so Matthews could get a look at the Russian helicopter. They loaded their rifles, ammo and put on warm clothes. Tony opened the door and was instantly greeted by the three big dogs and three fuzzy puppies.

"H.R., how about seeing if you can shoot some meat? We also need to find homes for these Aussies; we don't have the luxury of feeding this many dogs unless we find an abandoned truck full of dog food."

H.R. pointed out. "You do realize that you can eat dogs if you have to. I saw them do it when I was in Nam."

Tony shook his head. "Lord, I hope it don't come to that."

They hiked back down the trail toward the kiln because it was good clear walking, and then they cut up to the trail that led around to Mitch's Mountain. In no time they were walking on top of the mountain and looking down upon Mitch and Hannah's home.

Tony glanced over at Matthews. "I hope the news is good this morning. When we left yesterday, it was still up in the air if Hannah would make it. I sure hope we aren't digging a grave this morning."

"That would be too bad to even consider."

As they came down the hill, Bacon came bounding out barking. Tony called his name and he quieted, came up and smelled the other dogs on their clothes.

Hazel was out back on the kitchen porch smoking a cigarette. "You boys are up and at it bright and early this morning."

Tony nodded and tipped his hat. "How are things this morning?"

"Hannah made it through the night okay and awoke tired and hurting. We gave her some pain meds and managed to get her up and to the bathroom. I think she and the baby are going to be fine. It's just going to take a while for her to recover. Mitch is the problem. He keeps wanting to get up and roam around. With as much blood as Doc pulled out of him, he will be weak as a kitten for a few more days."

"I can't blame him for wanting to get moving. We are all in a fighting state of mind. I know I was fit to be tied when I got shot a few weeks back. My shoulder is still killing me, but I am sure glad to be moving again."

Mitch came creeping out the back door. "Tony, I want to thank you for what you did for Hannah and me yesterday. If you hadn't known exactly where to go get Doc, I wouldn't have found him in time to save Hannah."

"Hell, Mitch, you'd have done the same for me. I just wish I was a better shot. If I had been one, none of this would have happened. Is Spike around this morning?"

"No, he left last night after everything quieted down. If you need him, all you have to do is follow the stream down the hill for about a mile, and you will come to where he and his people are camped."

"No, I was just wondering. I wanted to apologize for questioning his loyalty."

Mitch grinned. "Don't feel badly. I started to shoot him a few days back when he came walking in here. Old Bacon saved him."

"Saved him?"

"Yep, Bacon is a hell of a judge of people. If Bacon is at ease around you, then you can't be all bad. He's a Catahoula Cur; they're impossible to fool. I swear he can read my mind. If he didn't think you were okay, you would have to shoot him before you could come on the farm."

"I believe it; maybe we can get some pups off him one day. Speaking of pups, do you think Spike and his people could use some dogs? We have three more of those little Aussies that are ready to go. We need to either find them homes or start fattening them up."

"Bring 'em over in the morning. Spike will be back with some of his brothers-in-law so we can plan a defense and come up with a battle plan. What brings you over so early?"

Matthews spoke up. "Is that Russian helicopter you have out back flyable?"

"It should be. All I did was disconnect the batteries and the emergency beacon before dragging it back there and hiding it. I needed to get it out of sight; do you know someone who can fly it?"

"You're looking at a helicopter pilot. Tony fished me out of the river after my helicopter was shot down. Would you mind showing her to me?"

"No, not at all; you head on out while I get my shotgun."

"Hazel, can you keep your eyes peeled and check on Hannah? Doc's still asleep in the recliner by the fireplace in the living room."

"Sure thing, I don't know a thing about helicopters. All I know is to try and hide from them."

Mitch strapped on his pistol, jacket, 12 gauge, a bandoleer of buckshot and slugs and followed Tony and Matthews out behind the barn. The pilot's and gunner's blood which had flowed from the seats and across the floor was dried to a dusky red stain. Mitch opened the battery compartments and showed the men where he had disconnected them and how he disabled what he thought was the rescue beacon. Matthews went over it from top to bottom and pulled some manuals from a case behind the seat. Everything was in Russian, but the diagrams helped him locate fuse panels and various systems that he recognized.

He pointed to the radio. "The radio frequencies should be the same as all aircraft use, and they can listen to it as well as we can.

I also see another set of radios that are probably for military use only. It's a shame we don't understand Russian. I'm going to kill this military frequency radio and hook up the batteries. I want to see if I can communicate with Bossier City from the ground. I may have to crank this baby up and get it three or four thousand feet up if the radio doesn't work here on the ground."

Tony could see Mitch starting to sag. "Matthews, Mitch and I are heading back to the fire."

"C'mon, Mitch, let's get you warmed back up; they tell me your blood is a little thin."

Mitch grinned for the first time in a day. "You're right. I'm pretty tired. I need to get some food in me. Hazel's friends, Harriet and Shannon, have breakfast cooked. For tough girls, they can sure cook. What do you think of everything that's taking place?"

"I think we may look back on these as the good old days before all this over."

Mitch and Tony walked back through the rusty screen door just as Doc came from the living room with an empty coffee cup.

"Mitch, I told you not to be up and about so quick. I want you to just sit around the fire and rest. Now get over there and sit down next to the kitchen fireplace, and we'll fix you a plate."

Harriet pulled a pan of homemade biscuits from the oven and put two of them on a plate. "I hope you don't mind, but I found some canned butter, Bisquick and grits. We gathered some fresh eggs and made sure the chickens were fed and watered."

Mitch nodded. "Thanks, Harriet, I can never repay y'all for what you're doing. As soon as they start setting, I'll try and supply every-one with chickens."

Harriet slathered the biscuits with butter and buried them in white gravy. The two eggs over easy sat in the middle of the pile of grits. A cup of strong coffee topped off the meal.

Doc took his plate. "Mitch, if we can get a few more meals down you like this one, you might survive."

Mitch finished his breakfast and took a plate down to Hannah. "Needless to say, you scared the daylights out of me."

Hannah tried to smile, but grimaced. "I am sore all over. From my chest to my insides, everything is sore and hurts. Did Doc say anything about the baby?"

"Doc seems to think the baby's okay; you just need to eat, rest and get well. We've got lots of friends to help now."

"How's our food holding out? We've got a lot of people eating?"

"We have a big food surplus right now. We're having a meeting tomorrow, and food production is going to be on the agenda. Now quit fretting and eat; I think Hazel and Doc are going to want to get you up and about."

"How long do I have to stay in the basement?"

"I'll ask if we can get you moved up to the bedroom."

"Thanks, Baby."

Tony had been waiting upstairs with Doc in the kitchen and was drinking a cup of coffee when Mitch returned with Hannah's empty plate. "Mitch, I'm going to leave Matthews over here working on the helicopter; I'm going to get back to the house. We'll see you in the morning, and we'll put some ideas together. Show Matthews all those handheld two way radios you have. We are going to have to work on a communication system."

Spike rolled out of his bed in the back of his bus. The bus was well insulated and warm, but it wouldn't be long before the propane was exhausted. They would have to locate a farm and hopefully a source of natural gas for the big generator that was now sitting on a trailer in the woods. Little Roger was sitting on the front couch in his pajamas eating a cookie out of an MRE. Spike fired up the diesel generator to top off the batteries while he showered and dressed. Lisa and Lacy, as usual, had a good breakfast ready when he came out.

Lisa looked at Spike and nodded in the direction of the child. "Roger hasn't said much since he arrived. He's still terribly unsettled after what has happened."

"I'll take care of him this morning. I want to call up the guys and get them started looking for us a home place around here. We're safe for now, but we will be out of propane quickly unless we can get our hands on a propane truck."

He walked over and sat next to Roger. "Roger, what do you have planned for today?" Roger just looked at the floor and shrugged his shoulders.

"Have you ever built a campfire?" Roger shook his head, "no."

"Let's get some biscuits and gravy in you and some hot chocolate, and we'll get a fire going. All the men will be around here in a bit for a meeting, and we'll need a good hot fire for our hands."

Lacy fed Roger some breakfast and got him changed into his warm outside clothes. "He's ready to go out and take on the world." She gave him a big hug and kiss.

Lisa followed suit. "Don't forget my hug and kiss."

Roger was grinning as he headed to the door. Spike winked at the girls as he followed Roger outside.

"Roger, let's find a spot away from the camper where we can rake away the leaves and little limbs. You don't want the fire to get away from where you're burning and catch the woods or our campers on fire. I want you to gather up a whole pile of little twigs and pile them up there in the middle. Then we'll pile on some larger sticks and limbs."

Roger soon had his fire ready to light. "Mr. Spike, I have it ready."

"Good job. You don't have to call me Mr. Spike. Just call me Pop from now on. Let's see if we can get this lighted."

Spike took out an old Zippo, spun the flint striker and had the fire burning. "Roger, your job is to watch the fire and make sure it doesn't go out. Look around under these trees and get us a pile of limbs over here on the side so we can add them to the fire as it burns down. Let me or our two ladies know if it starts getting too big or is trying to spread."

"Do you mean Mama Lisa and Mama Lacy?"

"That's who I mean. Can you tell them apart?"

"Sure, can't you?"

"Sure I can. How can you tell the difference?"

"It's easy. Mama Lacy has a little wrinkle next to her lip, and Mama Lisa has a tooth that's a little crooked."

"You are very observant Roger, but I wouldn't point out to them that Mama Lacy has a wrinkle."

"I already did. It's okay; they just laughed at me."

They pulled out some folding camping chairs from a compartment in the bus. Roger gathered up a big pile of pine cones. He was having a good time, and his troubles were no longer on his mind.

Spike knocked on the bus door. Lisa opened it and looked down at Spike. "I'm going to round up your brothers; keep an eye out for Roger. Try not to let him burn up the camper or the woods."

"Roger, you hang out here and don't wander off."

"Okay, Pop."

Lisa bent down and kissed Spike on the cheek. "Pop? Thanks, he needed cheering up. Also when you're out and about, see if you can put your hands on some lotion and face cream. Lacy is worried about getting wrinkles."

Spike grinned. "I'll round some up."

"Roger, you stay back from that fire; I don't want you falling in it. Do you see that little creek back there?"

"Yes, sir."

"If for some reason you or one of the other kids catches on fire, go jump in the creek and roll around in the water; it's not deep, but it will put out the fire."

"Yes, sir."

Spike walked out to the road and over to the next camper where Lucas and his family lived. Lucas's wife was named Misty, and they had a two year old daughter named Mandy.

Lucas saw him coming and stepped out of the door. "What happened yesterday? We were worried when we heard all the shooting in the distance."

"Carl Benson and his crew won't be a problem anymore. If you follow this stream a mile or so, you'll come to the road to the Henderson farm. We are actually parked on the east side of it now. Carl tried to take it late yesterday, and we killed him and his people. He almost killed the girl living there named Hannah. Doc was able to patch her up, and she should be okay. It's going to take a while for her to get well though. She lives there with her boyfriend Mitch Henderson. Doc used him for the blood transfusion, and as a result, he isn't in the best of shape either. Can you round up all your brothers and meet me at my camper. We've got to make plans; I've got to get back and make sure Roger isn't burning up the woods. I think I've created a fire bug."

Lucas laughed. "I was wondering where that smoke was coming from."

Spike got back to the fire and cautioned Roger. "Don't put a lot of wood on the fire. You want to keep it small so it won't make a lot of smoke. If that smoke climbs up out of these trees, we can be spotted by an airplane or helicopter. The trick is to keep a small hot fire and stick close to it to keep warm. Otherwise, you'll just stay warm toting wood."

The day was very cold. Spike checked his watch and realized that Christmas was only a week away. His watch unlike most watches was a self-winding, mechanical type made by Seiko. He obtained it and a box of a hundred more when he was in Iraq. Everyone would get one this year for Christmas. They were in one of his five containers sitting in the woods further down the road.

Lucas was the first to arrive around the fire. He brought his own folding chair and a chunk of seasoned oak for the fire. "I picked up a load yesterday from an abandoned pile out by the farmers co-op."

"Great. How's our fuel holding out?"

"We're in pretty good shape. We and four of Hazel's girls cleaned out Carl's stash. He had two five thousand gallon semis filled with gasoline and one full of diesel. We have an abundance of propane as well. We found a propane delivery truck and were able to fill it up from their bulk yard. We helped some old people fill their bottles and made a note of where they live. I can't believe how many people have just flat out starved to death. I am amazed at the number of strangers who have come through killing people and stealing all the food."

"That's why we are going to have to stay off the beaten path and stay on guard. Between the Russians and the murderers like Carl Benson, we are going to have to be careful."

Presently, all the brothers and a few of the wives and girlfriends were gathered around the fire.

Once Lisa and Lacy came out, Spike spoke up. "I wanted to give everyone a heads up on what's going on." Spike first looked around and then recounted what had taken place over at the Jackson and Henderson farms.

"What happened at Mitch's and Tony's could just as easily happen to us over here. I want all of the adults to be armed at all times when you are outside of your campers. I notice some of you ladies are not armed at this moment. From now on, I want you at least to be wearing a pistol."

They all nodded in agreement. "I met a helicopter pilot who is a Captain in the army. He was shot down by the Russians and picked up in the river by Tony Jackson and his wife. He says the Army believes that the Russians are taking and holding the East side of the country, and the Chinese PLA are coming in from the West side. They took out the grid in Europe and other parts of the world as well. That means we have one hell of a war on our hands. They are going to be interested in finishing off us stragglers. The U.S. Army has managed to take out all the airports to the west of here, and that only leaves New Orleans, Baton Rouge, Natchez, and Jackson that are near us and that can handle big jets. Captain Matthews was shot down trying to close the Natchez airport. Tomorrow, all the guys but Bob and Lucas are coming with me over to the Henderson farm.

I want Bob and Lucas to stay here on guard with you ladies. We will be planning our next steps after the meeting. This afternoon, I want to look over all the surrounding countryside and locate a permanent home for our families; any questions?"

Lucas's wife Misty spoke up. "Spike, who is our new family member?"

Spike caught Roger and picked up him up. "Everyone, this is Roger my new right hand man; he is living with Lacy, Lisa and me. If anyone needs help building a campfire, this is your man."

"Lucas and Bob, do you mind standing guard today? I want the rest of us to spend the day looking for a nearby empty farm where we can move. We should look for the oldest and most remote one we can find. If you spot a farm, look for a nearby gas well or a gas line under pressure that we can hook up to our big generator."

Lucas and Bob both gave him the thumbs up. Everyone dispersed to their campers and got prepared for the day. Spike showed Roger how to pour a bucket of water over the fire to kill it.

"We can't take a chance on the fire getting away and burning up the woods and our homes."

Spike thought back through the years to when he was a small boy. His Uncle Percy had taken him in after his mother died. He saw his Dad only one time and that was just before Spike left for Iraq. His dad had asked for a loan of a thousand dollars and that was the last time he had seen or heard from him, or the thousand dollars. Uncle Percy was the only Dad he had ever known. Percy had taken him camping and showed him how to build a fire when he was about Roger's size. That morning was a cold one just like this one when they had gone on a squirrel hunt and stopped to build a fire to warm up. His uncle had given him a puppy that turned into his squirrel dog. The little fellow was a cross between a beagle, rat terrier and what was called a mountain cur. Spike named him Buster. Many years were spent with Buster trudging up and down the hills and hollows hunting with Uncle Percy and him. Percy and Buster were now both long dead and were only memories. A box with Buster's collar and several worn out tennis balls for playing fetch was in one of the storage units. His Uncle Percy had died when he was in high school, and Spike had been living by his wits ever since those days long ago.

Spike knew that the bad part about running around in broad daylight was the fact that they were sitting ducks should an enemy helicopter choose to attack or if they passed a patrol or sniper. The only advantage, he had, was that he knew most of the roads and places to hide and take refuge. He wondered if Captain Matthews could get the Russian helicopter up and running.

Spike had always been a loner. Having all of his extended family looking to him for direction wasn't an easy task for him. He left Bob and Lucas to guard the camper site and paired the other four off and sent them in different directions to look for a suitable homestead. In the back of his mind, he remembered an old farm that had been occupied for many years. It backed up to the national forest lands and wasn't far from the river. The property had a large brick house, some fields and a huge old wooden barn. He recalled that the owner had struck it rich when they drilled an oil well on his property and that he was having the old home place renovated. The old man's nickname was Slippy, and he had rented several of Spike's storage units for his belongings while the house was being refurbished. Spike pulled out his map and showed Lisa and Lacy where he was heading.

"If I don't come back, at least you will know the direction from which I'll be walking." He also pointed out to them the location of the Henderson and Jackson farms should they need to find them.

29

H.R. HEADED OUT down the trail that led to the old kiln. He was wearing one of the Beretta pistols, and he had a .22 rifle that Tony had loaned him so he could go squirrel hunting. The goal for the day was meat for the pot. He walked until he reached the old cemetery and sat on a log within sight of it. He thought to himself about how lonely the old stones looked standing silent in the morning mist from the foggy river valley. The family resting there were long gone and forgotten by those they left behind; in fact, everyone they left behind were long gone by now. H.R. thought about his parents and brother that lay in the old church cemetery back in South Louisiana. His plans were to be buried next to them one day, but it would be unlikely that he would ever see the little church and cemetery again. As he sat and daydreamed, he reached in his pocket and pulled out a square of tobacco. This was his last square of chewing tobacco, so he would have to make it last. He unfolded the pocket knife that had been his constant companion for the past thirty years. Normally, he would cut off about a third of the square; instead he lopped off only about a fourth. He thought *four more chews, and that's it old boy*. He shoved it into his mouth and positioned it back in his jaw. He relished the sweet bitter taste. After a while, he projected a dollop of tobacco juice out past his knees and almost hit the toe of his boot. He remembered riding in the back of a pickup truck in Avoyelles Parish with his grandfather in the driver's seat. The summer was hot, and the road was gravel. He and his cousins always rode in the back of the truck.

A chuckle erupted from his throat as he thought of their looking as if they had freckles from his grandfather's spitting tobacco juice out of the window while they barreled down the dusty gravel road. Good days like that were all gone and would never return in this lifetime. About that time, a fat red squirrel came out of his nest in the cavity of the huge old oak tree that stood in front of H.R. The red squirrel slipped out on a broad limb and sat with his tail hanging over his back. H.R. took aim with the rifle, and the big squirrel fell dead on the ground. Since the weather was cold, H.R. wasn't in a hurry to skin and gut the squirrel so into the sack he went.

He walked further on until he reached the old kiln. Once again, he sat and waited until another squirrel showed himself. The rest of the morning netted six more squirrels and a rabbit. He gutted the rabbit because he had learned, from his old grandfather many years ago, that it was necessary. His final kill was an armadillo. He was told that they were good to eat, but he had never tried. The dogs would not turn their nose up at the critter once he was boiled and presented to them.

Tony was on the porch working on patching up some of the bullet holes in the house when H.R. came up holding the armadillo, by the tail, in one hand.

"Can't wait to see the look on Cheryl's face when she sees supper."

Tony turned and called. "Honey, come see what H.R. has brought you to cook."

She came out of the kitchen wiping her hands on a towel, took one look and said, "Not no, but hell no; I ain't cooking that thing!"

H.R. said, "All you have to do is clean it, cut it up and fry it."

"Did you hear what I just said?"

H.R. laughed. "I figure it will make some excellent dog chow. I hear you can eat them, but I never tried."

When he dumped all the squirrels and the rabbit out on a picnic table in the yard, Cheryl's eyes grew large. "I hope you don't expect me to cook those either; they had better be dog food too."

Tony laughed. "It's a new world, Cheryl; this is some really fine eating. H.R. and I will get them skinned. Do you know how to make dumplings?"

"Yes, I can make dumplings."

"You make the dumplings, and we'll show you how to fry up the squirrels and rabbit. You'll be surprised how good they are going to turn out."

They quickly cleaned the game, and boiled the armadillo in a pot out in the yard over a wood fire. They added a little salt from a block in the barn in case it needed a little extra seasoning for the dogs. A couple of dozen salt blocks were still stacked upstairs from when Tony's grandfather ran a small dairy at the farm.

The squirrel and rabbit dinner turned out just as they remembered, and even Cheryl agreed that they were much better than she could have ever imagined. Her biscuits and gravy, along with a bowl of beans, made a great meal. Larry's leg was very sore, but it didn't appear to be infected. They kept it slathered with antibiotic ointment and covered with a bandage. He kept himself occupied reading some novels that were on the bookshelf. He particularly enjoyed reading *Jernigan's War* and *Porter's Run*.

Holding up one of the books, Larry said, "This reminds me a lot of what we are going through now. We could sure use Dix and Porter right about now!"

Tony pointed out. "If you could shoot like them, you wouldn't be laid up here recuperating."

H.R. who had been standing guard near the front window called back. "Tony, Captain Matthews is coming back."

Cheryl chimed, "Just in time to finish the leftovers."

Tony opened the door. "You timed it just right; Cheryl has lunch ready. Did you get the helicopter figured out?"

"Yes, it's mostly like ours; I just had to figure out what was what. I was able to fire up the radio and reach Bossier. They want me to try and get that helicopter cranked and flying. I checked the fuel tanks, and they are about three quarters full. We need to locate some kerosene or jet fuel; otherwise, it's just going to be a one way trip out of here. I won't be able to do any sightseeing on my way back. We figure that they won't be shooting at one of their own helicopters. That will give us a shot at taking the Natchez airport. They also have intelligence that says that the Russian fleet is at the mouth of the Mississippi and in New Orleans. The oil in the Gulf has forced them to run up into the river. How was it out there when you left?"

Tony shook his head. "You can't imagine. I can't describe the ecological disaster that is unfolding. Our plans were to hang out in and around the Gulf for a couple of months to allow most of the killing and violence to subside. However, after the oil came, our only choice was to head upriver or sail through it and on to South America. We didn't realize that we were being invaded until we got well up the river."

"Do you have any idea where I can find some kerosene or jet fuel?"

"I can make diesel using kerosene. A person simply adds a quart of oil to eleven gallons of kerosene. I guess we could experiment with adding oil to gasoline to see if we could get a similar rate of combustion. When we have our meeting tomorrow, we can see what Spike and the other guys have to say."

H.R. scratched his sprouting beard. "I know a guy who rigged up a Coleman lamp to run on kerosene instead of Coleman fuel. You might be able to use Coleman fuel, but I doubt we're going to find enough to fill up a helicopter."

Matthews pointed to the kerosene lamp sitting on the kitchen table. "How much fuel do you have for your lantern?"

Tony shook his head. "I have less than five gallons, enough to run a helicopter about three miles."

"After the meeting tomorrow, we'll drag the helicopter out in the field, and I'll fire it up and head back to Bossier."

Reaching in his pack, Matthews pulled out eight hand held radios and a charger from the helicopter. "These are the handheld radios

Mitch took off the dead Russians. I found a charging cradle in the helicopter. Do you have an old volt meter that still works?"

"I've got one that came out of *Lucille*, the boat that we used to travel up the river."

"I need it to test the voltage of the power feed in the helicopter. I am pretty sure we can charge them using car batteries; I just need to verify the voltage before trying. We can't take a chance of burning them out. We also need to come up with a code when we communicate. My Pig Latin is a little rusty. Do you have any suggestions?"

H.R. grinned while petting his big black lab. "We can call this location, Gumbo after old Gumbo here; Tony can be Gumbo One, Cheryl Gumbo two, and so on. That might confuse them a little; they won't be able to associate people or places in the event they are able to look at court house records or telephone books."

Matthews pointed to his rank insignia on his coveralls. "I think you guys need to join the Army and be official units over here."

Tony started shaking his head, "no."

"I'm not willing to join the Army at this point. I will have no way of knowing if I am taking orders from the good guys or the bad guys. I've already come under attack from what should have been the good guys; that is why you are packing that M-4 rifle. I'm willing to help fight the Russians, American traitors and thieves, but it will be on my time and terms. I think it's wise to shut down the airports to heavy jets; that will put them on foot and on our terms. We'll also have to cut up sections of the interstate as well and drop as many bridges as possible. Any straight flat section of roadway will be useful to them. If they have an aircraft carrier and support vessels in the Mississippi, I would like to see them resting on the bottom. Our only way to defeat them is to shut down their supply lines and keep them demoralized by maiming them. I don't believe they'll be trying to send more vessels into the Gulf. That oil is only going to keep piling up."

Matthews saw that Tony had been giving a lot of thought to the problem. "When I get back to base, I'll convey your ideas."

Cheryl pointed to the fireplace. "Gentlemen, if we are going to live a medieval lifestyle, we are going to need wood. The propane isn't going to last forever, and I would rather have it to heat the bathwater than to cook and heat the house."

Tony looked around the room. "Guys, you heard Gumbo Two; let's see if we can get some wood cut and stacked."

They went to the barn, hooked up the equipment trailer to the diesel tractor and took it to the back of the pasture where there was a section of hardwood forest. They used chainsaws to cut up four large oak trees. Using wedges and malls, they split the wood and stacked it in pyramids next to the house. The effort took them all afternoon, and by the time the sun was trying to set, they were way past ready for the leftover squirrel and rabbit.

Spike's first stop was at the huge brick house that belonged to old Mr. Slippy. When he drove up, it appeared as though it had not been occupied for weeks. The porches had leaves blown up on them, limbs were down in the driveway and on the sidewalks, and no smoke was coming from the chimneys. The house was probably built back in the 1920's from the looks of the brick and shrubbery. The camellias growing around the house looked to be twenty feet tall. Two huge live oak trees sat on either side of the front yard; from their massive girth, they obviously predated the house by several hundred years. The huge limbs reached out and touched the ground around the trees. Live Oaks in the Deep South take a hundred and fifty years to reach maturity. They live a hundred and fifty years and take another hundred and fifty to die. These were near the end of their second hundred and fifty years. A huge Magnolia tree with a thick carpet of crisp brown leaves and seed pods lying underneath stood to one side of the house and towered over it. Not wanting to threaten the inhabitants, Spike tooted the Jeep horn and was greeted only by silence. He walked up to the front door and knocked; again there was no answer. He walked around the entire house; there wasn't a sound or any sign of life. The ancient farm buildings sat silent around the yard behind the house. The only sound being made was on the roof of the largest barn. A banging, loose piece of tin was being lifted and dropped by the gentle breeze.

The old brick steps to the house were worn where years of feet had favored the side nearest the entrance door. The large double French door looked in on an open walkway between the kitchen and the breakfast room. Spike cupped his hands and put his face to one of the panes. A large opening separated the walkway and had two pocket doors that were only partially extended into the space from each side. Above the doors, an artisan had carved an intricate piece of woodwork to fill and decorate the area. Mr. Slippy's lifeless body hung beneath the woodwork and in the middle of the opening. Spike recognized the old man from the unique mustache that he had sported over the years. Mr. Slippy had been dead only a couple of days. The cold weather had delayed decomposition. The door was unlocked so he went in and looked around. In a hospital bed in one of the downstairs rooms laid the body of Slippy's wife. She had obviously been an invalid and was bedridden at the time of her death. A note resting on the nightstand next to her bed simply read:

"Mamie has died and I have no reason or will to continue. We had a good life; if my children make it back or if anyone asks, please give them this note. Slippy."

Spike went through the house from top to bottom. There was ample food and supplies. He then went through the barns and outbuildings, and from the large second floor door of the barn, he could see in the back the oil well that made Slippy a rich man. It was about two hundred yards away at the rear of a pasture, and it had a pumping unit on it powered by a natural gas engine. The engine ran on the gas produced by the oil well. The pump pushed the oil into a huge oil tank where the oil could be pumped off into a tanker truck and taken to a pipeline or refinery. The tank was also designed to cut off once it was full so as not to overflow and create an oil spill. As a result, the tank was now sitting silent. The gas that normally powered the oil pumping unit would feed their generator. The house could contain at least two or maybe three families, and they had ample room in the back for the campers. An old family cemetery was located down a path leading away from the yard. The cemetery sat behind a short brick wall that had a gate in it. Plenty of room was left there for Slippy and Mamie. Taking a shovel from the backyard tool shed, Spike opened a large wide grave that would hold both of them. He moved their bodies to the grave and covered them over. He paused a minute and thanked them for their home, and asked God to receive them into his. A grave marker for them would have to wait because he wanted to get back and get the family moved.

When he reached the gate, he bent to pick up his magazine pouch and his rifle that was leaning on the brick wall next to it. A bullet narrowly missed his head. He heard the sonic boom the bullet made as it passed, and that was followed by the sound of a muzzle blast a moment later. The shot came from the direction of the house. The thick cover of woods on the other side of the cemetery wall would conceal as well as provide cover. So without waiting, he ran dodging the headstones and making a dive over the far wall. The timing for his dash to safety was perfect; a hand grenade that had been lobbed landed in the middle of the cemetery just as he cleared the wall. The explosion showered him with dirt and brick fragments, but he didn't slow down his run into the thick woods. He ran about a hundred yards and turned to his left to circle back to the road. He was really ticked that an attempt had been made to kill him. He ran another hundred yards before turning again. This track would take him back to the front of the house. After another fifty yards, he dropped to his hands and knees and crawled toward the house. He could hear behind him in the woods leaves and twigs breaking under the enemy's footsteps.

Although one part of him wanted to flee, he had an overwhelming desire to stay and kill. His entire life had been spent surviving. His adult life had been consumed with accumulating material wealth so that he could survive. He was a cool confident man whom people feared or associated with because of what he could provide. He didn't consider himself to be part of the community or any group; he was motivated by greed and lust. Looking back, he didn't like that version of himself; he found that he actually liked his brothers-in-law and their families. He found that he loved Lisa and Lacy. What started out as a cool thing to have identical twin girlfriends had grown into his family. At one time, he would have simply handed little Roger off to whoever would take him. The paradigm had shifted and along with it--himself.

He listened to the footsteps in the woods. He proceeded forward with the noise of the attackers off to his left rear. Before long, he was within sight of the house; the nearest towering Live Oak dominated his view. A number of men were busy going over the yard and house. All of them were in uniform, but the only vehicle he saw was his Jeep, and he had the key in his pocket. One man walked out drinking something from a cup. He barked an order, and another man quickly ran up and topped off the contents of his cup from a coffee pot he was holding with a hot pad. Spike clicked the safety on the M-4, put the orange dot of the Trijicon scope on the head of the officer and squeezed the trigger. The rifle bounced. He didn't wait to see the result, but centered on the body of the other man and squeezed the trigger. Both men were down. The second one was trying to crawl back into the house. Not wanting to reveal his position, Spike waited and resisted the urge to finish off the second man. He listened as he heard movement from behind and off to the left. The noise grew louder as the men made their way back toward the house. He was well hidden down in the ferns and among the wild blueberries and wild azaleas that surrounded him. He dug through the leaf litter and found the soft black earth beneath. It was cold to the touch as he dug out a handful and brought it up to where he could spit into it. Soon he had his face, hands and shirt smeared with the mud. He turned his olive drab cap around on his head so the bib would not interfere with his line of sight or side vision.

Off to his left, he saw the first of his stalkers slipping through the woods. Glancing back at the house, he saw that the man trying to crawl back in was now lying still. A head popped out around the edge of the house and disappeared as quickly as it appeared. A twig snapped as a second man ran forward and stopped a hundred or so feet in front of the first one. In due time, four men were leap frogging forward. All of them were focusing their attention in the direction of the house. He could clearly see the three who were crouching. He would have to hit them and then concentrate on the one running and hope that in all the confusion he could get him as well. He delayed shooting until they were past him and almost back to the yard. Just as the last man ran by the one in the rear, Spike fired upon the three who were waiting. The man running dived for cover as the bullet passed through the last man in line. Spike turned and fired on the front two and turned back to the one that dived for cover. He got a glimpse of him trying to crawl through the underbrush and shot him through his rear end which was exposed for a moment. He quickly turned back to the house just as the head popped out around the house again.

Knowing that all four men in forest with him had at least one hole in them, he turned his attention back to the ones he knew remained at the house. He had no way of knowing how many more there were. Not wanting to reveal his position, he waited in silence. The only noise he made was when he exchanged his partially expended magazine with a fresh one.

There were three probable scenarios that would unfold: they could fort up in the house and wait for reinforcements; they could make a run for it, or they could try to come for him. He was well hidden, but he would have liked to have had better cover because a stray bullet could easily find him. In fact, he was surprised that the woods had not come under fire. They were probably reluctant to fire because they were not certain as to the location or disposition of their comrades. All four of the men he shot were hidden where they fell. He heard one man moaning and yelling for help. He couldn't understand what he was saying, but it didn't sound Russian. In fact, it sounded more like the language he had heard being used in Iraq. He thought *could these be jihadists or Iranians working with the Russians?* He again saw the head pop out from behind the wall; this time it lingered a moment. He continued to wait. Then he saw movement on the far side of the yard near the big Live Oak on the opposite side of where he sat. He heard the rustling of the leaves under the big Magnolia that was on the other side of the house out of view. Off to the left, he saw movement as a couple more men entered the woods from that side. As long as they were moving, he knew their whereabouts. The thick leaf cover on the floor of the forest revealed their every move. If he moved from his position, he would lose the advantage of silence so he remained sitting in the bushes with his rifle at the ready. The head that kept showing itself behind the wall made a dash over and behind the far Live Oak. The movement on the far side of the yard materialized into three men who crept up using his Jeep for cover. From where Spike sat, he could see under his Jeep and see the feet and legs of the men using it for shelter. The man behind the Live Oak poked his head out and hesitated just long enough for Spike to place a bullet through it. Next, he shot through under his Jeep at the legs and feet that he could see. Two of the men were down, and the third was running and limping back toward the house. At that moment, the two in the woods started shooting in his direction. He rolled onto his belly in the leaves and resisted the urge to run. Bullets tore through the leaves and limbs above and around him. They were shooting wild hoping to hit or spook him into running; it didn't work. Spike wasn't the type to panic, so he waited. Everyone else but the two he was facing had holes in them. He heard them moving again in his direction; they wanted to flush him out. He heard the thud of a grenade; all he could do was stay low. The concussion hurt his ears, and he was showered with dirt and debris. He pulled out his pistol. The fighting would be close and fast from this point on. Through the ringing of his ears, he heard footsteps as they came closer. At about twelve feet, he saw the feet and legs of one of the men. This one was almost straight ahead, and he could hear the other off to the right. They once again sprayed the woods in front of them with fire from their AK-47 rifles. All the bullets were going over him so all he had to do was aim at the legs in front of him. He fired, and the soldier fell to the ground where Spike placed three more rounds through his torso. He heard the remaining soldier running, so he rolled to a sitting position and shot at the fleeing man. His pistol was empty, but before he could raise the rifle, the man stumbled and steadied himself on a tree. Suddenly, he collapsed to his knees and fell over on his side.

All at once, Spike felt as though someone had hit him in the lower right side with a hot poker. He heard the booming sound of the rifle shot. He spun and fired his rifle on full automatic; the man who shot him was stunned and fell back when the stream of bullets stitched holes across his torso. Spike looked around, found, reloaded his pistol and placed it back in its holster. He then replaced the magazine in his rifle and hit the charging button that loaded a fresh bullet into the chamber. If there were any men left, they now knew where he was, so he crawled past the dead and back to the cemetery wall where he stopped long enough to throw up and collect his wits.

He sat for a very long time and didn't hear or see anything. It was unlikely that he was going to bleed to death as he was still very clear headed, but the pain was significant. After sneaking around the property, he located two hand held radios that he chunked in the back of the Jeep. The last man he shot was the one he had wounded while shooting under the Jeep. A bullet hole through the side of the man's leg near the ankle answered his question about where the man had come from. Upon further investigation, he determined that the men were in all probability Chechen or maybe from Northern Turkey or possibly even Iran. All of them had a small crescent moon and star tattooed on their left hand near the thumb. He was surprised that they had the tattoos as they were generally frowned upon in the Muslim world. Maybe this was a concession for identification since they were fighting in a foreign land.

The backpacks that they were carrying indicated that they were a foot patrol, and they obviously had little tactical training; otherwise, they would have strung him up and would have taken pictures with his carcass. His men could round up all the weapons and gear as well as drag off the bodies when they returned to take possession of the house.

Off in the distance, he could feel and hear a helicopter crossing. He cranked the Jeep and backed it under the canopy of the huge Live Oaks. He grabbed the collars of the two dead men who had been lying next to it and dragged them back out of sight as well. The helicopter made a couple of passes but made no attempt to hover, land or fire upon the house. It was soon gone, so he cranked the Jeep and headed back to his camp. He sure hoped that Doc was still over at the Henderson farm. He figured that he could use stitching up. As intense as the pain was getting, he became fearful that a bullet had nicked something vital.

The trip back was tedious as he never realized how bad an old Jeep could ride. He pulled down the road to the campers and up beside his bus. At that point, he started to feel lightheaded, so he just sat down on his horn. Lisa, Lacy and little Roger came running out.

"Keep Roger in the bus he's not ready to see this again."

Lisa scooped Roger up and took him back in the bus while Lacy called to her brothers. "Quick, I need some help!"

Bob and Lucas came racing over. They stretched Spike out on a blanket so they could get a look at his wound. He grimaced as they pulled off his shirt, and Lacy cleaned him up with soap and water.

"I think you guys need to go fetch Doc; I'm probably going to need some holes plugged. Do you know how to get over to the Henderson farm?"

Lucas's wife came over and took little Roger to their camper so Lisa could come out. "You look terrible. What did they do to you?"

"If you think I look bad, you should see the other guys."

"Other guys, how many other guys?"

"I forgot to count with all the excitement, but I got 'em all."

Bob hopped in the Jeep. "I know the Henderson farm is at the end of the road. I'll go find Doc."

Heading to the Henderson farm, Bob disappeared in a fog of dust. The girls cleaned Spike up, propped him up on a pillow and covered him with a quilt to keep him warm.

He motioned for Lucas. "I found a big old house that has an oil well with a gas line in the back. There is also a pile of rifles, ammo and gear from all the men I had to kill. Lisa and Lacy have a map with the area circled. Just look for the big house on the right side of the road behind two huge oak trees. Send the guys down there to clean up the mess in the yard and in the woods and to recover the guns and gear. We can get moving right away. The patrol was on foot, and a helicopter that came over didn't stop. So I think we can be as secure there as we are here. The old house is solid brick so the walls must be two feet thick. They won't stop cannon fire, but they'll stop small arms fire."

Lisa told him, "Quit talking so much. You are weak enough without getting all exciting barking orders."

"Girls, y'all have to quit getting all worked up. If I were going to bleed to death, I wouldn't have made it back. If I die from something, it's going to be from infection or shock. You have to look at the good side of all this."

Lacy questioned. "Good side? What good side?"

"Well for one, we don't have to worry about our credit score any longer."

Lisa pinched his arm. "If you don't die, I'm going to kill you myself."

Bob rode up with Doc in the Jeep and Hazel was sitting in the back.

Doc got out and walked over to where Spike was lying. "They won't let you back in the camper?"

"They are afraid I'll die in there and stink up the place."

"Hold still while I take a look."

Hazel, get his vitals while I look at the holes."

Hazel took his blood pressure and his pulse; both were elevated.

Doc stated, "Hurting like hell I bet."

"How did you know?"

"Your pulse is way up, and so is your blood pressure. That's a good sign; it means you have plenty of blood to build up pressure."

"Doc, what do you think?"

"I don't know if you have a gut nicked or not. To find out, I've got to open you up. I can give you plenty of pain meds, but I can't put you out."

"Doc, what if we just wait as see if I get worse?"

"If you've got a hole in your intestines, you will die a horrible death in a few days from a massive infection. I'm afraid you are going to have to let me do some poking around. I recommend that we take you back to Mitch's and operate on you in his basement."

"How long will I be laid up, Doc?"

"You're a young man and obviously in great shape." He glanced at Lisa and Lacy then gave him a wink. "I would say you will be sidelined for a week before you are up and about. By the end of the month, you will be back moving naturally. It'll take about six months to start feeling normal."

Looking around at Hazel, he said, "Stay with him while we run back to Mitch's and get a truck or trailer we can move him on."

They transported him back to Mitch's house and operated on him in Mitch's basement. They moved Hannah up to the bedroom and put Spike in her old bed. Just as Doc suspected, the bullet had nicked an intestine, and Spike would have died if Doc hadn't operated.

30

CHRISTMAS WAS JUST five days away, but no one was in the Christmas spirit, except Cheryl. She found where Tony had stored the Christmas decorations and quickly had them displayed in the living room and kitchen. She talked Tony into finding and cutting the Christmas tree that now stood next to the fireplace. She had spent the previous evening shelling pecans and had made several pecan pies and a banana pudding from the dried banana chips in their remaining stash from the banana boat. So when they headed over to Mitch's for the meeting, she had goodies to give them. The weather had taken a turn for the worse during the night. Because of the storm, they would take the captured black Chevy truck over to Mitch's. They would leave Larry sitting next to the fire, and Cheryl intended to leave a slice of pie within his reach.

Tony and H.R. gathered up the little Aussie puppies. H.R. pointed out, "Better leave one of them, or she'll follow us all the way to Mitch's farm."

Tony looked over at Cheryl. "Which one do you want to keep?"

"I want the liver colored little male; I've already named him Sydney since he's an Australian Sheppard." They all laughed and climbed in the truck. The mama Aussie was concerned, but didn't follow.

Matthews was glad the weather was stormy. "With the weather this bad, they'll have all the helicopters grounded unless there is an emergency. I don't figure there will be any foot patrols out either."

When they arrived, Mitch told them, "Back the truck into the barn or park under the tractor shed on the side. I don't want to advertise that we have a house full of people in case there's a flyover."

They got out, came up on the porch and through the side door into the kitchen. Cheryl was smiling as she presented the pecan pies and banana pudding.

"Merry Christmas."

Mitch said, "I had forgotten that it was Christmas; thank you so much for reminding me. I don't think you've met everyone. I'm Mitch Henderson and all these men and ladies are Spike Hobbil's family. I'm going to let them all introduce themselves as I am still learning their names."

Four of the brothers along with Lisa and Lacy introduced themselves. Lacy motioned for her to follow. "Hannah's still in bed, so you'll have to come back here to meet her."

They walked into the room and helped prop her up on a pillow. A warm fire was burning in the fireplace, and Hannah tried to smile.

Cheryl came over and sat on the edge of the bed. "I hear that you've had a rough couple of days."

Hannah nodded. "It's been a rough month, and I'm afraid it's not going to end anytime soon."

Hannah looked over at Lisa and Lacy. "How's Spike doing?"

"Spike is being Spike. He thinks he should be able to start running around and driving all over the country."

Cheryl gave them a puzzled look. "What happened to Spike?"

Lisa nodded in the direction of the basement door. "I guess you haven't heard. Spike ran into a foot patrol and got shot yesterday. Doc had to go in and stitch everything back in place. He'll be okay; he just won't be back in fighting trim for a while."

All the men and Hazel gathered in the basement around Spike's bed.

Mitch, sitting on the bunk nearby, spoke up, "Guys, as you know we've got a war on our hands. It doesn't appear as though the Russians or the Carl Benson's of the world are going to leave us alone. I had hoped that hiding out here in the middle of nowhere was going to allow us to quietly ride out the storm."

Spike agreed. "I believe the Russians are planning on mopping up the remaining survivors. Every time I've run up on them, they started shooting first. It was a miracle I didn't get killed yesterday. They missed their first shot, or I wouldn't be here."

Doc asked, "You mean you were shot at more than once?"

"Several hundred shots and two hand grenades missed me. I don't think the ones that were after me had much experience."

Doc scratched the stubble of beard on his chin. "I figure the reason we haven't seen more refugees from the cities is because they have forced them to starve. For one thing, most of the people didn't have more than a few days' supply of food at the very most. Most of them would have been waiting for the government to bring in food and supplies which they couldn't deliver. Even if they tried to walk out of the city into the country, they would be doing so on empty stomachs. Most cars don't work, so they would be on foot. If the Russians are blocking the roads and bridges, most people will starve before they can get this far."

Tony made the point. "We were defeated before they landed their first men."

Matthews had been quietly listening. "Their strength is their ability to bring in men and supplies. We need to consider fighting a regional war. Right now they have an aircraft carrier battle group in the river below New Orleans; they can fly heavy jets into New Orleans, Baton Rouge, Natchez and Jackson. I don't know about the other airports in the country because our information is sketchy. I think the first thing we need to tackle is closing the Natchez airport. Once it's closed, they will have to travel cross country to get here. If we also take out the bridges, that will put them trying to get here on foot. They will be restricted by the range of their helicopters and will be further limited when we destroy their fuel supply."

Spike pointed out, "Their foot patrols will meet opposition. I am certain there are some outdoorsmen who are alive and mad as hell. I don't think the invaders have any idea what they are dealing with. I think they're out of their element; they don't understand the people or the country they're invading. All they know are those poor folks who live in the cities and work in cubicles and what they see on TV and in movies. They don't understand the real America."

Spike looked over at his brothers-in-law. "How's our move coming?"

Mike spoke up, "We have all the campers moved, and the generator is hooked up. Mr. Slippy had a gas line run off the well to his house so all we had to do was tap into it at the barn. We have the generator tied into an electrical panel on the barn."

Spike grinned. "How long before we can finish the move and what about all the dead men?"

Mike replied, "We can finish moving and packing up this afternoon. It'll take another day to get the sewer lines run; we've already got the water going. We are going to have a problem with wild dogs. When we arrived, a pack of twenty or so dogs was eating on the dead. We shot a few of them, and the others ran off. We picked up all the gear and dragged all the bodies off into the woods down the road. We found two more radios on the dead ones in the woods."

Mitch pointed out, "Mr. Slippy's place is only a couple of miles from here in a straight line through the forest. In fact, the old logging road that goes from the Jackson place to the old brick kiln continues on over to the back of old man Slippy's place."

Tony asked, "Now that we have a back woods road between the farms, what can we do about communication? As of right now, when we hear a shot, we don't know if it's a hunter or killers."

Matthews raised his hand. "We have eight Russian hand held radios. We need to figure out if we can charge them off of car batteries. I have a charger from the helicopter."

Mitch pointed to a workbench in the basement. "There are several old voltmeters on the bench. I'm an electrician, and charging them will not be a problem. I'll find out what voltage they need after the meeting. I also know that the Russians will hear us when we use them."

Matthews agreed. "That's why we are only going to use them for emergency communications unless we want them to hear what we're saying. We can misdirect them and ambush them when possible."

Tony spoke up. "We have already thought about that. H.R. suggested that we call our farm Gumbo after his old lab."

Mitch piped in. "This will be called the Mountain after Mitch's Mountain behind the house."

Spike added. "We'll call Slippy's place, Magnolia after the big tree near the house. If we are under attack, we can simply radio, 'Magnolia stat.' It's a shame we can't all speak Klingon or some unknown language. Do you think they could figure out Morse code?"

Hazel grinned at Doc. "Our place will be called the Clinic."

Mitch grinned. "I have an idea. When I was first learning to be an electrician, I was interested in some old radios and equipment my dad had. He used to work on televisions and electronics back in the day. He showed me how to read the value of resisters on the old circuit boards using a little jingle. Each color represented a number, and they had a little jingle to remember the colors and numbers. It read: Bad Boys Rob Our Young Girls But Violet Gives Willingly. The colors were Black, Brown, Red, Orange, Yellow, Green, Blue, Violet, Gray and White with each color having the numeric values of 0 thru 9. If we communicate, we can do it in pairs of colors. The letter A would be number 01 or Black Brown. The letter B would be 02 or Black Red. It would slow our communicating to begin with, but it would take them some time to figure it out and probably not at all since it would be just us using it."

Spike nodded his head. "Great idea; if we see that they are starting to hit the houses with attack helicopters or aircraft, we simply radio the phrase, SCATTER. That will be our warning to hit the woods and hide. You also need to realize that it is very dangerous to try and move at night. I know it seems like you are safer in the night, but they will have advanced night vision equipment."

Matthews pointed up. "I need to see if I can get that helicopter up and headed to Bossier. This weather will help me sneak out undetected. I'll be back in touch by radio, or we'll send someone in with radio and supplies. The code word will be TOOTSIE; the response word will be SAINTS."

"Mitch, will you write down your code so we can communicate with you until we can get you some encrypted radios?"

"Sure, it will only take a moment."

"I want you guys to consider taking down the major bridges. You can make thermite grenades that will cut through the girders and destroy them. All you need to do is take one part finely ground iron oxide, which is rust, and one part finely ground aluminum. Mix the two and put them in a pipe or metal conduit and wire it to the girder. Leave a hole in the cap so you can light it with a torch or with a magnesium ribbon as a fuse. If you don't hear back from me, you will know I didn't make it. You will have to destroy the airport and bridges and fight for your homes on your own."

Leaving Spike in bed, they went out to the barn where Mitch cranked a diesel tractor and attached a chain to the helicopter skids. He carefully pulled it back out into the field where it had originally landed. Matthews cranked the power unit that quickly had the turbine engines spinning to life. Mitch tested the voltage and removed the charging cradle for the handheld radios while Captain Matthews went over a checklist and made sure all the systems were working and the temperatures were in the green. Mitch handed him the radio code folded for his pocket. They all stood back and watched as Matthews buckled himself into the pilot's seat. He brought the blades up to speed and changed the pitch so that the blades started to bite the air. Slowly, the craft left the ground and drifted towards the woods. When the chopper was several hundred feet above the forest canopy, it disappeared heading north and west.

Mitch, with the help of Tony, made four charging cradles from blocks of wood and insulated screws. When they finished, they had charging cradles that connected to the twelve volt auto batteries in their vehicles. Mitch killed the propane generator in order to save fuel for the next time it was needed or for an emergency.

The ladies made lunch from the MRE's that Spike supplied from his storage container. The next topic was food.

Mitch started the discussion. "We have a lot of people eating. If we don't come up with a way to grow crops, we are going to be starving in less than six months. You know, it takes up to ninety days for crops to mature; so, we have to have seeds in the ground by March."

Tony agreed. "We need to have one or two folks hunting and fishing every day. We also need to get some winter crops in the ground, so we had better hit the old farm and ranch stores and get some sacks of seeds if there are any left."

Mitch pointed to some barrels in the corner of the basement. "I have ten barrels of red wheat and ten barrels of popcorn; I suggest that we take a barrel of wheat and plant all three farms in wheat. It will grow now, and we will have wheat to harvest by early summer. We can plant corn in the spring, and I have some heirloom vegetable seeds that we can plant for everything else. We'll have to save seeds from them to plant from year to year. If we each plant big gardens, we should have plenty to eat about the time our food storage starts to dwindle. We can also check any silos or railway cars to see what's in them. The other things we are going to need are animals. Look for pigs, horses, cattle, goats, and sheep; I'm afraid most of them have been killed and eaten, but you never know. I've got chickens, and as soon as they start setting, I can raise and share them as well. Until we have three or four big flocks, we can only eat eggs; once we have some large flocks, we can start eating the birds."

Tony nodded at Hazel. "Hazel's place is going to be the best place to hunt. It has or had a lot of deer and wild hogs; if we try to plant over there it will only feed the game."

Cheryl had been listening and spoke up. "When we are looking around empty houses and stores, you need to look for things that we'll need in the future like: brooms, mops, lye, vinegar, sewing needles, thread, playing cards, books and other everyday items. If you see some antique stores, look for an old foot operated sewing machine, hand grinders, butter churns and things like that. We are going to be living a medieval lifestyle quickly. Now is the time to be gathering pecans, so get in the habit of picking them up. Also see if you can spot some bee hives and sugar cane. Life will be much more pleasant if we have sweets to eat."

H.R., who had been mostly silent, said, "You can move the bee hives while it's cold, and they won't be fighting. I also know an old man who's just about out of chewing tobacco; if you run across any, I would appreciate your saving it for me."

Mitch grinned at him. "H.R., I'll swap you some pipe tobacco for meat; I hear you are a hunter."

"I believe I can figure out a way to chew pipe tobacco. You've got yourself a deal."

Mitch walked over to a shelf where his mother had stored trade goods and pulled off a large can of pipe tobacco. This is fourteen ounces of tobacco; I want the empty can back and a sack of squirrels."

"Deal."

Mitch also stated, "If any of you run across a priest, preacher or a Mormon Bishop, Hannah and I are looking to get married."

Cheryl piped up. "I think you may be in luck; I happen to know where there's a captain of a boat. I don't see why he couldn't perform the service."

Tony grinned. "Is there a family bible around here where we can record the wedding?"

Mitch headed up the stairs to a little reading room alcove off of the living room where he retrieved his mother's family bible that she kept at the farm. She also had a copy of the *Episcopal* book and *The Book of Common Prayers* that he retrieved as well. *The Book of Common*

Prayers had the traditional marriage vows that were used in most Christian marriage ceremonies.

"If you guys would give me a minute, I need to see Hannah and see if she is still willing."

Lacy and Lisa had been taking turns sitting with Hannah. She was awake and propped up on a pillow when Mitch came in.

"Ladies, could you give me a minute with Hannah?"

Lisa smiled and nodded at Lacy to follow her. "Sure, I'll be in the kitchen; I'm ready for some coffee."

Hannah gave him a puzzled look. "What's up, Hon?"

"I haven't ever asked anyone to marry me; I was wondering if you wanted to get married this afternoon?"

"Of course I do. Where did you find a preacher?"

"I don't have a preacher, but I have the next best thing--a sea captain. Tony is the captain of a boat and has offered to perform the ceremony. He's as official as we are ever going to get. We'll record it in our family bible just like they've done it for hundreds of years before there were courthouses."

Hannah fussed. "I look a mess; can you call Lacy and Lisa to help me fix up a little?"

"We can have it with me sitting on the bed next to you."

Mitch went to the kitchen and explained to Lisa and Lacy what he wanted them to do. They happily told him that they would come and get him when they were ready.

In a short time everyone, except Spike who Doc insisted stay in the basement, were gathered around the bed where Tony performed the ceremony. Mitch placed his grandmother's wedding band on Hannah, and they were pronounced man and wife. Tony recorded the event in the family bible and signed as a witness.

Spike called up to Tony. "Tony, I have a question?"

Tony went downstairs to the basement. "What's up, Spike?"

"I've got a question, how do you feel about a man having more than one wife?"

"I've never given it much thought; are you thinking what I think you're thinking?"

"What started out as a joke between twin sisters has gotten serious. I had a date with Lacy several years ago, and we went out a few times, but it wasn't anything serious. As a joke, they substituted Lisa without my knowledge to see if I would notice the difference. I pretended not to because it was fun, if you know what I mean."

"I take it the fun got out of hand."

"The next thing I know, they are arguing, and when they found out I could tell the difference, the 'you know what' really hit the fan. Then they got all worked up and asked me to make a choice between them. When I refused, it hit the fan again. To make a long story short, they both moved in, and it has somehow worked out. I can't make a choice, and I can't say I want to. Now that we have little Roger, I think we need to see about making it all official."

"This almost getting killed has got you to thinking, I take it? I jumped the broom on my boat. I don't want to die alone, and I've known Cheryl for years. She is one of the nicest ladies I've ever known. I'll perform the ceremony if you want me to."

"Great, will you send my girls down? I figure I need to talk to them first."

Lacy and Lisa came down, and Lacy asked, "What's up, Baby?"

"I've a got a question for you girls. I think you know that I love y'all more than anything. That's why I couldn't choose one over the other, and I'm not going to now. I would like to know if y'all would like to get married this afternoon."

Lisa grinned. "Are you asking both of us?"

"That's what I'm asking."

They both got on either side of the bed and gave him a big hug.

Tony performed the ceremony and added their names to the family bible along with his and Cheryl's. The girls' four brothers agreed that it was about time Spike settled down.

H.R. and Hazel joined the celebration. H.R. looked over at Hazel and she winked. "H.R., I don't want you getting all worked up over all this and proposing to me."

H.R. laughed. "Having a supply of tobacco is all the happiness I can stand in one day."

Everyone laughed and broke up the meeting. Doc double checked Hannah's and Spike's dressings, and all appeared well. He stressed that he didn't want them doing anything more than walking for a week. Doc and Hazel packed up and headed to Hazel's place. Spike's brothers-in-law headed back to finish moving the families; Lisa and Lacy stayed to help Mitch, Hannah and Spike. Little Roger would stay with Misty until Spike and the girls could make it home.

Spike stayed put for only two days before he insisted on getting up and out and back to Slippy's. Hannah was able to get around as well, so Lisa and Lacy left and joined him at the new house. Spike, the twins and little Roger occupied one wing of the big house. Since this wing had a couple of separate bedrooms and a bath, they could have their own private space.

Spike felt that the Russians would hold down their offensive until after Christmas; they were, after all, a mostly Christian people. The Islamic tattoos on the foot patrol were another matter. Because they had a quiet Christmas, they spent the day singing carols and sticking close to the fireplace. Little Roger occupied his time by playing with the little Aussie puppies he named Jack and Jill.

31

THE TWO RUSSIAN attack helicopters left the Natchez airport well before dawn with a full load of fuel and ordinance. They had the last known coordinates of the missing patrol, and they knew where the scouting party was hit at the fire tower about thirty miles from town. From five thousand feet and using their infrared cameras, they quickly spotted a half a dozen houses with heat coming from their chimneys. They concentrated their fire on the three that were nearest the river and to the location of the missing patrol. In ten minutes, all three houses were reduced to burning rubble. They then turned their attention to the other houses in the region that were showing signs of life.

When the helicopters' cannon fire hit the house, Mitch hit the microphone key and shouted SCATTER. That was the last thing he remembered before waking up in the basement.

Tony crafted a harness from rope and called up, "Pull him up slow."

Mitch could only see from one eye and was freezing cold. H.R. touched the trigger on the four wheeler winch switch and slowly pulled Mitch up and out of the ruins. Tony held on to the harness and kept it steady as he ascended from the hole with Mitch. When they had him up on level ground, Cheryl came with a blanket.

"Let's get him covered up before he goes into shock."

Mitch called out, "Hannah, where's Hannah?"

Tony covered him up. "We found Hannah first. We have her up on the mountain; she's bruised up, but she's okay. That big brick chimney in your bedroom is the only thing that saved you guys."

"What about everyone else?"

"All our houses are gone. Spike's brothers-in-laws and their families who lived out back in their campers are dead. Spike, Lisa, Lacy, and little Roger are okay. Lucas, his wife Misty and their little girl survived as well. The two foot thick brick walls shielded them as they ran out of the front door and took shelter behind some big oaks. We haven't heard from Hazel and Doc. Once we get you squared away, I'm heading over there to check."

"How's Larry?"

"Larry's shot leg may be broken as well. We have it stabilized and splinted and have him in the old shed down by the kiln."

At that moment, Bacon and Pinky came crawling out from under the debris; Pinky soon had Rover located and chased him off in the direction of the mountain. Mitch rolled to a sitting position and touched his blind eye.

"Is it just swollen shut, or is it knocked out?"

Cheryl got down on her knees and squinted in the early morning light. "It's swollen shut. You have a gash across your eyebrow, and we're going to need to stitch it up as soon as we find a first aid kit."

He tried to stand, but his legs gave way. "I guess I was conked on the head pretty good."

H.R. reminded him. "Don't forget you gave all your spare blood to Hannah a couple of days ago."

"Give me a second." He got on his hands and knees and crawled over to the four wheeler and pulled up to a standing position while leaning on it for support.

"They have finally made me mad! As soon as we can come up with some shelter; I'm going to start killing the sons of bitches. I tried my damnedest to just live back here on my farm and just survive. I realize now that it's not going to work."

H.R. pointed out, "They aren't going to stop. We can either start killing them as hard and fast as we can, or we can hide back here like rabbits and wait for them to slaughter us."

Mitch sat back down on the floor boards of the four wheeler. "Tony, y'all go check on Doc and Hazel. Do y'all have a vehicle?"

"Yes, that old black Chevy is still running. Are you okay?"

"Where's Hannah on the mountain?"

"She's up there at the campsite with the chiminea. We have a fire going, and she's in a sleeping bag."

"If y'all don't need the four wheeler, I'll take it up the mountain and find her."

Tony took Cheryl aside. "H.R. and I are going over to Hazel's; stay with Mitch and Hannah. I'll send H.R. to get you if I need you."

Mitch straddled the seat of the four wheeler and Cheryl sat behind him.

Tony gave Cheryl a tight hug and whispered in her ear. "He's taken one hell of a hit on his head. Get him settled, and see if you can locate our first aid kit. Keep your gun handy. Don't hesitate for an instant to kill a stranger."

"Don't worry, honey. If I see Spike or the girls, I'll tell them where you've gone."

"If you see him, tell him we'll be over to help after we check on Doc, Hazel and her girls."

Mitch gave the four wheeler some gas and in no time was up on the mountain and over to the old campsite where Hannah sat bundled in a sleeping bag next to the chiminea. Pinky had already found her; Bacon was following the four wheeler. Hannah burst into tears. Mitch climbed off the four wheeler and could only embrace her. As tears flowed down their faces, Bacon leaned up against them, and Cheryl burst into tears as well.

"Now, you've got me doing it." They both looked around and reached for her.

Hannah looked at Mitch. "You're hurt."

Cheryl said, "We need our first aid kit; it has a suture kit in it. Once Tony gets back, we can look for it."

Hannah asked, "Why did they attack us before daylight?"

Mitch backed up to the chiminea for warmth. "They are responding to attacks on their people. They are trying to finish off the stragglers; that's why they start shooting as soon as they see someone. They probably used their thermal imaging in their helicopters to spot houses that were being heated. I know we had a fire in the kitchen stove and had a fire in the bedroom fireplace. Did you and Tony have a fire or gas heaters on?"

"Yes, we kept a fire in the kitchen stove to heat the house."

"I know Spike and his people had a natural gas powered generator and gas heat in the house, and being Christmas, they probably had a fire in the fireplace. All three houses would have been lit up like light bulbs in their thermal imaging equipment."

Spike rode up in his Jeep. He had driven up the woods road and up onto Mitch's Mountain. Cheryl ran up to the trail and waved him down.

"They're down here at the old camp."

Spike slid to a stop and hopped out. "I just got off the radio with Captain Matthews. He'll be landing in the field in front of the house in about two hours. He is bringing us supplies and weapons. I told him what happened. He said to keep our heads down and hold tight. Where's Tony?"

"Tony has gone to check on Doc, Hazel and her girls."

Tony and H.R. pulled up to the smoking remains of Hazel's house. Doc was sitting on one of his medical supply cases that he had managed to save. He shook his head.

"They're all dead. I tried to save Hazel, but there was too much damage. The only reason I'm alive is because I was in the outhouse when they hit. All my medical supplies were in the front room, and I was able to drag most of it out through the front window. Hazel and the girls were in the back of the house and upstairs. I found Hazel and pulled her out front here, but she was just shot up too bad." He pointed to her grave.

Tony said, "We have more graves to dig. Most of Spike's people were killed. It was horrible."

H.R. clenched his fist. "Boys, I don't know about y'all, but I am ready to go get 'em. I'm fed up with all this hiding and trying to stay out of the way."

Tony agreed. "Doc we need to set you up somewhere out of the way. I'm with H.R., and it's time to unleash the 'dogs of war.' We are going to need you around to patch us up if we survive."

Doc nodded. "I agree boys, but I sure wish I could help with the killing."

Tony grinned. "Don't worry, Doc; if you can keep us fighting, it's the same as you pulling the trigger. We are going to have to figure a way to mass kill them."

Doc made a suggestion. "If we cut off their food and fuel like they did us, they'll start starving like we did."

"Doc, let's load your extra gear and get you back to Mitch's. He needs stitching up, and my boy Larry needs his leg looked at. It may be broken, but I'm not certain. We splinted it, and we have him off of it."

When they had Doc and his gear back at the campsite on Mitch's Mountain, Doc shaved off Mitch's eyebrow and carefully stitched the wound closed. He liberally filled the wound with antibiotic cream.

"I need you guys to check every empty house, store, boat and camper you can find and bring me every tube of antibiotic ointment or any other medicine you find. Carry a sack with you; also bring honey and white sugar. I can pack wounds with them as well. Most of the vets and feed and seed stores will be cleaned out, but look for antibiotics and supplies like syringes anyway. Pet stores will also have antibiotics, especially in the tropical fish department. Those small razorblade knives in the hobby and craft section of stores are good too; I can use them as scalpels. Also bring those manicure sets with the little scissors, eyebrow tweezers, etc. Check all the doctor and dental offices just in case they have some pain killer. If you don't know what it is, just bring it back. Once I run out of injectable pain medicine, it won't be easy for me to operate."

Mitch pointed in the direction of the old farm house. "If we can get into the basement of my house, there is a lot of what Doc is looking for. I can go in through the tunnel and retrieve it if the rest of the house doesn't collapse in on me."

Doc ordered. "Mitch, you aren't doing anything for several more days. You are still about half a quart low on your blood count, and you have taken one hell of a hit on your head. You have a concussion; tell us where the tunnel entrance is located, and we'll get it cleaned out and moved up here."

Spike hadn't said much. Like Mitch and the others, he was thinking. "Guys, the problem that I see is simple; we've got to take the battle to them. Captain Matthews will be arriving any time now. Once we see what he has brought us, we need to get it hidden out here in these woods and get some shelters built in the ground where we are out of the elements, but also out of sight of the thermal imaging."

Tony pointed at Mitch's Mountain behind them. "This is a very secluded spot. There are enough of the three houses and barns left to build an underground structure. If we cut into the mountain and build a house with a shed roof sloping toward the front, we can cover it with tin from the barn and rebury it; it would be thermally hidden, and the earth would moderate the temperature. Our solar system survived, and so did my camper in the garage. We can take it all down by the creek and use its pump to push water up here. We can build some outhouses and even set up the wood stoves outside to cook on. We just need to make sure they are cold before dark."

Mitch motioned again toward his house. "There are some tents in the basement as well. I suggest you start getting it cleaned out right away, and if you find my rifle and ammo, I would appreciate your getting them to me. All I have is the pistol that I am wearing. Look inside the old kiln; Hannah and I have some supplies buried under the leaves and debris. In fact, it would make a good shelter for a few people. I would clean it out real good; I wouldn't be surprised to find some rattlers hibernating in it. We also have several caches out in the cutover with extra food, guns and ammo."

Spike took his cap off and slapped some of the dirt off his pants. "Sounds like a plan; I still have a bunch of stuff in my containers. I think I can make up for any lost weapons and ammo; there should also be a lot of food left. As soon as we get the family put in the ground, I'll start moving it over here and getting it covered up. The containers are broken up, but there's a lot of undamaged stuff inside."

Tony pointed at the Jeep and the black Chevy parked up on the mountain. "How's our fuel look? Our truck is almost empty."

Spike pointed across the woods. "We have two tankers of gasoline, a tanker of diesel and a propane truck with a full tank. They are hidden about a mile down that creek off the road where we camped for a few days. They are out of sight and are still there unless someone has walked up on them. Even then, unless they have a tractor trailer truck that will run, they can't very well steal them. The tractor trailer truck we were using is badly shot up. It was still parked out back of the house where we had unloaded the shipping containers."

At that moment, they heard the sound of a helicopter approaching. H.R., Tony and Spike headed up on the mountain to see.

Cheryl started to go, but Doc cautioned. "Wait, let's be patient; it could be the Russians coming back. I need to go take a look at Larry's leg."

"Mitch, can I use your four wheeler?"

"Sure thing, Doc."

When Doc and Cheryl reached the crest of the mountain, they looked back in time to see the Russian helicopter coming in low over the trees, slow to a hover and land in front of the Mitch's old farmhouse.

32

CAPTAIN MATTHEWS KEPT the helicopter just above the trees as he approached from the west.

He told his co-pilot, "There's a fire tower off to the south. We are looking for a farmhouse on the edge of a big pasture straight ahead." Although he knew an attack had taken place, he was still shocked to see the grand old farmhouse lying in ruins and the big barn a pile of sticks. He thought *Mitch and Hannah couldn't have survived.* He brought the helicopter to the spot where he had taken off days earlier. He was relieved to see Spike, Tony and H.R. appear from the woods behind the remains of the barn. He and the co-pilot killed the engines of the captured Russian helicopter, opened the side doors and starting setting out crates of gear.

"Guys, you need to get this stuff out of sight as soon as you can."

H.R. turned. "I'll get the truck down here." He disappeared in a hustle back up the mountain.

Matthews looked at them. "Did Mitch and Hannah survive?"

Spike nodded. "They are bummed up badly, but they're alive; most of my people are dead."

"Damn, I hate to hear it. Guys like it or not, you are in the U.S. Army. If you are a Christian male and alive, you are in the Army. You will not be paid, and supplies are limited or do not exist. I am dropping off forty shoulder fired surface to air missiles. You also have five hundred thermite grenades to destroy machinery and infrastructure. Here are twenty Claymore mines and two cases of

C4 with timers and fuses. Do any of you have any idea of what this can do and how to use it?"

Spike spoke up. "I know how to use everything you are dropping off. The contractor I worked for in Iraq dealt with all of this."

Matthews glanced down at Spike's shirt that had a damp bloody spot. "Are you okay?"

"It's just a scratch. Doc patched me up, but my wound is still trying to ooze a little."

"Don't die on me. I'm putting you in charge; you are now a Captain in the Army. You will need to keep track of everyone else in your command, record their rank and give it to me when we talk again. I'm now a Major because all the other officers are dead, deserted or traitors. I don't mind the deserters since they went home to take care of their families. The traitors were primarily from the new officer corp. They believed in the communist dream before this event even happened. They also partnered with the militant Islamic groups here in the US. All those terrorist training camps that we were told didn't exist did and were funded by the Russians and the Iranians. Look for the little crescent moon and star tattoo on their hands."

Spike pointed to his hand. "They have the tattoo on their hand right here, or at least that was where it was on the ones I ran into."

Matthews opened one of the cases. "Here is a case with radios and two solar chargers. These radios are encrypted to one another and to us back at headquarters. I have included a dozen hand held units and two more powerful base units. I suggest you lock one of the base units away and hide it someplace in case one gets knocked out. If you lose one, call in the number so we can lock it out; otherwise, the bad guys can hear what you are saying. You should only encounter Russians and Islamists in this region. The Peoples Liberation Army from China is on the West Coast along with the North Koreans. North and South Korea are now reunified and is a province of China. I don't know about Japan, but I expect they are quickly becoming a Chinese province as well. Cuba has troops coming into South

Florida. The Russian fleet is stuck in New Orleans, and nothing is moving in or out of the Gulf."

Tony asked, "Were we able to hit them at all?"

"I'm sad to say; they pulled off a tremendous coup. This problem goes really deep, probably even to the office of the President. Some officers at the highest levels in the country refused to order strikes. In fact, right now, we are defying orders to stand down. We have taken our commanding general and the officers she, or rather he, appointed or promoted into custody. Our present leader was recently appointed after our former commander and his staff was sacked. They were trying to order American troops to fire on our own citizens. Only true American men can defeat our enemies and take back our country."

Tony was looking at the radios. "We can sure use these. How are we going to know if we are facing loyal American troops?"

"In this region you won't have much trouble. If they are with the Russians, kill 'em. We will be in close communication and hopefully know where each other are operating."

While inspecting his wound, Spike asked, "Any first aid kits in this gear?"

"Yes, I brought you everything but rifles, pistols and ammo. I knew that you were well armed when I left so I concentrated on things I knew you didn't have and things that you would need."

H.R. drove up in the black Chevy truck and backed it up to the first stack of supplies. "I sure wish there was a case of chewing tobacco in here."

The co-pilot, who had remained silent, spoke up. "I think I can help with that." He disappeared and came back with a carton of Beechnut chewing tobacco.

Matthews laughed. "I forgot to introduce my co-pilot, this is Buck Landrum. Where did you come up with a carton of Beechnut?"

"I found a case of it at the commissary before it was bombed; I've been using it to trade for stuff." Looking at H.R., he winked. "That's going to cost you two dead or maimed Russians."

"You got a deal, Buck."

Matthews looked over at the destroyed house. "I'm giving you guys a week to get yourselves put back together; then I want the Natchez airport shut down and the bridges closed. Remember to break up the sections of highway and interstate that a heavy jet can land on. We have taken out the Jackson airport, so that leaves Natchez, Baton Rouge and New Orleans."

Spike asked, "What about Gulfport, Meridian, Columbus and Pensacola?"

"Pensacola is under our control for now; the others including Keesler Air Force Base in Biloxi are destroyed. If we can shut down the Russians' food and fuel supply, they are going to starve to death just like everyone else. They have a significant anti-aircraft defense around those three airports, and the aircraft carrier at New Orleans is the most formidable."

Tony grinned. "I've been thinking about how we can sink it."

"Don't try to sink it just yet. We would like to trap it there and take it. We believe that they have nuclear warheads on board and that it has a nuclear reactor that can power a small city. Our nuclear capability is diminished or in the hands of the enemy now. Until we can re-engineer our bombs to get around the launch codes, we may need to capture theirs."

"Will our people know how to make them useable?"

"We won't know until we get our hands on them."

Spike spoke up. "I have a question. What about all the nuclear powered submarines all over the world? Surely they can't all be compromised or destroyed."

"We have lost communication with most of them. The new Admiral in charge of the submarine fleet had almost a year to replace the officers and noncoms in her hierarchy so we don't know what happened. Three submarines made contact, but without codes they can't launch. The last word we had was that these subs are attempting to rendezvous with our experts to work on a solution. They have to evade the Russian and our own submarines."

H.R. grimaced. "It sounds hopeless."

Matthews replied, "It's hopeless only if we give up. Those bastards killed my girlfriend, most of my family and almost everyone I know. I don't have but one thing on my bucket list right now."

They all nodded in agreement.

H.R. asked, "What about taking the wounded out? Do you have any hospitals?"

"If someone is critical and we're heading back to base, we can take them; otherwise, they are better off staying put. Our positions are open to being overrun or hit from the air at any moment. Once you get the equipment secure, radio back anything else you may need. I want to get this helicopter back before we get spotted. Good hunting, guys." With that he and Buck cranked the helicopter, became airborne and disappeared over the trees heading west.

Spike, H.R. and Tony took four trips to move all the gear back to the camp. After another two days, they had all the dead buried and the most of the contents of Mitch's basement pulled out. They made a shelter using wood and tin from the farmhouse and barn. Their evenings were spent in darkness with everyone sleeping in sleeping bags or under blankets. A layer of earth and leaves was placed over the tin roof to mask any thermal signature that could be seen from above. They were all rearmed from Spike's arsenal.

Spike instructed them on how to use the shoulder fired missiles and the thermite grenades. "Other than being heavy, the shoulder fired missile is simple to use. You simply unfold it, and it powers up. Get the target in sight, and pull the trigger until the red light appears. If it sees the target, the light will turn green. At that point, complete the trigger pull, and it will take over from there. Just make sure it's one of theirs and not one of ours; it won't know the difference. Then just discard the empty launch tube and hide. Everyone for miles will see the smoke trail pointing back to you and will shoot in your direction if they can. The thermite grenades are also easy to use. All you have to do is pull the pin and set the grenade on or in whatever you want to melt or burn up. The thermite will burn at about twenty-five hundred degrees until it is consumed. Setting one on the hood of a vehicle will destroy it. The thermite will burn through the hood, onto the motor and down into it until all the thermite is consumed. Tossed down a cannon barrel, it would melt though the bottom of it. Trying to douse it with water will only create steam; the thermite will burn on, no matter what."

Doc was thrilled with the medical supplies; he now had everything to treat injury and sickness in the field. By the end of the week, everyone was back on their feet with the exception of Larry who was on crutches. All the gear that was salvageable was under cover and secure. They estimated that there was enough food for one year if they didn't waste any. The old kiln was packed with supplies and had room enough for two people to safely sleep inside.

33

WITH EVERYONE SITTING on logs, they gathered around the chiminea as Spike stood. "As you know, all of us men are in the Army now. Major Matthews put me in charge; we're secure here until they hike in or spot us from the air. Under this canopy of pine trees, we are invisible to them unless they come over with thermal imaging at night. Make sure the chiminea and the wood stove are completely burned out and cold before dark. If they hit us here, we'll be catching minnows in the creek to stay alive."

Lisa raised her hand. "Is it true that Major Matthews said that women can volunteer?"

"Yes, you can volunteer, but remember I am in command. You are already trained to shoot and are armed to the teeth. So unless it gets desperate, the ladies will be guarding our gear and setting up equipment and food caches where we can retreat. I have to establish a command structure and tell them the names and ranks. Are there any ladies not volunteering?" No hands went up. "Ok, here goes and it's not up for argument. I am naming Cheryl a Sergeant over the ladies and Doc a Lieutenant over her. Hannah and the two little ones are to be protected at all cost. If I or any of the men give you the order to bug out, there's to be no argument. Tony, you and Mitch will be Lieutenants; H.R. a Sergeant under Tony, and Lucas a Sergeant under Mitch. Larry will be a Sergeant under Doc until he gets back on both feet; any questions?"

Little Roger stepped forward. "What about me? I can fight."

"Your job is to help guard Hannah and Mandy; you make sure that they are always safe and taken care of. Do you think you can do that?"

"Yes, sir." Everyone smiled.

"Now get over there and stay close to Mandy and keep an eye out for danger." Roger ran over to Mandy with his two puppies on his heels.

"The first thing we've got to do is establish some safe bug out locations. I also want you ladies to establish a bug out location that only you know about. You can't tell any of us where it's located. If one of us gets captured, they will use whatever is at their disposal, including drugs to make us talk. You need to be able to melt into the forest and get to a spot that has food, water, first aid, and shelter. Everyone but Tony, H.R., Mitch and Lucas can get back to what you were doing."

The three men set up a folding table just under the shed's roof, but where the sun light could hit it, and unfolded a map of the region. On it Spike circled the Natchez airport and the Concordia Parish airport near Vidalia, La. He also circled all the bridges on the roads and highways that would need to be dropped.

Tony asked, "I don't think we will have any trouble dropping the small bridges with the thermite grenades and C4, but we're going to have a hard time knocking out the bridges over the Mississippi. What kind of capability does Matthews have?"

Spike pointed to the stack of crates on top of the mountain. "We have enough C4 to take out one of the piers, but I would rather save the C4 to blow the bottom out of some ships or boats. If we can sneak onto the bridges, we can wire the thermite around the girders and weaken them. The weight of the bridge will collapse it; however, I think we need to concentrate on shutting down the airport. What are your ideas?"

Mitch spoke first. "I think we need to shoot those attack helicopters down as soon as possible and drop the bridges nearest to the airport. If we can catch one of those big jets on the runway, that would effectively close it until they can drag it off."

Spike remembered the big yellow bull dozer with the ripper behind it. "Across from my storage business was a construction company with a huge bull dozer with a ripper blade. If we could get that thing out on the runway, it could rip the runway to shreds, or if worse comes to worse, we could get the dozer out in the intersection of the two runways and set off several thermite grenades on it and some C4 under it. To remove the dozer and repair the runways would take them a few days."

H.R. pointed out, "I think we need to see how close we can get to the airport before we decide on our game plan. We might not be able to get within a mile of it. If that's the case, we can scatter out with each of us toting one of those shoulder fired missiles and wait for those helicopters or jets to come by. We'll need to travel by the most remote roads we can find and travel on foot from about two miles out."

They each had a hand held radio to communicate with each other and home. Spike pulled out a base unit and contacted Major Matthews. "Here are the plans, chief. We are going to make our way through the back roads to Natchez, find a place to camp near the airport and hike over to it from there. We're going to carry five of the shoulder fired weapons, and our plans are to locate the anti-aircraft defenses and shoot down some of the helicopters."

"The sooner you can shut down the runways; the sooner they start starving to death. Good luck."

"Thanks, we are going to need it."

They loaded enough rations to stay a week in the field. If they became separated, they were to make their way back to the trucks, and if the trucks were missing or compromised, they were to make their way back to the Mountain.

Spike and Mitch headed out in Mitch's Jeep, and Tony, H.R. and Lucas followed in the black Chevy. Each vehicle contained guns, thermite grenades, shoulder fired weapons and gear for each man. They also had extra fuel cans in order to guarantee a return trip. The Jeep waded through the creek and struggled a bit as it climbed up the bank on the far side.

Mitch commented. "Kind of feels like we're going on a deer hunt."

"We are going on a hunt alright; I just hope we can make our kills without getting killed."

When they arrived at the highway, they waited for Tony to catch up.

They did a radio check, and Mitch keyed the microphone. "Let's keep the radio chatter to a minimum. We don't know if the Russians can detect the signals. They aren't supposed to be able to listen to what we are saying, but we don't need to take any chances. Tony, give us about a two minute head start. We will rendezvous at Emerald Mound off the Natchez trace; you know the planned route."

The route took them across the Homochitto River. They turned on the old, winding, curvy river road that took them through the little town of Meadville. Spike glanced at the residue of the Blue Flamingo as he passed. He was certain that the remains of Pete and his men were still lying at the back door where he had killed them. They turned and took the back roads in the direction of Fayette, MS. Another country road led them through the small Civil War era community of Church Hill. The gravel road they were on plunged between high ridges on either side. This old trace road had been worn down into the earth by the hooves of countless horses and wagon wheels and had the appearance of a wide flat bottomed ditch. Slaves once walked down this very road and in all probability had cut the original road out of the wilderness. They crossed an old bridge that rattled and shook as they drove across. The boards were run lengthwise so that the weight of the vehicles would be spread over the cross members. Some boards were missing, and they were afraid that their wheels would drop through the bridge. Unfortunately, no county road crews would be around to repair the bridge again. Twice they had to stop and pull fallen limbs from the gravel road that led from the bridge before they could proceed.

Soon, they reached an intersection that took them away from the airport but would lead them over to their rendezvous point--Emerald Mound. Mitch paused when he spotted an old cabin up on a ridge in a pecan orchard. The cabin was an ancient structure with a front porch that was starting to sag. An old fireplace still leaned against one side. Tony caught up to them in the black Chevy and they decided that the cabin was a good place to conceal the vehicles. Emerald Mound was a little further down the road, but this place was too good to pass up. They quickly cut through the chain on the gate and drove up behind the old house. A quick look verified that it was indeed uninhabited. A farmer was using it to store hay. This would make an excellent place to camp. The farmer was unlikely to still be alive, and the cabin would be a good place to camp out of the wind. They left the shack with the vehicles out of sight behind it. As they proceeded on foot toward the airport, they checked out houses on the way. Most of the homes were empty, but a few of them contained the unburied dead. Other homes had a few fresh graves around them.

When they approached one house, an old man with a heavy German accent met them with a shotgun at his front gate. "Keep moving gents if you want to live."

H.R. recognized the old man. "Ivan, it's me, H.R.; don't shoot."

"I don't recognize you with beard and without your bird dog."

"As you can see, I am still hunting; just bigger game this time."

The old man opened the gate and motioned. "You need to come in and out of sight; patrol comes by every day at 4:00 pm."

They quickly went around the house until they were out of sight of the road. Ivan pointed at the road. "I wave when dey pass. Dey leave me alone; dey think I am crazy."

H.R. grinned, "Sounds like they know you."

Ivan shook his fist at H.R. and looked at the others. "He thinks he is funny; big comedian."

As Ivan disappeared around the corner, Tony looked at H.R. "Don't make him mad; he's liable to shoot us."

"No chance, he and I are good friends. We have hunted and fished together for years. There's a big lake down behind his house that is full of catfish and perch. I'm glad he's still alive; he can tell us what's going on."

Peering around the house and bushes, they watched as Ivan eagerly waved at the patrol coming by. The Ford Expedition stopped, and Ivan went down carrying a gunny sack filled with fish. He came back up with an empty sack and a can of coffee. He stopped again and waved as they sped away in the direction of the Indian mound. He walked around the house.

"Follow me. Leave your rockets by back door. I fix coffee."

H.R. introduced everyone and passed Ivan a pouch of chewing tobacco.

Ivan grinned from ear to ear. "I can get coffee from dem now and again, but dey won't part with tobacco. You need to sit tight until after 4:45 pm. That is when dey come back by headed to airport."

Mitch pointed at the road. "Where are they going?"

"Dey go to Indian mound and swap out crews manning anti-aircraft rockets. Are you planning on attacking airport?"

Spike rubbed his hands together as Ivan set hot cups of coffee in front of them. "We will attack if we think we can close it; otherwise, we are going to take a look and make plans."

Ivan came out with some cream from his goats and some honey from his hives. "Sorry, I don't have regular sugar or creamer."

Lucas who had been silent took a sip of the hot coffee. "You can't imagine how good this tastes to me."

Ivan nodded. "I know. I was small boy in Slovakia during World War Two. We lost everything, and were put in concentration camps." He rolled up his sleeve and showed the tattoo on his forearm. "My mother traded herself to the guards for food. I never saw my father after dat. Men were separated and sent to work in labor gangs. I remember the last Christmas at the camp. We ate two rats and a potato and felt guilty because we had more dan others. After we were liberated, my mother again traded herself for passage for us into Western Europe. From there we come to America. My mother died from complications of Syphilis. The nurse told me she was allergic to penicillin." He paused for a moment lost in thought. "Now it comes to America because we are governed by idiots, and voters are biggest idiots."

Everyone was quiet for a moment and savored the hot coffee. Spike sat his cup down and looked at the old man. "Ivan, we have been conscripted into the U.S. Army."

Ivan gave him a stern look, "The real Army or the one siding with Russians and Muslims?"

"The real Army; we are under orders to kill the ones cooperating with the Russians."

"Good, I killed three of dem already. I poisoned their coffee." They all looked at their coffee cups.

"Don't worry; if I was going to kill you, you would already be dead."

H.R. grinned. "I've eaten some of his cooking at the deer camp about twenty years ago; his chili will take you out. I'm still pooping fire."

Ivan died laughing. "You should have seen his face when he took first bite."

Spike nodded at Ivan. "Ivan, I think you have a basic grasp on what we need to do."

"You want to kill all Russians and shut down airport. Can I join up? I was Sergeant in Vietnam; I worked on a ground crew of planes spraying Agent Orange."

"Congratulations, you are back in the army at your previous rank. My rank is Captain, and Mitch and Tony are Lieutenants. There is no pay and few if any supplies. I can bring you a rifle, pistol and ammo."

"I need nothing, son. I just want to kill the sons of bitches. Besides dey know what I've got, and if dey come and find fancy rifle and stuff, dey just shoot me."

Spike asked, "Where are the Russians set up, and about how many are there?"

"There's about twenty-five hundred located at airport. Dey have set up tents and have about a dozen attack helicopters. Dey been keeping everyone bottled up in town to starve 'em out."

"We didn't bring that many bullets. Do you have any idea on how we can attack? The anti-aircraft fire has stopped our attack helicopters."

"I know how to kill 'em, but it ain't gonna be pretty or quick."

"What do you mean?"

"After Vietnam, I went to school on GI bill and got degree in chemical engineering. I worked with company building refinery and chemical plants. Later I work for chemical company selling chemicals to farmers and landscaping contractors. To cut to chase; I have herbicide product dat is basically odorless and colorless. If you're exposed to it, it will cause the lungs of human to crystallize in week or so. It will be horrible death for anyone exposed. If you take bath in it or drink it, it will kill you; nothing short of lung transplant will save you. Dey quit selling it back in 1981 after dey had some people get sick and die. There was also a local woman who murdered her husband with it. She fixed him hot bath and added it with bubble bath. It was big news here for a time."

Spike commented, "I don't care how they die at this point. How are we going to get them to bathe in it or drink it?"

Ivan grinned. "Dat's easy part; dey have to truck in water. With power out there is no city water. Dey bring in water by tanker trucks. The trucks run back and forth from house down the road that has water well. There are usually two runs a day. All it will take is one five gallon bucket of poison concentrate in the five thousand gallon tanker to kill 'em. I have three, fifty-five gallon drums of it along with some other stuff dat was left over from when I sold the chemicals."

"How are we going to get it in the tanker?"

"Dey don't guard tankers. Dey have pipe run out to road where dey drop off full one and pick up empty. The empty one is driven down road where dey have generator running to power electric water pump that fills it. The farm owners were some of first people dey murdered."

"How have you survived?"

"I'm crazy old man who showed up one day with stringer full of catfish at front gate. I took out my false teeth, let my hair hang down and my whiskers grow. I put on raggedy shirt and pants and mismatched pair of shoes. Dey think I'm old lunatic, but dey like fresh fish. I'm too old to climb on top of tanker with five gallon bucket of chemical."

"Can you show us where the tanker is parked?"

"Sure, load up missiles and bring them. I don't want to be caught with dat stuff here."

They loaded the missiles and followed Ivan down his driveway to the road. Once he verified that the coast was clear, they crossed over the road and entered the woods that surrounded an old farm.

Ivan instructed. "We're going to hide missiles in old truck dat was abandoned and rolled down into gully. Den we're going to go back and get a couple of five gallons jugs of chemical."

After hiding the missiles, they went back for the herbicide. Ivan had several empty five gallon jugs that had formerly held peanut oil. He put on some rubber boots, placed some protection over his eyes and pulled on a pair of rubber gloves that went up to his elbows.

"Stand back guys while I fill 'em up." He had a self-priming siphon hose that he put in the first barrel, and with a few shakes he had the chemical filling the jugs. When they were full, he capped the jugs off and replaced the bung in the barrel. He carefully rinsed the full jugs and the siphon hose. Then he washed his gloves and boots.

"If something happens to me you know where the stuff is and how to handle it."

H.R. looked around at the younger men. "Ok, you young bucks, this is where you come in. We need strong backs and weak minds. I've got your back."

Lucas picked up one of the jugs. "I think I heard my name called."

Ivan filled another jug with soapy water. "If you get any on you, you need to wash it off."

Spike grabbed a jug. "Ok, Ivan, are you ready?"

"Sure, we cross back across road and into woods. We go slow and stay under canopy of trees. Attack helicopters run all hours and have thermal imaging equipment. Keep ears peeled. If you hear helicopters, get down in bottom of gully. Dey make circle of airport when dey take off and land."

Spike shifted the jug from one hand to the other. "I forgot to ask. Are there any prisoners being held?"

"No, Russians don't take prisoners except young women. Dey kill 'em when dey are worn out."

Mitch grimaced thinking about them landing to pick up Hannah. "I hope they die agonizing deaths."

"If we pull this off, you get your wish, sonny. You can't fight 'em on their terms; there's too many of dem."

The vibrations of the helicopter could be felt before it was heard. One was coming into the airport. In the twilight they couldn't see it, but they could tell that it passed straight overhead. They continued on. If they had been spotted the entire gulley would have been engulfed in flames. They crossed a creek and made their way up the bank on the other side.

At that point, Ivan put his fingers to his lips and whispered. "We are within half mile of airport entrance where water truck is parked. This power line right of way parallels road which parallels airport grounds. We're close to lake where dey hangout when off duty."

Everyone nodded in silence as they carefully chose their steps and proceeded. A generator could be heard humming; the sound would help mask their movement. Men could be heard talking and laughing around a camp fire. The moonlight reflected off the small lake behind them.

A shiny silver tanker sat gleaming in the moonlight. As they neared the water tanker, they paused and watched as the full replacement tanker pulled into view and parked alongside of it. The smell of food hit them as it drifted from the mess tent. The driver hopped out and hooked up a large hose to the outlet on the fresh tanker and unhooked the hose from the empty one. When the exchange was completed, he left and headed over to the mess tent.

Ivan tapped Spike on the arm. "We're in luck; both tankers here."

"Ok, guys, get going. H.R. and Tony, stay here where you can see and cover us. Spread out a little."

Lucas, Mitch, Spike and Ivan quietly walked down the road. Both the tanker trailers had ladders leading up to the hatch where the filler opening was located. Mitch climbed up to the filler opening on the first one, and Lucas climbed on the second one. Without a word, Spike passed a jug up to Mitch and another one up to Lucas. The bright moonlight illuminating the filler openings made it easy to pour the deadly potent into the tanks. As soon as they were finished, they closed the filler openings and silently returned to the ground. In less than two minutes, the deed was done. All of them retraced their steps back through the woods and gullies. They said very little until they were back at Ivan's house.

Spike finally spoke. "I think we ought to do it again tomorrow night. There will be planes bringing in men and equipment. I think we should deploy again, and if we live, drop some aircraft on the runway with our missiles the day after that."

Ivan cracked the cap on a bottle of Wild Turkey bourbon. "Time for celebration." He raised his glass for a toast. "May all our battles be successful as dis one." They all tilted their glasses back and grinned.

Spike gave Ivan a salute. "Great job, Sergeant. We're going to head to the old shack, sleep and stay hidden until after 4:30 pm tomorrow afternoon."

Ivan grinned. "You welcome to crash here, boys."

"Thanks, but I don't want to take the chance of your having to explain why we were here. It's difficult to hide the extra activity taking place with this many people running around. If you take the first right toward the Indian Mound and go about a quarter of mile, we're in that old shack up on the hill to the left."

"I know where it's at; old man Priest Holmes stores hay there or did; looters killed him weeks ago. Since Russians moved in, we have no problem with looters. Dey shoot anyone seen on roads. You lucky you made it without getting caught."

"We took only back roads and shot the hell out of any Russian we saw. I figure they are concentrating on the main roads for now."

Ivan handed Mitch the bottle of bourbon. "Take dis; it'll help keep you warm."

Mitch grinned. "Thanks, Mr. Ivan, we'll be seeing you."

Spike gave Mr. Ivan thumbs up. "We'll be back after the 4:30 pm patrol comes by. I want to give them another dose before we officially close the airport."

They headed out about fifty yards apart. When they returned to the old shack, they got on the radio with the Mountain.

Spike keyed the microphone on the radio, "Anybody listening on the Mountain?"

The radio crackled as Doc answered. "This is the Mountain. How are you guys making out?"

"We are having a successful mission; I hope everything is quiet on the Mountain."

"We haven't heard a peep; we have completed every task you ordered and more."

"That's great, Doc. I need you to get on the base unit and contact Major Matthews. Tell him we have operations under way. If you or he doesn't hear from us in two days, he can proceed on hitting our target in one week from today."

"I understand. When do you expect to return?"

"We don't know at this time. Just tell the ladies that we are alive and well."

"Roger that; radio if you need us."

34

TONY LOOKED AT Spike. "I think we need to make a trip to Baton Rouge with the chemical as well."

"As soon as we close this airport, Baton Rouge will be our next stop. I surely hope they are using water tankers as well."

They sat in the darkness among the bales of hay that was stacked high along the walls. Somewhere in the straw they heard the rustling of mice. Having been disturbed by the entrance of the men, the straw had an earthy smell that hung heavy in the air. The moonlight streaming through the old windows gave them just enough light for them to open their MREs and to eat. Although the windows had been left open for ventilation, they would close them in order for the old one room shack to warm up.

Lucas spoke up. "I'll take first watch and wake Mitch in few hours."

H.R. piped up. "There's no need. My internal alarm is set, and I'll get up in a couple of hours and relieve you."

Tony asked, "Are you one of those people who can tell themselves to wake up at a particular time?"

"No, but my bladder is. Don't worry; it never fails to get me up."

H.R. dug a chew out of his tobacco pouch and shoved it back into his jaw.

Spike pointed at the tobacco pouch. "H.R., I wouldn't have taken you as a tobacco chewer."

"I'm not; I prefer a pipe or a fine cigar. My pipes are burnt up in my house, and I haven't run across any cigars. So when my nicotine craving hits, I feed it chewing tobacco because that's what I was able to scrounge up."

They all laughed, made beds in the straw and waited for the dawn. Sleep came easily since they had all reached the stage of being able to sleep when there was an opportunity. They were awakened once by a helicopter passing somewhere near, and each of them worried that the shelter on the Mountain was in danger.

Tony said what everybody was thinking. "I hope that pilot and gunner had a good long shower, and had an extra glass of ice tea with supper. Don't forget that all their Muslim comrades will be washing their feet before prayers. With a little luck, they've already had one good foot washing, and will be having another knocked out at daylight."

They dozed off with the satisfaction that justice was being served. Each one went to sleep with the thought of someone or something that had been lost. Lucas thought of his dead brothers and their families. Tony wondered if his daughter was alive, dead or a captive in one of their camps. Mitch thought of his beautiful wife, pregnant with his unborn child, sleeping under a shed in the wilderness. In his mind he saw the old farmhouse lying in ruins. He worried if Hannah and the baby would be okay. H.R. wondered if any of his friends and neighbors had survived; he also wondered if he would one day be laid to rest next to his mother and brother in the little church yard back home. Spike thought about Lisa, Lacy and little Roger. He relived in his mind the scene in the big bus where he found Roger; he reassured himself by pulling his rifle closer as he dozed off once again. The blisters on his sore hands reminded him of all the graves he had opened and closed in the last few days.

The morning dawned clear and cold. The anti-aircraft crew manning the Emerald Mound site was relieved around daylight. They watched from well back in the one room shack as the new Ford Expedition passed with the crew heading back to the airport.

Spike grinned. "I hope they enjoy their coffee when they get back. Guys, I think we need to reconnoiter the countryside and see if we can locate some sites where we can shoot down one of those jets as it's coming into the airport. If it's hit, they will try and land it, and with a little luck, they'll crash on the runway. We can also try shooting one trying to take off."

H.R. pointed out, "The problem with shooting them taking off is that we have to shoot over the airport fence or be on the airport grounds."

Tony chimed in. "Remember Ivan told us not to fight them on their terms. The helicopter pilots will be dead in a few days. I think we should shoot the jets down from a distance. In a week there won't be a lot of them left. If we can drop two or three jets and if all their men are dying, they may abandon this airport. Maybe we can locate the anti-aircraft rocket batteries and destroy them with thermite grenades if we can't figure out how to use them. The rocket crews will probably be dead. With enough debris on the runway, they won't be able to land any heavy jets."

Mitch nodded in agreement. "If they can't land a plane and we can keep the water poisoned, we won't have a problem. We can cut every bridge coming into the area so their only alternative will be to walk in on foot. I'm sure they can deliver troops by helicopter, but if we can find a few survivors willing to fight we can shoot most of the copters down."

At that moment the radio crackled, it was Lacy. "If anyone is listening, please answer."

Spike keyed the mic. "What's up, Hon?"

"A helicopter has landed in the field in front of Mitch's house. It's an attack helicopter. The pilot and gunner are just walking around it like they are checking on it; Doc is getting one of the shoulder fired rockets."

"Don't shoot, unless you're attacked. If you're discovered on the Mountain, we won't have a place of retreat. Those men will both be dead within the week. They have been poisoned by a slow acting agent. So please hold tight."

"Okay, I'll tell Doc what you said."

"Remember, don't panic and don't be too anxious to make a kill. They will both die a horrible death soon. Radio me back when they leave or if you have to kill them. Go ahead and send Hannah, Misty and the babies to safety."

"I'll radio back and let you know what happens."

"I love y'all. Be safe."

Everyone turned to Spike. "As you heard that was Lacy, an attack helicopter has landed in the field in front of Mitch's house, and they appear to be checking their helicopter. You heard me tell them to refrain from attacking and to send Misty, Hannah and the babies to one of the hideouts. I told them to do nothing unless they are attacked. I think the Russians are just checking on their machine."

H.R. pointed out. "They may be getting sick and landing to puke or something. They would probably take the opportunity to do a pre-flight check."

Doc returned to the top of Mitch's Mountain with one of the shoulder fired rockets. Lacy told him what Spike said, and Doc grinned.

"Look, one of them is coughing, and the other one looks as if he's trying to throw up. Did they say what kind of poison they fed them?"

"No, just that it was slow acting. I'm going to send Hannah, Misty and the babies to the secret site."

"I'll stay here in case I need to shoot them down."

Lacy went back down the hill and sent them to the remote camp-site. Lisa joined Doc back on the Mountain and watched the helicopter pilot and gunner climb back in. The pilot fired up the monster, and they watched as it rose to altitude and resumed its patrol.

Doc keyed the mic on the radio and reached Lacy and Spike. "The helicopter's gone. It looks as if it's heading back toward the airport."

Spike hit his mic button. "Good news."

"Spike, Lacy tells me that you were able to slip them something."

"I can't go into any details on the radio; just hold off on exposing yourselves to them in any way. Unless you are directly attacked, I would just stay hidden and continue with your fortifications."

"Will do; keep us posted."

Spike looked around the room. "We've just heard good news. The helicopter is gone and is heading in this direction. Maybe they are going to come in on sick call."

He pointed to HR and Tony. "I want you guys to slip through the woods and see if you can get to Emerald Mound. We'll want to know how to get there without exposing ourselves when the time comes to take them down. Mitch, Lucas and I are going to get around to the north side of the airport and see if we can spot any other anti-aircraft batteries or find a place from which to shoot."

Tony and H.R. loaded up and headed out the backdoor of the shack. They crossed through the pecan orchard that lay behind it and across the corner of the hay field. Some bales of hay were scattered on the far side. The old farmer was killed before he could complete his harvest.

H.R. pointed in an easterly direction. "I think the mound is off in this direction. I used to do a little quail hunting around here thirty or so years ago. I had my first Brittany back then. My wife left me, and all I got was the dog. I figure I was on the winning end of the deal."

Tony grinned at the prospect. "I wish I could have at least gotten a dog out of the deal when my wife took off."

"It looks as if you have a winner with Cheryl. Did you go with her very long before you got married?"

"No only a few weeks; it just seemed like the right thing to do, so I said what the hell and went for it. I'm glad I did it. I just hope we live long enough to have a life. There's something I can't understand, H.R. All I've ever wanted was a quiet life, a home to come home to, and peace of mind. Instead my life has been attacked from every angle. Everything from taxes to insurance has preyed on me

my entire life. Now I am hunting and killing men, and I am starting to enjoy it. I finally have people I hate, and I can do something
about it."

"You know it does feel pretty good hunting these bastards. I
spent my entire life trying to get to the point where I could go fishing or hunting once in a while. I paid off my house. I even had a small
winery set up in the old carriage house, and I finally started drawing
my social security and an annuity. Now, I am back to square one. At
least I am getting to go hunting every day. My goal in life was to be
buried by my mother and brother back in the little church cemetery
back in Avoyelles Parish. My new goal is to win this hopeless war."

"There's always hope H.R. In the deep recesses of my heart, I
wished to love again, and it has happened. I hate spreadsheets, and
now I don't ever have to create another one." He paused a moment
and continued, "I hope my little girl is safe."

H.R. lamented. "I never had children; I guess it's one of those
things I never got around to. One day I was a handsome bachelor,
and now I am an old man pretending to act like a young one."

"H.R., I think every life must be filled with regret and disap-
pointment. Everyone wonders why he or she is in this world. I believe
I know why we are here. We might not live to see victory in our life
time, but I know why I'm here right now at this time in history."

"You sure make it all sound noble and righteous."

"It is, H.R.; it is. The barbarians are here."

After another hour of walking, they were within sight of the
great Indian mound. It had been continually used by the Indians up
until the Natchez Indians were massacred by the French in the early
1700's. Now, it was occupied by another invading army. H.R. and
Tony held back in the woods where they could see the mound and
be unobserved by the troops who manned it. The mound occupied
eight acres and had another mound on one end where the Chief
could oversee the festivities and worship their Sun god. Tony and
H.R. could see the rocket battery at the very top of the ceremonial

mound. A generator was running and a radar antenna was spinning above it. The rockets were in a box that contained launch tubes.

Tony whispered. "If worse comes to worse, we can hit that box with one of our missiles; it would set them all off. That would be one hell of a fireworks display."

H.R nodded. "Just remember, Tony; we are looking at dead men."

In the meantime Spike, Lucas and Mitch who were fully armed, headed in the opposite direction. They took a road that ran beyond the lake located behind Ivan's house. They followed that road past several vacant houses. A starving dog barked at them from one of the houses. Further down the road, they passed a hunting camp, and finally, they came to a pipeline right of way. Following the pipeline to the left and east would take them back to the road leading to the airport. They turned west on the pipeline, but before they left the shelter of the forest, they heard a large jet coming in at about a thousand feet. It was making a slow bank. They stayed out of sight under the tree line. The jet was only visible for a few moments which was not enough for a missile launch.

Mitch pointed ahead to a path. "Let's see where this goes. It has to cross a road or a field where we can get a shot."

They spread out about one hundred yards apart on opposite sides of the pipeline. The pipeline was a hundred or so feet wide, and it went in a straight line over ridges and across gullies. They came to a point where it rose from the ground, and there were sidelines tied into it. These lines were either feeding it or diverting some of the gas elsewhere.

Spike noted, "Might be a good place for a thermite grenade if we need a diversion."

Continuing on they reached a large open pasture. The remains of a recently slaughtered cow lay in front of them. Buzzards that had been feeding on the carcass scattered and began to circle overhead. Tire tracks led off toward a gate several hundred yards in the distance. At that moment, they heard the engines of another large jet.

They backed into the tree line and watched the large jet for a full thirty seconds as it made a broad lazy circle before it spiraled down to the runway.

Mitch smiled. "They won't have a prayer; let's look around a bit more to make sure that they don't have snipers set up out here. This spot is too good to be true."

Lucas pointed. "Look, there's a solar panel on a post down the way and what looks like a camera set up. I'm glad we didn't go barreling off into the field."

Mitch agreed. "We don't have to even enter the field; we can shoot from right here. If we need to cross the field, we'll have to go around behind the camera and unplug it before exposing ourselves."

Spike stomach growled. "It's getting late. Let's break out an MRE, eat and get back to spiking the drinking water. I'm sure those two jets brought in some more thirsty men. We'll head back to the shack and get ready for tonight's run. I would like to hit both tankers at the same time, just like we hit them last night. Tomorrow, we'll take out the big jets and the Emerald Mound rocket battery."

They went back down the pipeline and entered the woods. They were hoping to find a secluded spot to relax and eat. They stumbled upon the remains of a plane crash that was decades old. The twisted frame was overgrown with vines, and a tree grew up through the mangled fuselage. There was no sign of the pilot or passengers. They ate their meal in silence and buried the garbage from their MREs under a log. The day was warm with the temperature in the fifties and no wind. As they approached the pipeline, they heard a shot ring out from the woods in front of them. A wounded buck emerged from the woods on the opposite side, collapsed and died in the middle of the pipeline right of way. Several men emerged from the opposite side; they were in Russian uniforms. One of them took out his canteen and took a swig. He took out a rag, wet it and wiped his face; he was obviously in distress as were the others. They all appeared to be unable to catch their breath, and all three were breathing through their mouths. The men quickly gutted the buck. They cut a sapling two inches in diameter and about five feet wide to use as a draw bar. A rope was tied around the neck of the buck, and the other end was fastened in the middle of the sapling. They headed back in the direction from which they came, pulling the buck as two plow horses would pull a plow. The third man carried their rifles and followed.

Spike whispered. "That was a close one. We could have been spotted. These pipelines make good places to deer hunt. I'm glad to see that they aren't feeling well. We need to keep spiking the water."

Mitch agreed. "You do realize that all they have to do is start landing men by helicopter. There are only five of us. They are bound to realize that they have been poisoned in a few days."

"I bet all that oil in the Gulf didn't enter into their invasion plans, and I'm sure there are more of our troops rebelling against our new officer corps than anyone anticipated."

They retraced their steps to the old shack and were joined by Tony and H.R.

Tony asked, "How was the hunting?"

Spike took off his cap and ran his fingers through his hair. "We found a great place to shoot down jets coming in for landings. How about you guys? Did you get to see the rocket battery?"

"We got to within shooting range; I don't think we will have any trouble taking it, especially if the men occupying it are busy succumbing to the poison."

With military time and precision the Ford Expedition came by and returned at 4:45 pm. They headed out right after it passed and arrived at Mr. Ivan's house. Ivan saw them as they came up his drive and met them to open the gate. He was wearing his lunatic costume since he had just talked with the passing rocket crew.

"The soldier boys not looking good; the one who does driving speaks little English; he says dey have caught flu. I told 'em rest and force fluids. I've already drawn up juice for night run. I started frying some fish. Soldiers didn't want any today since dey not feeling good, so we get to eat 'em. We got plenty of time. Let's eat, and you tell me what you found out." Ivan laid the fish out on a platter on his kitchen table along with some hushpuppies and a pitcher of sweet ice tea. "Eat up, boys; you going to need your energy to haul juice tonight and shoot down planes tomorrow."

Spike spoke between bites. "We found a spot about a mile down the gas pipeline where we can easily shoot down those jets as they circle in to the airport. We also have plans to take out the rocket battery on Emerald Mound. We haven't spotted any other rocket batteries."

Ivan took some tongs and made sure everyone's plate was full of fish. "The ones I know of are on Emerald Mound, one over on Foster's Mound Road and one at intersection of Hwy 61 and Natchez Trace Parkway. Remember; dey are all going to be dead in a week so don't take chances."

Mitch took a bite out of a hushpuppy. "If we don't shut down the airport to the jets, they'll just keep bringing in troops, and we won't be able to kill them fast enough. The only thing that has stopped an invasion here in the South is the oil spill in the Gulf."

Ivan looked surprised. "What oil you talking about?"

Tony explained to him what had taken place. "There won't be any shipping taking place in the Gulf any time soon."

Ivan grinned from ear to ear. "Then all is not lost. All we have to do is stop big jets from landing, and then the only places dey can land are at the big airports."

Spike broke in. "I don't know about the rest of the country, but the only airports open to them in this area are Natchez, Baton Rouge and New Orleans. Our guys have control of or knocked out all the others."

Ivan laughed. "Great news, now all we have to do is poison those airports."

Spike gave him a puzzled look. "You make it sound easy. As of right this minute there are six of us so called "commandos" taking on the Southern Russian Front."

"Is easy, you just killed about twenty-five hundred men; if successful tonight, several hundred more. Tomorrow you shut down airport and day after drop all main bridges around here. Is easy, we're kicking asses up here."

Spike questioned. "How do you propose we take the Baton Rouge and New Orleans airports?"

"The lights are out there as well. We take supply of herbicide. If dey have tankers, we simply repeat what we did here."

Tony asked, "What if they aren't using a tanker system?"

Ivan shook his head. "I don't see how you guys have lived this long. We inject it into system by tapping into water spigot. All we need is pump that will put out higher pressure than what dey are using. We simply pump directly from barrel or tank through water hose connected to open spigot. It will go right into water system; the result will be the same--dead bad guys. The land is flat around there; we can shoot down jets from anywhere. I don't care how many men dey have; Russians are looking for hundreds of men to attack. Dey won't be looking for two geezers, an old fart and three rednecks."

Spike agreed. "I see your reasoning. Let's get going. We need to treat the water and get ready to blow some of them out of the air in the morning. They'll be trying to fly out the sick, so the sooner we shut the airport down the less likely we will be found out. They can't stop the poison unless they run it though massive carbon filters. They won't have any on hand."

They repeated their steps, just as they did the day before, and right on cue the fresh tank of water arrived. The driver swapped the hoses and headed to the mess tent. Just like clockwork, they spiked the punch and headed back to the safety of Ivan's house.

Ivan reminded the guys. "Come; wash up just in case you have some chemical on you."

They all washed up, and Spike asked Ivan, "Do you want to participate in the shoot down tomorrow?"

"I'd love to shoot one down, but I'm almost eighty years old. If things get dicey I not able to keep up with you youngsters; the last thing I want is to slow you guys down or get in way. I go to Baton Rouge and New Orleans. I think my engineering skills come in handy once we get there. I want to take shot at aircraft carrier. It has to be sitting duck stuck there at the mouth of river."

Spike pointed towards the Indian Mound. "Ivan, we're going back to the shack; when you start hearing the shooting tomorrow, that'll be us."

35

THE NEXT MORNING they were up before dawn. The first order of business was to retrieve the five shoulder fired missiles hidden in the old abandoned truck down in the gully. They found the missiles just as they had left them. With each man packing a missile, they climbed out of the gully and up into the open hardwood forest. Back at the shack, they planned the attack.

Tony pointed in the direction of the Indian mound. "We have two options on the Emerald Mound's rocket battery. We can slip in and shoot the men manning it, or we can hit the rocket canister with one of these."

Spike nodded in agreement. "I wish there were some way to utilize those rockets, but we would have to know how to run the equipment, and all the controls are in Russian. I want Tony and H.R. to get in position to hit the Russians' canister of rockets with one of the missiles. When we get an airplane in our sights, we'll radio for them to fire one of their missiles into the canister. The resulting explosion should create one hell of a diversion. Tony, radio us when you get into position."

Retracing their steps, Tony and H.R. returned to the Indian mound. Since the missiles were heavy and they weren't as young as they once were, their getting to the mound took longer than they had anticipated.

H.R. questioned, "Do you think Ivan was referring to us as the Old Geezers?"

"I'm not sure H.R. You could very well be the Old Fart."

They both laughed and were relieved to finally see the Indian mound. As they expected, the generator was humming, and the radar dish was still turning.

Tony keyed the mic on the handheld radio. "Spike, we're ready when you are."

Spike answered. "We just got here, and all we have to do is wait for a target."

Lucas pointed at the camera and the solar panel down the way, "When are we going to turn that camera off?"

"We're not. It's set up to catch someone crossing the field, and we'll be doing our shooting from over here."

They spent the rest of the morning resting in the shade and waiting for a target. Several times they felt the beating of helicopter rotors and heard helicopters arriving and leaving the airport. When one of copters came into view, they resisted the urge to fire upon it. Near noon, they heard the familiar sound of jet engines. This time it was one leaving the airport, and they got a glimpse of it as it headed in a westerly direction. The jet made a turn south and disappeared. After another thirty minute wait, they heard the sound of another jet; this time it was coming into the airport. Just as the plane had the day before, this one make a slow bank as it spiraled in to line up with the runway.

Spike keyed the radio mic as Mitch popped open the missile control panel and sight. "Tony, we have a target; start your attack."

"Will do," Tony turned to H.R. "We're up; do you want to take the shot?"

"No, I'll stand ready to shoot anyone who pokes their head out; you do the shooting."

Tony flipped open the mechanism and the missile came to life. He aimed it at the canister of rockets and squeezed the trigger. The light turned red as he waited. A second later it turned green, and he finished the squeeze. The missile came alive and startled him with its sudden recoil and noise. One second it was coming to life in his hands, and the next second it was exploding on top of the Indian mound. As they had expected, the missiles set off a chain reaction in the rocket canister on top of the mound. The resulting explosion sent a shock wave that shook all the trees around them. Debris and dirt showered down on them, and a man's head landed about ten feet away.

A heartbeat before Tony squeezed the trigger on his missile, Spike squeezed the trigger of the one on his shoulder. The missile dashed away leaving a smoke trail; it ran true, went straight into the body of the big jet and exploded. The weight of the big jet carried it forward, but it was no longer in controlled flight. It rapidly lost altitude as the pilot struggled to direct it onto the runway. They watched as the smoking hulk disappeared from view; a moment later they heard the booming concussion of the huge jet when it hit the ground.

Spike yelled. "Okay, guys, let's move it. I'm sure they'll be heading this way once they figure out what happened."

They double timed back toward the shack by trotting down the pipeline until they reached the gravel road that ran back out to Artman Road. They heard the crunch of tires on gravel as a new Ford pickup came barreling down the gravel road. All three of them opened up on it and riddled it and its occupants. The truck careened off the road and overturned. In spite of the intense gunfire, one man survived and crawled back up to the road. He wasn't armed and was breathing so heavy that he was almost gasping. Mitch replaced the magazine in his rife, slapped the bolt release and popped him through the head.

Ivan who had been concealed behind a large pecan tree showed himself. He was carrying an old Winchester 30-30 rifle. "I told you it would crystallize their lungs; did you hear him trying to breathe?"

Spike lamented. "I wish we knew if that jet hit the runway."

Ivan shrugged his shoulders. "The only way we are going to find out is to look. Russians *expect* more trouble; it would be suicide to go look now."

Spike hit the mic button on the radio. "We dropped a big jet. How did you guys do?"

Tony answered. "We have the rocket battery and the men manning it scattered over about a half a mile. The upper part of the Indian mound no longer exists."

H.R. called out, "I hear helicopters returning."

Tony hit the mic again. "Helicopters are returning. Do you want us to engage them?"

"Only if they spot you; otherwise, we're going to save our remaining missiles for the jets and the other anti-aircraft batteries. Y'all beat it back to the shack. They'll be sending out patrols; we'll meet you there."

They pulled the dead Russian out of sight and covered the wrecked truck with limbs and pine boughs to hide it from the air.

Spike looked around at Ivan. "Do you think it's safe for you to stick around?"

"Face it guys; this is war. None of us are safe. At my age I might not wake up one morning; I had good run. My daughter and grandchildren are missing, and no way can I hope to find them in Toronto; I don't have to tell you what it is like up there in the dead of winter with no electricity."

"I'm sorry, Ivan. What about your wife?"

"She died when she couldn't get dialysis several weeks ago. She's buried in the side yard. I'm just getting started killing those bastards. I will carry sack of fish to the gate like I do sometimes; I can see from there. I have fish trap that stays full. I have feeling crew that comes by at 4:00 pm won't make it today."

Spike got on the radio to Tony and H.R. "I want to knock out the other two rocket batteries as quickly as we can. You guys meet us at the shack."

"Doc, are you listening?"

Doc responded. "I've been listening."

"Doc, get on the radio with Major Matthews and give him an update. We'll know in a bit if the airport is closed. One anti-aircraft battery is destroyed, and we have two more to go. We'll report later what we've accomplished."

"I'll let him know; be careful and good hunting."

Ivan turned to go. "Don't get yourself killed; remember soldiers will be getting real bad off by tomorrow. You saw how that last one was breathing. The Russians are heavy smokers and drinkers. I've watched Muslims sit around hookahs puffing up a storm. The smokers will be affected sooner and will die quicker. Remember, guys; this is not hundred meter dash this is 100k run. Don't get hopped up to make quick kills. There are only six of us until our guys get here. We have to take our time; fight on our time and terms."

Everyone looked at Spike who said, "Ivan, you're right. If the airport's closed from the crash, all we have to do is wait a bit and let them die."

Tony pointed out, "I noticed that the helicopters fly up and down the river. Maybe we can knock them off from my boat *Lucille*. I anchored her in the river, and I hope she's still there. The Russians won't be expecting attacks to come from an old sailboat."

Ivan left to gather his fish and put them in his gunny sack. He removed his teeth, greased up his hair and put on the worst shirt and pants that he owned. One of his shoes was a slip on tennis shoe that was wrapped in duct tape to hold it together; the other was a completely worn out golf shoe. He put on an old blue jean jacket that was at least thirty years old and an old baseball cap that he had found on the highway. He waited until after 4:00 pm and put his sack of fish in his old wheel barrow. He slowly started toward the airport. When he felt he was within hearing of the little airport lake and pavilion, he started talking out loud to himself. Soon he had a full-fledged argument taking place with an imaginary foe. Once he knew that he was being watched from the park, he stopped, put his hands on his hips and gave his imaginary foe a good cussing. He shook his fist and proceeded to argue in the most colorful German he could muster.

He shot the imaginary foe the middle finger and progressed toward the gate. Occasionally, he would stop and shake his fist at the imaginary foe in the road behind him.

The man at the gate spoke in very choppy English. "Not a good time, old man; everybody has flu, plane crash."

The Russian tried to cough but was racked with pain. He pointed to the huge pile of debris at the intersection of the two runways that was once the giant jet. The fire was still burning, and a column of black smoke was still rising to the sky. Ivan stood and admired the devastation with a look of horror on his face. He put on his most sad looking face and thought *I missed my calling; I should be great actor.*

He took the fish and laid them out in the grass and told the guard. "Eat, will make you feel better."

The guard waved him away. Looking back, Ivan counted twelve attack helicopters and three general duty ones. The most important thing he realized was that they were all on the ground. The spiked punch was doing its job. He headed back home arguing with his imaginary foe until he was past the park and out of hearing range of the men who usually hung out in the pavilion.

He was tired by the time he walked back to his house. He turned up his driveway and was relieved that Spike was sitting on his steps.

"How did we do, Ivan?"

"We did good. Big jet is resting at intersection of two runways and burning. Men are in agony; still think dey have flu. More good news- twelve attack and three regular helicopters on ground."

"Do you think we can hit the other rocket batteries tomorrow?"

"Sneak up and observe 'em from distance. I'd be surprised if they're even manned; you may not have to waste missile."

Ivan broke open a bottle of Russian vodka. "Don't worry; I got this before we spiked punch."

Spike shook Ivan's hand. "We couldn't have done this without you."

"Me neither."

"We'll be heading out early in the morning to knock out those rocket batteries; here is a radio so we can stay in touch. I'm going to send Lucas over here with a missile to stay with you. If you need to send him to shoot down something, do it."

"Thanks, I can use help. We'll get chemical drawn up to take to Baton Rouge and New Orleans. I also need torch, welder, high pressure washer, tools and equipment packed up to go."

"That's a good idea, Ivan, but we won't have time to scrounge up what we need. Get some rest. Tomorrow is going to be another busy day."

They passed the bottle back and forth a couple of times.

Ivan clapped Spike on the shoulder. "Get going, boy."

Spike headed back to the shack. When he arrived, he told the men about the airport being shut down.

He got on the radio with the Mountain. "Anybody listening on the Mountain tonight?"

Lisa answered. "We have been so worried. How are y'all doing?"

"Tell everyone that we are all alive and well. I need you guys to radio Major Matthews and tell him that we have shut down the airport. It is closed to large jets. We have destroyed one of the anti-aircraft batteries and should have the others demolished before lunch tomorrow. All enemy personnel are suffering from what they think is the flu. All their helicopters appear to be grounded. When we are certain that the anti-aircraft batteries are silenced, we will radio the news and proceed to destroy the main bridges coming into the area. Our plans are to advance to the Baton Rouge airport for the second phase. We'll be traveling by water; I hope that Tony and Cheryl's boat *Lucille* is still where they left it."

Lisa replied, "Everything is okay here; we haven't seen or heard any helicopters since early this morning."

"That's wonderful news, but don't let your guard down. After we knock out the rocket batteries, we're going to take down some bridges and head back. We'll see you in a couple of days."

As they sat in the darkness, the radio came to life, "Is anyone listening? This is Lisa."

Spike answered, "We hear you. What's up?"

"Major Matthews congratulated you on your success. He wants to know how long before he can start bringing in troops."

"Tell him that after we knock out the anti-aircraft batteries, he can start immediately. His troops should be able to head in tomorrow afternoon. Find out how many men they are sending. Be sure to tell him to remind his guys to not drink or use any water at the Natchez airport or from the water tankers located there."

They opened another MRE for dinner while they waited for her return call. The radio came back alive.

"I'm back. Can you hear me?"

"What did he say?"

"Captain Matthews will be coming in with thirty or more men to occupy and secure the airport. He asked that you call him about a good landing spot near the airport."

"We'll call tomorrow after we shut down the remaining anti-aircraft batteries."

Spike spoke to the guys between bites. "Lucas, I want you to take your missile and head over to Ivan's house in the morning. He is going to need some help gathering up everything he needs to take with us. He wants to help us poison them in Baton Rouge. That old man thinks outside the box. I have no doubt he could handle them by himself if he were ten years younger. If you spot a jet or a helicopter and think you can drop it, take the shot."

"Tony, I want you and H.R. to go over and knock out the rocket battery at the intersection of Hwy 61 and the Natchez Trace. Mitch and I will look for the one on Foster Mound Road. I'm not sure of the location, so we will have to search for it. Be careful. If the rocket battery is manned just hit it with a missile. If it's not, set off the thermite grenades on the important parts; we are going to do the same. Your number one goal is knock out that rocket battery. If you don't use your missile and see a helicopter or airplane, you are free to take the shot. Since all the helicopters seem to be grounded, I am planning on driving around there after midnight. It's too far to carry those missiles by hand."

Tony pointed out, "They shouldn't be too hard to locate; all you need to do is listen for a generator running. The one on Emerald Mound had a generator powering the radar antenna and equipment."

Mitch looked up from his meal. "That's good to know."

Spike grinned. "H.R., when that alarm bladder of yours goes off, wake me up, so we can head out."

"Don't worry, Captain; it hasn't failed me in years."

36

THE RAIN STARTED during the night; the rain drops hitting the old tin roof serenaded them as they slept. A chorus of snoring from around the room was led by H.R. and supplemented by Tony and Spike. Mitch finally stirred when an overly ambitious mouse tried to get a leftover cookie out of his shirt pocket. Lucas who had been standing guard was sound asleep. Mitch slapped at the mouse and grinned as it scurried for safety. He hoped that Hannah was safe and warm at the Mountain. In his mind, he made plans on rebuilding the old farm house. Many of the timbers were salvageable since they were made from heart cypress wood. He worried that the pine lumber would rapidly decay now that it was exposed to the weather.

Right on schedule, H.R. quit snoring and headed for the back porch. The old door creaked as he pulled it open, and everyone started to stir. Without a word, everyone got ready to go. Mitch walked to the front door and pulled it open. It had sagged on its hinges and dragged the floor as he forced it open. The rain hitting the roof drowned all noise from the night. A steady stream of drops came off the porch roof in what would become icicles before the day was out. The weather was turning colder; it would probably keep any patrols or snipers huddling next to their fires. They put on their heaviest gear and went out to the vehicles where they loaded the missiles and their guns. Lucas opened the gate and waited until the vehicles came through before closing it and returning to the shack to await the dawn.

Tony and H.R. drove out with the headlights off and at a dead slow speed to avoid running off the road. They also wanted to keep the noise of the truck engine to a minimum. The smell of Beech Nut chewing tobacco filled the cab as H.R. dug a chew from the tobacco pouch. They followed the road until it turned to gravel, and they coursed their way toward the parkway. This section was at one time the road leading to an old plantation. Both sides of the road were lined by huge Live Oaks. A break in the clouds allowed the moon to stream through. They could see the Spanish moss hanging like the beards of old men from the limbs. They reached the Natchez Trace Parkway and stopped long enough to get their bearings. The moon shining down the wet black roadway gave it the appearance of a waterway. They turned toward the highway and continued on. They came to a sign on the road and stopped long enough to read it using a match. Just as they had hoped, it read that Hwy 61 was one mile ahead. This was perfect. They ran the truck to the next spot where they could leave the road. A small grove of Cedar trees stood at the top of the right of way. They drove the truck up behind them where they gathered their missile and weapons. A light mist was turning to ice on the small limbs and on the surface of the truck. Each of them was wearing their foul weather hunting gear, and H.R. wore his Gor-Tex duck hunting parka. Tony wore an oil skin drover hat and a camo poncho under which he carried the electronics portion of the missile. H.R. carried the rifles. Both had pistols and knives on their belts and vests.

Even though the temperature was plummeting, they were warm; their clothes blocked the water and breeze. The mist was coating all the tree limbs with ice, and they were starting to sag. The roadway remained thawed as it had not gotten cold enough for the ground to start freezing. When they were within sight of the highway, they began to hear the drone of a generator.

Tony pointed at the bridge. "There, I thought I saw a flash of light."

They quickly moved to the north side of the road to where they could melt into the forest if necessary. As the dawn arrived, the mist was trying to form a light crust of ice on their clothing and hats. H.R.'s moustache had a slight coat of ice trying to form on the tips. Their breath fogged as they pulled gloves from their pockets to protect their fingers. Peering through binoculars, they observed the rocket battery. They could see a little movement; the Russians were still trying to man the rockets.

Tony pulled out the radio and hit the mic. "Looks as if they are still trying to man the site up here on the highway. Do you want us to hit them now or wait until you are in position?"

Spike answered. "If you are within range, just stay put; we'll try and hit them both at the same time."

"Good thinking. If one is hit, the other will be on alert."

Spike and Mitch stopped and killed the engine on the Jeep. They stood outside and listened. They could hear a dog somewhere off in the distance. A light breeze was blowing across the ice in the trees which made the ice produce a crackling sound. They cupped their ears and finally heard the sound for which they were searching. Off in the distance in the direction they were driving, they heard the sound of a generator. Each time the wind slacked off, they could hear it.

Mitch said, "Let's drive another half a mile and stop to listen."

After a while, they stopped the Jeep again and listened. The sound was coming from around the bend in the road. Spike turned the Jeep up a driveway and parked next to a mobile home. The decomposed body of a man and woman lay in the front yard. The hair was still visible on the now faceless skulls, and the mist was freezing on the remains. The front door of the trailer was open. If anyone were inside, the cold would have forced them to close it. The ice crunched under their feet in the gravel driveway as they walked toward the woods next to the house. They could hear the generator very well once they were on top of the hill. Walking through the woods brought them to the edge of a large field that bordered the road. The rocket battery was set up in the field next to the road. While still in the woods, they stopped and used binoculars to observe the site.

"I don't see anyone there, Spike. The generator is running and the radar antenna is spinning, but I don't see anyone." The trailer on which the generator was mounted had a small enclosure on the back.

Spike turned to Mitch. "We're going to hit it with a missile. I'll call Tony and H.R."

He keyed the mic. "Tony, light her up."

Tony cautioned, "Don't get too close. It's one hell of an explosion. Duck as soon as you pull the trigger."

"Don't worry we will."

Spike turned to Mitch. "Take your shot; aim for the canister of rockets."

Mitch sighted in on the canister and squeezed the trigger. The light turned red and then green. He finished the pull on the trigger, and the missile sprung to life. Mitch dropped the launch tube and they retreated into the woods just as the shockwave arrived and almost knocked them down.

H.R. and Tony heard the echo of the explosion in the distance.

Tony pointed. "Light them up H.R.; that's our signal."

H.R. took the shot and watched the missile strike the canister. The rocket battery practically vaporized when the ordinance all went up at once.

Spike got on the radio when he heard the explosion echoing across the county. "It sounded like your attack was a success."

Tony keyed the mic. "It's going to take more than duct tape to put that back together."

"Meet us back at the shack, and we'll decide what to do next."

Spike keyed the mic again. "Is anyone listening back on the Mountain?"

Doc answered. "We've been listening."

"Call the Major and tell him that we have knocked out the three known anti-aircraft sites, and we await his instructions."

"I'll radio him and let him know."

Lucas and Ivan were busy drawing the herbicide up in five gallon buckets when they heard the explosions in the distance.

Lucas grinned. "That sure is a beautiful sound. After what they did to our families, I want to see them all dead and not just the ones here."

"I feel same way I felt when Nazis destroyed my family and my country. What Nazi didn't destroy; Russians destroyed when they come."

A fire burning in a large metal drum warmed their hands as they took a break from drawing up the cans of herbicide. Ivan and Lucas admired the 10 five gallon cans of herbicide lined up ready to be moved. They were still glistening from having been rinsed to remove any residue that may have gotten on the handles.

A helicopter could be heard coming in. Ivan pointed to the missile Lucas had leaning up against the side of the house. "Grab it and follow me. I always wanted to see one work. That might be more men coming in."

Ivan set a metal lid on top of the burning barrel, and they headed down the hill behind his house. Ivan carried his and Lucas's rifles, and Lucas carried the missile. The house sat up on top of a ridge near the road. The land fell away into gullies where water drained into the creeks and rivers. What had once been a huge gully had been dammed up to form a large lake; at the bottom of the trail, sat a pier that led out into the lake. A small aluminum boat was sitting upside down on the bank nearby.

Ivan pointed to the sky. "Helicopters always circle across lake before landing at airport; get that thing ready."

They started out on the pier and almost slipped on its ice covered surface. When Ivan stomped on the pier and cracked the ice, small pieces skidded out from under his feet. Icicles hanging under the pier broke away and landed with splashes in the water. Lucas opened the sight, and the missile came to life. Just as Ivan had said, the big twin rotor job made a slow lazy circle. Lucas pulled the trigger, acquired the target and fired. The missile left in a cloud of smoke. They had to move back up the pier to see around the smoke and to see the missile hit the big helicopter. The missile hit the helicopter just below the jet turbine engines and detonated. A split second later, a secondary explosion, from ordinance loaded on the helicopter, detonated and blew the helicopter into three pieces. It fell into the end of the lake near the dam. It was soon completely submerged in about thirty feet of water. Only bubbles and smoke gave evidence that anything had taken place.

Ivan shook Lucas's hand. "By golly, dat's what I call shooting. I hope you have more missiles."

Lucas nodded. "Yes, we do. Now let's get a move on and finish getting your gear ready to go."

"I ready; dis is most fun for me in long time."

Walking back up the ridge, they were aware of their feet crunching on the sleet and ice on the ground. They had failed to notice any precipitation on the way down.

Ivan pointed at their feet. "Wonder we didn't break our necks."

Lucas just shook his head and grinned. "Too much excitement; now, let's go find some more to kill."

Halfway up the hill, they ran into Spike and Mitch. Spike pointed to the empty missile tube in Lucas's hands. "You realize that you don't have to keep toting that thing once you've fired it."

Lucas grinned. "I guess I forgot in all the excitement." He heaved it down the embankment and into the woods that surrounded the lake.

Mitch pointed at it as it tumbled down the ravine. "Someone will be selling that in a pawn shop as a war relic one day."

Spike hit the mic on the radio. "Tony, how are y'all making it?"

Tony answered. "We just got out of the truck; we're back in the shack."

"We'll be there in a minute."

"Doc, if you're listening, I need to know if you've heard from Major Matthews."

"I was just getting ready to call. He said they would be landing two choppers with fifty men. He will need a secure landing site somewhere near the airport in three hours."

Tony broke into the conversation. "Tell him to look for a hayfield north of the airport next to a pecan orchard. We can light a bale of hay when he gets near. As wet as it is, there should be plenty of smoke."

Spike agreed. "Doc, call him and tell him where to land; we'll be ready to receive him. Tell him to fly in from the north."

"I'll tell him. Good luck. Everything is safe here; everyone is warm and fed."

"Thanks, Doc."

Spike turned to them. "You heard the man. Let's get back to the shack, eat and secure the hay field for landing."

Ivan clapped him on the shoulder. "Get going. It won't take long to load my stuff when we leave."

"Okay, guys, let's saddle up and get ready for our guests."

37

MAJOR MATTHEWS GOT on the radio when he was within sight of the Mississippi River. "Spike, are you guys ready? We'll be there in about twenty minutes."

Spike keyed the mic. "Come in well from the north. We have knocked out all the rocket batteries that we know of; there could be one we don't know about to the south of the airport."

"We'll be coming in at tree top level from the north."

"Look for the smoke; we're not far from Emerald Mound."

Spike looked over at the guys. "Light her up. They'll be here in fifteen minutes."

H.R. flipped open his Zippo lighter and ran his thumb over the flint striker. The lighter produced a blue and yellow flame about an inch above its stainless steel chimney. When he touched it to the bourbon soaked bale of hay, it lit up, and a column of white smoke climbed into the sky. With Lucas, Mitch, and Tony scattered around the field, there would be no surprises.

Major Matthews wasn't piloting the big twin rotor helicopter, but he was standing behind the pilot and co-pilot and pointed out the column of smoke. "Put her down there."

The big helicopter came in and gently set down in the field. A second copter settled down a couple of hundred feet away. The ramps were already open by the time the copters touched down, and men poured out. H.R. killed the fire and smoke by pouring a jug of water on the hay bale. The men immediately set up defensive positions to guard the helicopters. Both helicopters were quickly unloaded and emptied.

Matthews saluted Spike and his men. "Good job, guys. Before we get this show on the road, I want to take a minute to look at the airport layout."

Spike pointed to the shack. "Let's go into the command center and get out of this weather."

They all went in where Matthews pulled out a map that showed the airport. Ivan showed them the location of the guard shack, the mess hall and the barrack tents and pointed out several locations where they could approach the airport.

Ivan then explained. "Do not drink any water or get any of airport water on you. The herbicide we spiked water with makes lungs crystallize. Everyone there is deadly ill, except ones who came yesterday. Dey are walking dead men, but dey can probably still fight."

Spike interrupted. "They are probably expecting trouble since their rocket batteries were knocked out this morning. I wouldn't be surprised if reinforcements are coming in by helicopters from Baton Rouge or New Orleans."

Matthews pointed to three entry points on the map. "We're going in here, here and here."

"Spike, I want you guys to stay here with the helicopters. After securing the airport, we'll scatter our men out with surface to air missiles to defend it."

Breaking into three teams, Matthews' troops hit the airport from the east, west and north sides. They mowed down the tents with machine gun fire and attacked the buildings with the shoulder mounted missiles. They encountered little resistance and took the facility with no losses to any of their forces, and as a result, they captured the Russian attack helicopters and ordinance.

After a brief time, one of the pilots of the American helicopters approached Spike. "It's done. We're going to fire up these birds and land at the airport. Do y'all want a lift?"

"No, we have vehicles. We'll meet you there."

Spike, Tony, Ivan, Lucas, H.R. and Mitch watched as the big helicopters lifted off and disappeared toward the airport. The woods grew quiet.

Ivan said, "I sure hope dey don't put us on burial detail."

Mitch laughed. "That's going to be a job."

They piled into the Jeep and the black Chevy and started to the airport.

Ivan pointed to his driveway. "I had enough excitement for now. Drop me at my house; I'm ready for some hot coffee by fire."

Lucas handed him his handheld radio. "Hang on to this; I'm sure Major Matthews will have some questions that only you can answer."

"Thanks; just have him call if I can help."

They dropped the old fellow off, and he went up his driveway with renewed energy. He looked back and watched as the vehicles disappeared toward the airport. He walked around to the side of his house where there was a flower garden. In the middle of it was a grave with a homemade concrete marker. He had engraved her name and the dates of her birth and death in the concrete. He stood over her grave and spoke to her with tears dripping off his chin.

"Mama, I helped turn back first wave of Russians. I haven't heard from our little girl or grandbabies. If I'm alive come spring, I'll leave on foot or by horse. I have no hope of getting there in winter."

He walked into the house and put on a small pot of coffee. He sat at his table, drank his coffee and finished off the fish and hushpuppies from the night before.

When Mitch's group arrived at the airport, they went into the small terminal building. Major Matthews was pouring over the maps that he had unrolled on a folding table near the plate glass windows. The weather was still terrible; icicles were hanging on the eaves and off the blades of the helicopters. A large jet sat empty on the tarmac; it was stranded because the crashed jet blocked the runway. The sleet was piling up on the grass, but it had not started accumulating on the runway, roads, or sidewalks. A detail of American soldiers had located a tractor and an equipment trailer and were removing the dead Russians to a ravine down the road. An arsenal of AK-47 rifles and other gear was being created in one of the least damaged buildings. As the soldiers scavenged what was usable, they stored away all canned rations. The tankers were emptied, and the water lines were drained.

Major Matthews pointed to the map. "I expect if they intend on keeping this airport, we will be hit by carrier jets or attack helicopters. I want to move some of those Russian helicopters away from here; we're going to use them since we are already running out of ordinance. I don't want them destroyed if the Russians decide to strike the airport."

Mitch asked, "What do you want us to do next?"

"The immediate goal is to shut down the invasion in this region; we can't stop that until we stop the heavy jets from coming in. The oil spill has shut down ships coming into the Gulf. All this may be futile since the Chinese and Koreans are still coming into the country, and we think the Russians are entering through Alaska and Canada. With that being said, about twenty-five percent of our forces have seized control and ousted their treasonous officers. The pro communist forces in our military have been unsuccessful. Most of our men have either gone AWOL and headed home or have overthrown the bad guys. We think that seventy-five percent were defeated, AWOL or surrendered. So that leaves us, the remaining twenty-five percent to fight."

H.R. asked, "Does that twenty-five percent include us former civilians?"

"No, it doesn't. We're hoping that guys like you will turn the tide. Twenty-five percent of our armed forces is nothing to sneeze at, especially since we are all mad as hell. Vengeance is a strong motivator. We don't have a single man who hasn't lost people to the murderers. Now, getting back to Mitch's question, I want you guys to try and reach Baton Rouge airport and shut it down. You guys were successful because you are not coming in as a strike force, and you fought in an unconventional method."

Tony nodded. "We don't like getting shot at if we can help it."

Spike pointed to the map. "Our plans are to travel back down the Homochitto River in the jet boat, get on *Lucille,* if she's still there, and head south. Once we reach a point where we can leave the river, we'll do so and head inland. We'll have to leave someone on the boat to guard the gear and chemicals until we can figure out how they're set up."

Captain Matthews stated, "We have ten men with the shoulder fired missiles spread out in every direction and our two transport helicopters are heading back for more men and equipment. We'll take care of the Russians in town. Do you know where there may be others?"

"Yes, they are probably at the fire tower out on Hwy 84 this side of Meadville again. I'm not sure if they drank the water, but if I were a betting man, I would say, 'yes.' I don't know how many of the Muslim brothers are roaming the countryside either. Assuming we are able to knock out the Baton Rouge facilities, what are the plans?"

"Baton Rouge is not going to be easy to take and keep. It is only about a five minute run by fighter aircraft from the carrier at New Orleans to Baton Rouge. We want to capture that carrier undamaged so we can put the lights out in Russia, China, and their Middle Eastern allies. To put out their lights, we need nuclear weapons. Ours were compromised by our former leaders, and the ones we control have no launch codes. We have a few experts taking them apart and trying to reconfigure them so we can detonate them. Those intact big jets may have to be repurposed to become missiles to deliver the warheads."

Spike asked, "Do you want us to start dropping bridges with the thermite grenades?"

"We'll take the ones out around here; I want you guys to drop the two over the Homochitto River on Hwy 33 and the ones on 61South. We need to get the water working; do you think Mr. Ivan can help us get the poison out of the system?"

"We'll find out."

Spike hit the mic on the radio. "Mr. Ivan, are you listening?"

"Ivan here."

"Ivan, Major Matthews needs to know if the water system can be cleaned out?"

"Yes, he needs to dump all water in tankers and completely fill and dump three or more times. After tankers are clean, he needs to flush water lines by running a couple of clean tankers of water through entire water system. That means open every faucet and spigot in airport, including water heaters. Otherwise, dey will be committing suicide. He needs to guard tankers too. I would fill and leave one inside airport fence. It took two tankers a day for Russians; it won't take that much for just fifty men. Runoff will run into little lake by airport. I wouldn't eat fish out of there for at least a year; give it time to breakdown in environment. Remember, don't even wash hands in airport water; it will kill."

"Understood, I will order all the water dumped immediately. Thanks Sergeant, keep up the good work."

"Ivan, out."

Major Matthews set the radio down. "I want you guys to get back to the Mountain and get your families some shelter squared away; plan on heading to Baton Rouge in seven days. That will give us time to move in the rest of the men and equipment and support you in the effort."

Spike, Lucas, H.R., Mitch and Tony returned to Ivan's house where they loaded the chemicals and Ivan's gear in their vehicles and headed to the Mountain. Taking the same roads as before, they retraced their steps. A lot of trees and limbs had fallen from the weight of the ice, and the roads were crusting over with sleet, but their four wheel drive vehicles were able to navigate the hazardous roads in stride. When they reached the old wooden bridge, they had to take precautions because one slip here would have them careening into the ravine below. The ice crunched as the tires of the Jeep rolled onto the boards. Careful not to brake or accelerate, Spike kept the speed steady and made the crossing without slipping. Tony waited for Spike to get completely across before starting the attempt. From inside the enclosed cab, they held their breath as they heard the sound of crunching ice and creaking wood.

Ivan said, "Don't lose control and kill us. I have more Russians to kill before I go."

Everyone laughed as they crossed to the other side. The trek up the hill on the gravel road was equally as treacherous. Spike's Jeep was cutting ruts that were only made worse as Tony followed. If they were forced to stop here, they could not continue. Only the momentum of the moving vehicle took Tony's truck through the deeper ruts and slush.

Once both vehicles were out of the bottom, they made it to the paved roadways. Even these roads were now covered in sleet and ice; fortunately, they did not meet any traffic. In this weather, any wayward enemy patrols would in all probability be hold up around a fire. They only spotted one or two houses with smoke coming from a chimney or gas flue. As they had learned, this was a good way to get spotted by enemy thermal imaging and get shot.

Spike asked Mitch, "Since we have knocked out the helicopters operating in this area, what do you think about our moving back into town until we can find new houses or rebuild in the country?"

"What do you have in mind?"

"My big old house out on the highway should still be standing. It has six bedrooms and two baths. We can turn the living room and library into bedrooms as well. There's enough room to get everyone moved in, and if not, there are still some campers and motor homes in my storage yard. I think my natural gas generator is intact, and we should be able to get it moved over and running. We need to stop and get some heat going in it so the pipes won't freeze and burst. It will beat leaving the girls in the woods."

"Sounds good to me; I could use a hot bath."

Mitch got on the radio with Tony in the truck following them and told them the plan.

Lucas keyed the mic. "The generator did not take a direct hit; the gas line feeding it was severed so the generator just quit. Spike's bus didn't take a direct hit either. Since no one was in it, we had it parked on the far side of the barn, so it was out of sight. We can move it over if we need it."

"That's good news; follow us over to my house in case we run into trouble."

The trip back to Meadville was quiet and slow. The sleet was several inches thick on the road, and snow had started falling. The old house was just as they had left it. A quick run through found no one and no damage. The doors had been left unlocked, and nothing was missing. They lit the space heaters that were scattered throughout in the house and made a quick run around the storage yard. One storage unit door was open; someone had apparently made it back to claim their belongings.

When they returned to the house, Spike watched as Ivan backed up to one of the heaters. "Ivan, I want to leave you here with your gear. Will the chemicals freeze and be damaged?"

"Chemicals won't freeze unless it gets below zero, and it won't get that low around here. Do you need me to help you guys make move?"

Spike instructed, "Mr. Ivan, I want you to guard your stuff and keep the house safe. We're going to unload all our extra gear. You make yourself comfortable. There's a bedroom downstairs that you can use until we get the girls moved. I think it will be best if we let them decide who goes where. I don't want to interfere with their nesting if you know what I mean."

"I feel better just dealing with Russians. I dealt with wife for almost sixty years; it was not always pleasant. I notice Airstream trailer in back, can I look at that?"

"Sure Ivan. The propane tanks should be full, but I'm not sure if the battery is hot. You have full run of the place. You can stay in it if you would be more comfortable. We'll try to have the girls and generator back tonight."

They unloaded Ivan's chemicals and extra gear in one of the storage units and got him squared away in the big house. They put the extra food in the kitchen and drove off with Mr. Ivan waving from the front porch. They called Doc on the radio and told him to tell the girls to start packing and to get ready to roll.

The trip back to Mitch's Mountain was uneventful. The trip across the Homochitto Bridge was slippery as it was fully coated with ice. When they reached the road to the Mountain, they had to stop numerous times to move limbs from across the road and the lane leading to Mitch's old farmhouse. The little creek was still flowing, but ice was forming along its edges. They drove past the remains of the old house, around the side of it and up the trail on the Mountain.

They pulled up to the camp and were greeted by all the dogs. Hannah came walking up and smiled at Mitch. "It's about time you came home; I thought you had run off after knocking me up."

"Can't say I didn't consider it."

She punched him and gave him a big kiss. "I managed to get our clothes and lot of stuff out of the house. I stored much of it in the tunnel."

"You shouldn't have been doing that."

"I took my time, and Doc said it was alright so long as I didn't do any lifting. I just picked around in it; Lisa and Lacy helped. Little Roger helped carry things out for me."

"We're going to move to Spike's house in town. We don't expect to have much trouble now that we've killed most of the Russians at the airport."

Tony asked, "Where's Cheryl?"

"She is over at y'all's old house with Lacy; they've been salvaging everything they can. Larry's still laid up; however, he can get around on crutches so long as it's flat land. He's down in the shelter sitting near the fire."

Lisa came running up with Doc behind her. "Spike, you had us worried; you should have called in more often." She gave him a big kiss.

"I couldn't, Baby. I didn't want them to be able to pinpoint us or you if they had some way of tracing the direction."

Lucas went down to the camp where he greeted Misty and Mandy. He gave her a big kiss and hoisted Mandy up on his shoulders. "Mandy, where's Roger?"

"He went with Aunt Lacy and Ms. Cheryl. They needed a man to protect them."

"Oh, I understand."

Doc waited until all the ladies were finished greeting the men. "Well, how did the poisoning work out? What exactly was this poison?"

Spike grinned. "It worked like a charm. It is a herbicide that when mixed with water crystallizes a person's lungs if they come into contact with the contaminated water."

"How many did y'all kill?"

"We're estimating over twenty-five hundred."

"That's going to be one hell of a mess to clean up."

"Thank the Lord that it's cold and some other men are tending to it. We've just got to get geared up to go and do it again."

They left Lucas to help Doc get everyone packed and ready. Tony and H. R. drove down the road in the woods to the remains of Tony's house. Cheryl came running over to the truck and buried Tony with kisses.

Little Roger put his hands over his eyes and said, "That's what Mama Lacy and Mama Lisa do to me; you better get used to it."

Lacy asked, "Can we get a ride back to the camp?"

"Sure, as soon as we get the trailer hooked up, we're going over to Slippy's place to meet Spike and Mitch. We're moving back to y'all's house in town. We've got to pick up the generator."

Cheryl asked, "What about the Russians?"

"Very few, if any, are left alive. With the help from Ivan, we managed to pretty much wipe them out. Major Matthews and about fifty men cleaned out the rest and took possession of the airport. They are busy flying in a lot more men and ordinance."

"Honey, how long before you head out again?"

"How did you know I was leaving?"

"Easy. When you've been married as long as I have, you just know these things." Tony grinned, kissed her and gave her a tight hug.

They hitched his equipment trailer to the black Chevy. By the time they made it over to old Slippy's place, Mitch and Spike had the natural gas generator ready to load. They had it loaded, moved to town and running before nightfall. They then concentrated on moving their ordinance and getting the bus moved. The ordinance was put in several of the empty storage units well away from the house but within range of their rifles should they need to defend it. After seeing the damage that the missiles could do, they had no desire to have a chain reaction explosion that could destroy the house. Larry took the downstairs bedroom so he wouldn't have to navigate the stairs with his broken leg. The married folks each had their bedrooms, and Mandy and Little Roger shared the last one. Doc and H.R. elected to take the bus, while Ivan took the Airstream camper.

All of them had long awaited showers, and they ran the laundry machines overtime. Everyone relished the hot showers and the warm beds. Rover, the cat, was locked in the house so he wouldn't leave and head back to Mitch's Mountain. After he was fed a couple of times, he would stick around for good. Bacon, Pinky and the other dogs soon made themselves at home under the porches. No one would sneak up on the house with a yard full of dogs. A half dozen chickens and a rooster were turned loose in the yard.

The next few days were spent moving the contents of Spike's containers into storage units and hooking the bus and the Airstream trailer up to plumbing. The final task was moving four wheelers, tractors and other equipment and supplies that could be salvaged into the units. After five full days, everyone and everything was moved in and settled.

On the sixth day, Spike had all the men in his den around his big table. "H.R. and Doc, I want you guys to stay here and guard our gear and families. Although we have the bug out locations in and around Mitch's Mountain to evacuate to in an emergency, I want you guys to establish some around here as well."

H.R. nodded in agreement. "If we lose the airport, the Russians will be looking for survivors again, and we need to keep an eye out for patrols that may still be running loose. We can't assume that all of them were poisoned. Also, those Muslims could be washing their feet in and drinking river water."

Spike agreed. "They can only carry so much food on their backs, so unless they have a supply truck with them, they will be getting hungry quickly."

Mitch interrupted. "Remember; don't get in a shootout here in the house. Every gun they carry will shoot right through this house and out the other side."

Spike looked over to H.R. "H.R., I seem to remember that you owned a construction company for quite a few years and took up guiding as a hobby when you were getting ready to retire."

"That's true."

"This house had a root cellar when it was built. I think the opening to it was in the kitchen pantry. Do you think you can take up the linoleum in there and open us an escape hatch? The house sits on a four foot tall brick wall foundation, and the storm cellar has a brick wall as well. I believe it came out under the back of the house years ago. The bricks on that side appear to have been added where a door was located at one time."

"I'll have it opened up before lunch. Do you have any tools?"

"Lisa and Lacy can show you which storage unit has all my tools. The rest of us are packing up and heading down river in the morning. We are going to need fuel for the jet boat, diesel for Tony's sailboat, batteries, food for several weeks, plus all of Ivan's gear. I don't think the jet boat will hold it all."

Tony mentioned, "We can always load up some aluminum boats and drag them behind us. We'll need to carry some saws to cut any trees that might be lying across the river and those we can't jump."

"Great idea; Mitch, you and Tony go down to the warehouse behind the Blue Flamingo; Carl Benson had some vehicles and boats stored back there. I seem to remember him having several old green, flat bottomed, aluminum boats. In Bude on the east side of town, was an old boy who worked on boats and outboards. If he's still alive, find out what he needs and work a trade. He might have been run off or killed by Carl. I sure wish I'd popped a cap on Carl when I first had the chance."

Mitch simply said, "Let's lock and load. We can't get back to living until we finish the killing. I'm ready to wipe the sons of bitches out, and that includes killing the Carl Benson's of the world. I could be home in bed every night with a beautiful woman; instead, I've been shot at, blown up and run half to death. I'm fed up and ready to go."

Tony grinned, "Us too, brother; us too."

38

THE JET BOAT ran like a champ as it powered its way down the Homochitto River. It was loaded to the gunnels as were the two fourteen foot aluminum boats behind it. Mitch's crew had most of the C4, and shoulder fired missiles scattered among the three boats. No one boat held all the gear that they needed. In the event they lost one boat, they would have duplicate gear in the others. They each had a double pack of ammo, their rifles, pistols, knives and packs. They were lucky that the river was elevated from all the rain, sleet and snow. Most of the trees and limbs were submerged which make for an easy ride for them. They put ashore when they passed under the first bridge. The steel girders were in the form of huge I-beams that spanned the space between the bridge piers. An aluminum ladder stowed in one of the small aluminum boats allowed them to reach the beams that supported the superstructure above. They chose the span that was over land as they hoped they could return home using the jet boat and the river. They placed thermite grenades every two feet on each of the I-beams under the bridge and pulled the pins.

Spike cautioned. "Don't look at the light; it will burn your retinas."

The grenades fired and started melting their way through the huge I beams. The steel melted and poured in a stream that fell to the sand below. Small limbs, brush, leaves and driftwood were soon blazing away from the molten steel falling on to them. The beam that was fired first was the first to go, and as it did, it caused the other side to twist and moan as it became distorted. In just a few moments, the weight of the bridge tore the molten beams apart.

Tony gave them the thumbs up. "One down; three to go."

The next three bridges came down just as the first one had. The demolition of the bridges only consumed a portion of their thermite. Of the original three hundred thermite grenades, they still held two hundred. They rode downstream from the last bridge and pulled over long enough to call Major Matthews.

Spike keyed the mic. "This is Spike calling Matthews."

The radio crackled. "Matthews here; how are you progressing?"

"All four bridges are down; we are proceeding to the river to see if we can locate Tony's sailboat. How are things going on your end?"

"We've shot down several helicopters attempting to come in. I have men scattered out five miles in every direction, as well as snipers in place to intercept any that might try to land. As far as we can tell, every one of them got a good dose of Ivan's chemical. A patrol came in yesterday and surrendered. We have them under guard; I don't look for them to survive the day."

"How many men have you landed?"

"We have three hundred men on the ground. If you guys can slip in and poison the ones in Baton Rouge, we'll be in a position to work on the carrier. The carrier has a forty-five day cycle before it has to be resupplied. We are within range of their fighter jets from the carrier and their helicopters in Baton Rouge. They can only be resupplied by the big jets coming into New Orleans and Baton Rouge. We are slowly getting men with shoulder fired weapons within range of both the airports. As of right now, they are spiraling in from high altitude to reduce the time they are exposed to our fire. The problem we have is a lack of men and missiles. We have about twenty-five hundred of the missiles left in our arsenal."

"I know the Russians have satellite surveillance. Have we been able to access any of our satellites?"

"I am certain they are looking at us right now. Our satellites are damaged or have been sabotaged by our traitor officer corp. I am frankly surprised that we haven't been hit by jets from that carrier. We are keeping only a minimum crew here at any one time. I am keeping them scattered around the county. The only Intel we are getting is from ground intelligence such as you guys. The only reason you were successful was because you didn't show up on their satellites. I'm counting on you doing it again."

Spike responded, "I don't think they realized they were poisoned; the fact that they thought they had the flu worked to our advantage."

"If you guys can figure out a way to close the Baton Rouge airport and block the fuel delivery to the helicopters, we will have them bottled up in New Orleans. They will be limited in what they can do with helicopters because of their limited range. The carrier jets are another matter. I am training pilots to fly the Russian helicopters. We are learning as we go because no one has been trained on them, and all the manuals are written in Russian. The translating is going slowly with no internet. We are using a tourist translation book from a bookstore."

"Matthews, be sure to let us know when you start flying those helicopters and the jet. We don't want to accidently shoot down the good guys."

Mitch pointed out. "I don't think we need to shoot down any of their aircraft unless we are being attacked. The less attention we can draw to ourselves the better. Once we get to *Lucille* and start south, we can sit down and pour over the maps to see where we can sneak in."

After another hour of slow travel, they approached the point where the Homochitto River entered the Mississippi. The huge river was menacing as they powered their away into its current. They quickly found the opening into the old river and charged up the old channel. They were happy to see *Lucille* still at anchor. A large flat bottomed aluminum boat was tied up to her. They killed the engine on the jet boat, and each man had his weapons at the ready. Using oars, they silently paddled up to the old boat. Lucas climbed over the fan tail, and with his pistol drawn, he went in. A moment later he motioned for them to come aboard. He was holding a Russian pistol by the barrel and had an AK-47 in his hand.

"There's one dead Russian on the floor, and another one is on his last legs on the front couch."

They quickly boarded and went in to find the one on the couch gasping for breath.

Ivan pointed to their canteens. "Dey must have filled canteens at airport before coming here. Go ahead flush water tanks and lines on boat three times just in case dey brought water to fill tanks. We can't take chances."

They passed the dead Russian over the side and looked at the one gasping for breath.

Ivan walked over to him. "Speak English?" The Russian didn't respond.

"Sprechen sie deutsche?" Again there was no response, only gasping.

Mitch looked at Spike. "What do you want us to do with him?"

Spike looked over at the Russian. "The same thing he would do with us. Throw him overboard. Don't shoot him; we don't want to draw any attention to ourselves."

Ivan pulled a razor sharp, British commando knife from a scabbard on his leg. "I know where to stick him. Get him outside and hold him over rail on his back."

Mitch and Lucas dragged the Russian over to the rail where Ivan took the knife and with the skill of a surgeon inserted it between the man's ribs and into the heart. The man stiffened and almost immediately went limp. Ivan wiped the blade on the man's shirt.

"Dump him; he's dead."

With a splash, the body hit the water and joined his comrade on the way to the river. Without missing a beat, Ivan walked back into *Lucille* and dropped his knife in the sink. "Let's get this water dumped before we slip up and get it on us."

Tony had been looking over the boat. "It looks as if they took good care of her. Ivan and I will dump and flush the water system; you guys get our gear unloaded and stowed."

Tony cranked the generator and turned on the taps in the kitchen, lavatory and shower. The little water pump hummed away as it pumped the tank dry. When it was empty, he closed the taps and turned on the water filter and refilled the fresh water holding tank. At Ivan's insistence, they filled and drained it four times for good measure. They took the Russians' canteens, removed the caps and threw them overboard. The sun was getting low so they decided to stay put for the night. Ivan washed off his commando knife and returned it to its scabbard.

The weather had cleared. The snow and sleet had subsided, but the bitter cold was still holding on. The Russians had equipped *Lucille* with a lot of can goods. Ivan quickly went through and threw overboard anything that could have been prepared using the airport water including bread and anything with a screw top lid.

He reminded them. "You saw how dey died. Take no chances. You understand?"

They all nodded in agreement as he went to the stove. "I'll cook; you keep look out and rest."

Ivan cooked biscuits from scratch, and along with the freeze dried food from Spike's storage, they had a good hot supper. All was quiet on the lake, and the cabin was warm as they sat around in the dark. They called in an update to Matthews and waited for the dawn.

38

AFTER HE HAD removed a set of shelves from over the side and back of it, H.R. soon had the hatch to the old root cellar exposed. At one time, shelves had been built only on the left side of the room. Sometime in the past, the hatch had been nailed shut, and shelves were built so that the entire room could be used as a pantry. Linoleum and, later, vinyl flooring had been placed over the floor and the hatch. After he had removed the layers of flooring and the shelves, the hatch's opening was revealed. Its old hinges creaked as he took a crow bar and forced it open. A set of brick steps fell away into the darkness. He pushed up the hatch and held it open using the crow bar as a prop. He lit a kerosene lantern that was sitting on the top shelf of the pantry and descended down the steps into the room. Entering the room, he realized why it had been so thoroughly sealed. A pair of skeletons lay to one side. Both skulls had what appeared to be bullet holes in them. The clothes were mostly rotted away. One of the skeletons still had a gold pocket watch and chain. He looked up to the opening of the cellar in time to see little Roger peering down at him.

"Roger, go fetch Doc and tell him to come see me."

Lacy looked down from above. "Find anything interesting yet?" H.R. handed up the gold watch. Lacy took it and turned it over. "Did you find anything else?"

"Just the skeleton wearing it and someone else."

"You're kidding; I always told Lisa I thought this house was haunted."

Doc arrived and H.R. grinned. "Lacy, can you find me a box or a sack that I can put them in? Doc, come on down; you've got to see this."

Doc looked over the remains. "Looks like a man and a woman; both were shot through the head." Pointing to the man's skull, Doc continued his examination. "He had money at one time; look at the gold crowns on his teeth."

They pulled down an extension cord and lit the cellar with some lamps. There was more to the root cellar than met the eye. A set of brick steps led up to an opening that had been bricked closed. On either side of the steps were iron rails that sat atop the sides. This opening would have opened to the outside and would have been accessed from under the house. To the left of it was a corridor that descended downward with a corresponding set of rails that were the same distance apart as the ones on the stairway. A large steel door sat on a rail over that opening and could be slid across to block it. This opening had a large piece of structural iron on which the foundation of the house rested. The corridor beyond had a domed brick ceiling, and from the angle where it descended, it was obviously below ground level under the side yard. The stairway with the rails was about twelve feet long, and this opened into a much larger room with wood kegs set on cradles made of brick. The kegs were placed two deep down both sides of the room. Cases of glass jugs and bottles lay on a bench behind this. Another corridor led away to the rear and dead ended at another doorway that had been closed with a brick wall.

Doc tapped on the barrels. "Sounds like they are all full."

H.R. tapped a plug in the side of one of the barrels loose and stuck his nose to the opening. "Whew, Doc, take a whiff; we've struck gold!"

Doc put his nose to the opening. "I'll be danged; it smells a lot like bourbon whiskey, and it's probably been down here since prohibition. Those rails were used to roll the barrels up and down the stairs."

"These barrels have the word Mathiglum branded on them; seems like I heard my uncle refer to Mathiglum."

"Yes, I remember hearing about Mathiglum. It was made from fermented honey and brown sugar."

"I bet it will taste pretty good after aging in those barrels all this time. You don't see the door to a humidor around here do you?"

Doc grinned. "Let's keep looking."

They removed the skeletons and swept out the space. An old Smith and Wesson pistol lay on top of the bodies. Two spent cartridges were found in the cylinder. They buried the remains of the couple on the back of the lot and proceeded to break through the brick wall at the end of the passage. After opening the passage and removing the earth, they had an exit tunnel that opened out in the side of the ravine behind the property. The ravine was littered with the remains of old bottles and crockery that had been discarded in the past. Now, the debris was overgrown with fern and vines. The opening was completely hidden from view, and the steel door on the inside still closed to cover the opening. They moved food, supplies and weapons into the space with the whiskey barrels. They had created a safe place to retreat if the house came under fire.

Lisa wiped off the gold pocket watch and opened it up. A small photo of a young woman stared back at her from the inside of the cover. She wound the stem, and the watch sprung to life. Roger grinned when she placed it to his ear so he could listen to it ticking. Hannah smiled as she watched.

Lisa looked up at her. "I'm glad to see that you are feeling better."

"I am feeling a lot better; Doc says I can start doing more so long as I'm careful. Can you believe they found skeletons in the basement?"

"I imagine that there are a lot of skeletons for people to find lying around now. I can't wait to hear what Spike has to say about what we found."

They spent the rest of the day in speculation as to who the dead people were, and how the root cellar had once been a whiskey bottling plant.

That evening, they all sat around the fire, and the adults each had a small glass of the Mathiglum.

Cheryl commented, "As soon as we get some extra flour and eggs, I'll make a whiskey cake using this."

The next morning H.R., Lisa and Lacy finished cleaning out and moving the rest of Carl Benson's stash of food and supplies into the storage units where they could keep an eye on them. Larry sat in a chair out on the back deck with his deer rifle. From there, he could see the front gate to the storage yard and down one entire side. The barricades were still in place, but at this stage of the crisis, they thought it would be unlikely that anyone would show up. The possibility of a large armed group existed, but each day that passed meant there were less people alive to attack.

Doc made a run down to a medical supply house in town the next morning. He returned with a wheel chair and a set of real crutches for Larry.

"Now you can get around a little better until that leg gets healed."

"Thanks, Doc, that'll be a great help."

Larry rolled the wheel chair through the back door of Spike's den and out onto the porch deck. Doc handed Larry his deer rifle and set an extra box of cartridges for the .308 Winchester on the table next to him. The dogs milled about as soon as Cheryl showed up with some waffles, honey and coffee for Larry.

Doc went back to his car and returned with bag of diatomaceous earth from the swimming pool supply department of the old hardware store.

Larry pointed at the sack. "What do you have planned for that bag of filter material?"

"Those dogs are going to get loaded with fleas. I'm going to dust them with it before the weather warms up; the diatomaceous earth will kill fleas and insects. The dirt is composed of microscopic sea shells and will get in between the insect's joints. Imagine how you would feel if you rolled around in broken glass."

"Well, how about that. You learn something new every day."

Bacon stood and shook. The dust drifted off in a cloud, and he snorted as he trotted down the steps. He stopped short, barked and trotted toward the storage yard. A group of men were heading through the front gate.

Larry turned to Doc. "Get the family in the hole."

39

THE MORNING ON the river dawned cold and clear. A brisk wind across the water made their ears sting as they began preparations to get under way. They transferred the contents of the two small aluminum boats into the large aluminum boat that the Russians had tied off to the back of *Lucille*. The aluminum boat was outfitted with a Kubota diesel engine that had been liberated from a tractor or piece of equipment. It was mated to an outdrive from a bass or ski boat. The fuel tank on the boat appeared to hold about twenty gallons. There were two fifty-five gallon plastic drums of diesel fuel, two more empty ones and a small battery powered fuel transfer pump on board. The fuel tanks on *Lucille* were already full. They transferred the empty barrels to the aluminum boats and then pulled them up and out of sight on the bank. The willows completely hid the boats from view. After reviewing the maps of the river and the airport, they determined that a canal was located across the river from Southern University at Baton Rouge. Near the university was a rail line that worked its way around through a switching yard and then to a refinery tank farm that sat due north of the airport. If they could climb up on one of the tanks, they would have a platform from which to shoot at aircraft, as well as a spot to observe the layout and location of the occupying army. Ivan pulled out a duffel bag that he insisted on bringing. In it he had a Russian flag and Russian uniforms.

He handed the flag to Tony. "Put flag on mast hanging off back of boat. Everyone put on Russian uniforms and hats. Don't worry; I wash. Dey are warmer than your clothes."

Lucas dryly pointed out. "Don't they execute spies if they're caught?"

Ivan laughed. "What do you think will happen if dey catch us anyway?" Everyone laughed as they donned the Russian gear. "If dey fly over, just point to ear and shake your head 'no' like radio is out. If dey come in close, blast 'em out of the air."

Spike commented as he pulled the Russian hat down to cover the top of his ears. "Also be on the watch for Americans taking a shot at us. I'm going to notify Major Matthews of what we're doing so they won't be tempted to shoot at us."

After Spike called Matthews with an update, Tony and Mitch took the big aluminum boat with five rockets. Ivan took the helm of *Lucille*; he also had five rockets on board. Spike and Lucas followed in the jet boat with the remaining rockets. The chemicals and the grenades were also distributed among the boats. They spaced the boats out about two miles apart on the river. If one came under attack, the others would be close enough to join the fight, but not so close as for all of them to be attacked at once. They decided to put *Lucille* in the middle position. The smaller boats were much faster and more maneuverable. Being smaller and faster, they could respond to any threats to *Lucille* much quicker. The wind on the river was fierce since it had an uninterrupted path across the mile wide expanse. Even with their heavy winter gear, the exposure was brutal. To save fuel, they ran the boats just over an idle; they would let the river do the work of carrying them south. They used the engines to keep them straight in the current and to guide them around any trees or debris that they encountered in the water.

Tony and Mitch were in the lead boat. In the distance, they heard and then spotted a helicopter coming up the river. It was one of the heavy attack helicopters with rockets in pods suspended under the fuselage. It was flying about a thousand feet above the water as it cruised up the river. It made a lazy circle around them and spiraled down to just a couple of hundred feet from them and hovered. Tony pointed to his ear and shook his head "no." The pilot rocked the rotors and pointed to a sandbar down the river.

Mitch turned to Tony. "What do we do now?"

"You've got about thirty seconds to fire one of those missiles."

Mitch hefted a missile and opened the mechanism. The missile came to life. He squeezed the trigger, and when the green light glowed, he finished the squeeze. The missile detonated when it entered the exhaust of the helicopter's left engine. The craft seemed to collapse as if a rope holding it above the river had suddenly broken. The huge blades chopped the water as it plunged into the river which quickly consumed the helicopter and the men trapped within.

Tony grinned at Mitch. "Good shooting, Tex. Call the others and tell them what happened."

Ivan answered the radio first. "I hear explosion. What happened?"

Mitch explained while all the others listened. "The attack helicopter was fooled by our uniforms long enough for us to fire on it with a missile. I hope they didn't have time to report. I believe they were heading toward the airport at Natchez."

Matthews who had been listening responded. "If they had time to report, you will be having company really quick. Those big helicopters can fly over two hundred kilometers per hour."

Spike came on. "If they do, we'll have to try and splash them as well."

Matthews came back on. "Continue the mission and be on alert; that could have just as easily gone the other way."

As they approached the crash site, thousands of bubbles and small pieces of the helicopter were popping to the surface from where the current was dragging it along the bottom. The jet fuel from its tanks was forming iridescent circles on the surface of the water as the fuel globules erupted on top.

They spent the rest of the morning and into the afternoon traveling downstream and staying alert for attack.

Spike hit the mic and called to Tony and Mitch in the lead boat. "Start looking for a place where we can hide these boats."

Tony radioed back. "There are a lot of derelict vessels and old cuts off the channel that we'll be coming up on; I'll radio when I find a spot."

They motored on for a couple of hours. When they approached a large sandbar, a woman was standing waist deep in the water, and on the sandbar, a pack of large dogs was barking and lunging at her. She was swinging a long piece of driftwood at the dogs. The dogs continued to bark and plunge at her, but she drove them back to the bank.

Tony turned the boat. "Mitch, shoot 'em."

Mitch shouldered his rifle and emptied the magazine on the pack. Out of the nine dogs, two got away. The large pack consisted mostly of pits. Several of them still had collars, and one was dragging a chain. The lady appeared to be in her fifties. Her short blond hair had a hint of gray, and she had intense blue eyes.

"Thanks. You guys came along just in time."

Tony said, "How long you been out here?"

"I've been in the water for about ten minutes. They jumped me up on the levee, and I fought them off with this stick."

As they helped her into the boat, they saw that her lips were quivering from the cold.

Tony hit the mic on the radio. "Ivan, we have a passenger for *Lucille*. We're on our way back; we have someone who needs warming up. We have a young lady who we just fished out of the river that needs some dry clothes and hot coffee."

Spike radioed back. "We'll come up and take the lead."

Mitch put his coat over her shoulders and she looked up at him and smiled. "You look like Russians, but you don't sound like 'em."

"Ma'am, I hope you won't be disappointed, but we aren't Russians or working with them. In fact, we fully expect to be attacked by them at any time."

Although she was wet and disheveled, her beauty shown through as she huddled down in the bottom of the boat in order to stay out of the wind.

"My name is Dawn LeBeaux from Walker, LA. I can't thank you enough. Those damned dogs would have just waited until I collapsed from cold and dragged me from the water."

"I'm Mitch Henderson, and this is Tony Jackson." Tony gave her a nod. "Tony and I are from up near Natchez; we're in the U.S. Army."

She looked around. "You wouldn't have anything to eat would you? All I've had in the last three days is a piece of cornbread that I took from an old man down the river. We negotiated a trade for a piece of the cornbread, but I welched on my part of the deal."

Tony grinned. "You're going to fit right in with us."

Spike and Lucas waved as they powered past in the jet boat to take the lead. Spike called on the radio. "Get her warmed up on *Lucille,* and I'll find a place for us to put in."

Lucille came into view. The diesel engine in the big aluminum skiff ran smooth and strong. Tony rode past *Lucille* and brought the boat up alongside against the dock fenders. Mitch tied off to the rail and climbed over the side. With Tony and Mitch assisting, they helped Dawn climb aboard.

Tony pointed. "Dawn, this is Ivan. Ivan, this is your new passenger. We fished her off that sandbar on the right that we're coming up on."

"Welcome aboard, Ms. Dawn. We get you warmed up and fed."

Tony turned on the cabin heater and lit the hot water heater. He heated a pot of coffee, opened an MRE, and heated the contents. Dawn eagerly consumed her meal and drank her coffee.

Tony instructed, "The water is hot; get in there and get a good hot shower. Here are some spare clothes until we can get yours cleaned up. That front cabin has a good warm bed. After your bath, you can sack out if you're tired, or we can feed you some more."

She smiled, "I can't believe you'd do all this for me. Everyone else is desperate. The Russians are shooting anyone outside of the city and a lot of people in the city. People are starving to death, and the ones that aren't starving are robbing and killing. About three days after the grocery stores were cleaned out, the people went berserk."

Tony pointed to the bathroom. "If you need to wash anything out, you'll have to do it in the bathtub. We can run a clothes line out on the deck."

"Thanks; I'll see you in a bit."

The radio crackled, and it was Spike. "About three miles past that sandbar there are two grounded towboats, a huge string of barges and river debris piled up on the west side of the river. We can tie up to one side. No one will notice us at night, and probably not even in the daylight. I just hope they don't have a satellite focused on us."

Mitch pointed out. "I think if they were concentrating on us, we would have been hit by now. A carrier jet could have been here in about ten minutes, and an attack helicopter in about twenty."

Ivan pointed down river. "Look, there are the grounded towboats and barges."

As they looked, Spike and Lucas waved from the jet boat. They came in alongside and tied up to one of the half submerged tows. Spike tied off to the opposite side of *Lucille* and climbed aboard. Lucas and Mitch stayed on board the boats and on guard.

Spike asked, "What's this about you rescuing damsels in distress?"

Dawn came walking out with her hair combed back.

Tony laughed. "I never miss an opportunity. I want you to meet Spike Hobbil. Spike, this is Dawn LeBeaux."

Spike put out his hand. "Glad to meet you, Ms. Dawn. I think you need to know that we're heading to do battle. You are probably as safe here as anywhere tonight, but I can't say what we'll be facing in the coming days. So you are welcome to stay with us, but you'll be danger. We can outfit you and put you ashore between here and Baton Rouge if you like."

"Thanks for helping me, but I have lost everything. I have lost my husband, child, grandchildren, home and as far as I know all of my friends and relatives. My son was in New Jersey; they didn't even have a gun because they were afraid they would get arrested. Do I have to tell you what their life expectancy was? My husband had a heart attack and died while fighting in the yard with a looter. My house was burned down when looters torched the neighborhood. I crossed the river in a canoe that I found a dead man in. I overturned the canoe and lost my gun and food. If you guys are going into battle, take me; I volunteer. I have one question, 'can I get a gun?'"

"I'm the Captain leading the mission. You will start as a Private; your job will be to guard the boat. We have the base station radio here on *Lucille* so you'll need to relay messages between us and headquarters. If you see that the boat is going to be boarded, you'll need to shoot the radio or throw it in the water to kill it."

"What kind of battle are five men going to put up against thousands of Russians and thousands of looters?"

"Well to keep it simple; our job is to shut down the airport so they can't land the big jets."

Ivan spoke up. "We're also going to kill several thousand Russians."

She looked around at them. "You're serious; you mean to tell me that you five are planning on shutting down the airport and killing thousands of Russians?"

Ivan nodded. "Yes, that's about it."

She looked around at them. "Do you guys think you could spare a little food and a gun? You can just drop me off on the bank over here in the morning? At least I'll have a chance; you guys are going to commit suicide."

Ivan grinned. "We don't fight fair. All we have to do is shoot one or two big jets down on runway. Once the big jets can't land, dey start starving like everyone else. We have couple of other tricks up our sleeve."

Mitch spoke up. "It's sort of like committing suicide to not be killing 'em. We tried staying hid on our farms, but that didn't work. All it resulted in was getting a bunch of our people killed and our houses destroyed. They almost killed my wife and unborn baby. We are through hiding; we are in the Army under Major Matthews. A number of our military have joined the Russians, so we're fighting communist Americans and Russians. The Chinese People's Liberation Army and the North Koreans are coming in from the West Coast, and the Cubans are coming into Florida."

She looked up. "Then it's hopeless."

Ivan spoke up. "There are people like us all over the place. In Germany there were Jews who fought back. Once everyone realized dey were going to be exterminated, dey started resisting. When you have nothing to lose, it changes the way you look at things. When dey shut off the lights, my wife died. My daughter is stranded in Toronto. I'm going to search for her when it's warmer, but we all know that almost everyone up there is dead by now. I was there one winter when it was thirty below zero; one in a thousand will have survived. No heat, no food, millions of people and a large part of them being fed by the government; dey wouldn't have had a prayer."

A big tear ran down her cheek. "That's what has happened to my son. The government and the gun control nuts in New Jersey have killed him."

Spike interrupted. "We still have about twenty-five percent of our forces left. A Russian aircraft carrier is stranded at the mouth of the river because of the oil. Our goal is to shut down the Baton Rouge airport to stop them flying in men, food and equipment. That way the real American Army can concentrate on New Orleans and capturing the carrier."

"What oil? Why not just sink the carrier?"

"We can't sink it because we want to recover the nukes so we can turn out their lights. Our nukes were rendered inert by our communist officer corp. The carrier battle group is stranded in the river because of a huge oil spill in the Gulf."

Ivan grinned. "There is always hope. Winter has them stalled in North, and we are kicking their tails here in the South. Remember; every American gun owner that is still alive is shooting at them. Once we have airport here and New Orleans knocked out, dey will starve to death pretty quick. Dey have to drop supplies and men by parachute to resupply after that, and we'll still be shooting them."

She said, "I'll do my part. I'm not giving them a free ride after what they've done. I wish I could shoot the man I stole the cornbread from."

Spike pointed to the AK-47's leaning in the corner and the Russian pistol belt. "Lucas, get her outfitted with a rifle and pistol. Tomorrow she can practice once we are out on the river."

Even though it was cold on the river, they kicked off the heat and power after they had their evening meal. They relied on their warm clothes and the tight boat cabin to stay warm. They didn't want to fall victim to a helicopter with thermal imaging.

40

HANNAH CALLED FROM the door. "Bacon, get back here." Bacon trotted back to the foot of the steps and turned back toward the men with a growl rumbling from his chest.

H.R. commanded. "Hannah, hold that door while I get Larry wheeled back in."

H.R. made sure Hannah, Misty, Mandy and Roger were down in the shelter. Larry followed behind them on his crutches. The girls were armed, and Larry had a 12 gauge shotgun. Doc, H.R., Lisa, Lacy and Cheryl were all armed with the AR-15 rifles and were wearing pistols.

H.R. reminded them. "If they start shooting, get down in the hole or hide behind the cast iron heaters. This is a wooden house, and it only offers concealment, not cover."

Doc was still standing on the deck as the men approached. There were no less than a dozen, and they were scattered out. This wasn't their first time to come up on an occupied house. Half of the men held back from the house or positioned themselves near or behind cover.

The man in front stepped forward. "We don't want any trouble. If you folks want to live, you're going to have to come out here and surrender. We have you surrounded."

Doc could hear the dogs barking from around the back of the house as well. "Can you tell me to whom we are going to be surrendering?"

The man grinned. "I'm Clay Garrison, and I'm in charge around here now. We'll start shooting in about two minutes if you folks don't just come on out empty handed."

"Give me a minute; I need to talk to the others."

Doc walked back in the door. "Everybody in the hole, grab the radios, guns and ammo; we ain't going out there."

They quickly went into the hole; once they closed the hatch, a rug stapled to the hatch's door covered any evidence of the hole's existence. The door was barred from the inside as a precaution. They then retreated to the safety of the barrel room. Without a word, Doc, H.R., Lisa, Lacy and Cheryl headed out through the tunnel. When they were in the ravine and had the outside door barred, they worked their way down to the ravine's bottom.

H.R. told the ladies. "Doc and I are going to slip around where we can shoot. We can't let them get their hands on the missiles, thermite or our food. I can't fight and look out for you ladies."

Doc nodded in agreement. "I want you girls to act as backup."

Lisa pointed out. "Doc, Lacy and I are good shots; we grew up with a bunch of brothers and a dad who took us hunting. Spike has been drilling us on tactics and on keeping our heads down."

"Okay, we don't have time to argue. This ravine runs down along side of the house and the storage yard. I want us to scatter out about one every hundred yards. There are five of us and at least a dozen of them. Cheryl, you and Lacy head down the ravine toward the backyard; I'm sure they think they have us surrounded. Don't just blast away at them; aim and hit them. I don't care if the only shot you have is a foot or an ear. Get a hole in them. If there's more than one that you can see, take careful aim on your first target; fire and then get on the next one. Don't wait to see if your first shot connected. You can go back for a follow up when you have taken a shot on every target."

H.R. reminded them. "Shoot from cover. If they decide to just blast away at the woods, a stray bullet can kill you. We will only have about five seconds to kill them. Concentrate on killing them; don't think about what you're doing. Just hit your targets. If we had surrendered, you ladies would be getting raped about now, and the rest of us would be dead. These are bad guys. They are no different than that bastard Carl Benson. These aren't men or Americans--they're animals. Get in position; we have to start shooting in about five minutes. Radio when you are in position, and try to hold off until you hear Doc and me open up."

H.R. took a position nearest the men; the others scattered out along the ravine. When they were in a position to shoot, all of them radioed; H.R. crawled up over a gravel bank where the excess gravel from the driveway had been dumped.

Their leader started yelling. "You've ten seconds to get out." He turned around to the men behind him for reassurance. "One, two, three, four, five, six, seven, eight...."

H.R. didn't let him finish; he had the dot in the Trijicon sight aimed where it would pass through the man's torso. Then, he shot another man who was standing next to a storage unit and was aiming his rifle around the building. The bullet passed through the man's exposed arm. Suddenly, H.R. became aware of the others firing and of men falling and running. He got back to the task of looking for targets. The men were firing wildly at the house, and finally, they began shooting at the wood line where they were being fired upon.

From down in the barrel room, Hannah quietly cried as the muted sound of gunfire echoed from above. She reached down and caressed the small baby bump that only she could see and feel.

H.R. got on the radio. "Is anybody hurt?" Everyone answered, but Cheryl.

Lacy hit her mic. "I'll check on her; everyone, keep your heads down."

H.R. hit his mic. "Doc, cover me. I'm heading over to the storage yard."

H. R. broke from cover and sprinted down the fence line. Several shots rang out from somewhere in the front of the storage yard; none of them struck home, but in firing the shooter revealed his position. Doc and Lisa both opened on the shooter's location. The shooter tried moving, but he couldn't stay on his feet. He rolled down into the ditch on the opposite side of the road. H.R. then ran toward the gate and shot the dead and wounded ones on the ground as he ran past them and through the gate. Once he was through the gate, he ducked left and ran behind the row of storage units that lined the side of the yard. He reached the corner unit, got down on his belly and peeked around. From this spot, he saw men jumping into trucks down the highway. Kneeling in position, he started firing at the retreating vehicles. He continued to fire as long as they were within sight. Afterwards, he walked over to where he could see the shooter who had fallen and rolled into the ditch. The man was separated from his rifle, but he held a pistol. H.R. could see that he was gut shot.

H.R. asked, "Do you want to drop that pistol?" He was answered by a bullet's being fired at his head. H.R. once again asked, "Do you want to me to leave you out here gut shot in the ditch, or do you want to put that gun down and answer my question?"

The guy said, "I'm out of bullets; finish me."

H.R. moved down a bit and peeked over the edge of the ditch. The slide on the man's pistol was in the open and empty position.

He took aim at the man and stated, "I'm going to leave you out here to die in this ditch unless you tell me who you people are and where y'all are camped."

"We all escaped from the Wesson Penal Farm. There were thirty of us who started out. There are only seven left after today; they won't be coming back this way. We were camped at an RV dealership over near Brookhaven. All we spotted when we watched the last two days was that fellow we talked to, a crippled man and several young women. We didn't know you had men hid out in the woods."

"It's a shame y'all had to die for nothing." H.R. popped him through the head and gathered his rifle and gear. He made a quick walk around and counted seven dead and two who were unconscious, but still breathing; a shot to each head quieted those two.

Lacy made a round through the back yard and found three that she and Cheryl had killed. She then found Cheryl who was unhurt and shaking from the adrenaline rush.

"I can never get accustomed to shooting and killing. I think I killed two of them; I dropped my radio."

"Is this the first time you killed anybody?"

"Yes."

"Me, too. I'm not bothered by it though."

"Me, neither."

Cheryl looked around and found the radio down the hill where it had come to rest when she dropped it. That no one was hurt and that the only damage to the house was the door, wall and windows of Spike's den was a miracle.

Doc went in, tapped on the hatch and called down. "It's over; the bad guys are gone."

Misty opened the bolt and pushed the lid up where Doc blocked it open with a prop, and every one climbed out.

Larry asked, "How many?"

Doc pointed out back. "We killed three in the back and nine in the front. Looks like four or five got away."

"Do you think they'll be coming back?"

"Not after the shellacking we gave them today."

Hannah asked, "Do you think it will ever stop?"

Doc lamented, "It won't stop any time soon."

H.R. came in. "The one out on the road told me they had escaped from the Wesson Penal Farm, and he didn't expect the others to come back for him. I need the key to the storage unit with the weapons. I've gathered up their weapons and ammo; I need to get them put away. Then we've got to drag those dead bastards down the road. What a bunch of dumb asses."

Lisa just shook her head. "I guess they've got away with intimidating everyone up until now or killing them before they could shoot back."

H.R. and Doc cranked up the tractor that Spike had used around the property; took the bodies down the road and left them in the ditch.

H.R. turned to Doc, "I don't know about you, but I could sure use a good shot of that Mathiglum."

"H.R, we've had an exciting morning. I still can't believe what has been happening since the lights went out."

"I'm afraid it's a long way from being over; it's going to be one hell of a ride. Let's hit the Mathiglum, call Spike and the team and tell them what happened."

41

D OC CALLED THE team and reported to them and Major Matthews the events of the day. Everyone was concerned and was glad that the bad guys lost one more time.

Mitch said, "I'm ready to get this show on the road so we can get back home."

Tony pointed to the front cabin. "Dawn, you take the front cabin, Ivan, take the other one, and the rest of us can take the couches. I'll take the first watch."

Spike nodded. "You heard the man; tomorrow's going to be a busy day."

The cabin was dark, and other than a lot of snoring, the evening was uneventful. They were awakened by the sound of helicopter blades beating the air. Mitch who had been standing guard out on deck slipped back through the door. Everyone was awake and listening as the sound grew loud and then finally faded away.

Tony commented, "My bladder took a cue from H.R. and woke me up about an hour ago. What time is it?"

Mitch laughed. "It's 4:30 am. I hope we have a productive day."

The only light came from the radio console at the helm, but it was enough for them to see around the cabin.

Pulling his suspenders over his shoulders, Ivan came from the rear cabin. "Remember, guys; this is the 100K run. We don't get in hurry. We get killed if we get in hurry. Today we attempt to reach Baton Rouge. If we don't, we hide, we eat, and stay on guard."

As soon as it was light enough to see, they cranked the boats and powered back into the river. Tony and Mitch again took the lead in the big aluminum boat; Ivan and Dawn took second place in *Lucille*, and Spike and Lucas brought up the rear. The weather was warming a bit; clouds were once more building from the southwest. The fog on the river almost obscured the banks on either side, and as soon as it socked in, it would protect them from being seen from the air.

All of a sudden, a deep rumbling that sounded like thunder echoed in the distance. It grew steadily louder and soon drowned out the sound from their engines. The surface of the river erupted in small waves as one would expect from a storm; however, the wind on the river didn't change. Sandbars on either side of the river melted into the churning water, and trees on the bank swayed and fell. What appeared to be storm clouds were forming to the north as the sky grew dark, and the fog dissipated.

Spike radioed to the team, "Everyone, back to *Lucille*! Ivan, turn *Lucille* around and head her back into the current. I think we need to hold our position in the river until we figure out what's taking place."

Ivan made a slow turn in the river and had *Lucille* slowly making headway north. Both of the other boats were quickly tied along either side. Ivan kicked the throttle up a bit to keep the boat centered in the river and to match the speed of the current.

Spike asked Ivan, "What do you think is happening?"

Ivan watched as the first of many huge swells met them coming down the river. "It's an earthquake, or a massive nuclear bomb has been detonated."

Mitch pointed to a huge section of the levee off to their left as it disintegrated, and they watched as the river rapidly poured through the gap with a torrent.

"An atomic bomb could only do that if it were a direct hit. Kick the throttle up a bit, Ivan; we're losing headway."

Although Ivan kicked the throttle wide open, they were barely holding their own.

Tony pointed out, "This boat wasn't designed to take on this kind of current. It's a sail boat, and it only needs an engine for maneuvering and short trips."

Spike said, "If the current get worse, we'll have to rig up a tow line from one of the other boats."

Again the rumbling grew louder. Because it was so loud, they had to yell to be heard over it. A huge geyser of sand and water erupted near the eastern shore. Spike took his binoculars and concentrated his attention northward. He passed the glasses so the others could see. Debris was starting to fill the river. Towboats and barges, that were previously tied or derelict along the banks, were now torn loose and were heading south with the current. Huge cascades of bubbles were coming up in every direction as methane deposits beneath the river were released. One eruption came up directly beneath *Lucille* causing her to drop low in the water; the boat recovered when a swirl in the current saved her from sinking.

Tony ordered. "Break out the life vests; they're stowed in the box outside the door."

Tony took the helm and steered the boat to the east to avoid the first tow floating downstream towards them. Another cascade of bubbles erupted in front of the tow, and they watched with unbelieving eyes as the huge vessel simply fell into an invisible hole in the water.

Ivan explained, "When water is full of bubbles, it creates void; water is displaced by the bubbles. It's as if boat is trying to float on air." Ivan pointed upstream. "Russians are no longer our immediate problem."

They turned their attention upstream. Lightning flashed and connected the river to the dark clouds above. A huge fireball erupted from methane gas in the vicinity. It was soon extinguished when a runaway barge floated over it. The smell of sulfur filled the air, and the sky grew darker. The river was rising as the current increased, and the rumbling raged. The rumbling died away, and soon the only sounds were the running of the engine and the snapping and falling of the trees on the bank as the rising water ripped them from the soil. The current was increasing to the point that they were unable to make headway or maintain their position in the river.

Tony told Spike, "We need to rig a bow line and start towing with one of the other boats. Use the big aluminum; it has a diesel engine, and we have plenty of fuel for it. We may have to use the jet boat as well."

They secured the big aluminum boat to a bow line which was attached to *Lucille* and as a result they began to make headway. Lucas and Mitch were manning the aluminum boat so they could relieve each other at the helm. Spike powered up the radio and tried to call Major Matthews and home, but all he heard was static.

Ivan pointed out, "Radios will probably not work until atmosphere clears. We need to concentrate on staying alive. At least we don't have to worry about attacking Russians or Baton Rouge; Mother Nature is doing that for us."

The river continued to rise the rest of the morning and to cascade over the levees into the Louisiana delta. Just as suddenly as the tumult had begun, it ceased, and the river slowed and came to a stop. Huge flocks of birds were flying aimlessly in every direction. Animals were swimming around in the debris. They saw a possum hanging on to a piece of driftwood. Mitch shot a wild boar trying to climb aboard the aluminum boat. They idled the engines in the boats, but they were fearful about turning them off. In the distance, they could hear more rumbling. The sky was dark, and the sun was almost blacked out. They could see that the current was changing and moving in the opposite direction. Their movement was only evident by watching the river bank.

Tony called to Mitch and Lucas. "Let's get the boats turned around; this ride is just starting!"

Mitch kicked the throttle up on the big aluminum boat, and just before the current started speeding up, he slowly towed *Lucille* around so that it was facing south. Over the next hour, the current picked up speed. They had both vessels' engines straining to maintain their position; as before, they had to dodge debris and derelict river vessels heading north on the river.

Spike looked around at Tony, Ivan and Dawn. "We've got to find a place to get out of the channel; we won't survive the night out here on the water."

Tony agreed. "Take the jet boat, run up the river and see what you can find. There has to be a canal or bayou off the river that we can get in."

Spike climbed into the jet boat, and since it didn't have a propeller that could be damaged by debris in the river, he headed north at high speed. A jet boat is propelled by the engine powered pump sucking water through an inlet in the bottom of the boat and forcing it through a water jet that directs the thrust through a nozzle protected behind the transom of the boat.

Spike found the perfect place--an old bayou that was open on the west side of the river. He ran the boat up into the bayou for several hundred yards before he made a broad turn and headed back toward the river. The water started to ripple as the jet boat's hull transmitted the fresh tremors through the bottom of the boat and through the soles of his boots. He shoved the throttle wide open and ran back down the river where he found the team barely maintaining their headway.

He came alongside. "Follow me; I've found us a spot."

Following Spike in the jet boat, they turned the boats and headed back north on the river. They anchored *Lucille* in the middle of the bayou with the aluminum boats tied on either side. They gathered in the cabin, and Ivan broke out a bottle of whiskey.

"It's time for a little nerve tonic. We had great stroke of luck today."

Mitch gave him a puzzled look. "What do you mean, Ivan?"

"Russians will not expect us to attack. If dey had source of water other than tanker truck, it is now interrupted. If dey had a working airport, it's now busted. I bet all runways are cracked beyond repair. Aircraft carrier is probably floundering in changing currents of river. See if you can reach Major Matthews. We need to attack or try to take that carrier now. Russians won't be expecting us to hit them in middle of all this. God has handed us victory."

Spike grinned. "You're right. Let's fire up the radio, check on our families and call Matthews." There was no answer from their home.

Mitch pointed out, "Their power could be down if the natural gas lines are broken. It will take them a while to get a generator fired up from one of the campers and the radio hooked up. There is no reason to panic at this point."

Major Matthews answered the radio. "Matthews, here; are you folks still alive?"

Spike keyed the mic. "It has been awful exciting out here on the river. How are you guys making it?"

"The airport runways are destroyed; it's a good thing that we are operating with helicopters. We have plenty of fuel for now, but the countryside is torn up badly. The New Madrid fault has cut loose again and has destroyed every bridge that we know of on the Mississippi. This earthquake is much worse than the one that hit back in the early 1800's. The Mississippi River is flowing into the delta lands of Louisiana, Mississippi and Arkansas. We sent out recon flights up and down the river. Our guys spotted you, but they didn't try to radio. They said you guys were pretty busy fighting the river. I'm glad you made it."

Spike asked the Major, "Can you send someone up to my place to check on our families? They're all staying at my house out on Hwy 84. Look for the mini storage facility on the east side of Bude. Take an American helicopter because they'll probably shoot down a Russian one."

"I'll divert a flight right away."

"Major Matthews, Ivan has a good idea; I want you to listen to what he has to say."

"Sure, put him on."

Spike handed the mic to Ivan. Ivan took the mic and squeezed the button with his thumb. "Matthews, this is Ivan. I tell you what I told team. We have been handed wonderful gift. Earthquake now occupies Russians' every thought. Last thing dey would expect is for us to hit 'em. We head in as planned; dey are bound to be using tanker trucks at this point for water. If you take assault team directly to aircraft carrier, you should be able to take it. You could land Russian helicopters on deck. You need to attack now while ground is still shaking. We are heading in as soon as river calms down so we can travel."

"Ivan, I'm taking your advice. I'll assemble a team and attack immediately. I have just been handed a note. Tell the team that their families are okay. The house survived the earthquake, and they are restoring power. One of our teams landed at the house and called in the good news." Everyone rejoiced over the report.

Ivan handed the mic to Spike. "Thanks for the good news; it's still pretty dicey down here. We can't do anything with the current in the river as fierce as it is right now. Our plans are to ride it out here in this bayou, so unless the levee collapses next to us, we should be alright here."

"Do you expect more aftershocks?"

"I'm no expert, but I would guarantee that there will be more."

Dawn interrupted. "I was a history teacher before the lights went out. When the New Madrid earthquake hit back in the early 1800's it started out with tremors and lasted over several months. The later shocks were as intense as the first ones."

Spike who had been holding the mic spoke. "Matthews, did you hear what she said?"

"Yes, I take it you have a new team member."

"Yes, add Dawn LeBeaux to our team. We picked her up on the river before the earthquake."

"Welcome to the team; guys, I am mounting an assault to take the carrier this afternoon. Proceed with your mission. Keep me posted so we can support one another if possible."

Ivan took the mic once again. "Don't forget; attack even as earthquakes strike. Dey will never suspect."

They spent the rest of the afternoon riding out the tremors. Some tremors were worse than others. The river continued to flow backwards as it filled in the delta lands and whatever chasms that were opened up by the quake. The methane bubble cascades continued to erupt keeping them in constant fear that the boats would sink. As a precaution, they anchored the big aluminum boat with provisions further down the bayou in case they lost *Lucille* and the jet boat. As the sun went down, they sat in the cabin wondering what the night and next day would bring.

42

HANNAH PEERED OUT from within the empty mini storage building after the first lull in the tremors. Just as it had on the river, the earthquake was preceded by a low rumbling in the distance. The old house shook, but remained solid; it was built back in a time when wood was in plentiful supply. It was framed with true two by four studs. The exterior was sheathed with cypress boards that started life as two by six boards that were tongue and grooved and nailed on forty-five degree angles. Each wall of sheathing was angled opposite of the adjoining wall. The same was true of the floors, except they were resting on two by twelve floor joists. The process was repeated on the inside walls, and these were covered in real wood paneling. The roof deck was no exception; it too was sheathed on the diagonal. The house could withstand an earthquake and most storms. Its foundation could collapse and drop it to the ground, but no matter what happened, the house would remain solid. The real danger to the house would be ruptured gas lines and pinched electric wires starting a fire.

H.R. came walking up. "I've pulled the electrical and cut the gas. The furniture is scattered all over the house, and most of the cabinets have dumped their contents, but the house is still okay. I think we need to stay out here in the units until these tremors stop."

Doc called from the storage unit where he was stitching up Lacy's arm. "What about the Mathiglum? We aren't worried about the house."

Everyone laughed, and Lacy pondered. "I wonder how the men are fairing out on the river."

H.R. pointed out. "Those guys are pretty resourceful; it would take more than an earthquake to get them. The only thing an earthquake is going to do is slow them down, divert them, or open up an opportunity for them."

Lacy watched as Doc clipped the suture on the last stitch. "Thanks, Doc."

"We'll pull those stitches in about a week. Meanwhile, I'm giving you a shot of penicillin. Try not to overdo it for a while. That was a deep cut, and I don't want you to aggravate it."

Little Roger piped up. "Don't worry, Doc; I'll take care of her."

They moved some beds and chairs into the storage units. The tremors came and went; the metal building that housed them creaked, rattled and shook, but it held firm. The concrete slab under it cracked, but the slab held together because the embedded wire mesh in it did not fail. The gully that ran next to the property had a spring that ran a trickle of water year round. Now the spring was flowing vigorously. Pressure from somewhere beneath the earth was pushing the water to the surface. For the time being, they had shelter, fresh water, food, medicine, guns and ammo.

A helicopter began to circle the house. H.R. hefted one of the shoulder fired missiles and waited. The helicopter circled again and landed in the roadway in front of the storage yard. The American flag was painted near the tail. The pilot came out, and H.R. recognized him as one of the pilots from the airport.

The pilot grinned. "I knew you would be too ugly to kill."

H.R. laughed. "You mean to pretty to kill."

"I just talked to Major Matthews; he asked me to check on you guys. Your men are doing okay out on the river. They are safe, and I just need to report on how you are making it."

"Tell them we are alive and well; the house is okay. I am waiting until the shaking stops to try and hook the electricity and gas back up. What do y'all think has happened?"

"The best we can figure is the New Madrid fault has cut lose. It has torn up the Mississippi Valley. All I know is that we are being ordered back to the airport as soon as I checked on you guys."

"Tell them we are safe."

Lisa came running up with two glass jars that had been mayonnaise jars in their previous life. "One's for you guys; the other is for Major Matthews. Don't try it unless you are ready for bed, it's Mathiglum."

"What in the world is Mathiglum?"

She grinned. "You'll find out."

H.R. and Lisa stood back and watched the pilot get back in the helicopter. The co-pilot waved from the cockpit. The blades which had been slowly spinning soon spun up to speed. The pilot changed the pitch, and the blades started biting the air. Dust rose and circulated as the craft overcame gravity and rose above the treetops. Lisa and H.R. squinted through the dust that enveloped them. The limbs of the pine trees bowed to the column of air being driven down onto them by the chopping of the blades. The copter headed west and disappeared. The sound of the helicopter's blades could be heard long after it was lost from sight.

Hannah met them as they walked back. "What's up?"

H.R. grinned. "The guys are okay and safe; the pilot told me that they were just checking on us. I told them to report that we are fine. They think that the New Madrid fault has caused this earthquake. The word they are getting is that the entire Mississippi Valley has been affected. Other than that, we know as much as they do. Something is going on because he said that they had been ordered back to the airport."

At that moment they heard the rumbling in the distance. The ground started to heave and pitch. The little spring in the gully next to the property turned into a fountain, and the gully turned into a stream of muddy water. They all three sat down where they were standing because it was impossible to stand. The shaking continued for another six minutes. More trees fell, and the big house on the hill across the highway collapsed. The bulldozer parked next to the construction company disappeared into the ground as the plasticized earth opened beneath it. They looked back at their house and watched as it shook, but it remained standing.

After checking on everyone, H.R. went over to the old house and walked around it. Several of the windows were cracked; the foundation wall had a few vertical cracks, but otherwise it was intact. H.R. entered the house and found that, other than a couple of stuck doors, it had survived remarkably well. He walked over to the gully next to the property and marveled at the stream of steaming water bubbling from the bottom. It had started to clear as the muddy turbid water ran downstream on its journey to the river. Fog rolled off the water where the cold winter air met its surface. The geologic changes beneath the surface of the Earth had to have been dramatic. There was no hope in using the natural gas as every line had to have been broken. There was also little chance of even using the roadways anytime soon. He watched as herds of deer aimlessly ran down the highway; their world had come unglued. He grinned when he realized that a small herd of cattle were following the deer.

He quickly called to the ladies. "Quick, get out here I need some help."

They came running, and he pointed to the herd. "We need to get them behind our fence; our lives will be a lot easier if we have cattle."

Cheryl looked puzzled. "How are we going to get them to follow us?"

"They aren't going to follow us. We're going to have to get behind them and herd them through the gate. Bring your guns."

With the help of Bacon and the Australian Sheppard mama dog, they soon had the cattle headed into the back lot which bordered the gully that was now a stream. The lot had about five acres of uncut grass. The cross breed herd had four cows, three calves and a yearling bull. Now all they needed were some horses and mules. The fact that the cattle hadn't been killed and eaten before now was a miracle.

Doc came out and admired the herd of cattle. "Great work, guys. H.R. there's a portable building next to the construction yard across the highway. Do you think we could empty it and drag it over here?"

"Sure the tractor will easily handle it."

"Let's get it; we can turn it into a smoke house. With all the rabbits, deer and wild boar running around, we should be able to fill it with meat."

"That's a great idea, Doc! Our stock of freeze dried food and MREs is going to run out quickly at the rate we're using them."

The building was a twelve by twenty four foot metal framed building. It was full of plumbing equipment. They transferred all the equipment to a vacant bay in the remains of the construction company's metal building. The old John Deere tractor easily dragged the portable building across the highway and pulled it near the house.

Doc stood back and looked at their work. "This is a good spot. We can watch it from the house or the campers, and we can move it again if needed. H.R., you take your gun and kill us some game; the girls can help me rig up wires and racks for the meat."

Little Roger who had been watching and listening asked, "Can I help hunt us some meat?"

H.R. grinned. "I tell you what Roger. If you'll help guard the place while I hunt this afternoon, I'll take you in a few days and start teaching you everything I know."

Roger smiled. "Thanks." The little fellow turned and headed back to where the ladies were cooking over a wood fire in a barbecue pit. Bacon and two of the puppies followed his every step. H.R.'s old dogs stayed near because the years were working on them.

H.R. pointed at them. "Those old boys were just about retired when all this started; they're only good for barking and eating scraps now."

Doc reached down and scratched the old lab behind his ear. "I don't know about you, but I sure sleep easier having them around. These dogs don't miss anything going on around here."

H.R. left with Cheryl and Lisa following. H.R. carried his .308 deer rifle. The girls carried a couple of the Remington 870 shotguns, and all of them wore pistols as well.

H.R. pointed in both directions down the highway. "I want each of you to walk down the highway in opposite directions; don't get out of sight of the yard. Don't shoot toward the yard, or each other. If you shoot a deer or pig, aim for their chest, head or neck. I'll come running if I hear you shoot. If you hear me shoot, just stay put; I'll come get you if I need help. Also there are a lot of wild dogs running loose. Don't hesitate to kill them; especially if a pack runs up on you, they are no different than those criminals who tried to take us a few days back. They will kill and eat whatever they can catch, and that includes us, the kids and the cattle."

Cheryl grinned. "I guess we can eat dogs if we have to."

Lisa shook her head. "Sure hope it don't come to that."

H.R. pointed down the road. "Lisa, get up on that rise and find a spot where you can see. Just sit still and quiet."

He turned and pointed down the road in the opposite direction. "Cheryl, you head up next to that big tree on the hill. We are meat hunting. Don't worry if it looks like Bambi or Thumper; this is serious."

H.R. watched as they took their positions. He headed down through the woods. He avoided the downed timber and followed the new creek that had been formed from the hot spring that flowed near the house.

Before the day was out, they had three deer, two hogs and a dozen or so rabbits hanging in the smokehouse. A charcoal grill with a small oak fire burning in it had the portable building full of smoke, and the meat on the racks in it was absorbing the smoky flavor.

H.R. took a pull from his bottle of Mathiglum and looked across the fire at everyone sitting around it. "Folks, I can't much remember a fuller day in my life. I'm so stiff from all the running for my life, chasing cows and shooting game. I can hardly move."

There were more tremors, but none of them were strong enough to scare them.

43

HOVERING JUST ABOVE the water in his copter, Major Matthews had his night vision headset on as he flew down the Mississippi River. He kept the speed low as he approached runaway vessels. He elected to fly around them as opposed to going over them. When he reached the bridge at St. Francisville, he found that most of it had collapsed and was sitting in the river. An island of debris was piled up against it, thereby creating a vast logjam to the south. His co-pilot relayed what they were seeing to the other two helicopters flying with them and to the three groups that were following at five mile intervals behind them. The first group was comprised of captured Russian helicopters from the Natchez airport. The second group held men with missiles. Major Matthews listened through his headset as the first wave behind them notified the team they were leaving the river and heading to the Baton Rouge airport. Off to the east, he could see a huge fire raging away.

The commander of the team heading into the Baton Rouge airport called in as they approached. "The field of oil storage tanks north of the airport is burning out of control. The runway appears to be busted up in sections; it will no longer function as an airport for anything other than helicopters."

Matthews keyed the mic. "Stay out of range until we commence the assault on the carrier. We'll let you know as we are going in."

The flight down to New Orleans took another ten minutes; the aircraft carrier near the mouth of the river was just ahead. The Sergeant leading the assault team had come in from Bossier to join

Major Matthews the day before. He came forward and plugged his headset into the Russian radio and flipped it on. Immediately, the radio came alive with a Russian from the carrier hailing them as they approached. The Sergeant was born and spent a big part of his early life in the Ukraine. His older brother had disappeared into the Russian prison system many years earlier.

He answered in Russian, "*This is Dmitry Gorbechouv. We need to make an emergency landing. We are out of fuel, and we can't land at Baton Rouge. The airport is ablaze.*"

The Russian on the carrier answered, "*You can't land here. We are an aircraft carrier, and we are fighting to stay afloat from the earthquake.*"

Dmitry answered, "*We have three helicopters loaded with injured, and we are out of fuel. We have no choice. Where on the deck do you want us to land?*"

"*Permission is granted; we are clearing the deck.*"

"*We are lighting the deck; land one on each end and one in the middle.*"

Dmitry turned to Matthews. "We're in; they want one on each end, and one of us in the middle."

Matthews hit the mic key. "I'll take my ship and land in the middle; Nelson, you land on the rear, and Blake, land on the front. When we are all on the deck, we'll depart and kill everything that moves. My team will assault the bridge. We have to secure the ship and the nukes and clear the deck so that the next wave can land. Standby; I have the ship in sight and am going in."

He once again keyed the mic. "Guys, you can hit the Baton Rouge airport in sixty seconds."

"Good luck, we are commencing our attack."

Matthews took the helicopter in and turned it so that the doors faced the stairs and doors. He paused in a hover long enough to let the other two helicopters reach the deck. Keying the mic, he commanded, "Hit 'em; it's show time."

Dmitry flung open the door and dropped the first three crewmen that were approaching the helicopter. In no time, twelve men were out of the copter and firing on the carrier crewmembers.

Matthews yelled to Dmitry. "Get back in here and keep your head down. I am going to need you on their radio as soon as it's secured." He powered back up, took the helicopter airborne and landed it near the tail in order to make room for next wave that was now landing in the middle of the carrier. These helicopters held seventy-five more men and equipment. They lifted off as soon as they had disgorged their men and cargo. The following three helicopters repeated the process. The last helicopter held the nuclear experts and the marine engineers whose job it would be to secure the carrier and the nukes.

Matthews' radio crackled. "Baton Rouge is secure."

"Great, get down here and sink every vessel that is floating anywhere near this carrier and make sure the banks are clear as well. I want men and missiles placed where they can drop any Russian jets they see. We don't know how many aircraft they may have deployed or if they are in contact with them. I am certain we are under satellite surveillance, and it will be a matter of minutes before a response is ordered."

"We have you in sight and are commencing operations. We will deposit men and missiles down the levee with orders to shoot at any jet aircraft. We are going to be out of fuel soon."

"As soon as you finish, land on the levee nearby and await orders. We will refuel you as soon as we secure the vessel and determine if there is jet fuel."

Matthews' radio came alive again. "Major, the bridge is secure. I am sending a man down to get you and Dmitry. We have also secured the radio room and need someone who speaks Russian."

"Good job; we're on our way."

Explosions were going off up and down the river as the carrier support vessels were hit by the cannon and missile fire from the two combat helicopters that had arrived from the Baton Rouge airport attack. The third helicopter in their group had men and missiles that were dropped off up and down the river levee for several miles in each direction.

Matthews and Dmitry passed dead Russians and a few dead and wounded Americans as they ran to the man meeting them. With their rifles at the ready, they ran toward the door. Bullets ricocheted around them; all three turned and fired on a Russian that had been hiding near an anchor winch on the deck.

The trooper said, "Sorry, Sir, we thought it was secure."

"No worries; we got him."

They made it to the bridge where they had several Russian officers secured and sitting on the floor. The radio was sounding frantic. Matthews pointed to the mic.

"Dmitry, you're up."

Dmitry got on the radio and in Russian answered, "*This is Lieutenant Dmitry Gorbechouv. We have had a fire on board; the radio officer and his men are injured, and the officers are battling the fire. Who am I addressing?*"

"*This is Commander Polovichsky. I am aboard the tender* <u>Leningrad</u> *we are under attack.*"

"*We can't assist. How bad are you hit?*"

"*We are sinking.*"

"*You'll have to stay and try to save it; we will assist when possible.*"

Matthews looked at him. "Well, what did he say?"

"It's the <u>Leningrad</u>, it's sinking."

"Good, get on the radio and call for their aircraft; see if they have any jets or helicopters in the air."

"*This is the aircraft carrier* <u>Khrushchev</u>. *I am Lieutenant Dmitry Gorbechouv. I need all deployed aircraft to respond immediately. We are on fire, and I am in command of one of the firefighting teams. The radio operators and senior officers are injured. Respond.*"

They received no response. Matthews pointed to the officers tied up against the bulkhead. He looked over at his trooper nearest the door.

"Find me a fire axe and bring it here." The man left, and he turned to the three officers tied up. "Which one of you is the Captain?"

The two to the left both glanced at the one on the right and none of them said a word.

The one on the right said, "No speak English."

Matthews glanced over at Dmitry. "Ask them in Russian which one is the Captain."

Dmitry repeated the question in Russian, and again they were met with silence. Matthews grinned as the man with the fire axe showed up.

"Dmitry, they don't speak English and don't know who the Captain is. You and I both know that they have radioed the attack, and there is in all probability attack aircraft coming from the Atlantic. So I am going to speed this process up a bit. Dmitry, ask the Captain here once again if he is the Captain and if he speaks English."

Dmitry repeated the question, and the Captain said defiantly, "Nyet."

Matthews took the axe and split his skull to the teeth. "I read where a pole axe could do that in medieval battles."

The Captain's body convulsed in its death throes and covered his two companions in splattered blood. Matthews grinned as he put his foot on the dead Russian's chest and pulled the axe from the split skull.

He glanced over at the remaining two. "Gentlemen, which one of you two is second in command? Do you speak English?"

The one on the end nodded. "I'm the Executive Officer."

"Good, now we're getting somewhere. Do you have any desire to live?"

"Yes."

"Good." Matthews pointed to the other officer and told his men take him into another room and keep him safe and secure.

"Yes, sir."

He looked at Dmitry. "Get the Exec on his feet."

Dmitry pulled the Executive Officer to his feet.

Matthews stated, "We are going to remove the nuclear warheads from this vessel; you can either help us and live or die like him. What's it going to be?"

The man glanced at the axe that was still dripping blood and started shaking. "I don't want to die."

"Good, now calm down, and get on the loudspeaker. Tell your men to stand down, drop their weapons, put on their life vest and proceed to the fantail of the ship. Where is the officer in charge of the nuclear warheads?"

"You are holding him in the other room."

"Will he follow your orders?"

"Yes, he is my brother-in-law."

"Make the announcement. Remember; Dmitry speaks Russian, and I am in no mood for anything but your enthusiastic cooperation. Dmitry, I want to be certain he understood what I said so repeat what I just said to him in Russian and remind him that I don't bluff."

Dmitry repeated everything in Russian. They cut his hands loose, and three men held their weapons on him. The Executive Officer wiped the Captain's blood off his face on his shirt sleeve. He flipped a switch and keyed the mic and in Russian gave the command.

"This is Commander Boris Polaski. The Captain is dead, and I have assumed command. This ship has surrendered to the US forces. You are to stand down; we are all now prisoners of war. You are ordered to put down your weapons and put on your life vest. All officers are to move your men to the stern of the ship and await further orders. Do not resist in any manner; do not compromise any equipment, but dismantle any traps. I will personally shoot anyone who disobeys."

Matthews looked at Dmitry. "Did he do what we asked?"

"Yes, sir."

Matthews got on his radio and told the men what to expect. "Don't hesitate to kill any of them who are not complying."

He turned to his men guarding the Executive Officer. "Secure his hands and bring in the other officer."

In short order, they had the Exec's hands re-secured, and they ushered in the nuclear weapons officer. Matthews looked at Boris as they frog stepped the nuclear weapons officer back onto the bridge.

"Boris, tell him what we are doing in case he didn't hear or understand. Does he speak English as well?"

"Yes, he speaks it better than me."

"Good, what's his first name?"

"His name is Viktor."

Boris explained to him in Russian what had taken place. Matthews looked directly into Viktor's eyes.

"Viktor, I am going to put you with my nuclear experts; Dmitry reads and understands Russian. This is very simple; we are going to remove the nuclear weapons from this vessel. Which crew members do you need to assist?"

"They are dead. Your soldiers can assist, and it is all automated."

Boris spoke to him in English. "The only way we are ever going to see our family again is to fully cooperate. Do as they request. Do not deviate in any manner."

Viktor looked at the dead Captain lying in the pool of blood and appeared sick to his stomach. "I understand, Boris."

Matthews nodded. "Good, we all understand one another."

Matthews got on the radio. "Are all the Russians surrendering?"

When everyone responded with a "yes," he turned to Boris. "Are there any political officers or implanted spies that you know of?"

"If there are, no one, but the spy himself, will know."

Matthews keyed the mic. "Dmitry, make sure the area is completely secure. A spy or a political officer that we don't know about may be lurking around. Make sure the bombs and ordinance are secure. We don't want to have them booby trapped and detonated before we offload the nukes."

Matthews watched as they left the room. "Boris, where is your family now?"

"They are living in the south of Russia near the Ukraine border where Viktor's family has a farm. It is in the middle of nowhere. What are you going to do with the crew?"

"I'm not planning on executing them unless we have no other choice. I will not hesitate to kill every one of you people if I don't retrieve the nuclear devices. How many of the devices are on board?"

"We have two dozen cruise missiles equipped with nuclear warheads. The ninety-seven remaining missiles are equipped with fifteen hundred kilo conventional warheads."

"Where are the launch codes?"

"Ours don't work like that; there are three officers with keys. Any one of us can activate the warhead. We activate them prior to deployment by switching on a special transmitter using the key. The transmitter is in that blue box on the panel. The key opens the box, and we send the command by pushing the button."

"I thought it would be more complicated than that."

"There's no need so long as everyone thinks it's more complicated than that. It has to be activated by the bomber crew before the command button will work, so it takes the mission commander and one of us three officers to fire it."

"Why are you making it so easy for us?"

"I desperately want to see my family again one day."

"If you and Viktor continue to cooperate, I will see what I can do. You will be our guest for the foreseeable future."

Eight Americans were killed and eighteen wounded. An undetermined number of Russians were killed and wounded. The Americans took another hour to remove the nuclear and conventional cruise missiles and transport them off the carrier. The political officer tried to sabotage the ordinance, but he only managed to blow himself up when a hand grenade got away from him. There was enough jet fuel on board to refuel the helicopters for their trip back upriver. The tremors continued, but the immense aircraft carrier floating in the river was able to handle the stress of the waves and debris. All the Russian aircraft were destroyed with thermite grenades, and a time delayed bomb in the bottom of the ship soon had it sitting on the river bed. The oil from the Gulf surrounded it as the river continued to run backwards. Its upper decks were well above the surface of the river. The Russian sailors were dutifully sitting on the fantail as the last of the Americans left in the helicopters. The radios were destroyed, and smoke was starting to billow from the bowels of the vessel. A flight over the New Orleans airports showed that the Lakefront Airport runway was destroyed, and the Louis Armstrong Airport was underwater.

Matthews looked over at Boris and Viktor. "We left all the lifeboats and survival equipment intact. You guys just need to sit back and enjoy the flight."

Matthews was piloting the same helicopter he was flying when he landed on the carrier several hours earlier.

He keyed the mic on his radio and spoke with the other helicopters. "Guys, I am certain that attack aircraft will be arriving at any minute. The Russians have satellites trained on us, so we need to disappear. Go to your predetermined evacuation points and proceed to hide your craft. Then, wait for orders. They can't remain over target for long and this far into the continent. Natchez airport, prepare for incoming; I want men with missiles ready to intercept any jets they can shoot down."

The sun was peaking over the horizon off to the east. Matthews' helicopter carried two nuclear cruise missiles and one of the three transmitters used to activate the warhead; as well as a half dozen targeting computers from the jet fighters. The other two aircraft had the remaining two transmitters and the targeting computers as well as an officer who was schooled in their use. They now had a fighting chance. Dmitry unscrewed the lid on the jar of Mathiglum and took a sip. He passed it to Matthews.

"Take a sip, Major; it's Mathiglum compliments of the Mitch's Mountain Guerillas." He changed the frequency on his radio to the Mitch's Mountain frequency and keyed the mic.

44

OTHER THAN THE continuing tremors, the night was quiet on the bayou. The radio crackled as they were rising to see what the day would bring.

"Matthews here, did you guys survive the night?"

Spike keyed the mic. "We're still alive and well. How did it go last night?"

"The mission was a success; you now have new orders. As soon as it's safe to do so, I want you to go home. The Baton Rouge airport is no more. The Russian aircraft carrier is sitting on the bottom of the river, and the airports at New Orleans are destroyed or under water."

"Great news; we'll head back as soon as it calms down."

"Stay alert; we are expecting Russian combat jets to respond. Be prepared to use your missiles or to get off the boats."

"We're going to stay put until the river calms down. We are starting to see some oil from the Gulf. The river level is continuing to drop; we'll keep you posted."

Ivan grinned. "I told you dey would not expect attack. In World War II American bombers were crewed, armed, fueled and tied down on runway facing typhoon wind. They flew planes into wind while sitting tied to ground. When wind subsided, dey refueled and immediately took off for attack. The last thing Japanese suspected was attack just as typhoon ended."

They stayed put and watched as the river continued to flow north for the rest of the day. The following day, the river changed direction and started to flow south again. Instead of a huge torrent, the flow was now greatly reduced. Gone were the whirlpools, huge trees and derelict vessels; the river resembled a large bayou. It was now a placid steam that was less than a quarter of mile wide.

Dawn looked puzzled. "I don't understand what has happened."

Tony pointed upstream. "The Mississippi River has been trying to change course since back in the 1950's. Just south of Natchez are the old river control structures and a hydroelectric power plant. Those structures were built to relieve pressure on the river. I expect the Mississippi is now running down through the Atchafalaya River Basin or what used to be the Atchafalaya River Basin."

Spike looked around at the rest of the men. "I guess this means the war is over for us for a while. Ivan, you look disappointed."

"I was looking forward to killing more Russian bastards."

Dawn patted him on the shoulder. "I know how you feel. Now that you're heading home what are y'all going to do about me?"

Mitch just shook his head. "I guess since we have another mouth to feed, let's just throw her overboard." Everyone burst out laughing.

Tony put his arm across her shoulders. "You're welcome to come back with us if you want. Unless Major Matthews needs us to embark on a new mission, we'll be trying to farm, raise some food and rebuild what's left of our lives."

Ivan spoke up, "I've got to find a couple of horses or some mules. My plans are to travel to Toronto and look for my daughter."

Tony said, "My daughter was in the New York City area. All I can do is wait to see if she makes it back. I know she's not going to be in the apartment she was living in."

Dawn agreed, "My son was in New Jersey. There's no way I can carry enough food and ammo to go look for him. I wish I could've left a note telling him where I had gone, but at the time, I had no idea where I was going, so I am stuck never knowing."

Spike pointed at the big aluminum boat with the diesel engine. "I think the best thing for all of us is to get back home and let the country settle down. I'm certain that Major Matthews will manage to turn off the lights in Russia and China. It will take years, if ever, for the roads and bridges to be repaired across and approaching the Mississippi Valley. I imagine we can make a run back down the river with that big boat and leave a sign for your son with a map to our place. I do think we need to give the remaining Russians time to starve and get picked off by the locals before we attempt to do it."

Ivan added, "I think we need to get with military and set up some sort of alphabetical list of who is where so that survivors can find each other. It would be better doing that than blindly searching. When word gets out, people will start looking at list and adding names to it. Once we get some sort of communication set up we can duplicate list and send it by courier to other bases where it can be updated, copied and sent back."

The tremors were mild in comparison to the earlier ones from the days before. They heard jet aircraft several times, but they didn't see anything to shoot. As a precaution, they held tight for another day.

On the third day, they slowly headed out. They spread the boats out with *Lucille* in the middle. In the remains of the old river channel, huge sand and gravel bars were left on either side. The corpses of thousands of trees lay on and protruded from the sandbars. Pieces of plastic and insulation from destroyed structures hung in their limbs and roots. Boulders, having been washed down eons ago from previous floods and earthquakes, could be seen in portions of the stream.

They took the jet boat in tow in order to conserve its fuel for the trip back up the Homochitto River. They wanted to have enough gasoline to make it back to Franklin County. They still had two drums of diesel for the diesel engines in *Lucille* and the big aluminum boat. Spike and Tony joined Ivan and Dawn on *Lucille,* while Mitch and Lucas led the way with the big aluminum boat.

Tony lamented. "I wish we had brought more gasoline for the jet boat."

Spike pointed out. "We have plenty of fuel to do what we planned, but if anything unforeseen comes up, we'll quickly exhaust our safety factor, and I don't want to have to abandon it. I'm not so sure this war is over. I'm sure the Russians, Chinese and Cubans still have many thousands of troops firmly entrenched. Even if they knock out the electrical infrastructure of both countries, we'll still have to contend with two sizeable armies."

Dawn commented, "It's beyond belief what has taken place. The odds of the oil spill followed up by an earthquake are almost too much to believe. I wonder what historians will say about all this."

Tony shook his head. "You realize that if Matthews is successful; there will be little chance that any of this will be recorded. It will be an oral history for a few generations. I expect the world will be in a pre-medieval situation very soon. Wandering minstrels will travel about entertaining people with tales of what has taken place."

They arrived at the point where the bulk of the Mississippi River flow was diverted to the west. The old river control structure was no longer there. A vast lake that couldn't be seen across was in its place. Sections of the levee remained, but they were now big green islands in a sea of brown water. These islands would erode into the river over time. Before the levees were constructed, the Mississippi River covered what is known as the Louisiana and Mississippi deltas. The rich farmland was created by deposits of sediments from the spring floods that filled them every year.

Tony pointed out. "We may be walking back to Franklin County. I'm afraid we may be unable to locate the mouth of the Homochitto River. If it's been rerouted, we may have to try to leave the river somewhere near Natchez."

As they continued, they began to realize that Tony had been correct. They couldn't locate the mouth of the Homochitto River; they were forced to continue north. As night approached, they found a cut off from the river on the east side and went in. The current was very calm, so they anchored in the middle and poured over their now almost useless maps.

Mitch put his finger about where he thought they were. "We may be in Butlers Lake; it's an oxbow off the river and was part of a wildlife management area. When its light enough, I'll bet we can see some signs on the trees."

Tony asked Ivan, "Ivan, if we have to go back on foot, how long do you think it'll take?"

"Will take couple of weeks; it's not distance we have to worry about. You have to realize every road is broken and every bridge is down. All those little bridges we have driven over and under will probably be down. Every gully will be challenge."

Mitch asked, "Spike, do you think we can get a helicopter pickup from Major Matthews?"

Spike looked up with a worried look on his face. "I don't think it will be a problem. I just don't want to focus their attention away from finishing off the invaders. I'll call him and see if he can spare us a ship."

Spike keyed the mic. "This is Captain Spike Hobbil calling for Major Matthews. Can you read me?"

Matthews came back on. "Spike, what's up?"

"Sorry to bother you, but we have a little problem; we can't get back up the Homochitto River to get home. What are the chances of our getting a helicopter pickup?"

"Where and when do you want a pickup?"

"We're in Butler's Lake for the night. It's just a few miles south of Natchez on the river."

"We can probably arrange a pickup at the park just south of the bridges. That section of levee is still intact. You can leave your boats; our guys can use them in policing the river."

"Everyone's curious about the mission. Is there anything you can tell us?"

"For security reasons, I can't breathe a word. If you'll radio when you reach the park, we'll send a chopper."

"Thanks, it would've taken us a couple of weeks to walk home. Send a big one if you have it; we still have most of our missiles, gear, and six people."

"We can handle it; call us when you get there."

"Thanks, Major. Hobbil out."

Spike turned to the group. "It looks as if we'll be going home in the morning."

Ivan added, "Even though war is over here in the South, doesn't mean war is over. Unless we stop 'em in their home countries, we will be colonized rapidly." Tony agreed. "The only thing we have going for us is the fact that they can only get to our region by walking or by helicopter at this point. I know we haven't been gone long, but it sure seems like a long time. I want to get back and start rebuilding my farm."

That night was almost free of tremors. The few that occurred could only be felt through the hull of the boat. The next morning, they headed out of the inlet and pushed through the limbs and debris that had accumulated where the lake narrowed and entered the river. The smell of decay filled the air from the corpses of dead animals and marine life lying in the river. Rotting vegetation that had been buried in the bottom of the river and in sandbars was now released, and the process of decay had begun again. When they were out in the river, the going was easier. The flow of the current was slower as the river was now spread over a vast delta that extended from the Natchez, MS, bluffs to the hills near Harrisonburg, LA. Survivors and animals were taking refuge on the hundreds of Indian mounds that covered the region. After a couple of hours, they reached the park alongside of the river. It was now an island. The remains of the two bridges at Natchez were resting in the river with an island of debris piling up behind them.

Tony pointed to the debris field piling up behind the bridges. "Let's take the boats to the other side of the levee behind the parkway.

When enough debris piles up behind the two bridges' superstructures, it'll break loose, and I don't want to be swept away with it."

Spike got on the radio with Mitch and Lucas who were leading the way in the big aluminum boat. "Head around to the back side of the park; we don't want to be downstream when the pressure from the river forces the pile of debris to break free."

They turned just south of the newly created island, powered around to the west side and nosed the boats in to the bank. Spike, Tony, Mitch and Lucas made a quick run over the park and looked for anyone surviving in the buildings.

The newly created island was uninhabited. Spike came back and got on the radio. "This is Spike Hobbil; we are ready for retrieval."

Matthews answered. "Good news. Hold tight; we'll be there in about thirty minutes. I am bringing y'all back here so we can go over what has taken place."

"Can't wait to hear what you have to say."

The helicopter came in over the remains of the two bridges and settled down on top of the old levee adjacent to the three boats. Three troopers came out and helped them move and stow their equipment in the large twin rotor helicopter. Once the transfer was complete, the three soldiers stayed with the boats.

The helicopter blades spooled up to speed with dust and debris obscuring the boats as the copter rose and drifted away. The copter headed north above the river, and when it reached altitude sufficient to clear the bluffs, it headed to the airport. The flight was only about ten minutes. They circled in and landed near the remains of the small terminal building. Matthews came out smiling.

"I wanted to give you guys an update; c'mon in. We'll take you back home in a bit."

They all gathered in Matthews' office where he pulled out a map of Europe and Asia.

Matthews pointed to the map. "We managed to set off eleven of the twenty-four nukes over Russia and Asia. They're in the same shape as we are. We also used the conventional warheads to take out a significant portion of their forces that are here. We've had to battle some of our rogue army units, and there is still no word on our carriers or remaining submarine fleet. We can only assume they are gone. Without a way to re-supply, none of them can operate for much longer than a year."

Mitch asked, "Where does that leave us?"

"After the earthquake, the middle section of the country is only accessible by helicopter or horseback, so there shouldn't be any invaders coming this way. You guys can go home until we need you again. Russia, China and North Korea have been neutered, and a lot of their forces are stranded here with no re-supply. Cuba is being hit right now."

Ivan asked, "Can you use some herbicide to poison 'em on the East and West Coasts?"

"We may have to use it, but for now we have them trying to live off the land. They are in the same shape as we've been and will be starving to death quickly. With the lights out back home, they are limited on getting re-supplied. We're still shooting at every jet in the air, and we'll nuke their bases if we have to. They still have a navy, but the problem is they don't have a lot of targets left over here."

Spike lamented. "When we Americans aren't killing each other, we're killing them."

Matthews grinned. "Don't forget; we have a bunch of arrows left in our quiver. We are setting up the government here in the territory we have taken and can hold. We will be following the constitution and will hold elections in a couple of years."

Dawn raised her hand. "Major Matthews, I have a question. Can we set up some sort of registry that we can share with all the other bases to register survivors so we can locate our missing families and friends?"

Matthews nodded in agreement. "That's a great idea. You start it, and I will see that it is carried forward. I want you to set up a courthouse of sorts to record marriages, property descriptions and such. Y'all are not only officers and soldiers in the U.S. Army for life, but you are the official government for your area. You will be the police, judiciary and local government. Decide among yourselves who does what. If someone needs killing, you are authorized to carry it out. There is no shortage of bad guys running loose. You older folks will remember Matt Dillon on *Gunsmoke*; that's what your job is for your region of the state. Don't take any crap off of anyone. Is there anything that you need?"

Mitch said, "We don't know what we need at this point; we'll know more once we get home."

Ivan pointed in the direction of his home. "I want to find out if my house is still there."

Matthews spoke up. "It's still intact, and so is the little bridge between here and there. I'll have someone load you and your gear and take you home when you're ready."

As they spoke, a continuous convoy of helicopters was bringing in equipment, men and supplies.

Ivan left for his house with a radio and everyone else got back in the helicopter that had picked them up and headed to Spike's house and storage unit complex. They settled down in the road in front of the house and were greeted by H.R. who turned and gave the thumbs up to the others who were hiding. Doc leaned the shoulder fired missile that he had been hefting up against the building where he had been hiding. Roger came running out to Spike who lifted him up on his shoulders as Lisa and Lacy joined them.

Hannah came up, hugged Mitch and said, 'Thank God, you are safe."

He gave her a big kiss. "How's our baby growing?"

"The baby and I are fine now that you're home."

"From the way things are looking, I may get to stay for a while."

Tony introduced Dawn to everyone, and H.R. was quick to offer her a tour of the place.

45

HANNAH SHIFTED THE little girl to her other hip. "You're getting to be a big girl."

Mitch called down from the roof of the farmhouse. "Be careful, she's getting heavy, and you are pregnant. Don't overdo it."

"Don't worry so much. The roof is looking good; I've always loved a shake roof. I can't believe it's been two and a half years since the lights went out."

"It seems like a lifetime ago."

Bacon let out a bark, and they looked up to see H.R. and Dawn riding up in their wagon that had been a boat trailer in its previous life. The two horses stopped at the water trough and drank while H.R. pumped water from the hand pump on the old cistern.

"Y'all sure have got if fixed back up nice. Old Betsy here is going to have us a new colt in about a month. Before long, we'll all have horses."

Mitch lowered his hammer and nails from the roof with a rope and bucket. "I'll be over this afternoon to start bumping on your roof."

Dawn wiped the sweat from her brow. "Did you hear the good news? Ivan's daughter and grandchildren showed up at his house last week, and I got word that my son and his family are alive and in West Tennessee. They are going to build a flat boat and try to come down the Mississippi River."

Hannah lowered little Mary Ellen to the ground. "Play with Pinky while I let my back rest."

She walked out to the wagon. "This is a week of good news. We found out yesterday that Cheryl is pregnant, and Tony is strutting around like a spring rooster."

Mitch walked over to the pump. "H.R., let me spell you on the pump. How are Spike and his family doing?"

"They are doing fine. Lisa and Lacy are both expecting again. Doc has set up his practice in that old contractor's building across the street from the storage yard. He even found a couple of good looking nurses to help him. It's a combination barroom and clinic. He's turned out to be a pretty good vet too. People are starting to use the storage yard as a trading post and courthouse. The hot spring is still flowing, and everyone swears it has curative powers. We soaked in it last night, and I've never felt better."

"What's Larry up to?"

"Larry found a girlfriend so you girls will be helping plan a wedding before long. He turned into a great sheriff."

Hannah asked, "Any word from Major Matthews?"

"He said the world has pretty much gone silent. With no electricity in North America, Europe and Asia, civilization is now limited to communities. This is the new medieval ages. Centuries will pass before mankind can get back to where they were. Most of the aircraft are grounded, and the Army only uses them for emergencies, because spare parts are nonexistent and very little fuel exists. Most of the men have gone home."

Mitch looked around. "I don't know about you guys, but I hope it never gets back to the way it was."

They looked across the big field that was now covered in corn and that was almost ready for harvest. A fat hen came running by with a rooster in hot pursuit, and everyone laughed.

The wind blew across Mitch's Mountain as it had for eons. The huge pines were still standing, and the little farm in the wilderness still sprouted and nurtured life.

Read on for an exciting sneak peak of:
JERNIGAN'S FINAL BATTLE
Third in the *Jernigan's War* series

Jernigan's Final Battle

Chapter 1

Dix's breath fogged as he exhaled in the cold Ozark Mountain air. Standing on a rock outcropping, he peered down the valley. He squinted as he sighted down Fox's arm. "I see it now."

A wisp of vapor rose from what appeared to be a rock perched on the side of the mountain. Fox pointed farther up the valley. "Do you see that big pine tree on that hill up there?"

"I see it; what about it?"

"That ain't no pine tree; no pine tree that tall and big is that perfect."

"I see what you mean. That's an antenna array; I see the satellite dish in the top. They've disguised it to look like an eagle's nest. I'm going to radio Colonel Miller and tell him what we found. We've already lost three groups who've come up here to check this out. I want to get in a report before they find and kill us. For all we know, they already know we're here and have people on their way to intercept us."

"Dix, tell me again; why we're not back home hunting, gathering and watching our children grow. Rachel was none too happy when you decided to come traipsing up here. My wife Bonnie is fit to be tied; who's going to feed and care for them if we don't come back?"

"Fox, all I agreed to do was come up here and look around. I don't have any plans to start fighting again."

"You didn't have any plans to get remarried, settle down and start raising kids either. How'd that plan work out? Shouldn't we have some kind of transportation other than our two feet?"

"Fox, I can't help it if our engine blew in the Jeep. At least we made it almost all the way here before we got stranded. I have Porter coming from Louisiana with a string of mules. He came over to help get Cooney moved over to his ranch in Texas. He's agreed to come up and help us look around and bring us back."

"Are you sure we can't find a running vehicle and drive back or a river we can get on and float back?"

"Fox, how come you have become so civilized; has having a wife and baby settled you down?"

"I guess it has; I had given up all hope of ever having a life when the collapse hit. I sort of turned into an animal. The only thing I wanted to do was clean out the roaches that destroyed our country."

"I was the same way, and I thought we had killed them all, but then we discovered this nest of them hiding in these old mines up here in the Ozarks."

"Who do you figure they are, Dix?"

"I think we know who they are. They aren't members of the new Constitution Army. I think they are remnants of the communist American government and their willing accomplices in the government and media. We discovered them by accident when Colonel Miller sent a squad up here just to investigate the area. They disappeared, as well as the next two squads."

"I heard rumors of a huge underground shelter somewhere up here that was set up and stocked in case of a catastrophe."

"I heard about it too. There was a cable TV show that explored conspiracy theories. When they finished the show, you felt silly for even considering such a thing. Turns out most of the theories were correct. It looks like this one is real as well."

"What's your plan, Dix; how are we going to keep from disappearing like all the others?"

"There are only two of us here; we aren't going to start anything, and we are going to keep quiet. If I see we need help, I'll call Colonel Miller, and we'll get our old team up here."

As Fox turned to head back into the woods, he slipped on a loose piece of rock. Dix jumped to his rescue, and in the process fell and slid down hill with him. The distinctive pop of rifle rounds passing inches above them answered the question about their discovery. They stayed low and crawled on their bellies up the side of the ridge until they were well into the cover of the forest.

Fox turned to see on Dix's face a look that he knew so well. "I guess this means we are finished looking around, and we're ready to get shot at some more?"

"I guess so, Fox, let's high tail it back the way we came and find a hole to hide in."

They were double timing it up the ridge toward the road where they left their gear when they were stopped dead in their tracks by a deep voice from in the shadows of the woods. "Fox White, what in God's name are you doing up here? You're going to get yourself killed."

Both Dix and Fox had their rifles aimed in the direction of the voice. Dix was aiming the old Springfield 1903 and Fox pointed his trusty old 30-30 deer rifle.

Fox grinned. "I'd recognize that voice anywhere. Jonas, I figured you'd make it if anybody could."

Jonas seemed to appear from nowhere as he slipped from his cover and met them on the trail. "Y'all had better follow me now; they will be here in about five minutes. I heard the shooting; they don't usually miss. I already stole your gear; you can pick it up back down the trail."

Dix grinned. "If us old farts hadn't almost fell off the side of the mountain, they would have. Old Fox here took a tumble, and I came after him just as they squeezed off their shots."

They followed Jonas down the side of the mountain and retrieved their packs. Jonas stopped and took some pieces of meat and hung them every so often on a fishing line with a #10 fish hook attached. Fox gave him a puzzled look.

"Don't look surprised; listen."

In the distance they heard dogs barking and baying. Jonas pointed. "They'll try and run us to ground and close in for the kill. We'll wait on the next ridge until the dogs get into these baited hooks. We'll be able to shoot from up there." As they passed, he raised some lines that would catch the men about chest high.

Fox looked at Dix. "We could have used him down in Vicksburg."

Dix and Fox were breathing hard as they followed Jonas up the ridge. They stopped just short of the top. Jonas pointed to where he wanted Fox and Dix to hide. "I'll start with the ones that are bringing up the rear. Fox, you aim for the front ones, and you with the Springfield start in the middle. I don't want all three of us shooting the same man. It makes a terrible mess."

As they separated, Fox said, "Jonas, this is Dix Jernigan."

"I heard of you; I thought you were dead."

Dix grinned. "Came close to it a time or two."

They waited on the side of the ridge; rocks and bushes provided excellent cover and concealment. A short time later they heard the men with the dogs. Just as expected, the dogs were soon tangled, yelping and impaled by the sharp hooks. Several of the men were also cussing as they too became snared. Jonas whispered. "There are usually about a dozen; give them time to gather. That's the only trail; don't shoot until I do. If any of them come in from behind us, follow me into the cave behind me and move quick! I'll blow the entrance, and we'll head out the back door."

Silently, they watched as the other men caught up. Four men took up a post to cover the others while they untangled themselves from the fish hooks. Jonas motioned for Fox to take the two on the right, and Dix to take the two on the left. Jonas flicked the safety on his ancient Remington deer rifle and aimed at the chest of the last man he could see. He squeezed the trigger, and the rifle bounced.

THIS BEGINS THE THIRD BOOK OF THE JERNIGAN WAR SERIES. PLANS ARE TO HAVE IT COMPLETED IN THE COMING MONTHS. IN THE MEANTIME, I HOPE YOU ENJOYED MITCH'S MOUNTAIN. Ken Gallender..............

51985653R00245

Made in the USA
San Bernardino, CA
07 August 2017